# ALPHA OF MORTAL FLESH

*Darkmourn Universe*

## BEN ALDERSON

*To my mother, **my warrior**. Who faced pure evil and survived it.*

# CONTENT WARNING

*Please be aware this novel contains scenes or themes which readers may be triggered by. This book deals with the topic of domestic abuse, gaslighting, physical abuse, mental abuse, control.*

*Other content warnings are as followed:*

*Toxic relationships, murder, loss of family members, death, abuse, manipulation, anger, grief/grieving, depression, profanity, adult scenes, adult themes, blood/gore, mentions of suicide.*

## ❧ 1 ❧
## 25 YEARS BEFORE

*rip. Drip. Drip.*

D Warm droplets of blood fell across my upturned face. If I closed my eyes, it would have been like looking up into a storm cloud as it unleashed an abundance of rain. But this wasn't rain. Rain was not sticky. Rain did not tack in my eyelashes. Rain did not taste like old copper coins.

I pinched my eyes closed, flinching with every drip that splashed against my skin.

*Drip. Drip. Drip.*

I couldn't look away. Mumma's eyes were wide and all-seeing above me. Her face was squashed into the floorboard that separated us. Dead eyes peered through the gap, bloodshot and discoloured.

Mumma had such pretty eyes, even when they sang of death.

*Drip. Drip. Drip.*

I clamped my hand over my mouth. My mind

commanded me to scream, but I couldn't. The dead would hear me. Just as I could hear them sucking, slurping. Pappa would have slapped the back of my hand if I ate like that. Smacking one's lips whilst chewing loudly on a meal, it was not good manners. The dead didn't care what noises they made. They had no manners when draining their prey.

*Drip. Drip. Drip.*

As Mumma's blood dribbled through my little hands and spread across my lips, I couldn't help but ponder why the dead craved blood with such desperation. The copper tang was vile. My stomach cramped, and I felt as though I would be sick. I wished to spit it out and scream and scream. But I couldn't. No. No.

As I stared deep into Mumma's eyes, I remembered what she said as she hid me beneath the floor. *Keep quiet, Eamon, don't make a sound.*

*Drip. Drip. Drip.*

My skin itched where her blood spread. I wanted to scratch at my face and rub away the gore, but it was the only thing smothering my scent from the vampires. My hair was drenched by it; my eyes were blinded by it.

*Drip. Drip. Drip.*

Where were the Crimson Guard? They would come. They should come and save us.

*Drip. Drip. Drip.*

The blood ran dry by the time the vampires finished drinking from my parent's corpses. So much time passed that the blood no longer bothered me. I was frozen to the spot, looking up through the gap in the floorboards as they creaked with the monsters' movement.

*Drip. Drip. Drip.*

One of them boasted about the taste of Mumma's blood. Fresh peach, it said. The other thought Pappa tasted like vintage wine. I thought they would leave, but they didn't. They were in no rush. No one was coming for them. I recognised the familiar sound of a chair scratching against the floor as they took a seat. Whilst I was hidden beneath the floorboards, covered in Mumma's blood, the monsters sat at our family table and laughed with full bellies.

*Drip. Drip. Drip.*

They laughed.

*Drip. Drip. Drip.*

They sang.

*Drip. Drip.*

I had been hiding for so long, I felt as though my body would never break free of this position. Spiders welcomed me into their domain, crawling over my bare feet and blood-coated face. I used to hate spiders. Now they were my only comfort.

*Drip. Drip.*

The monsters leave, not because the Crimson Guard had come for them, but because dawn had arrived. With the light of day, it ushered them out of my home. Mumma watched me. Her skin looked blue. I used to think she had pretty eyes, but now the whites were grey, and the blue looked like it bled out from their circles.

*Drip. Drip.*

Light spilled in from above. I lifted my hands before my face. They were not red as expected. It looked as though I dipped my hands in rust. The blood had dried to a flaking brown stain. The Crimson Guard were still not here.

*Drip. Drip.*

Night came again. Sick covered my chest and face, mixing with Mumma's dried blood.

*Drip.*

Three times, the world above the floorboards had brightened with daylight. It was on the fourth day when my saviours came. They came when there was nothing left to save.

*Drip.*

I hated them.

*Drip.*

Vampires. The Crimson Guard.

*Drip.*

They were all monsters.

*Drip.*

I hated them.

*Drip.*

I...

I...

I do *love you, Rhory Coleman.*

It's strange how such words hurt far greater than the physical pain left in their wake.

Eamon always seemed shocked when he spoke them to me. His piercing sky-blue eyes would glisten with tears of regret. He would look from his hands to the part of my body he'd chosen to mark during his blackout of rage, and whimper as though he was the one with a body riddled with pain. For such a towering broad man, in those moments he was more akin to a child looking between their favourite broken toy and the hands that tore it in two. I recognised remorse; I thought. If only for a moment, which made the bitter taste of fault hard to swallow.

He never said sorry. No. It seemed Eamon could not allow such a dirty phrase to grace his lips.

All of Darkmourn would tell me how kind he was.

Which made the understanding of *why* he acted with such ferocity towards me confusing. Kindness caused bruises, broke bones and drew blood.

I couldn't pick up bread from the bakery in town without being told how wonderful Eamon was. Even during my frequent visits to the local medic, they'd remind me about the many great things Eamon had done for them. It was those encounters I found most difficult to hear when I was forced to lie about how two of my fingers even became shattered in the first place.

*That is one nasty bruise you've got,* Jameson would say, pointing his finger towards my swollen eye.

I would smile and exhale the lie with such ease, one would have thought it was rehearsed. *The door picked a fight with me and won.*

Jameson would tut, smile and dismiss it. And no matter how many times I visited, or how many aliments I collected across my body, he never questioned me. No matter how ridiculous and fictitious the excuses became.

Of course, it was Eamon who left those marks, but I couldn't ever say that. Not out loud. And it wasn't because I was scared about what he would do to me. The days of fearing him were long gone. It was what others would say. And how I would be looked at, like a crazed fool, for even suggesting Eamon Coleman had such a capacity for evil.

No one would ever believe Darkmourn's leader of the Crimson Guard—the man tasked to protect every living creature from the monsters of the world—was that very thing to me.

*My* monster.

*My* devil.

*My* husband.

*But he loves me*, I reminded my reflection. Which made sense, because love had only ever caused me pain.

My fingers had only recently healed, making my movements awkward as I tied the velvet laces of my scarlet cloak around my neck. The splint and cloth bindings had been removed days ago, and I couldn't ignore how skeletal they looked. Thin from the lack of use, like the fictional description of a witch's finger. Fitting, I thought.

The thick band of iron and gold spun around my emaciated finger. I hardly spared it a thought before my heart dropped into the pit of my stomach. There was a time looking at the ring filled my chest with breath, and my mind with the wonders of a future with the man I loved.

Now, it simply reminded me of the harsh truth of my reality.

"You must be looking forward to getting some fresh air, Rhory."

I turned my back on the scratched glass mirror to regard Mildred, who stood in the foyer before me. Mildred had been in my life for as long as I could remember. The Coleman residence wouldn't have been the same without her stout, hunched body shuffling across the waxed oak floors. She was part of the furniture, as Father used to explain. Which I always disliked, because Mildred was far more than that. She was, to me, the soul of this house with its countless rooms all empty as the next.

I almost folded in on myself at seeing her again.

"Eamon called you back?" I asked, not meaning for my voice to sound as relieved as it did.

"He did indeed," she replied with a smile that tugged the wrinkled corners of her mouth upwards. One thing about Mildred, she had been old for the twenty-seven years of my life. She had the same nest of wiry, grey hair and a face that bore more resemblance to the surface of a melted candle.

"Poor soul!" She rushed towards me, waddling like a duck on two of the same feet. "Bed bound for all those days. I almost demanded to be let back in so I could care for you myself! But, of course, that would not have been necessary since your darling husband has kept you fed, bathed, and rested. Lovely man, that Eamon. You are very lucky to have him."

I allowed Mildred to fuss over me, not stopping her as she reached towards the poppy-red curl of my hair that fell before my eye. With a motherly brush of her finger, which smelled of pine oil and lemon, she moved it out of the way.

At least I knew what excuse Eamon had spread about my imprisonment whilst my fingers had healed. It had been a long while since he blamed my absence on an upset stomach. Mostly because when he hurt me, the damage was easily concealed. This last time was a lapse in his judgement, one he would likely not allow again.

Or would he?

"Never mind that," I said, lifting my fingers to her shoulders. They felt like dough in my hands. I wanted her to envelop me in her arms so I could melt into the safety of her motherly aura. "I'm glad you are back. How about I fetch you a tea before you start, and you can update me on all the books you have devoured during your time off?"

It was Mildred who had encouraged my love of reading. From when I was a child, she had smuggled books past my mother, and we had discussed the stories in great detail. Reading was an escape, one that we both thirsted for.

Mildred waved me off, pushing me with unseen strength towards the main doors at the end of the shadowed foyer. "Go, Rhory, get going with you. Your skin looks as pale as death itself; some sun might do you well. Bring some of that lovely glow back to those cheeks of yours. If you would wish to entertain an old woman, you can do so tomorrow. But today, I would be happier knowing you were out of this house."

"Are you sure?" I asked, almost expecting she would go back on her word.

"I'd rather you were not under my feet whilst I caught up on weeks' worth of neglected dust since I last stepped foot inside this house." She drew the feather duster from her belt, unsheathing it like a sword. With a great swing, she clobbered my arm with its soft end. If she noticed me flinch, she didn't mention it.

"Go, go, go."

My back thumped against the door. The chill of the autumn breeze slipped through the cracks, tickling across the back of my neck as though seducing me with the promise of the *outside*.

"Will you stay for supper?" I asked, hopeful. *Please say yes, please say yes.*

Mildred pulled a face, one that would've been best carved into the expression of a statue in mid-contemplation. "Dearest, I have a feeling I'll be cleaning from now until sunrise tomorrow. Although Eamon wouldn't allow that, would he? Darling man, the moment he walks in that door, he will relieve me of my duties. Such a caring soul."

I shook my head, the same pesky curl of red hair falling back into place over my eye. "Indeed."

A cloud passed behind Mildred's honey-coloured eyes. For a moment, her brows furrowed in wonder, searching for something that my face must have given away without me realising.

"Is something bothering you?" she enquired, eyes trailing me from head to foot. "If you are still feeling under the weather, I could see you back in bed, and then I'll rustle up some soup for you."

From the pits of my belly, I dredged up a mask to adorn. One that eradicated weakness. An expression which oozed—*I am fine*—in abundance. "And what, I leave the patrons of St. Myrinn without a visit from me? How could I possibly deprive them of my presence?

After the past couple of weeks, I am surprised the infirmary has stayed afloat without me."

Mildred's face cracked into a smile. "Only if you're sure. If Eamon thought I sent you on your way whilst still unwell, he would have my guts for garters. He cares greatly for you, you know."

I took Mildred in my arms before she had another moment to contemplate the wince that shattered my mask of strength in two. There would've been a time, years ago, that I buried my face in her forest of silver hair and inhaled the scents that clung to her. I was far too tall for that now. So, I rested my chin atop her head and held on tight.

"It's just so good to have you back," I said.

"Oh, my darling." She expelled a breath, her concern melting away like butter on a hot spoon. "I've missed you too."

Over her shoulder, in the distance of my home's entrance, sat the tall-standing mirror. I caught my reflection in it. Wide, unblinking eyes stared back at me, with a mouth drawn tight, all exposed by the golden glow which encompassed my hands.

Light spilled beneath my splayed fingers as though I held onto a star. A shard of sunlight grasped in my very palm. The magic was cold, like dipping my hands into the bottom of a frozen lake. But there was nothing painful about the light. It was peace. An emotion that reminded me of the sensation of snow falling upon my upturned face. The brushing of flakes as they tickled across my skin, before melting and leaving the icy kiss as a physical memory.

My power didn't always feel like this. Sometimes it pained me. Stung like the needle of a bee. Burned like the wick of a flame on skin. Shattered like finger bones beneath a hammer—

"Go on, get out of my sight, sappy fool," Mildred cried, pulling away suddenly, drawing me from the sudden, horrific memory.

The magic spluttered, winked and died out, all before she would've noticed anything was amiss.

"Don't tire yourself out too quickly. A woman of your age shouldn't be overdoing herself," I said, gripping the brass knob of the door with a firm hand. I forgot, for a moment, of my aching fingers. It shot a stab of pain up my arm. I drew blood as I bit down on my tongue to stop myself from yelping. It made hiding my pain easy when Mildred whacked me with her feather duster once again.

"Cheeky boy." I heard the mellow laugh in her tone. "If you were any younger, I would've made you eat soap for such a remark."

I yanked the door open, allowing autumn to spill into the foyer with its crisp wind. Leaves the colour off rust, wine and gold, shot towards and skated across the waxed flooring with ease. Mildred barked out a swear word that would've made the drunkest patron of our local tavern look like a saint.

"Who needs their mouth washing out now?" I

retorted, skipping out of the threshold before a third smack of her weapon of choice reached me.

Mildred's deep rumbling chuckle followed me down the three steps from the door, along the overgrown pathway of shrubs and reaching rose bushes, and out onto Darkmourn's main street. The childish joy it filled me with lasted until the screeching garden gate slammed closed behind me.

I hated lying to Mildred. It pained me. But I knew I could never burden her with what truly happened behind the closed doors of my family's home. It would break her, and I needed her whole. Selfishly, if it meant lying kept her laughing and… safe, safe from his gaze, then I would keep it up.

It wasn't like lying was a new concept between Mildred and me. I had been doing it to her since as long as I first learned to do so much as crawl.

Mildred didn't know of my magic. My heritage, beyond being the only son of the founder of Darkmourn's Crimson Guard, was a secret. Which, Mother would tell me, was very different to lying. Keeping secrets came from a place of protection.

When in reality, I knew otherwise.

It was tradition, when I navigated Darkmourn, to glance towards Castle Dread. I found myself drawn to the ominous place, like a moth to a flame. It sprouted in the distance. A dark scar across Darkmourn's landscape, and memory. A smudge of gloomy stone, stained-glass windows and the remnants of scaffolding from the recent renovations. Every year, it seemed the castle grew bigger. Swelling like the pregnant belly with more *halflings* imprisoned inside its walls.

It was a place my mother swore to keep me from.

Eyes down, trained on my scuffed boots, I pulled the red cloak over my head and moved with speed.

The sooner I reached St Myrinn's Infirmary, the better.

I remembered the day I was asked to identify the lumps of torn flesh and bone, as though it were yesterday. It wasn't the memory that haunted me, but the way death invaded my senses. How it clung on, refusing to give me any reprieve.

It had taken months for the smell of my mother's bloodied corpse to leave me. *What a mess.* That had been my first thought as Jameson, our family's personal physician and lead practitioner at St Myrinn's Infirmary, pulled back the blood-stained sheets and revealed the parts of the body beneath.

Then there weren't any other thoughts that followed. Only a mess of grief as the reality of what I looked upon crashed over me.

There was a slick, wet sound as the material tugged at ruined flesh, pulling loose bits back with it to expose the hollowed-out insides and the ribbon of guts that dribbled out onto the metal table. I'd vomited down my wedding suit. Over and over, my body expelled the day's joy and festivities. How could the happiest day of my life end in such a way? Ana Coleman, my mother, was laid out on a metal cot with skin of alabaster splattered with gore and grime. Only hours before my mother had raised a glass to me and my husband. Now she was scattered across a metal table with her legs beside her and her chest open and empty of what should have been inside.

As I stared down at her, vomit spread down my chin and tears sliced scars down my cheeks. I wanted Father to be with me, but his mind was already broken, and Jameson feared what would happen to him if he saw his wife like this. Eamon had kept him in the hallway beyond this room. I could still hear him. My father, whispering his pride and happiness to Eamon, whilst not knowing where we were and what had happened.

My father's mind had not been his own for years by this point. Mother had cared, night and day, for him. Now she was dead, I feared what would happen.

I'd vomited again. My throat burned with the bile conjured from heavy contractions gripping my stomach.

Eamon didn't waste time in convicting a rogue vampire for my mother's brutal murder. Days later, the nameless vampire was hung for all of Darkmourn to see as he screamed and pleaded his innocence. He hung from the noose, pale neck pinched by thick rope, as we all waited for the sunrise to come and claim him.

And, the worst part was, I had believed his innocence. I believed the vampire, who supposedly tore my dearest mother to shreds, because of the… blood.

There was so much of it. I couldn't understand why a vampire, whose requirement for blood was limited by law, would leave so much wasted. The foyer to my home was covered in it. Hours later, Mother still oozed blood across the metal table in the cellars of St Myrinn's Infirmary.

To me, it made little sense.

I had told Eamon my concerns, and it was the first time he showed me the monster that lurked beneath his perfectly crafted illusion. He had gone from the man who stole my heart to the one that held it in his hands and squeezed as he refused to listen to my disbelief. Eamon said I was blinded by grief. That I was a fool, stupid, pathetic—all because I refused to believe her killer was brought to justice.

The vampire was killed anyway.

He died, screaming for his innocence, and the case was closed.

"Keep going," the sleepy scrap of a girl mumbled from the bed before me. The crack of her tired voice drew me out of the painful memories. I gave into its siren pull, thankful to be reminded that it was all behind me.

"Where did I get to?" I said, tracing my finger across the page of the book resting across my lap. My mind had wandered to old memories, making it hard to locate where I had stopped. The girl, Sallie, giggled through a yawn as she watched me struggle.

"Is the story boring you to sleep, or are you just that tired?" I asked.

Sallie did a good job at widening her eyes as she pleaded. "It is the best story ever. It could never bore me!"

I closed the book as another yawn overcame her. Her milky teeth were stained a blush pink. Even the corners of her little mouth had the remnants of dried blood from her last coughing fit.

"Good," I replied. "That is the most precious thing about stories. They wait for you. And this one will not run away. So, how about you get some sleep, and we can pick up again tomorrow when I am back?"

"Will you come back *this* time?"

Her question had the power to break me. I leaned forward, chair creaking beneath me. The book became an afterthought as I deposited it on the sheets crumpled beside her. Then I took her hand closest to me, the one that always seemed to reach out when I read to her.

"Sallie, I promise."

She blinked heavily, turning her head to the side until she faced the ceiling instead of me.

"You promised me before, and then you didn't come, and... and. And you forgot about me."

Phantom pain speared up my two fingers. It was only a hint of the agony I had felt when Eamon shattered the bones, but it was enough to have me hissing through my teeth. "I could never forget you, Sallie, never."

"I hurt, you know," Sallie said, a jewelled tear rolling

down her swollen, colourless cheek. "No one could take the pain away but you. And you left me."

Sallie didn't know of my magic. Nor did any of the other patients that frequented St Myrinn's Infirmary. The ones whose discomfort I softened, and pain I blanketed, during my visits. If anyone knew, I would have been thrown into Castle Dread, never to help anyone else again.

Sometimes, that didn't sound like such a bad outcome. To be taken from this life and kept from returning. But that was a selfish wish, one I squandered quickly.

"Well," I drew the word out, offering Sallie a warm smile. "How about I don't promise you again since I'm the world's worst promise-maker. Instead, I would suggest a contract between me and you. One which legally binds me to return to your side come morning and finish that story you love so much."

Sallie scrunched her eyes closed. It was her way of pretending she couldn't hear me. "Con-ter-acts…" I almost chuckled at the way she echoed the word back to me, fumbling over its newness. "Mummy said they're for old people and vampires. Not for me."

She wasn't wrong, I had to give her that.

"A deal?"

Sallie peeked one eye open and shook her head defiantly, golden hair spilling around the feather-down pillow that propped her up in the bed.

"Okay then, I suppose there is nothing I can do—"

Sallie's eyes burst open as a gravelly cough clawed

itself out of her throat. Her sudden jolt tore my hand forward. But she didn't let go. Not as the whites of her eyes bulged a dark red, and blood splattered across the sheets before her.

"It's okay, Sallie. It's going to be okay." I opened myself up to Sallie's emotions. Taking a deep breath in, my magic roused deep in my core; like a butterfly cracking out from its cocoon, it awoke in a flurry of spreading wings.

I *felt* her turmoil and pain. It struck me like an arrow into my chest. Claws cut into my lungs, echoing the very agony Sallie was currently lost to.

This was what I visited St Myrinn's for. For this very moment, and the peace I could offer. It made me feel less useless. My being here gave me purpose. I recognised how selfish it was, but still, I returned. Because if someone couldn't take away my pain, how all-consuming and haunting it was, then I could at least do it for others.

I had been visiting St Myrinn's since Mother was killed and Father was moved here to be cared for daily. It took a year for his mind to kill him and return him to my mother's side in death. Even without him here to visit, I came anyway. It made me feel closer to him.

Sallie cried out, gasping for air as the coughing fit subsided for a moment. I sunk the fangs of my magic into her hurt and dragged it out of her like a dog to a bone. Sallie's coughing spluttered and calmed. Blood spread across her lips, dribbling down the sides of her mouth as though she was a vampire and had just completed a feed. But it stopped bursting from her ruined lungs the disease slowly ate away at her.

The small lines on her face melted away. I watched the hint of a smile return to her pink-stained mouth and even her eyes seemed to widen without effort. Slowly, as the storm of her pain continued to thrum within me, Sallie relaxed. Laying back into the pillow, her eyes drew heavy. I separated her exhaustion from her agony and fed it back to her.

I removed her terrible emotions, allowing more pleasant ones to replace them in their void. To give Sallie some form of peace, I harboured the pain and claimed it for my own.

❦

I didn't wish to leave Sallie's side, but the sky beyond the infirmary was growing dark. If I didn't return by nightfall, Eamon would come and find me himself. And that thought alone had me dropping Sallie's hand and leaving her in the grips of painless sleep.

Jameson must have sensed my presence as I reached the main atrium of the building because he raised his hand in farewell. At least, that was what I thought before he called out my name.

"Rhory, can I borrow a moment of your time?"

My rushed steps slowed as I glanced hesitantly between the deep maroon sky and Jameson, who watched me expectantly.

"I really should be getting home…"

"Just humour me, for a moment."

I swallowed a hard lump in my throat. "It's Eamon, he doesn't like me staying out past dusk."

Jameson's grin beamed at that. "I hardly imagine there is any human, vampire or witch, that would wish to see you harmed knowing the man that waits at home for you."

It was not those who lurked in the darkness of night that scared me, but the very man who waited in the warmth of my home. But I couldn't say that. And I hardly thought using Jameson as an excuse for why I was late would prevent the lashing of Eamon's belt.

That very excuse didn't work the last time.

"What is it I can do for you?" I asked, unable to keep the annoyance from my tone. If Jameson noticed it, he didn't react.

"I've been meaning to ask this of you, but of course, you have been… out of action for a while." He looked to my broken fingers, marvelling at how well they healed. I could almost hear his inner praise, gloating to himself about how his work alone had seen my fingers heal straight and with little scarring.

Unlike Mildred, Jameson didn't need to be told I had fallen ill with a stomach sickness. He was so blinded by infatuation for Eamon, he would never have questioned my disappearance being a result of my husband.

"I have something for you. Here." He plucked a torn, aged parchment from the pocket across his chest and held it out to me between two fingers.

"What is it?" I caught the hint of scrawled, untidy

writing between the folds as my firm question spilled out of me.

"He said he needs aid with his grandmother. The note explains it. Pleasant chap, he was. He said he heard of the wonders and effects your visits have had on our patients at St Myrinn's and wishes for you to offer the same for his grandmother."

"Grandmother," I echoed.

"Auriol Grey. She lives in a cabin outside of Tithe's old wall. Directions can be found on the note, as well."

Tithe was an old village that was once surrounded by a wall that kept the monsters out and the humans in. Since the covenant between the humans and vampires had been signed in blood, there was no need for such separation of our kinds. Which was odd why Auriol Grey deemed Tithe a place to live when it had been abandoned many years ago.

"You said a man gave you this?"

Jameson nodded. "Indeed. Didn't catch his name, but he said you would know him."

I pulled a face which screamed how untrue that statement was. "And you are confident he asked for me?"

One of his plucked brows raised and his lips screwed into a pout. "You can't turn it down."

"Pardon?"

Jameson stepped in close, looking towards a gaggle of bed maids who rushed past us in a cloud of hoods and aprons. "Rhory, funding for St Myrinn's has dried up. Since Lord Marius has suggested the opening of healing facilities at Castle Dread, it seems the more mundane route of medicine is being forgotten."

I shook my head, unsure how the Lord of Vampires, the creature that ruled over the undead of Darkmourn, had anything to do with me and this note.

Reading the confusion across my face, Jameson continued. "Money, Rhory, I have been offered an abundance of it if you visit Tithe and provide care for this Auriol Grey. Your father had always been such a supportive sponsor for our infirmary, but I'm afraid the reserve he left us is running out. This." He jabbed at the note currently strangled within my fist. "May just save us."

There were so many things I wished to say. I felt the excuses tingle across the tip of my tongue, begging to be released. Except, I didn't have the courage to speak my mind the way I wished.

"I'll think about it," I replied finally.

"Rhory—"

"Tomorrow," I said. "Give me until tomorrow. Of course, I would need to pass this by Eamon. If I was to go elsewhere, it would make him... worried. He likes to know where I am."

Jameson bowed his head, the dull light from the brass chandelier above casting a ruddy halo across his balding scalp. "Certainly. Although Eamon is a man of pure heart, if you explained that an elderly woman requires your company to ease the suffering of age, then he would not refuse you the visit."

*He would, if he so wished.*

"Tomorrow," I repeated then turned on my heel with a gentle yet blatant air of dismissal around me.

"Or you could stick your hand into your pocket, Rhory Coleman, and show some of that generosity that has seemed to perish alongside your father?"

I stilled. A cold rush flooded up through my body, and back down again, until my legs were ice and my bones as dense as stone.

Behind me, I heard Jameson fuss over himself and the words that his lack of self-control spilled. Not that I hadn't contemplated this myself before Jameson had said it. It'd been three years since my parents had died and the money which was left to me had fallen into the hands of my husband. Even if I wished to dig my fingers into the piles of coin that came with my family name, I couldn't.

Eamon had it locked, with the key secure and far away from me.

Guilt coursed through my body and soul. It was thick as tar and as hot as boiling oil. Just as I had that fateful night when I stood in this very building looking at the brutalised body of my mother, I wished to scream.

"I've spoken out of line," Jameson mumbled beneath his breath.

"Forget about it." I couldn't bear the silence that would have followed if I didn't say something.

"No, I was wrong to say such a thing."

"I will do it," I said, speaking from the raw place of guilt that would make even the strongest of men do another's bidding. "Tomorrow, I will go to Tithe. For your sake, I hope it gives you what you desire."

"St Myrinn's thanks you," Jameson said, reaching out and squeezing my upper arm. My body cringed at the contact. "As it always has, and always will."

"Auriol Grey, do not deviate from the path."

Perhaps it was my anger that diluted Marius's warning, or was it the rush of sickness that spread across my stomach? Regardless, I didn't *fucking* listen. I would scorn the day that bastard wolf bit me. From the moment its fangs sank into my arm, tongue lapping at the oozing blood, I would never forgive myself for stepping one foot off the path.

My mind was elsewhere as I exited the grand doors of Castle Dread. I never looked back when I left Lord Marius's domain, not because I feared what I would find but more because I just hated the ambiance. It was all cobwebs and dust and was so fucking cold.

Night still dominated Darkmourn, but dawn would arrive soon. I had always found the early hours of day the most beautiful, but today I was far too angry to care for its splendour.

It had been ten years to the day when the covenant

between living and death was signed, and my brother had let me down. Arlo had promised to return to Darkmourn with his husband, Faenir, to celebrate our success.

Darkmourn had never been the same since that fateful day when the treaty was signed.

But, not to my surprise, Arlo had not arrived. I had waited in the presence of vampires, peering meekly into my glass of red wine, trying to convince myself it was not blood whilst trying to conjure a good enough excuse not to drink it. I had hoped Arlo would distract my hosts from seeing me tip the wine into the nearest plant pot, but that didn't happen, because Arlo never arrived.

Arlo was older by a few years, but I couldn't help but feel as though he was younger. He had spent his youth protecting me, and then nothing. Of course, that was not my story to tell. My story was far more… mundane.

I kicked through the wisps of mist which clung to the castle's outer grounds. Ghostly shadows danced across the floor, obscuring the gravel path that crunched beneath my feet. I was far too focused on my disappointment from the evening's festivities to notice when the crunching of my footfalls ceased. I didn't notice when the ground had grown soft with dewy grass.

Not until the wolves were upon me.

As the first rumbling growl echoed though the dark, I protectively cupped the doughy swell of my lower stomach. The baby was only a handful of months old, but I already felt overwhelmingly protective of them, now more than ever.

The wolf parted from the darkness as though it was born from it. Shadows clung to the thick hide of dark fur. Silver droplets of saliva fell from its open jaw, every single pointed tooth flashed in my direction.

I had been aware of the shadow hounds that lurked the grounds of Castle Dread, wolves that were cursed alongside Marius all those centuries ago. Sometimes I could hear them sing all the way from my home on the outskirts of Tithe. Even now, as the wolf padded on large paws towards me, I couldn't help but admire its deadly beauty.

The mist had devoured the stone path I had stupidly stepped from. Even if I wanted to find it, I couldn't, not without taking my eyes off the creature which prowled towards me. There was only one I could see, but I heard the rest. They waited in the shadows, watching as a diligent crowd viewed a show. Yipping and snapping jaws were their applause as this brave beast picked on me.

I drew the stake from my hip, one I always kept close when breaking bread with the undead. Thrusting out the point towards the monster, I bent my legs and readied myself to run or fight.

"Now, now," I cooed, as though speaking to a child. "Steady yourself, pup."

The wolf snarled, splashing drops of saliva across its thick neck. It must have been the alpha of its pack. Even I recognised the command rolling out of its jaws; the sound kept the other wolves at bay. This would be the one to attack first, the rest of them would have the scraps.

I was fully prepared to drive the stake into the beast's neck and run. If that was what it took, I would do it. Gods knew I needed to get out some of my frustration from the evening. And it was not fear I felt. Instead, I buzzed with adrenaline that resulted in a strange sense of calm to settle over me.

I took a deep breath in and gripped my weapon tighter.

The wolf's eyes burned like molten gold. It stopped moving, gaze flickering from the stake, then back to my face.

"Yes," I sang. "That is a good boy."

It walked back and forth in a line, regarding me with narrowed eyes as I praised it.

"I am going to leave you in peace, just as you are going to leave me. I'm afraid you'll not be feasting tonight."

Damp grass flattened beneath each careful footfall backwards. Every time I put my boot down, I longed to hear the tap of stone beneath it.

One hand was still outstretched, pointing the stake towards the wolf whilst the other held the faint swell of my stomach.

I would have told Arlo tonight that I was expecting. All day I had pondered what his reaction would be to finding out he was to become an uncle. Part of me convinced myself that the news would make Arlo visit more often. And yet he did not show. Disappointment was an understatement. It was fury that I truly felt, even if I didn't want to recognise it. Which was why, if this creature lunged, I would be ready. In some sadistic way, I longed for it. At least something about the evening would be exciting.

"You wouldn't like the taste of me anyway," I said softly, refusing to take my eyes off the creature. "It has been days since I have kept down a meal, and longer since wine has passed my lips. I would be unseasoned and bland. Trust me."

The wolf tilted its large head. For a moment I caught some recognition in its expression.

"My mistake," I said. "I should have focused on where I was going. The nurse at St Myrinn's told me my brain may grow as foggy as a bog, the larger the baby grows."

What did I think to achieve, having a conversation with the unholy creature before me? Of course, it couldn't understand me. The only conversation it knew was hunger. Something I sympathised with since I found out I was with child.

The wolf followed at a distance. It never allowed too much space to grow between us. Just when I believed it would forget me and move on, it padded forward.

"You're such a handsome beast," I said, swapping my tactic to one of compliments. If the wolves were anything like Lord Marius, stroking their ego would work enough as a distraction.

I was wrong.

"Such big eyes you have—"

The wolf threw itself through the air, shadow and night blending as one. I stumbled back, falling over my feet as the monster's jaws split wide. Time slowed, and I refused to scream. All I thought of was my baby and the stories I prayed to tell it.

I bit down into my lower lip, blood bursting across my mouth as though I chewed down into a ripe fruit. The wolf latched onto my wrist. At first there was no pain, only the lapping of a rough tongue against my broken skin.

Then the agony came, like wildfire. It overcame me. Devoured me. Enough to set each of my bones ablaze.

I swung my spare arm wide. It took two powerful stabs for the stake to drive into the wolf's skull. Only then did it release my wrist. I had to pry it from me, then push the weight of the dead wolf from my lap where it rolled over into a heap at my side.

The pain was murderous, but I refused to scream. I wouldn't cry out for help.

I fell back across the ground as the beast's burning poison spread from my wrist, up my arm and across every muscle and through every vein. The rest of the shadow hound's pack still watched in the darkness. I felt them, stalking and waiting. In time they would come for me, picking the crumbs and leftovers from the beast I had just killed.

Soon enough, the sky was blessed with pink and oranges of a new day. I watched the sun rise, hand on my belly and arm covered in my blood, waiting for the wolves to come and claim me.

They never did.

I picked myself up. The ground swayed. I blinked,

and I was in Darkmourn, walking the streets before the world truly woke up. I blinked again, and I was in the forest, walking the path to my home where my beloved waited for me.

Relief flooded through me as I caught a flash of the cottage through the trees. A home he had built for me, for us. The trance I was in broke as I lifted my knuckles to the door and knocked. Before they rapped against the door for the first time, I noticed something. The pain was subsiding. My wrist, although covered in blood, showed no marks or wounds.

My skin was pink with fresh skin.

Although my outer body was fine, my insides still ripped and tore. Even the baby, deep within me and no larger than a bean, stirred. The cramp followed swiftly, spreading across my torso and stomach. I almost excepted the spotting of blood between my thighs. I had been warned about what the pain could mean if it ever happened. But this was different. It was not the baby.

It was... hunger. And not for blood.

This hunger was primal. And my stomach longed for the soft chew of flesh.

## ❧ 5 ❧

D arkmourn was an entirely different world at night. When the sun set beyond the town, and the human residents of Darkmourn curled up in their beds behind locked doors, it was the dead who came out to play.

Vampires roamed the night as though it belonged to them.

I pulled the cloak tight around myself, fending off the evening autumn breeze. It ruffled through my hair, so cold that even my teeth chattered, no matter how I tried to grit them closed.

All around me, fellow humans clambered on chairs and short-wooden ladders to prepare the town for its evening dwellers. One by one, the stained red glass lampposts were lit. The glow bathed the streets in an ominous haze of scarlet.

My pace quickened, and I buried the coiling discomfort Jameson's words left within me as I raced towards my home. I was late. And I dared to contemplate how Eamon would react when I returned, far past the time he allowed me out.

I thanked my lucky stars that Mildred would be waiting. At least she would hold off the wrath, perhaps even dilute it.

The red glow cast down from the many lampposts was not the only thing that changed when the sun departed and gave way for its silver counterpart. If I navigated the poorer, more clustered streets on the outskirts of the town, I would have found deep bowls of blood left upon doorsteps. Offerings to the undead, who left bags of coin as thanks.

Blood faired more than money. Its value was steep. But it was illegal to trade, not that it stopped those humans, in desperate need, from taking a knife to their skin and flaying it just enough to fill a mundane kitchen bowl.

Because of its illegal nature, there was no saying how much coin the vampires would leave as payment. It was a gamble. One I was thankful I would never have to partake in. Even if Eamon had cut my ties to my family's fortune, he would first kill me than let me bleed for the undead.

Up ahead I heard commotion coming from the White Horse. The tavern was named after the steed which Death was believed to ride upon. Humans stumbled out into the street, shouting thanks to the landlord inside with stomachs full of beer. Many still carried the glass tankards home with them, not wishing to waste the pricy drink just before the town's curfew was about to begin.

Inside the White Horse, the landlord would be busy swapping out barrels of ale for those containing blood farmed from livestock. Cows, pigs, chickens... it didn't matter what animals were slaughtered to provide the vampires something to drink, as long as it was not human.

Darkmourn's history suggested the vampires had spent years drinking blood from rats once the humans were kept safe within their walled dwellings, like Tithe. It was that fact which was part of the motivation for the Covenant to even be drafted.

They needed us. So, it was best to live in harmony than separated.

The Coleman's residence came into view as the drunk singing from the White Horse's patrons faded behind me. I picked up my pace into a slow jog, as if it would stop me being late. Perhaps, if Eamon saw me out of breath and hair plastered to my forehead with sweat, he might just be more understanding.

The wrought iron gate screamed on its hinges as I pushed it open. My skin crawled at the sound, alerting even the undead within the towering three-story houses that spread down my street, that I had arrived. If they could hear it, Eamon would have.

By the time my hand pushed against the black-painted door, my heart was in my throat threatening to strangle me. I hesitated. If only for a moment, nails digging into the already flaking paint.

*Breathe.*

If only someone had the power to take my emotions away. To remove my fear as I entered my home.

I was welcomed by the glorious scents of cooked food. One step inside the foyer and my mouth was watering profusely. The air's warmth suddenly made me feel overheated in my cloak.

"Eamon, I'm home," I called out, grappling with the lace ties at my neck. I hated how meek I sounded. My voice barely echoed in my home, as if it knew I was not worthy of it.

Silence reverberated around me. I stretched my mundane hearing out for signs of Mildred's heavy shuffling of her feet. By the smells that oozed within the dusty air of the foyer, dinner must already have been prepared.

"Mildred?" I called out, inhaling the pungent aroma of roasted chicken, potatoes baked in thyme and carrots bathed in spices. How I missed her cooking. For a moment, I forgot I was late, or the events at the infirmary had even happened. The smell alone conjured a smile and a hearty rumble of appreciation in my stomach.

"She isn't here." A voice purred from the darkness. "I dismissed her hours ago."

Dread traced its frozen finger down my spine as a shadow departed from a doorway to my left. There was once a time when seeing Eamon at the end of the day was something to look forward to. We had been in these exact positions before, except I would have run across the foyer and thrown myself into his arms.

Now, it filled me with dread. I'd much rather run away from him than towards him.

*But you can't,* I reminded myself.

I recognised his smile first. Wide and proud, displaying almost all of his perfectly lined white teeth. Shadows peeled from his face slowly, exposing his cobalt eyes followed by the high cheekbones and the subtle divot in his perfectly carved jaw.

Eamon's jet-black hair was slicked back away from his face. The flames from the chandelier above revealed that he had recently washed, which was not uncommon after a day's shift running the Crimson Guard. He would clamber into the scalding water of a bath, only to leave it once it had grown tepid.

He wore a loose white shirt, unbuttoned down to reveal the hard chest that lingered beneath. The sleeves were rolled up to his elbows, and in his hand he gripped the stem of one of my father's beloved wine glasses that had been blown for him as a gift during his marriage to my mother all those years ago.

We only ever drank from them when we had something to celebrate, which unnerved me beyond imagination.

"Mildred said she was staying for dinner—"

Eamon strolled towards me so suddenly I flinched backwards. The door pressed firmly into my spine.

"Are you disappointed, Rhory?"

I swallowed hard, not wishing to inhale too deeply.

Eamon was so close I couldn't ignore the heavy aura of lavender that seeped off his skin and hair. It was sickly. The type of smell that burned your nose and throat on the way down.

There was a time I used to long for his scent. I would've found it on my hands and my clothes and smile at the thought of the man that left it on me.

Now it haunted me, alongside the sweeter memories.

I wished to say otherwise, but I retorted with a single word. "No."

Eamon's gaze stalked me from head to foot. I felt the question glossed across his thin, red lips. "Where have you been?"

"I—I…" My chin dropped to my chest. It was easier to look at my boots than into his bright, inquisitive eyes. "Jameson asked to speak with me. I told him you would've wanted me home, but he was adamant he needed a moment of my time."

I almost closed my eyes in preparation. Scrunched them closed to protect myself from the hand he would likely raise in punishment.

When nothing happened, I hesitantly glanced towards him. Eamon rocked back a step and lifted the lip of his glass to his mouth instead. "Well, I am sure *your* tardiness will not be a bother again. Come, let us eat. I have some good news I wish to share with my darling husband."

Eamon swept away, back towards the door he had slipped from. Our dining room waited on the other side, which led straight through to the kitchens at the back of the house. By the smells of food that weighed heavily on the lower ground of our home, I knew the table had likely been set.

Eamon must have sensed my hesitation to follow. It was not by choice that I didn't fall into step behind him. My body had betrayed me, refusing to move from my place against the door.

"Come." His command was short. Unignorable. I almost relaxed at the sudden anger behind it. I expected it with the first thing he had said to me, not the last. The presence of the nasty side of Eamon had finally shown itself, and I felt at ease. It was better facing the monster than waiting for it to strike.

"It would be nice to eat before the food grows cold," he said.

My bones creaked as I took that first step away from the front door. Still, I couldn't muster a word to say to him.

The dining table stretched the length of the room. It was so large it could have seated at least twenty dinner guests. Mother and Father used to host Darkmourn's nobility at the turn of every season. The feasts they put on, with the help of Mildred of course, would be all that was spoken about amongst their friends, and Father's colleagues at the Crimson Guard. Our wine cellar would be raided, only to be filled again by the time the next celebration begun.

All those chairs had been removed from the room, leaving only two left. One for me, and one for Eamon. He could have sat anywhere but chose his place directly beside me. Every time his knee brushed mine beneath the table I stiffened.

"Are you not going to ask me about my day?" Eamon raised Father's celebratory glass up as if he was hinting the question I should ask.

I always found that my movements were rigid around my husband. Whatever I did, whether it was cutting potatoes on my plate, or walking at his side... I did so carefully. Carefully was certainly the right word.

I lifted the napkin from my lap and dabbed at the gravy that stained the corner of my lip. I did so because Eamon grimaced as though disgusted by my table manners. For my husband, there was never a hair out of place or food on his face. He was above that.

"I trust it was good, considering we are drinking one of Father's oldest wines and from his special glasses," I replied, forcing a smile that never reached my eyes.

Eamon took a deep swig of his drink. He didn't stop for breath. Not until the flakes of red wine sediment was the only thing left at the bottom of the glass. "Seven of our most wanted killers were found today."

What little appetite I had faded immediately. "Seven?"

"Yes. Those vampires think they can hide from us," Eamon barked a laugh, "Pathetic."

"Will they go to trial?" I didn't know why I asked it when I knew the truth. Darkmourn had not seen a public trial since Eamon took over my father's role of Head of the Crimson Guard.

"There is nothing to discuss. They are murderers,

Rhory. Monsters. One less vampire on Darkmourn's streets is one step closer to purifying it completely."

"One less killer, do you mean?"

Out of the corner of my eye, I caught Eamon shift his head around to look at me. I felt it, two eyes boring holes directly through my skull. "Oh, Rhory, of course that is what I meant."

"Good," I replied, mouth dry.

"Is that it?" Eamon slammed his glass down upon the table so hard, I was surprised when it didn't crack. "You know how restless my days make me, yet you do not share my celebration."

"I'm sorry," I said calmly.

"Do you even care for the effect this job has on my—"

"Temper?" I interjected, shocked that the word slipped past my walls of inner control.

Eamon's face flushed red. His chest rose and fell dramatically, and he didn't blink once as he regarded me.

But he didn't tell me I was wrong.

Before he could act out on the thoughts that clearly poisoned his mind, I raised my glass that had been left untouched until now and spoke with as clear of a voice as I could muster. "To my husband, Eamon Coleman, may he be successful in his *hunt*."

"Did you doubt otherwise? Rhory, I *shall* always be successful." He didn't join me in my cheers. Instead, he clutched his knife and fork as though they were weapons in his arsenal. "It would all be much easier if the

Crimson Guard didn't have to pass authority through Lord Marius. The clean-up of the vermin of this town would be completed in one bloody night. Instead, I am forced to wait."

Eamon's hate for the vampires seemed to have begun after the brutal murder of my mother. But I believed it started long before that, although he would never have admitted it.

The Crimson Guard, under my father's lead, were a force that protected both the humans and vampires of Darkmourn. Since Eamon had sunk his nails into them, it seemed the scales of justice always tipped towards the living.

I would never have said this aloud, but I thanked the stars that Lord Marius had his say in those the Crimson Guard brought to justice. His sway would have saved many unnecessary slaughters at the hands of my husband.

If my father could see the obvious corruption of his Crimson Guard, he would roll in his grave.

"I can still see the bruising," Eamon said, after finishing the mouthful of roasted chicken in a matter of a few chews. I thrusted my hands beneath the table, not wishing for his eyes to linger on my fingers.

"They are fine," I blurted, feeling the heat rise in my cheeks. "No one noticed."

"But what if they did?" Eamon asked. "You should have stayed at home until it had completely faded. I shouldn't have let you out today."

The tension rose between us, sharp and electrifying

as a summer storm. I panicked, knowing what was going to come. With Eamon, I always waited on the edge of a knife, unsure which side of his tolerance I would fall into.

My knuckles rapped underneath the table as I drew them back out again. The golden wedding band caught the amber glow of the burning sconces as I reached across and took Eamon's hand in my mine.

His mouthed parted at the sudden touch. I gripped on, feeling the urge to let my power out to calm him. But I restrained myself, not wishing to know the truth of how he felt inside. Instead, I let my emotion bleed out of my wide eyes as I leaned towards him.

"Darling," I whispered, the word only for him. "I am fine. No one noticed, and if they did, they wouldn't question the bruises as it would seem everyone in Dark-mourn knows I am cursed with a never-ending spell of clumsiness. I thank you for letting me out today. I needed it."

Eamon contemplated my words in taut silence. His teeth ground against one another, the muscles feathering in his jaw, as though he chewed what I had said, deter-mining if he could taste sincerity or the lie that it actu-ally was.

"I'm good to you." It wasn't a question, but a state-ment. One with no room to contest, not that I would dare.

"I know you are. You have my best interests at heart."

Slowly, Eamon's raised brows lowered and the tension around his mouth smoothed out.

I wondered if he saw how my other hand shook as I raised it to his face and placed it there. My fingers tickled against the short hair at the side of his head. Grey strands of hair mixed among the black, exposing the ten years of age Eamon had on top of me.

"What you do for me, for Darkmourn, is something undeniable. I know you will complete your work and we can celebrate together."

Eamon exhaled the remaining tension out of his nose. The corners of his lips turned upwards, giving me a glimpse of the man that I had met all those years ago. How his cerulean eyes had been so kind. He always looked at me as though I was the only person in the room, the world.

What I thought then was admiration and love revealed itself to be a nasty possessiveness. My skin crawled at the knowledge.

"You should get some rest," Eamon said, pulling away from me. I allowed my hands to drop awkwardly to the table as Eamon stood from it. He took the empty glass, and the burgundy bottle of wine in each hand. "Come morning, I'll be gone by the time you wake."

Relief swelled in my heart, but I bit down on the inside of my lip to stifle it from showing on my face.

"You work too hard," I said.

"Someone must. I have a town to protect." Eamon moved to the door. My eyes tracked him as though I was his prey, hiding in the shrubs as my predator passed.

45

"Will you be joining me tonight?" I asked, holding my breath for his answer. It was rare for Eamon to share a bed with me. I couldn't remember the last time his body had provided me warmth at night, not that I wished for him to do it.

The dread of where he would sleep was only another worry that cursed me during the day.

"Not tonight," Eamon replied.

I tipped my head in a bow.

"I *do* have your best interest at heart, Rhory," Eamon muttered, his gaze landing on my hand, to the fingers he had not long broken. "Everything I do is for you."

"I know," I replied. It was all I could say.

Eamon paused, as though he had something else he wished to say to me. Then he moved from the room, his knuckles white as he grasped the neck of the bottle.

I waited, steadying my breathing, and listened to his footsteps move through the foyer, up the curved stairway and across the landing far above the dining room. Only when the door closed to his personal room did I relax.

Even if this peace only lasted until I next saw him, I held onto and cherished it.

## ❦ 6 ❧

It seemed autumn had awoken today and chosen war.

As I walked towards my destination, the note Jameson gave me gripped in my fist, I battled through the season at every given turn. Frigid winds nipped at my ears. I drew up my red cloak and held the hood over my head for protection.

Leaves billowed from the bending trees lining the path towards Tithe. They were like the heads of spears, all varied shades of golds and jewels. I was attacked from all angles and couldn't do anything to stop it.

There was no denying the beauty of the season. It brushed the world in a shade of warmth and gave it a song of crunched leaves beneath feet and the whistle of winds.

I would've preferred to enjoy the drop in temperature if I was inside my home, curled by the fireplace with a book from Mother's personal library. Perhaps with a glass of mulled cider to warm my stomach and one of Mildred's muffins laced with maple syrup and topped with pumpkin seeds. Except that would mean staying home, and the guilt that woke me hours before had made me draw the note from yesterday's clothes before it forced me out the door towards the forgotten town of Tithe.

I remembered Father telling me stories of when the great wall that surrounded the commune of Tithe— keeping its occupants safe from a world ravaged by vampires—was finally torn down. He had only just been born and didn't remember the events first-hand. But, like much of Darkmourn's twisted past, the story of its destruction was added to the ever-growing storybook. Those tales were repeated to children with caution and warning. His parents had recited the tale to him, just as he'd recited it to me.

During my youth, me and my friends would run to Tithe, clamber over the rubble and used the deserted town's streets and buildings as our very own playground. We whispered about the elves that used to frequent Tithe, even daring one another to touch the tree in Tithe's centre, the very place those fey beings were told to have come through.

The elves had not been seen in years, but I imagined adults still used their memory as a warning to children who misbehaved.

*Do not be naughty, or the fey will come and snatch you from your bed only to replace you with another.*

Of course, my parents never used such a concept to

threaten me into behaving. Not when my mother was the very product of such a thing. Not completely human, and not completely fey. They called them halflings, but history called us by another name: Witches.

But being called a *witch* was no different to being a devil. The stigma was one of the many reasons Jak Bishop, eternal mate to Lord Marius—collected halflings as though they were coins, and he was a magpie with a thirst for gold.

Witches belonged to Castle Dread. Unless you knew how to hide from its all-seeing eye. Father, being the Head of the Crimson Guard, had the power and authority to keep those prying eyes from me and my mother. But it was not his will that kept us from Castle Dread. When his health declined, it was Mother who kept her strong thumb down on me, ensuring I was safe.

If it was not for her, I would have been taken years ago.

The only other trusted with the knowledge was the man who stole my heart. Eamon. At first, we all believed he could be trusted. Oh, how wrong we were.

No one knew what happened to the witches. Only that they never came back. It was as if the castle devoured them whole, keeping them from ever returning to Darkmourn's civilisation. Eamon reminded me of that often. So much so that I no longer took his words as a threat, but silently begged him to make it a promise.

The life Castle Dread offered must be better than what currently faced me at home.

I found the supposed path towards the cabin on the outskirts of the woods, just shy of Tithe's shattered stone-wall. Never had I ventured in this direction during my adventures to Tithe as a child, and nor had anyone else by the look of it. The woodland had overgrown; the worn path buried by debris, roots and foliage.

I wrestled myself through the skeleton hands of trees. One particularly low-hanging branch dug its spindly fingers into my cloak and threatened to pull it clean off. It seemed nature didn't fear the Crimson Guard. Anyone else would have seen my cloak and kept their distance, which was why Eamon ensured I wore it at all times. The colour marked me as his. His property. And I knew what he would do to me if he ever saw me without it.

I was thankful for the thin twig that snapped back and slapped across my lower face. It caught my chin quickly, drawing me out of those dark thoughts.

The deeper I drew into the woodland, the darker it became. By the time I found the cabin and the low light spilling beyond the windows, it was like dusk had fallen over the world whereas it must have only been midmorning.

*Who would live this far from everything?* The thought haunted me as I closed in on the front door. It was shrouded in climbing vines that had turned a russet brown.

Someone must have dwelled inside because the chimney pot billowed with a dark cloud of grey.

I knocked on the door, three times. The sound of my raps filled the woods. It was so loud that birds burst from their hidden perches in the surrounding trees. For a moment, far off in the distance, I was sure I even heard the howl of a wolf.

Silence responded. No one called out for me to enter, nor could I hear movement from inside.

After a moment, fear reared its ugly head. How stupid could I have been? One note, and the promise of funding for St Myrinn's. That was all it took to draw me here. Standing before the derelict building, I couldn't fathom how anyone inside could give so much more than a single coin to the infirmary.

The note crumpled in my shaking fist. I grew uncomfortably hot so suddenly. The warmth spread across my neck, my palms and even coiled across my chest until sweat blossomed across my forehead.

I almost missed my footing as I stepped back from the door. The sound of leaves screeched painfully loud as I stood on them. I winced, pinching my eyes closed as I continued putting distance between me and this place, my footsteps heavy with trepidation.

Father always said I was too trusting. He was right in so many ways, but it seemed even he was cursed with the same blindness as I.

Just as I was prepared to leave with haste, my eyes wrenched open at the sound of groaning hinges, and the door before me swung inward. A man stood in the threshold, an expectant glint in his eyes. Eyes the colour of molten gold.

"Rhory Coleman?" His deep voice seemed to silence the woodland entirely. I felt the power of his voice travel up from the ground beneath my feet. It took me a moment to discern that he had said my name, for it sounded so familiar on his strange tongue.

I swallowed hard, unable to draw myself out of the dark gilt pools of his eyes. Instead of forming a word in reply, I raised my arm out before me, the crumpled note suddenly exposed between my fingers.

It was all I could muster to explain my presence.

"So, Jameson *is* a man true to his word," the stranger said, one corner of his mouth drawing up into a smile. When he finally removed his gaze off me, I felt my marrow soften. My knees almost gave way from relief, or disappointment, I was not sure.

The man looked to the crumpled note, one thick dark brow raised. He didn't glance back to me when he said, "You better come inside."

"I am here to see Auriol Grey," I said, trying to force as much confidence into my voice but failing; it cracked as though I was merely a boy. He smiled at that. Smiled. Full lips, shadowed by an equally full beard, tugged upwards. It was the colour of warm sand, as was his hair which was drawn back into a bun at the back of his head.

"Yes, that is what I requested." Lines creased around his eyes as they naturally narrowed.

Heat rose in my cheeks at his reaction. "Is she here?"

"As I have said, come inside and I will take you to her."

Once again, as he spoke, the world grew silent. As if it, like me, hung off every word. There was a slight bit of annoyance radiating off him, proven by the subtle roll of his unnatural eyes.

"Excuse me," I said, chin lifted as my gaze widened whilst I regarded him. He currently blocked me from entering. Unless he wished for me to barrel through him, there was no way I could enter the cottage.

As though breaking out of a trancelike state, the man stood to the side of the doorway, giving view to the rickety hallway his broad figure had blocked. He waved a hand, mimicking the gesture a lord would have provided to the person they wished to dance with.

"After you," he murmured.

My limbs felt as though they waded through mud. Each step towards the cottage's threshold was stiff, but I managed it. I almost excepted the stranger to move out the way, but it seemed he wished to make me as uncomfortable as possible. His sly grin only proved my point, his gaze tracking the red glow which stained my cheeks.

He was tall. Very tall. The man had to bend his neck forward so the top of his head didn't bump across the doorframe. As I stepped in, shoulder almost brushing his abdomen covered in leathers, I had to bite back my gasp.

Instead of biting it back, I choked on it.

"Do you know my name?" he asked, expectantly.

"Unless you have told me and I ignored you, then no."

Disappointment winced across his expression, if only for a moment.

"Calix," he whispered beside me, body leaning in to ensure I could hear him. "Perhaps knowing my name will dampen your *fear* of me."

I could have sworn his nostrils flared. Was he... sniffing me? I stumbled forward, slightly out of his reach, only to feel more unnerved knowing I had my back to him.

"Should I fear you?" I asked, stumbling over my words enough to answer him.

"That would depend."

I didn't dare look at him, but I could certainly feel his gilded eyes boring holes into me.

"Calix, you gave Jameson the summons for me, did you not?" I said.

"Indeed, I did."

I forced a smile, feeling the skin on my face crack with the involuntary expression. "Then may I see Auriol? Or do you insist on keeping me from her?"

Calix exhaled slowly, sizing me up from head to foot. "Straight ahead. You'll find her on the last room to the left."

"Is she... troubled?" Troubled? My brain was so *scrambled* that was the word I had picked!

"Terrible," Calix replied, his smile slipping until his

face looked as though it had never known a smile before. "Go on ahead. I will follow right behind you."

I suspected he thought that would make me feel more at ease, when it had the complete opposite effect.

Wishing to get this visit over with, so I could return to Darkmourn with enough time to scold Jameson and get home before Eamon ever knew I had been here, I paced away from him. All the while, I felt his stare on my back.

My skin erupted in gooseflesh, and the hairs across my arms stood on end. As if sensing my discomfort, Calix emitted a low chuckle from behind me.

Except, it sounded more like a growl than anything else.

## 7

Nestled within the mounds of feather-stuffed pillows and ivory bedsheets, an ancient-looking woman waited. Her piercing eyes tracked my every movement. One was as bright as the summer sky, whereas the other was the richest of browns. Wire-framed spectacles balanced on the end of her neat nose; an old book laid out across her lap.

I could not place an age on her. She looked older than anyone else I had seen before. Her face was set with deep wrinkles, her hair the colour of freshly laid snow. Even her skin seemed translucent and lacklustre of colour. If it wasn't for the life that screamed out of her two mismatched eyes, I would have believed she was merely a corpse.

She leaned forward from the pillows. They had been stacked behind her hunched back to keep her upright. I could have sworn I heard every joint and bone creak in song.

"We have a visitor, Grandmother," Calix called out from behind me, making me jump.

The old woman, Auriol Grey, looked me from boot to head and exhaled a raspy breath. "What good is a visitor who doesn't bring me cake?"

My cheeks stained a deeper red, if that was even possible.

"Hello, Rhory," Auriol said, voice as clear as her gaze. "I should thank you for coming all this way to see me."

I stood in the doorway, hands clutched before me to give them something to do. My entire being buzzed, knowing that Calix lingered behind me. Like an unwanted shadow, he haunted me.

"Jameson passed me your summons but didn't specify how I could help."

Auriol narrowed her eyes, screwed her face up and patted the bed at her side. "Please, come closer. My hearing is not as famed as it once was."

As if sensing my hesitation, Calix leaned in and whispered, "Don't worry, her days of biting has long passed."

I couldn't dispel the feeling of deep-rooted discomfort. My soul was screaming at me to conjure some excuse and leave, never to see this place and the strangers it harboured again. But the note weighed heavy, back in the pocket where I had returned it, reminding me of why I had come here. Although, looking around this room alone, I couldn't understand how the Greys had the means to offer St Myrinn anything worthwhile, especially not money.

Calix hovered in the doorway as I paced towards the old woman, his prickling gaze never once left me.

Dust riddled the air. My nose tickled. The two bay windows at the west of the room were closed, and the curtains half-drawn. I almost had the mind to open them, if not for Auriol but for my sake.

No matter how I felt, the closer I got to the bedside and the smaller Auriol became in her perch, the more I felt unhappy that she was here.

"Forgive me if I come across rude, but this doesn't seem like the best place for someone of your… experience to live."

Auriol's laugh rumbled like a storm through a forest. The sound was more feral than pleasant. "Wise choice of words, dear boy. I could almost hear you say *age* beneath it."

I looked down, feeling as though I was scolded by a teacher.

"Is there a problem with my home? From where I sit, it is pleasant enough. Calix sees I am well cared for here."

I couldn't help but read the undertone of her comments and the mockery that seemed to thrum between Auriol and her grandson.

"Then may I ask why you called upon me?" I asked, unsure where the confidence came from. "I mean, the note was clear. You asked after me by name, it could have been any of the infirmary's healers or carers, I am simply a volunteer at St Myrinn's—"

"I am well aware of your charitable position, Rhory Coleman, and that is not why I asked after you. I hear you deal in pain, and I have an abundance of debt which I wish for you to collect."

Auriol looked down the length of her nose at me. Her bright eyes were alight with knowing. I couldn't hold them for long. Instead, I focused on the book in her lap, trying everything not to expose the panic that overcame me.

"I'm sorry, but I don't know what you are referring to."

"*Halflings* have a scent you know," Auriol said, nose twitching. "It is enough to fill a room, pungent and demanding."

I stumbled away from the bed. Instinct fired through me, scolding my urgency to get away from them. But there was nowhere to go. Calix stood in the doorframe, his broad body blocking it entirely. And there was the imprisonment that Auriol's gaze locked me in. It was heavy and all-encompassing.

"Do not worry yourself, Rhory. One's secrets are best kept by those familiar with secrets. Yours are safe here."

I shook my head, swallowed the lump in my throat and forced the fakest of smiles which cramped my cheeks. "You've got it all wrong. I think my coming here has been a mistake. I am sorry, Auriol, there is nothing I can do to help you."

"Calm yourself down, child," Auriol scolded. In a strange way, her clear annoyance silenced me. The feeling of displeasing her outweighed my worry. "Your panic is going to give me a migraine. Calix, make yourself useful and fetch some tea."

"Grandmother," Calix said, a hint of warning in his tone.

"*Leave* us to talk."

I glanced to the stoic mountain of a man. He ran a calloused hand through his length of honey coloured hair. A strand fell from the messy bun and draped across his face. "Would that be wise?"

"Your presence clearly unsettles the poor boy." Auriol waved a hand in dismissal, as though sending a dog away to its bed. "Shoo. Away with you."

Calix must have sensed the pure command in Auriol's ancient voice. He fell into the shadows of the corridor at his back. It seemed the cottage muffled his footsteps, swallowing any sound beyond this room entirely.

My blood thundered through me, echoing in my ears as though someone held a shell up to them. They knew. They knew what I was. But what caused my body to crash with anxiety was wondering what they would do with the information. I felt as though I had walked into a cobweb of iron with my eyes closed.

"If it is money you want from me..." I spluttered, ready to divulge that her attempts would be in vain because Eamon had my fortune locked in a chastity belt of his own design.

"Do I look like I need money? As I have told you, I have pain which I desire a reprieve from. Age is not kind. And you, from my knowledge, are the only one to offer me relief in the comfort of my home." Auriol gestured to a chair pushed into the corner of the room. "Fetch that and take a seat. I'm sure you would love to get this over with and return home before dusk."

I hardly took my eyes off the strange old woman as I followed her command and brought the chair close to the bed's side. The legs screeched as they were dragged across the worn wood-panelled floor.

"How did you know?" I asked, whispering as if the whole of Darkmourn could have heard.

Auriol reached out a hand across the bed. Her skin exposed rivers of blue and red veins hardly hidden beneath. Her arm was as thin as a twig, the skin melting from the bone as it sagged down with gravity. "I knew your mother, Ana, very well. In fact, there was a time when I knew you, Rhory Coleman. Although it would seem you *have* forgotten that all together. That is the curse of youth. Your minds are so busy that you can hardly remember what you ate for supper the night prior."

My mind had numbed to most of what Auriol had said. It was focused solely on the name she had spoken.

"You knew my mother?" I repeated. It wasn't a question for the old woman, but I felt the need to say it aloud myself to make it real.

"I did." Disgust tugged down at her face. For a moment, even the whites of her eyes dulled as her mood sobered. "It was terrible to hear of her…" Auriol hesitated. "Passing."

Grief always stalked me, lingering just over my shoulder. In moments like this, it struck hard and sudden. A sharp pain stabbed in my chest as Auriol continued speaking.

"I kept her secret. I promised to take it to the grave but did not expect it was her grave in which I spoke of."

There was no knowing if Auriol lied just to make me trust her. But the way her emotions clouded across her face, it was familiar. It seemed the old woman was whisked away, to another place and time, whilst the memories of my mother haunted her.

I couldn't find the words to reply. Instead, I took her hand in mine. It was frail and as fragile as glass. "Then I trust the same sentiment applies to me."

"Certainly, although I hope it is my grave this time. That is if Death ever deems me worthy enough for the peace it keeps from me."

Somewhere in the darkness of the forgotten cottage, a stove kettle whistled to life.

"Well," I said, lifting the lid on the power within me. Gold light emitted from my palms and the light seeped into Auriol's skin. There was something so freeing of showing my power so blatantly. I felt… seen. "Until Death lays their judgement on you, let me take some of this pain away. It would be a wasted journey if I left without helping."

Auriol's pain was physical. I closed my eyes and sensed her discomfort. It lingered between every joint.

There had been others at St Myrinn's whose body suffered with age, who I had helped during my visits. But nothing compared to the agony I took on for this woman. Hers beat any others by tenfold. It was so sudden and sharp. I sucked in an inhale and dug my teeth into the soft skin of my lip.

We sat in silence. Auriol grinned as I clawed the pain out of her body, whereas I felt as though mine was being torn apart. In the darkness of my closed eyes, I felt my skin split open. My bones cracked and splintered. Whatever this pain was that ruined her small, hunched body, I could have sworn it was inhuman.

"That is more than enough." Auriol pulled her hand out of my stiffened fingers, breaking the link between us. I didn't know how much time had passed, only that a silver tray of bone mugs waited on the cabinet beside me, milky tea still steaming with heat.

Calix had been in the room, all without me knowing. My skin prickled at the thought.

"Thank you," Auriol purred. It seemed she sat up straighter. The apples of her cheeks had flushed with vitality. "I cannot remember the last time my body felt so… light."

I went to stand, but the room swayed.

"And I do not think I can recall a time that I felt so much pain," I said.

"One grows used to it," she replied.

I couldn't imagine how that was possible. "St Myrinn's can help you. Give you longer term relief. I really think it would be wise if you—"

"That won't be necessary," Auriol interrupted. She pulled a face, which deepened the lines across her forehead. "You know, I always found it strange why Darkmourn's infirmary was named after the woman who sold my brother out and nearly had him killed."

"Pardon?" I spluttered, head still pulsing with agony.

"Ignore me," she replied, ending the conversation before it had even begun. "My brother would be the first to tell you I was always the hardest to please. Tea?"

I passed her a cup and picked one for myself. The handle was warm to the touch. The liquid inside was almost clear, all besides the flakes of mint that had fallen to the bottom. I inhaled the smell, desperate to have the tea wash away the lingering pain Auriol had left inside of me.

"I see you are familiar with the ball and chain? Your husband, Eamon is it?"

Her mismatched eyes had settled on the golden ring on my finger. I had the urge to place my hand between my thighs so she could not look at it. One mention of Eamon, and I felt the atmosphere shift. I wondered if Auriol sensed it too.

I nodded, noticing a dull, diamond encrusted silver band on Auriol's finger. "It is. What would be the name of your spouse?"

"Unimportant," she replied, smiling over the lip of her cup.

"That is a strange name, and where is *Unimportant*?"

"I ate him."

Tea burst up my throat, choking me. By the time my

breathing had steadied, my eyes streamed with tears and my lungs were raw.

I waited for her to tell me she was joking, but that never came. Instead, she continued sipping her tea with eyes never once leaving me.

Until now, I had wondered why I didn't remember Auriol. If she was a family friend, why had she not been around? Surely, I would have remembered such an eccentric soul. Or perhaps that was the very reason I didn't recognise her. Maybe my mother distanced herself because of the very nature of this old woman.

"Dusk arrives in the wood long before it graces Darkmourn's clear skies," Auriol said, filling the silence. "I think you should take leave. I wouldn't wish for Eamon to be forced from his duties at the Crimson Guard just to come searching for you."

"There is nothing more I can say to entice you to visit St Myrinn's?" I asked, placing my half-drunk tea back on the tray.

"Rhory, I am going to *pay* the infirmary just to keep me out of its grasp. I am fine, just as I am and have been."

I smiled, itching to leave. Her mention of providing donation to the infirmary was enough confirmation that my good deed was well and truly over. "I thank you for your generosity on St Myrinn's behalf."

My eyes kept falling back to the shadowed door, expecting Calix to be haunting it once again.

"You know where to find me," I said, offering her a smile as I edged away from the bed. I knew, deep down, if she reached out for me to visit again, I would soon burn the letter than do as it asked.

"Oh, I certainly do. But I will not require sending a summons for you again. You'll be back soon enough."

Her words unsettled me.

"Goodbye, Auriol," I said, finality plainly clear in my tone.

I could see the doorway now, right at the end of the corridor beyond the room. Calix was nowhere to be seen, but his presence lingered in every shadow.

"You have her eyes," Auriol called out, the sorrow I had seen earlier returned once again. "So bright, an emerald would be jealous."

I resisted the urge to lift a hand to my face.

"Your eyes are the windows to your heart. Not your soul. That is guarded, I can sense that."

I held Auriol's stare, not wishing to be the first one to drop it.

"There is much I must protect myself from." As soon as I said it, the pressure constricting around my chest loosened a little. Auriol would not know what I meant by that, but I did. And I had never given myself the chance to voice such a thing before.

"Stay safe, Rhory Coleman. There are monsters in Darkmourn, the likes that you could not even comprehend."

"I know," I replied as I took my leave.

I paced out of the cottage into a world of brass and golds and ran directly back towards the very monster Auriol warned me about. All the way back to Darkmourn, through the dense underbelly of the wood, I kept my pace up. Not because of my desperation to return home. It was the lurking presence at my back that kept one foot in front of the other.

Only when I exited the expanse of towering pine trees did I finally hear it.

A howl.

## 8

The last I remembered—before sleep claimed me—was the muffled humming of Mildred from somewhere within my home's many rooms. To stop myself from thinking about Auriol and Calix, or the impending doom which had settled in my chest, I latched onto the sound and allowed it to lull me into a false sense a security.

Until I was woken, abruptly.

There was no discerning if a noise pulled me from my dreamless slumber, or it was the sudden silence that spiked fear from me. What I knew with all certainty was something was terribly wrong. Bolting upright in the bed, the sheets barely covering my modesty, I scanned the dark room. The only light was that of the ominous red glow of Darkmourn's nightly world, spilling through the thin crack between my heavy stone-grey curtains.

Disorientated, my panicked eyes waded through the shadow cloaked room. My heart dropped when I saw my bedroom door was wide open. Then the thudding organ split in two when my eyes fell to the man slumped on the reading chair, legs spread and elbows leaning on both armrests.

"After everything I have done for you," Eamon said. His voice was deep and slurred. I could practically taste the sting of spirits that muddled his speech.

I gripped the sheets and brought them up to my chin. It did little to still the wave of shivers that overcame me.

"Eamon," I rasped. "What is wrong?"

He leaned forward, the chair creaking in protest. The crimson glow bathed over his twisted, furious face. His eyes were wide, his mouth pursed and colourless. In his hand he gripped the neck of an almost empty bottle. It seemed more like a weapon in his hold than the means to quench a thirst.

The cold claw of dread sliced down my spine.

"I am going to ask you something, and you are going to make sure you tell me the truth. Do you understand?"

I couldn't form the words to reply, so I nodded meekly. Eamon caught the way my gaze flickered to the open door. He stood, swayed on his feet, then walked to it. It closed with a sickening click.

I knew what was coming. Even though my mind raced for what possibly had caused the lashings I would soon endure, I could foretell the future in those moon-wide eyes of his.

"Is Mildred still here?" I asked, not wishing for her to hear the screams Eamon would soon conjure. Part of me didn't fear it. In a strange way, I almost felt relief that it was finally here after weeks of tiptoeing around the *beast*. I'd soon rather face it, knowing it would be short-lived and a time of reprieve from the pain would follow.

"No," Eamon snapped.

I swallowed, cold relief creeping across my neck like the grasp of a hand.

"I saw Jameson this evening and imagine my confusion when he told me you had not visited St Myrinn's today. My Rhory would never deviate from my rules. I had the right to call that man a liar. But is he? A liar?"

Bile crept up the back of my throat. It took great will to keep it at bay whilst I contemplated my answer.

"I can explain…"

Eamon shot forward, bottle raised high. His shout rocked the very rafters of our home. "Then do so!"

I threw my hands up and shielded my face, squeezing my eyes shut. Only when no pain followed did I open my eyes and lower my shaking fingers. When I did, I saw the long-drawn smile sliced across Eamon's face.

"Jameson asked a favour of me," I replied, voice trembling as violently as my hands. "I tried to tell you last night—"

"Quiet." The mattress creaked as Eamon added his weight to it. No longer did he hold the bottle like a knight wielding a sword. Now he simply sat. "He said. But what I cannot understand is why you agreed. You owe that man nothing. I am your husband, not Jameson.

How is it you seem to follow the commands of others who do not care for you, yet you choose to ignore me? Do you wish to hurt me, Rhory, is that what you are trying to do?"

"Not at all." I reached out for him. Eamon's shoulders had hunched forward, as though his misplaced sadness weighed heavily on them.

As my fingers brushed his sticky, sweat-damp shirt, Eamon struck forward. He had tricked me into his trap, leaving me helpless and uncovered. Eamon threw his arm towards my face. His entire weight must have been behind it, because the force blinded me. Pain burst across my skull. I didn't register how my teeth were jammed into my lower lip until the blood nearly suffocated me.

Suddenly, Eamon was atop of me. His powerful legs straddled either side of my waist, pinning me down. Not that I would fight him. It never ended well when I did that, so I kept still and compliant as my lip bled wildly into my mouth.

Eamon leaned down over me, teeth bared like a rabid dog. The bottle was still gripped in his large hand, the other had taken my wrists and pinned them above my head.

"Care to tell me where you went?" he growled.

I turned my head to the side as much as I could, wincing at every drop of spit that touched my skin.

"Tithe," I spluttered quickly, repeating the word in hopes it was clear. I didn't wish to give him any reason to prolong this punishment. "Tithe."

"You little fuck!" Eamon slammed the bottle into the bedding beside my head. I felt the power in the thud that vibrated through every feather-stuffed in the mattress. "I give you rules to protect you and you defy me. It is though you ask for this. You like it, don't you? Is that why you disobey me, because you beg for me to punish you?"

Tears sliced down my face as a sob wracked through my chest. All I could do was lay there, whilst my torn lip spread blood across my teeth, and the skin of my wrists bruised beneath Eamon's grip.

"No, no. Please," I begged. "I don't mean to upset you."

"Don't you?" He knocked his forehead into mine and held it there so all I could look into was his wide, feral sky-blue eyes. I inhaled deeply, drawing in the sickly scent of lavender mixed with whatever harsh spirits he had drunk. "What was so important that you picked Jameson over me? I should kill him for—"

"He told me of an old woman, someone who needed me to visit to help with their pain!" I shouted, arching my back to try to force him off of me. He held firm. Eamon knew what he was doing, holding my hands above my head. It stopped me from reaching for his skin and manipulating his emotions.

One touch and I could absorb all of his fury. I could take it away and fill that void with something kinder, more loving. So many chances I had before this night to do that, and only once had I ever tried.

I still bore the scars across my shoulder blade, left from his teeth.

"What woman?" His voice had calmed as he asked the question.

I felt the need to hold her name back. To protect it somehow. Names had power, that much was known. Revealing such a thing would turn Eamon's sights on them.

But maybe…

"She knew Mother and Father," I spat, almost laughing at the revelation. If Auriol had known my family, she must have known Eamon. He had been as much a part of it since I was barely eight and he the eighteen-year-old, fresh faced, Crimson Guard recruit who was more known for being my father's shadow.

Eamon completely released my wrists. He rocked back, still straddling me, but instead stared down at me with an inquisitive look across his face. "Who was it?"

"Auriol Grey," I started, watching the recognition deepen the lines across his furrowed brow. "Jameson gave me a note that said she requested my visit. He said she would fund St Myrinn's, and I was made to feel as though I could not turn it down."

"Auriol," Eamon seethed through gritted teeth. I cared little for the spit that flecked across my face. "Grey."

"Yes," I said, "Eamon, I'm sorry I didn't listen. I should have told you—"

The glass bottle smashed across the wall at the head of the bed. I barely had the time to close my eyes before shards rained down over me. Something wet dropped over my cheek and I hoped it was the spirit in the bottle, and not my blood.

Hands gripped down on my throat, thumbs pressing into my soft skin. I gasped like a fish out of water, but the air refused me. My lungs burned with fire.

"You'll never leave this house again," Eamon bellowed. I only hoped someone beyond the house would hear and come to help. I often thought that, but no one ever came. "I gave you freedom you never deserved, never!"

Stabbing jolts of pain exploded within my skull. I reached up and tried to claw his hands away, but he held on with a grip of iron. Eamon hissed when my nails drew blood, but it was no good. He seemed to thrive off pain. His hands tightened, his thumbs dug deeper into my throat and the world seemed to slip away.

The darkness behind my closed eyelids was both peaceful and welcoming. I didn't feel pain or panic as the starless night engulfed me, claiming me as its own.

"You made me do this!" Eamon screamed. "This is your doing. Not mine."

For a moment, I *felt* his fury. In my weakness, the door to my power could not be kept closed. It crept open enough, just a crack, that I was certain gold glowed from my fingers. If I had the strength to open my eyes, I would have seen it.

Instead, it stole my peace away and buried me in an emotion I would never be able to comprehend. Eamon's fury was as hot as a fire's heart, as sharp as a fork of lightning. Beneath it, I felt something else. *Panic*. I could not discern if it was my emotion reflecting at me, or his. But what I recognised was its power and strength. It careened into me, smashing me into the darkness and banishing me into a realm ruled by agony.

Just as the world slipped away, the pressure was torn from my body. Air flooded back into my lungs, threatening to burst them entirely. I grasped at my throat, no longer feeling hands upon me. My skin was raw. I coughed and gasped, my throat shredded to ribbons.

Eamon was still shouting, but I didn't care. It didn't matter. He likely melted into a puddle of guilt, pleading how much he loved me and how sorry he was.

None of it mattered. What was done was done, and it would happen again.

It was only when another voice registered that I dared copen my eyes. I rolled my head over slowly, wincing at the bruises that likely spread hungrily across my skin.

Eamon had his back to me. He was still shouting, facing something unseen in the door's direction.

"By the creed of the Crimson Guard, you will be drawn and quartered for breaking into my home!"

Every beat of my heart rumbled like thunder across my chest. It was so fast, I thought it would explode free from its confinement of ribs and flesh.

"Didn't I warn you before—"

A low laugh vibrated through the darkness, interrupting Eamon's frantic shouts. It tickled across my skin as I pushed at the bed in my attempt to sit up. Every muscle and bone screamed in resistance, but I fought on, fuelled by the wish to see who Eamon threatened.

Mildred? No. Gods, no.

The thought alone dampened my discomfort, enough for me to shift myself and get a better look at the door, to the person standing in it.

"If you wish to see morning, Eamon," Calix Grey growled, his eyes glowing a bright gold that would have made the stars jealous of its vibrancy, "I suggest you move out of my way."

## 9

For the first time, I felt Eamon's fear. It was an emotion I didn't think possible for such a man, but here he was, riddled with it. And I didn't need to touch his skin to know it, not when the emotion cascaded from him in undulating waves.

"I was wondering when you would break and come for him." Eamon stood straight, his shoulders rolled back and chin high. Whereas Calix held my husband's gaze, I watched as Eamon slowly slipped a hand into the belt of his trousers, flashing the hilt of a short dagger.

Calix prowled forward with the confidence of a man adorned in countless weapons. Except, from what I could see, he was without a single one.

"So, *this* is what you do to him? All your effort has led to this. The Leader of the Crimson Guard delights in causing harm to those he loves… as well."

My heart thundered in my throat as Calix risked a glance at me. His rich amber eyes traced across my bare chest, to my hands clutching the sheets at my waist and then back to my face. Pity slowly drew down his thick brows.

"What I do with my belongings does not concern you," Eamon spat, edging his body in the line of Calix's sight.

"But what you do with *mine* concerns me."

Eamon snatched his hand back from his belt and produced the dagger in a swift gesture, the dull blade held out before him, the tip aimed directly towards Calix's chest.

"One more step…" Eamon warned.

I winced when Calix threw his head back and roared with laughter. He clapped a large hand to his chest as though to catch his breath. "And what do you plan to achieve with that? I cut my meat with blades bigger, you fool."

Fear slipped back into Eamon's posture. This time I couldn't so much as feel it, but I could see it. His hand shook, knuckles paled white, as he gripped the blade's handle. Eamon stumbled back a few steps as Calix continued to move into the room, undeterred by the blade.

"He is mine…" Eamon spluttered; his voice was octaves higher than normal. It seemed Calix's presence had gripped him by the balls and squeezed.

"By all means," Calix spared me a look which sang with unseen pain, "You can have him."

Surprise leaked from Eamon at Calix's dismissal. "Then who brings you here this time?"

"You know who I want."

"What is to say he still lives?" Eamon said, goading Calix.

"Oh, *he* lives."

Who was it they spoke of? The thought was as sudden and lingering as the bruising Eamon had left around my neck.

"Get. Out," Eamon sneered, baring his teeth like some rabid animal.

Calix pointed towards me all without caring to look my way again. "Give me who I want, or I am taking him. It would be a fair trade after all."

It was Eamon's turn to laugh. My skin itched with discomfort as both men glanced towards me. I wished to draw the sheets above my head, pinch my eyes closed and pretend I was somewhere else.

"No, no, no," Eamon sang. "He is mine."

"Care to stop me?" Calix raised both hands out to his sides as though welcoming Eamon to try. And try, he did.

Eamon shot forward, his frantic growl giving him away. I screamed out, unsure if it was because I worried for him, or for Calix. *Or myself.*

Calix moved at the last moment. He side-stepped the blade, turned his broad body towards Eamon's outstretched arm and grabbed it. Eamon was torn from his feet as Calix heaved him forward.

I cried out as my husband's body slammed into the wall beside the open door. The dagger was still in hand, but soon slipped out of unconscious fingers. Eamon's body left a dent in the wall's plaster. Debris and dust, old paint and splinters of wood, rained down upon his unmoving body.

All the while, Calix showed no sign of effort. His breathing was steady as he looked down upon the body, a smile creasing his beard-shadowed face. "How I have wished to do that."

"Get out!" I screamed at Calix. It clawed out of my belly and filled the room. Even the volume surprised me. "Get out! Get out!"

Calix snapped his attention towards me, confused. "Unless you wish to alert every Crimson Guard in Darkmourn, I suggest you stop shouting!"

But I couldn't. My panic urged me to scream and shout, whereas it froze my body to stone in the bed.

"Eamon!" I cried out, wishing for him to wake. A small trickle of blood oozed from his hairline, staining the blond a harsh pink.

"Shh," Calix urged, suddenly beside the bed. He clapped a hand over my face, muffling Eamon's name from passing my lips again. "Stop it!"

Calix didn't remove his calloused hand, not when my tears danced across the dips and curves of his fingers and traced around his wrist.

I couldn't take my eyes off my husband. His chest rose and fell slightly, but it was not his welfare I cried for. It was the fury that would follow. The anger he would hold when he woke. I cried for myself. Knowing my skin would endure his embarrassment in the form of pain.

He would take this out on me. *That* was why I called out his name.

"Listen to me," Calix whispered, trying to make me look at him. His face was so close to mine. It was impossible to look anywhere else but his moon-wide eyes. I inhaled deeply, smelling pine and earth on his fingers. If I closed my eyes, I would have believed to have been in the heart of a wood after a summer storm.

My breathing was ragged, and my shouts had died down. I sensed hesitation in Calix's soft touch. He didn't wish to hurt me, but also didn't want me to ruin whatever plans he had.

"Promise me you are going to stop shouting," Calix murmured. "Promise me that, and I will explain everything."

He searched my tear-blurred eyes for that promise, because gods knew I couldn't speak it aloud with his hand still muffling me. I nodded my head sharply, as much as his grip allowed.

Calix dropped his hand from me and stumbled back. He withdrew so suddenly it was as though I had burned him.

"He… he will kill you for this," I said, throat sore from my anxiety and Eamon's necklace of bruises.

"I know. There is much you do not know, and I am sorry it has come to this." Calix didn't look sorry. In fact, his expression had hardened into a mask that revealed no emotion. His gaze was distant. "Can you walk?"

The question caught me off guard.

"You either walk, or I will carry you out of here."

"No," I snapped my refusal, gripping onto the sheets across my lap as though they had the strength to keep me in this bed, "Don't you touch me."

"So be it." Calix shot forward again. His hands slid beneath me. Effortlessly, he hoisted me from the bed. I gasped as his rough hand brushed the soft skin under my thigh. The widening of his eyes, and the way his mouth parted open, suggested he had not expected me to be completely naked.

"Get your *fucking* hands off me!" I shouted out again. It only rushed Calix more. He drew me towards his chest, one hand digging fingers into my skin and the other wrapped around my shoulder, to stop me from fighting back. "Eamon!"

My husband didn't respond. He was left on the floor, breathing but unconscious. If he witnessed me in the hands of another man, his heart would have stopped beating entirely.

"I'll ask you again," Calix grumbled into my ear. His cool breath sent a shiver down my naked spine, and conjured gooseflesh to erupt all over me. "You are welcome to walk, or I will carry you."

"Tell me what you want from me," I said, baring my own teeth. "Then I have adequate knowledge to provide you with an answer."

"You," Calix said, not a single hint of a smile on his powerful face, "You are my hostage. However, unlike your caring husband, I do not wish to hurt you in the process of what must be done. So, walk or carry?"

*My hostage?* Why didn't the words sound as horrifying

as it should? I looked to the four walls of this room and pondered what prison would await me when I left this one. I could have clawed my nails down Calix's thick neck or tangle them into his length of honey-coloured hair to pull it from the root.

But an odd calm rushed over me, and I replied, "I'll walk."

Calix put me on the ground, the bedsheet trailing around me like the dress of a bride. I sensed his control, and he fought against the urge to look me up and down. Instead, he kept his deep eyes on mine. "You can have a moment to gather any home comforts you wish to bring with you. And some… clothes perhaps."

"There are no such comforts here," I replied, jaw aching as I gritted my teeth.

"Clothes then, and quick. I'd like to leave before Eamon wakes, or his Crimson Guard come searching for the cause of your screams. Our carriage awaits."

I hurried to dress my naked body. Calix didn't turn away, which made me rush quicker. He stood guard at the door, beside Eamon's slumped body, his tapping foot like the ticking of the grandfather clock in the foyer downstairs.

My cheeks reddened as I clothed myself. I had turned my back to him, offering myself some reprieve from my embarrassment. By the time I was dressed in the slim leather breeches buttoned at my waist, and the red corset was slipped over my long-sleeved cream tunic, my hands didn't stop shaking.

If I could just get outside, then I could scream

bloody murder. It was clear Calix would do anything to get me out of this house, but the second we left I would make sure the whole of Darkmourn heard me.

I hardly had my boots on when Calix shouted. "There is no more time, come!" He had moved to the window, peering out between the crack of two curtains to the red glow bathing the streets beyond.

Another voice joined his from the door he had not long stood guard at. I expected it to be Eamon, returned from his forced slumber to stop me from becoming an *unwilling* hostage.

A woman stood there. Sheets of long, straight black hair fell across each shoulder, parted down the middle of her head. Not a hair out of place. Her skin was as pale as snow, her lips colourless in contrast to the burning red of her eyes. My blood buzzed in my veins, panicked by the final detail of the woman I noticed. Two, pointed teeth were longer than the rest, and rested slightly over her lower lip.

"The Crimson Guard are minutes away from storming this building," she hissed, hardly sparing me a glance.

"Millicent, how many?" Calix asked as his deep voice rumbled like thunder.

"Enough that the dance would not be enjoyable for us both," Millicent replied. "Get him into the carriage. Now!"

In a blink, she was gone. Her speed... her eyes and teeth. The deathly glow of her ice-white skin.

"You heard the vampire," Calix said, putting a name

to what my mind refused to believe she was. He too had moved quickly, and without sound. "It's time to go. And I think it best I reclaim the standing offer for you to walk. You'll come to learn I am not one to keep promises."

With one swift move, I was back in his arms. The ground fell away from me, and I threw my arms around his neck to steady myself from the suddenness of it all. His grip on me was not as hesitant as it had been when I was naked. He held me as though I was his most prized and coveted possession.

"He will kill you for this," I repeated to Calix, sparing a glance to my husband splayed across the floor.

"I'm counting on it," he replied.

Then Eamon was lost to the blurring of walls, floor and shadows. My stomach jolted violently at the speed. I scrunched my eyes closed against the sickening speed. Only when the world stilled, and the kiss of cold night graced my sticky skin, did I open them again.

A carriage waited at the end of the path from my house. Millicent was sat at the front, leather reins wrapped three times around both hands, connecting to the towering steeds of night before her.

I took in a breath, readying to shout out with all the air in my lungs.

"Inside," Millicent barked, red eyes silencing me. I saw hate in them. Danger. It made me cling to Calix against my better judgement whilst he forced me into the carriage, without any fight or resistance from me.

## 10

Darkmourn passed in a blur beyond the window of the carriage. There was only the screaming of the wheels slicing across the cobble street and the whipping of leather against the hinds of horses to occupy the thundering of my heart.

Calix didn't speak, not even to utter a single word of comfort.

It seemed comfort was a strange concept to the man who burned holes into me with his eyes. Not once did he look away from me, sitting on the velvet cushion seat in front of him. I didn't have it in me to enter a competition of stares, so I stared aimlessly out the window.

It was easy to lose myself in fear. With everything that had happened, it was hard to truly grasp the reality of my situation. But now, as Castle Dread was no more than a speck in the dark distance, it overwhelmed me.

I drowned in it.

My breathing became ragged, my eyes filled with

tears. The cushion beneath me groaned as I dug my nails into it. And all I could think about was Eamon. I could picture his wrath, when he woke, to find me gone. Missing. Already I prepared myself for the blame of this situation. My skin prickled with discomfort of the hand that would surely strike me. The booted foot that would drive the air from my lungs, and the hands around my throat that would keep the air from returning to them.

Beyond the window, the towering sentinels of trees revealed themselves. It was so sudden, I flinched away from the glass with a rasped gasp.

I pinched my eyes closed and lost myself to the storm inside of me. In that moment, I did not understand the world around me.

Hands found my thighs. The touch was reassuring in the dark, enough for me to open my eyes and regard the man kneeling before me.

"He cannot hurt you," Calix growled. There was something ancient and feral in his stare. "Not anymore."

I opened my mouth to explain to him how wrong he was, but all that came out of me was unkept breaths.

"Rhory, I need you to calm yourself down."

How was it this man's voice had the ability to sink deep into the frantic part of my soul? I felt him try to rein it, like a wild mare. The feeling was so strange that it caught me off guard… it was almost familiar.

All without removing his eyes from mine, Calix reached for my hand and pried my fingers from the cushion. A new thought seemed to demand my mind for a moment. He was so… warm. So… alive. My stiffened bones melted like butter over flame at his touch. I gave him no resistance as he guided my hand then took it in both of his.

Perhaps Calix sensed my thoughts, because his fingers tightened and he said, "Do it."

Those two words were as clear as his calm demeanour. It was that emotion I desired. I thirsted for it as a vampire thirsted for blood.

Blinking through the tears that continued to blind me, I opened myself up to him. There was no hesitation.

Golden light seeped from my fingers. It glowed like a star, captured in Calix's hands. The light blazed between the cracks of his fingers and bathed us each in the warmth of light. It banished the shadows that clung to the proud bones of Calix's face until every pore and strand of hair could be accounted for.

I did not borrow his calmness. I stole it. I clawed it from him, swapping my storm of anxiety for this blessed emotion.

His face creased with discomfort as I forced my anxiety into him, filling the space his calm had once claimed. Brows furrowed, and his full mouth thinned into a taut line of tension, but he didn't pull away. His hold on my hand tightened, refusing for me to pull away even if I desired.

My tears dried up. My breathing slowed and mind stilled. All the while, I watched as Calix struggled with the emotions I forced upon him. And he did it, all without complaint. He swallowed the acidic bite of the anxiety, warring with it internally.

"That is enough," I whispered, pulling my hand from him. All at once, the light dissipated until the carriage was coated in shadow once again.

Calix rocked away from me. The muscles in his arms bulged as he gripped the seat behind him. He used the leverage to seat himself. He slouched in on himself, his dark brows furrowed deeply until his entire forehead was cursed with worry lines.

"What a useful little trick," he said, tired eyes surveying me.

With my mind no longer clouded with fear and panic, I asked the only question I deemed important. "What do you want from me?"

"Straight to the point," Calix muttered. He lifted a lazy fist and rapped it on the wooden panel his head rested on. A hatch slid open almost immediately, revealing the burning red of Millicent's eyes.

I let Calix's calmness falter for a moment as the vampire looked directly across the carriage to me. Captured in the nightly winds, her sheets of obsidian hair whipped around her angular face.

"Have we lost them?" Calix asked.

"Of course," Millicent replied, rolling her eyes at the question as though it was the most ridiculous thing she had heard. "Is that a lack of confidence I hear in your voice?"

"Far from it," Calix replied. "Simply wondering why we haven't reached our destination yet."

Millicent bared her teeth, the two elongated points nipping at the skin of her lip. "Auriol's orders were clear. *Little Red* cannot be conscious upon arrival. It puts us all at risk."

Her use of the nickname shocked me. I had not heard it in years, not since my father had passed. It had died with him, yet here was this vampire speaking it without knowing the power it had over me.

"I know," Calix replied plainly.

If it wasn't for Calix's calm that still captured me, I would have reached for the handle of the door and thrown it wide.

"It's locked." Millicent glowered, drawing my attention from the door handle and back to her. Amusement burned in her eyes only to disappear when she slammed the hatch closed, leaving us alone once again.

"Don't mind her, Millicent has justified reasons for her lack of trust," Calix said. "But she is right, you cannot know where we are going."

"Why?"

"Because you are our hostage, and in the hostage rule book, being unaware of your whereabouts is pretty high on the list."

I swallowed hard.

"What do you want from me?" I repeated, this time my words as sharp as a blade.

"It is not what I want from you, but what I want from having you. Don't worry, *Little Red*, you'll get your answers soon enough. For now, we still have the issue about what I am to do with you if we ever want Millicent to stop taking us on this detour of Darkmourn's landscape. Trust me, she is stubborn enough to ride until the sun rises and burns her to ash. I rather enjoy her company, so we better figure this out soon."

"I thought she made it clear," I replied, sensing the chill of uncertainty slice up my neck.

Calix narrowed his gilded eyes, making them darker in colour and emotion. "I am not in the mindset of knocking you out cold."

"Thank my lucky stars. I was beginning to believe I'd been handed from the hands of one abuser to another."

He winced, as though my words had slapped him. "I am nothing like *him*."

"Yet you've broken into my home and taken me from it?"

Calix leaned forward, elbows resting on his spread legs. "Would you have preferred I left you?"

It was my turn to wince. My facial reaction and silence were answer enough.

"Right," Calix added. "Now, may I?"

From his pocket he withdrew a square of material. He folded it neatly into a thin length and held it towards me.

"And what are you going to do with that?"

I couldn't discern if my silver tongue was a result of my situation, or if the confidence had slipped into me from Calix when I had invaded his soul and swapped our emotions. I certainly hadn't spoken like this to anyone before. Or, at least not for a long time.

There was once a time when Mother would say my tongue was sharp enough to cut stone. That sharpness had dulled the night she died. Until now, it seemed.

"Blindfold you," Calix said; his voice was barely a whisper.

"Pardon?" I looked to the cloth he held out as though it was a viper that could strike me.

His laugh was deep and rumbling. It came from far within him and caused the skin on my arms to prickle with bumps.

"Did I stumble over my words?" Calix leaned forward more. "You can decide, if you wish for me to do it or you can do it yourself."

Not wanting to feel his touch again, I shot forward and tore the material from his grasp. His hand was left hanging out before him, fingers curling slowly inward.

I kept my stare pinned to his as I lifted the material. His smile was the last thing I saw as I brought the blindfold to my eyes and tied the length in a knot behind my head.

"Good boy," Calix drawled from the darkness that now blinded me.

My mouth became parched at his praise. I almost choked on it, finding the two words harder to swallow than the reality that I had become his hostage for some unknown reason.

"Sit back and enjoy the ride," Calix continued; I sensed the smile in his words. "We will reach our destination soon. Then you will get your answers."

"Good." It was all I could manage as I leaned back in the seat and folded my arms over my chest.

"You're welcome, by the way." Calix sounded so close as he spoke. If I had torn the blindfold from my eyes, I was confident he would have been inches from me because of the smell of forest and rain infiltrating my nose, and the soft brush of his breath.

"For kidnapping me?" I asked as my cheeks filled with crimson heat.

"For saving you," he replied.

"Eamon is my husband," I snapped, not willing to hear the pity in Calix's tone. "You have not saved me from anything."

"This…" A coarse finger traced the tender skin of my throat. My breathing hitched. I didn't need to look in a mirror to know the skin had bruised, Eamon's fingers imprinted in blues and dark purples. "…suggests otherwise."

## 11

Calix guided me from the carriage. There was only the scratch of material across my eyes and his warm, firm hand pressed into my lower back. Now and then short bursts of light shone through the top of my blindfold, like a glow through the crack of a narrow door. Then it was gone, and I was lost in darkness.

It was easier to rely on my other senses to help give me some clue as to where Calix led me. At first, the crunch of autumn leaves screamed beneath each of our footfalls. But that soon gave way to a patter as we walked across the smooth edge of stone. We had found some sort of path, or road. Soon enough, the sound of our footfalls echoed all around us. I knew we had entered some sort of tunnel from both the sound and the way the air seemed to grow thicker and damper with each inhale. I expected a reprieve, that we would come out the other end and be greeted with the much-needed kiss of fresh air. But I was wrong. The ground beneath my feet sloped downwards and the echoing only intensified. Even my heavy breathing and Calix's low humming became unbearable in the strange place.

We walked for an age until my thighs ached and my feet seemed peppered with blisters. At some point I lost my bearings completely, feeling that I was alone on this odd journey into the darkness without light to guide me, only the desire to not stop. Then Calix's hand would shift on my back, fingers drumming in rhythm, as if to remind me he was there.

I almost forgot the vampire's presence until she spoke. It seemed she had the ability to glide across the earth, with little need for making sound. Her footfalls were as silent as her breathless body. "Auriol will desire to know about this, Calix."

"Oh, I know."

Shivers trailed down my spine at the closeness of Calix's whisper.

"Then would you wish to do the honours to wake her and tell her what you've done?" Annoyance graced Millicent's stoic tone. There was something scolding about the way she spoke to Calix, as if she was his mother, and he, her son.

"Does my grandmother scare you, Millie?" Calix retorted, using a nickname for the vampire that was poisoned with jest.

"Only a fool wouldn't fear Auriol," Millicent snapped.

"Exactly why I wish for you to be the one to inform

her of this evening's events," Calix replied. "If she doesn't already know, that is."

It took a moment for Millicent to reply. Her silence unnerved me. Calix's deep chuckle suggested he sensed my emotions as if he had my abilities.

When the vampire replied, she was further away, her voice muffled by distance, but as clear as newly forged steel, "You owe me."

"Add it to the list," Calix retorted.

We continued walking, me blind to everything but the symphony our breathing made and the choking intensity of the damp earth-filled air, Calix humming his tune to entertain himself.

It was cold in this place. The chill was deeper than what winter gifts to the air. It was the type of cold that came hand in hand with the dark, so intense that it belonged in the furthest parts of the deepest lake, where sunlight could never reach.

I was thankful for the thick red cloak I had taken with me. The cloak that I had worn since the death of my father, with its gold trim around the hood, was a symbol to his position in the Crimson Guard. Many had wondered why Eamon, now taking the mantel my father once possessed, didn't insist to wear this very cloak himself. Whereas I once believed it was my husband's wish for me to have something of my father, I now knew it was simply a way of marking me. Possession of the Crimson Guard, it screamed. Possession of Eamon.

He would have thought this cloak and the meaning behind it would have made me untouchable.

I laughed suddenly, the sound echoing around the dark.

*How very wrong you were, Father.*

The direction we took changed suddenly. There were turns. Left and right, right and left. Sometimes it seemed we turned corners in circles, as if Calix had attempted to trick me. However, I didn't sense that would be the case.

Perhaps it was his borrowed calm, that still rallied within me, which tainted my vision of him.

"Rhory," Calix said as we slowed to a stop. "We can take this off now."

His fingers tugged at the knot of material at the back of my head. Although he had not stopped touching me since we left the carriage, the new place his fingers graced still made me quiver slightly.

I squinted against the flare of light before me. It took me a moment for my eyes to settle, enough for me to distinguish the glow was not the sun but a burning torch. Fire hissed and spat whilst it devoured the oil-soaked head as it hung on a sconce beside a large metal door.

Calix allowed me a moment to gather my surroundings. As I had thought, we were within some form of tunnel. Dark stacked bricks glistened with water, mould and moss. The glow from the sconces revealed the arched brick ceiling above my head. A droplet of stale water fell from the ceiling where it splashed across my cheekbone, startling me.

"If I asked where we are, I guess you wouldn't tell me," I said, drying my cheek with the back of my hand.

"Darkmourn," Calix answered through a grin, his deep voice echoing all around us.

I fought the urge to roll my eyes, finding it easier to look anywhere else but his intense gaze. "No, would have been an easier answer."

"I'm not one to lie, Rhory."

Gods, he really was leaning heavily into his sarcasm, using it as support to hold him in place.

"Are you planning on having me stand here or…?"

Calix leaned close towards me. I stiffened as his face neared mine. A surprised gasp broke out of me. The sound deepened his grin, only to make me feel foolish when his arm snaked out behind me and reached for the handle to the metal door. With a push, it opened. The hinges wailed, demanding oil.

"If I had a red carpet to roll out, I would've." Calix swept his muscular arm towards the shadows of the room beyond the door. "Welcome to your holding cell."

It should have filled me with dread, but as the glow of the sconces filled the room before me, I felt nothing of the sort. Firelight raced across the modest dwelling, revealing a large fourposter bed with mounds of pillows and rumpled sheets tangled atop the mattress. The dark wood furniture had been pushed up against the walls, cabinets and tall wardrobes that seemed more like doors leading to magical worlds within.

Carpets covered the slab stoned flooring, overlapping one another in contest. Even the walls were draped with rugs to conceal the evidence of leaking bricks and patches of moss.

The glow of fire shifted, stealing my attention back to Calix. He had lifted the burning torch from the sconce and drifted into the room without invitation. I waited at the threshold, awkwardly watching as he shared the flame with waiting candles throughout the room. By the time he was finished spreading his fire, the room held some inviting warmth.

"This should be comfortable enough for you to get some rest," Calix said, as if his simple suggestion could erase the fact I was now his hostage.

"Do you concern yourselves with the comfort of your prisoners?"

His eyes sparked with golden fire. "Should I not?"

I shrugged, feeling self-conscious beneath his devouring gaze. "What do you want from me, Calix Grey?"

He flinched. "My wants do not matter in this circumstance. Auriol can answer those questions come morning, but until then you need to rest. Regardless of what you think, I'm not a monster." He paced towards the door, needing to put as much distance between us as possible. "I'll return for you come morning with food."

The thought of being left alone caused fear to spike within me. It encouraged a desperate plea to burst out; it stopped Calix dead in his tracks, "Wait!"

He stilled, glancing over his shoulder enough to see me. "Is *my* room not up to the standards of a Coleman?"

I swallowed hard. "This is your room? Here?"

"Indeed," he replied.

I wished to ask him where he was to stay, but the question failed me. "Shouldn't you be chaining me to a wall? Isn't that what captors do to their victims?"

The torch cast shadows across Calix's face. It gave him a sinister glare as he slowly smiled at me from his place by the door. "Now, tell me why I would wish to give pleasure to my victim, if that is what you think you are?"

My mouth dried at his comment. I ground my teeth together, trying to keep the impression of strength when, in fact, my insides had turned to sludge and my knees threatened to give out at any moment.

Calix reached for the door, this time to close me in.

"I could escape, you know!" I snapped. "Nothing is stopping me."

There was no lock on the door on the outside, only two small sliding bolts on the inside. I could keep him out, but there was nothing stopping me from leaving.

"And pray tell, what would you do then?" Displeasure flashed across Calix's face. I had yet to place an age to him, but the threads of silver within his honey-coloured hair and beard suggested he had passed his thirtieth year. "Even if you could work out the maze of tunnels and find yourself in the fresh grace of Dark-mourn's landscape, would you run home? Back to *him*?"

"My husband?" I asked, voice high and light. "Is that whom you refer to?"

"Yes," Calix replied, voice as cold as the brick walls surrounding me. "*Him.*"

I didn't need to answer his initial question. The answer, although not spoken aloud, was obvious. No, I wouldn't run back to Eamon. And Calix knew it.

"What you should understand, Rhory, is tonight should never have happened," Calix stared straight into my soul as he spoke, "Eventually, we would have been in this situation, your being here and what that means for us all. But that shouldn't have been tonight. I understand you have questions and deserve answers... but I ask that you wait for tomorrow. It is best to come from Auriol herself."

I should have refused. Should have slammed my foot into the ground and demanded every detail that Calix kept from me. The hows, and whys, burned through my mind like a wildfire in summer.

"One thing," I said as Calix closed the door. "Just tell me one thing. It is the least you can do."

He surprised me by nodding, when the grimace and tension in his jaw suggested he wished not to tell me anything. "Fine. Ask your question."

"Why did you come for me tonight if it was not supposed to happen?"

Fury pinched Calix's strong brows forward as his nose scrunched. His pale pink lips pulled back from his teeth, enough to mimic the expression a vampire gave before sinking teeth into human skin. Except, Calix was no vampire. I had felt his warmth, the heartbeat that thundered in the tips of his fingers.

"I heard what he was doing to you," he replied finally. I blinked and was back in my room at home, with Eamon above me and his hands wrapped around my throat. The bruises seemed to burn with agony as Calix's eyes brushed over my neckline. "Rhory, I am many things, but I couldn't just leave knowing what was happening to you."

I dropped my eyes to the floor, finding the memory and the truth of his words too harsh to bear.

Then he asked me a question: "How long has this been happening?"

I wanted to tell him that it didn't matter. To inform him that the happenings in my home, in my marriage, had nothing to do with him. Or anyone for that matter. But when I opened my mouth to tell him just that, I replied with the truth, "Since my mother..." Grief struck again, promising to strangle me. "Since their influence could no longer protect me."

I stood in the middle of the room, feeling as though the entire place was about to cave in on me. Calix gripped the metal door, using it to hold himself up, or hold himself back; I could not tell which, only that it practically groaned beneath the force of his hand.

"Don't tell them," I snapped. Calix didn't owe me anything. There was no reason he would care to harbour my dark secret, but I found him agreeing without question.

"It is not for me to tell," Calix said. I sensed there was more that he wished to share, but the metal door swung closed, and he was gone.

Calix left me alone. Except that wasn't entirely true. His scent was everywhere. It lingered in the air. It stained the sheets I slowly climbed into on shaking legs and arms.

I forced myself to close my eyes, with no idea if it was day or night or if my body was as violently lost as I was in this strange, tunnelled place.

## 12

I woke beneath the glare of burning red eyes. My mind took a moment to differentiate them from cauldrons of endless depths filled entirely with blood. I choked back a gasp, gripping the sheets of my bed with iron fingers. *Calix's bed*, I hastily reminded myself. Beneath the vampire's watchful gaze, the comfort of the feather-stuffed bedding suddenly dissipated, leaving only the sensation of being weighed down by someone's attention.

"Oh dear. Did I wake you?" Millicent asked, reclining into the downy cushions of the aged reading chair. The leather of her trousers squeaked as she crossed her legs with dramatic flair.

"Yes," I replied, throat dry, and unsure on what else to say.

Millicent smiled, flashing the two sharp points of her canines as her lips drew back. There was nothing friendly about the expression. The smile never reached her eyes, which still hadn't left me. "Well, I apologise."

I didn't need to touch her skin to sense the dishonesty that dripped from every syllable she spoke.

"Rhory, isn't it?" Millicent's gaze narrowed. I was completely trapped beneath it, like a mouse in the paws of a bloodthirsty cat. "I see Calix decided against the suggestion of chains. He has always been more… pragmatic with his choices, however I can't help but sense he has had a lapse in judgement. Door unbarred. You, in his bed no less. What next, will he be offering to spoon-feed all his prisoners?"

Hostility rolled off her in formidable waves. As Millicent off-loaded her spiel at me, her upper lip continually curled upwards until her face was screwed in a snarl.

"Does my presence offend you?" I asked.

Even I was surprised by my question. I no longer had the dregs of Calix's calmness I had drawn from him the last time I was awake, but still this confidence was new. No, not new, but simply buried for a long time. Lost.

"Offend me?" Millicent's laugh cracked the air like lightning. It was so sharp it whipped at my bare soul. "Come on, Rhory, don't play the idiot. You know who I am."

"Millicent, isn't it?" I sat forward, knuckles turning white as my hold on Calix's sheets tightened. I could tell from her pinched expression she didn't like me using her own tone back at her.

A darkness passed behind her eyes, turning them almost black. The air shifted, bringing with it a new scent of lilies. Then she was before me, inches from my face, with teeth so close my blood retreated into the far corners of my body.

Fury brought some semblance of scarlet to her cheeks. So brutal, it defied her dead flesh and gave her a sense of humanity.

"Look at me," she demanded. The vampire moved with fluid grace and unnatural speed. Her nails pinched the skin of my chest as she took a handful of my shirt and tugged me towards her. Naturally, I reached for her single hand and clasped it with both of mine. It was the extra leverage I required as she practically tore me from the bed and held me aloft.

She was cold to the touch. As I pinched my eyes closed in fear, I remembered the same chill in the skin of my mother as I held onto her hand the last time I had seen her in St Myrinn's morgue.

"Please," I begged, turning my face away from her. "Whatever I have done, I'm sorry!"

I opened up my magic to her and instantly regretted it. The hate that slammed into me was as powerful as a wall of stone. I felt my bones crack at the impact and immediately drew myself out.

It had been many years since I had last been so close to a vampire. During the days when my life wasn't poisoned by Eamon, my family would host Darkmourn's vampiric nobility in our home. Mother and Mildred would conjure feasts that even the dead couldn't turn their noses up to. Then came Eamon. After my mother's murder and father's shortly followed death, the last vampire I had been close enough to see was the man who hung for a crime I didn't believe he committed.

"Open your eyes," Millicent sneered. "I do not have your powers, *witch*, but I can sense a mistruth better than any hound. Let me see it."

I didn't feel like I could refuse her. Prying my eyes open, I couldn't do anything but look directly into the pits of blood-red orbs that were now inches from my own.

If Millicent needed to breathe, she would have taken a hulking one at that moment. "Do you know what you took from me?"

My skin grew sticky, my heart thundered with the agony of my impending doom. All I could do was answer her again.

"I don't know, but I see that I have caused you great pain. Millicent, I'm—"

"Don't you dare. Your apology is unwanted if you do not know what it is you must be apologising for."

"Then tell me," I said, recognising the pinch of my skin across my already bruised neck.

Millicent parted her dark rose painted lips to answer me. Before a sound came out, her head snapped towards the closed door of the room. Her ears pricked at a sound that was out of the mundane reach of a mortal. Then she released me. I fell back into the bed with a thump that jarred through my body. When I looked up again, Millicent was sitting in the chair with her legs crossed and gaze focused on her nails as if they were the most interesting thing in the world.

That was when I heard the footsteps. Only a few seconds later the door creaked open, and Calix stood beneath its frame.

"Good morning," he said, eyes boring into me.

"Evening," Millicent corrected, all without looking up from her nails.

Calix snapped his head towards her, a look of surprise betraying his face for only a moment. It melted into one of fear which had him looking back towards me. It was only when he saw me again did he relax.

"I told you not to come," Calix said with false calm; he stared at me as he spoke to the vampire.

"And *I* do not abide by your commands, Calix."

"I asked for company," I added quickly, steeling my face and holding back any hint that I was lying. "Millicent found me exploring. I was lost, and she kindly returned me back to the room. Since then, we have just been... catching up."

"Catching up?" Calix raised a single, thick brow.

I threw my legs over the side of *his* bed, planting my feet on the cold ground; it helped the room stop spinning so violently.

"Is that so?" Calix sighed, looking from both of us with an expression of distrust.

Millicent glanced to Calix, a hint of her snarl returning to her pristine face. "You could have at least guarded the door. Your judgement is clouded."

I felt the unspoken thrum around me like winds

coiling around my legs and arms. There was something in the way they looked at one another, then to me, that revealed a secret they both wished not to speak aloud. Did it have anything to do with what Millicent accused me of?

"Auriol wishes to see us," Calix said, ignoring Millicent's comment about his judgement.

Millicent stood, clicked her head from side to side and faked a yawn that I hardly imagined the undead were privy to. "You can go without me. I have had enough of Auriol's fury to last me a lifetime and the next. Plus, I need to hunt. Our little *catch up* has built a rather burning appetite."

Millicent cut her gaze to me. I swallowed the lump in my throat, making the most audible gulping sound.

"It's been a pleasure… Rhory."

Calix sidestepped the door without a word. Millicent mocked a bow before she passed, disappearing into the shadows of the tunnel system beyond the room.

"Are you alright?"

I forced a smile at Calix but couldn't hold his gaze for long. There was something intense about it that had me preferring looking at the ground instead. "Should you be concerned about the welfare of your hostage?"

"Others would say I shouldn't, but I do."

His answer was plain. Simple. It spread a warmth across my chest, one that I wished would leave me.

"Regardless of my treatment, I *am* still your hostage. Your kind words and offerings mean little to me when you have stolen me from my home."

"You are not wrong. And if you would like some answers, then I suggest we make a move. By sunrise, I must leave you for the day."

I wished to ask why, but I couldn't show such interest.

"I want to go home," I said, almost stamping my foot like a spoiled child.

"That is not how this works."

Pacing across the room towards him, I made it a few feet from the door when Calix pointed to the ground beneath me. "Perhaps you should put something on your feet, unless you wish for me to carry you again?"

I turned my back on him, quick enough that Calix couldn't watch the scarlet spread up my neck and across my face.

"I'll wait for you outside," Calix said, his voice dripping with warmth.

Hunger cramped my stomach, causing it to roar.

"What was that?"

I faked a cough, rushing to grasp my boots that waited beneath Calix's bed. "Nothing."

Calix released a laugh that echoed through his room and the tunnels beyond. "If you are quick about it, you may find that some warm tea and cake waits at our destination. And before you ask, no. Not all our hostages are fed cake. Just you."

"Lucky me," I whispered to myself.

Calix heard me, replying loud enough for every dust mite to hear, "Indeed."

The blindfold was removed when we stepped out of the dank air of the tunnels, into the blessed chill of the nightly breeze. We continued walking a short while before we reached our destination. Twigs and leaves crunched beneath my footfalls. Calix even found it necessary to turn me around in circles a few times before removing the blindfold. *Just to be sure*, he had said.

Auriol's cottage was before us, the dark forest cocooning us entirely. I turned around, trying to search for the direction we had come out of the tunnels from, but it was no good.

"I've slept for an entire day?" I asked, studying the dusk-bathed sky above the thick canopy of trees above.

"Just about," Calix replied, reaching for the brass knob of the door. "My grandmother comes alive when the moon is high. I would have woken you sooner if she was able to host a conversation, but her age exhausts her."

I nodded, glad that his focus shifted to the soft glow of candlelight in the corridor beyond.

It wasn't that I had slept for a day that worried me. It was that I had been kept from Eamon for a day that did. As I watched Calix's broad back ahead of me, I had the urge to turn and run. Surely Eamon's wrath would dilute if I ran back to him now? The longer I was kept, the more kindling would be added until his blaze would spill over.

Pain jolted through my chest.

"Care to join me?"

I looked up, breath ragged, as Calix watched me with obvious concern. Before I gave into my desire to run, I fought against myself. Each step into the cottage was hard. Only when the door swung closed behind me did I feel like I could breathe again.

The cottage's air was filled with the sweat aroma of tea. It wafted in clouds that clung to the corners of rooms. Mint, camomile, ginger. I could taste the scents on the back of my tongue with a single inhale.

I had never met my grandparents on either side of my family. They had died when I was too young to hold my own bottle. I had often wondered what it would have been like having them and could imagine that it would be like this. Hearth warmed houses, tea and the smell of cooking that seemed as part of the furniture as the floral décor I now passed.

Auriol was nestled within her bed, as she had when I had first seen her. It seemed she hadn't moved, but there was more energy to her mismatched eyes as she lifted her attention from the book held in her crone-like hands.

"I knew we would see each other again, but not so soon as this," Auriol said, taking the round spectacles from the bridge of her nose and placing them on the hardcover of the book on her lap. "First, let me apologise for my grandson's actions. Know that he did not act on my authority, but his own, no matter how misplaced it is."

Calix tipped his head, unable to hold Auriol's gaze.

When she regarded him, she did it with anger and disappointment. Those expression's relaxed when she focused back on me. "Come, sit with me. You must be hungry, and I know the tea will help."

Not wishing to offend her, I stepped away from Calix's side towards her bed. As I passed him, he leaned in and whispered, "She doesn't know about Eamon."

A chill sliced down my spine. There was no keeping the discomfort from my expression.

"Your presence bothers the poor lad," Auriol barked. "Calix. Make yourself useful... elsewhere."

I heard him retreat without comment, leaving us alone once again.

Auriol's eyes fell on the bruises at my neck. "Which one did it?"

I lifted a finger and traced the sensitive skin. "It is my fault."

"Nonsense," she replied. "However, I know hesitation well. No need to tell me, I will see both Calix and Millicent punished as one party since they were both at fault for taking you."

"Please," I blurted. "Don't do that."

She narrowed her gaze on me. I sensed her reluctance to let it go, so I took hold of the conversation and changed it.

"Wasn't this always your plan?" I asked. "Taking me from Eamon. Having me as your hostage?"

There was no hesitation when Auriol replied, "It was, in time."

"Then why wish to punish Calix and Millicent, when you wanted this outcome?"

"Shouldn't you wish to see them both punished? They stole you from your home, your husband. We are keeping you against your will for our own gain. You, of all people, should wish to see them flogged for their actions."

She was testing me. I could see it, like a glint in her eyes.

"Why?" I asked, choosing to ignore her question. "Tell me what it is for, then I can answer."

"Eat something first. And drink. Once I see the bottom of your mug, I will tell all."

Her hand shook as she gestured towards the set-up of cake and tea at the bedside. I didn't waste time to slather the thick slab of pale sponge dusted with sugar and filled with smooth jam. I devoured it quickly. The tea washed it down. It was cool enough to knock the entire mug back. I cared little for the sprig of fresh mint that followed.

"Now tell me," I said, clearing my lips with the back of my hand.

"Yes," came a voice from the doorway. I didn't need to turn to know Calix had returned. "He deserves to know."

"Okay, okay," Auriol said, wincing as she shifted in the bed. Three pillows were propped behind her to help her old bent frame sit up. Calix rushed forward to help her, but she batted him off with a wave of her hand.

"Rhory, we need you to see that something is

returned to us. I promise, beneath our hands, no harm will come to you, but you must know that your being here is a plan that has taken years to complete. Of course, it was not entirely prepared before my grandson decided to flood your home and snatch you like some common criminal. However, here you are. And thus, the plan must begin."

"You are a bargaining tool," Calix added, at the displeasure of Auriol, "A means of a trade."

"Trade? For what?"

"In a manner of speaking, yes. My grandson, Calix's younger brother, was taken from us. We are under the understanding that it was your husband, Eamon and his Crimson Guard, that are behind the abduction. We had believed he was killed, but recent information suggests that Silas is alive and if we ever wish to see him returned home, we must do so by using you."

"I don't understand," I admitted as a storm captured my mind and twisted it into a vortex of thoughts.

"I will put it plainly. Eamon will know you have been taken from him and he will know why. Until he returns Silas back to me, I am afraid you cannot go home to *him*. Our terms will be sent to Eamon and they shall be clear. One for the other." As Auriol spoke a heavy sorrow weighed down on her. It aged her before my eyes, deepened her wrinkles and dulled her eyes with a milky sheen.

"You are going to send me home?" I asked, already knowing the answer as I looked up at Calix. Not once did he take his gaze off of me. It was what I had asked for, but the thought unsettled me deeply.

"Yes," he replied, voice deep with regret.

"Eamon loves you," Auriol said. "We know your importance to him, likely the only thing with enough leverage to give me back my Silas. Someone who is equally important to me."

I found tears filled my eyes. There was no discerning which emotion pricked them into existence, but I couldn't find it in me to fight them.

"Eamon is not as controllable as you believe him to be," I said, looking back at Auriol. "I'm sorry, but you will fail. If he really has your grandson, I will not be the person to sees that he returns home to you."

Auriol's shoulders sagged. "I do hope you are wrong."

"When?" I asked. "When do you hope to begin this bargain of yours?"

Auriol and Calix shared a look, one that spoke volumes.

"After the turn of the full moon," Calix answered me. "We will both be…"

"Indisposed," Auriol answered for him. "Then we will send our terms to Eamon. Until then, Rhory, I promise to provide you as much comfort as possible. It is the least we can do."

"And if he doesn't do as you wish?"

Calix placed a hand on my shoulder. The touch surprised me, but I found I didn't flinch. There was something familiar about the weight of his hand. My body recognised it, but I couldn't place why.

"Then you stay until he does. No matter how long it takes," Calix said.

I stood, knocking the empty mug of tea from my lap where it smashed into pieces across the wooden floor.

"Take me back," I demanded. "Take me back to the room."

Calix looked to his grandmother, for the permission she granted with a nod of her head.

"I am sorry," Auriol said. "I wish I could tell you this was a hard decision to make, but I cannot lie to you. Not you."

I didn't wait to hear the rest. None of it mattered. I left the room, knowing that Calix followed close behind me. He didn't stop me as I burst out of the cottage, leaving the tendrils of comfort behind for the cold of night. Perhaps it was because he knew I couldn't go anywhere, or that he knew I wouldn't.

There was only one person who would suffer the consequences of this bargain. And that was me. All I could think about was Eamon and his reaction to when I was finally handed back to him. My skin prickled at the promise of pain that would soon welcome me home.

## ❧ 13 ❧

## 4 YEARS BEFORE

My tongue traced across the back of my teeth. It brushed over the dead flesh caught between them, coating it with the taste of spoiled skin and blood. No matter how much I swallowed, the sickly tang of copper would not ease. It stained my cheeks, my throat, and thrashed within my stomach with every slight movement.

Vaguely, through the roaring in my head and the settling of my human bones as they fused back together, I was aware of the cold gore spreading down my chin, my neck and coating my bare chest.

I should wash before anyone found me, but I didn't dare move. My eyes were entirely fixated on the two vampires I had killed. Through it all, just looking at the torn flesh and tooth-scarred bones, I felt a swell of pride. I did that. I killed them, and they deserved it. If I could have done it over and over, I would have.

My grief was so fresh, so new, that I had hardly

recognised it for what it was. Hours had passed since Calix and I found our parent's slaughtered by their vampiric friends. Friends who now lay, body parts scattered throughout the forest bed, before me. And the grief was only starting to seep in.

My ears, still keen from the recent shift, picked up a snapping of wood far off in the darkened forest. I snapped my head towards it, nose flaring to catch a scent on the subtle wind which raced around the thick trunks around me.

Was it Calix? He knew what I planned to do and threatened to come after me. Or perhaps it was Grandmother. Auriol would have been able to stop me with a single command. I gathered, from her silence, she wanted me to avenge her daughter's murder as much as I longed for it.

That was the difference between Calix and me. My brother didn't have it in him. He couldn't kill anyone. He fought the beast inside of him, whereas I welcomed it.

There was another crack of wood, followed by the heavy step of a boot as it ground leaves into the dirt. I opened myself up, allowing my ears to pick up the rhythmic steady beat of a heart. One heart banged far greater than the others as it was closer.

I was all but naked, with nothing but the blood of my parent's murderers to warm me. Yet the vampire's blood was nothing but a frozen presence against my burning skin.

"I know you are there," I called out, throat slick with vampire blood.

Through the darkness, from behind a wall of thick oak trees, stepped a man adorning a cloak of dark ruby. His hair was as black as night itself, where his eyes were the colour of the clearest of summer skies. He was tall and carried himself with confidence. Shoulders rolled back and spine pin-straight, the man moved through the forest towards me as though he owned it.

This man was part of the Crimson Guard, obvious from the cloak tied around his neck, and the way his watchful gaze slid over the discarded corpses of the vampires and then back to me. He held a jewel of scrutiny in his blue eyes, which filled me with a claw of dread.

"What a mess you have made," he said, voice as smooth as silk. I felt as though I could drown in it.

I steeled my jaw and levelled my eyes with his. Something about it made him smile, viciously.

"Have you come to arrest me for my crimes?" My voice echoed through the dark, repeating back on myself until it faded to a silent whisper.

The man pulled at his red cloak as through righting it on his shoulders. He pouted his lips and drew his brows down into a deep frown. "And why would I do that?"

I lowered my eyes back to the corpses that separated us. "Because I have murdered someone."

"More than just someone I gather," he replied, not even a wince across his face as he looked to the mutilated body parts, then back to my blood-soaked and naked body. "Care to tell me how you have done it?"

My teeth forced themselves closed. I didn't dare open my mouth, because I could not tell him. I wouldn't. It was the very reason my parents had been murdered in the first place. They trusted their friends enough to reveal our secret, and that secret led to their death.

"Your name, at least."

The silence haunted me.

"Silas," I said finally, voice cracking, as I lost myself in the endless pits of his stare. There was something alluring about him. Perhaps it was his stillness, or the lack of care that I knelt in the leaves before him, naked and covered in blood. Or maybe I was drunk. Drunk on the adrenaline left in me from murder and revenge.

One thing I knew for certain was the man's heart skipped each time he allowed his gaze to leave mine and trail my body. His reaction to me was intoxicating.

"I admit, I am rather disappointed," he said. "I was hoping to be the one to kill these two this evening."

His words stole my breath away.

"Why?" I muttered. "Should you not be protecting them?"

"Who from? Monsters like you, or monsters like me?"

Slowly, as though proving he was not a threat, the man unclasped the red cloak from his shoulders and extend it to me.

"Take this," he said quietly. I felt his restraint as he

kept his eyes on mine. "Cover yourself up before you catch your death."

I regarded the offering, deciding whether to accept or refuse. The stranger made my mind up for me as he stepped carefully over the gnawed arm of the vampire and brought the cloak to me himself. As he settled it over my shoulders, the air picked up his scent and washed it over me.

I inhaled the pungent waft of lavender. It was as though I stood in a field of it. The brush of his knuckles across my bare skin sent an alarming shiver through me. This man, whoever he was, screamed danger. Why was it I was so completely stuck by it?

"Did they deserve it?" he asked, standing at my side and looking down at my chaos.

I inhaled sharply, now smelling both him and the blood of my victims.

"Yes," I said, finding it the easiest word I had ever said. "They... they killed my parents."

The man hissed through gritted teeth. Then he draped a warm arm across my shoulder, until his hand gripped my bicep to steady me. "Then I have no questions. All crimes must be answered for. And between me and you, Silas..." he spoke my name, extending each syllable as though he hissed like a snake, "We are no different. I am sorry for your loss. Come, let us get you cleaned up, and this... dealt with."

He attempted to move, but my feet were rooted to the spot.

"Who are you?" I asked, eyeing him as distrust stormed within me.

"My name is Eamon," he said, whispering as though it was only me and him in the entire world. "And I too lost my parents to these vile monsters."

Eamon reached a hand to the side of my face where he brushed his fingers over the tacky blood that coated it. He hardly blinked as he drew it to his nose, sniffed and then brought it down to his trousers where he cleaned it off.

"When my parents died, I was the one who was covered in their blood. I am glad to see you covered in the enemies." Eamon gestured to the scattered remains at our feet. "Come on, let us get you somewhere safe. The woods are a dangerous place."

His comment was edged. From the glint in Eamon's eyes, he knew the forest caused me no danger, not when I was the beast which lurked in it. As Eamon said, I was the one covered in the blood of vampires. And Eamon had yet to question why I was alone, naked and caught red-handed, let alone how I killed them. But I felt the question lingering. It would come.

"What are you going to do to me?" I asked, unable to hide the shake in my voice.

Eamon pouted as the lined skin around his eyes softened. "I am going to see you are cleaned, and the bodies are burned. Then we can have a discussion about how it is you came out in the woods and murdered two vampires... all alone."

I exhaled, searching his bright eyes for a reason to run. "Why does it matter?"

"Because we need someone like you."

"Who is we?"

Eamon smiled, leaned his forehead into mine and spoke. "The tides are changing. Our enemies align. Silas Grey, come and let us talk in a more suitable place. I want to hear about it all. Believe me, you can trust me."

And he was right because I allowed myself to slip down the stream of his charm, all the while not realising I had never been the one to tell him my surname. In the days which followed, I was far too deep in revealing all my secrets before I realised Eamon's first slip up—the first of many.

## ❧ 14 ❧

I quickly became aware that I was walking with no real knowledge of my destination. And Calix knew it. Every time I looked behind me, he was there. A shadow, lurking at my back whilst always keeping a distance.

I picked my pace up. Twigs scratched at my face, lacing my skin with small kisses of pain but I didn't care. On I pushed, fighting my way through the dense woodland with only one desire. *Don't stop.*

The forest swallowed me whole. It bathed me in its darkness and welcomed me into its belly. Nothing scared me more than the thought of home, yet I found myself trying to find it. I searched my memory of the directions Calix's note had provided but couldn't grasp the image. My mind was a storm of revelations and accusations.

Eamon had someone hostage. Calix would use me to get him back. I was a pawn on a gameboard I never asked to play.

Cold air stabbed at the back of my throat with each inhale. My feet stumbled awkwardly over roots and mounds of Gods knows what. But on I pushed, defending myself from the branches, vines and earth that fought hard to keep me within its hold.

"Rhory, wait," Calix finally called out for me. His voice was void of warmth. In its place was a tempered command. I felt the urge to listen to him as though it was the natural thing to do. *No*, I reminded myself, *Keep going.*

He could have stopped me. We both knew it. Calix was far stronger. It was not impossible to imagine him catching up, throwing me over his shoulder and carrying me back to his underground dwellings.

What held him back?

I could have been walking for an age before I finally stopped. Frustration bubbled up my throat, exploding out of me in a cry that brought the forest alive.

By the time I turned to Calix, he too was standing still. There was distance between us, so much that I had to squint through the dark to even make sense of his features. Only his eyes were clear. They no longer held the soft honey glaze, but now blazed like two beacons of burning gold.

"Please take me back to him," I said, breathlessly.

"Are you certain that is what you want?"

I could hardly calm myself enough to ease the thudding of my heart. "As if you would even allow it."

"I would," Calix replied slowly. "If that is what you wanted, I would take you back myself."

My laugh surprised me. The narrowing of Calix's eyes revealed his discomfort the sound caused.

"I don't believe you. You heard what Auriol said. What *you* already know."

"Tell me," Calix said. "Say it."

"You need me. You need me so you can trade me to see your brother returned…"

"And I am sorry if I gave you the impression that I was your knight in shining armour, come to save you from your awful life."

I hadn't felt anger like this since the first time Eamon raised a hand to me. My bravery to even allow such an emotion had died long ago. The feeling was so fresh and familiar that it took me back to that day.

It was the morning of my mother's accused murderer's execution. Eamon didn't wish to hear my pleas of the vampire's innocence, to acknowledge that I didn't believe the vampire was at fault for her death caused him too much of a headache. I had barely got five words out before his fingers had slapped themselves across my mouth, and the other ran across my scalp where they knotted with my hair.

"*Enough*," he had hissed, splattering spit across my face. "*That's fucking enough.*"

Even if I wanted to scream back at him, his harsh palm prevented that. He must have seen my desire in my wide eyes because his grip on my hair tightened until I could hear strands breaking one by one. I was frozen in shock, surprised and worst of all… fearful, an emotion I never thought possible to be conjured by Eamon.

"Rhory." I drew out of the memory to find Calix inches before me. "I shouldn't have said that."

It took me a moment to pull myself from the nightmare. Where my body was and my mind had been were two entirely different places. I had no recollection of Calix reaching me, nor when he put both hands on each of my shaking arms.

"You couldn't save me from him," I replied finally, speaking through the sorrowful lump in my throat. "No one can. Don't flatter yourself for even a moment, Calix."

I was highly aware of his closeness now. His warm touch reminded me of just how cold I was. The long autumn nights were far more deadly than winters. They made you believe they didn't have the power to freeze one to the bone by distracting with jewelled toned leaves, when in reality it was lethal.

I waited for Calix to say something else. It was the way his eyes flinched that told me he had something lingering on the tip of his tongue. Just before his lips parted, he dropped his chin to his chest and sighed.

"How are you so certain Eamon has your brother?" The question had been at the back of my mind until now. In a blink, I traced through my memories for any sign or familiarity that suggested Eamon was truly responsible for Silas's abduction.

"Because I know. And I am sorry if that answer is not good enough, but that is all I can tell you."

My mind told me to pull away from him and continue my blind journey back to Darkmourn. To Eamon. But something stopped me. Was it the warmth his touch gave me, or the way it seemed to cut through my emotions and give me some sense of grounding that kept me from listening to my better judgement?

"What would Eamon want with your brother? Make me understand… I deserve as much."

I sagged forward when Calix was the one to break contact. My shivering intensified immediately at the lack of his touch.

"You are not the first to be blinded by his charm."

I was caught in the web of Calix's gaze. My power reared itself to the surface, conjuring a glow of gold that illuminated the minimal space between us. Usually, I would have to touch another to sense their true emotions, but Calix's was so powerful they rolled off him in undulating waves. His helplessness had the power to barrel me over. But it was the undertone of guilt that unnerved me the most. Touching him wouldn't answer the question as to what he felt guilty about, but I was prepared to find out.

"What has this got to do with Silas? With Eamon?"

"Silas and Eamon." He paused. "They——"

Discomfort coiled around my heart and squeezed. Jealousy burned at the back of my throat.

"Are you suggesting my Eamon and Silas…"

"I am."

I turned away from Calix, not wishing for him to see the storm of emotions pass, one by one, across my face. I silently questioned if I believed Eamon had such a capacity for loving another. The answer came quickly to me.

Eamon wasn't capable of love.

"You could have reported this to the Crimson Guard directly. If Eamon has kept your brother hostage, they would have the authority to help you!"

Calix shook his head, long strands of his unkept hair falling around his face. "They are as corrupted as the man who heads it."

"You are wrong about them," I replied. The accusation hurt more than the idea of Eamon in love with another. The Crimson Guard were good. They stood for everything right in the world. Their entire existence was a product of my father's devotion and heritage.

It broke my heart to think Eamon's poison had not only slipped into my life, but into the very legacy of my father's efforts.

"I can imagine this is a lot for you to take in." Calix placed a careful hand on my shoulder, reminding me he was there. When I faced him, my knees grew weak to the pity he looked down at me with. It conjured bile to creep up my throat and sting with every swallow.

Calix saw me as weak. As something which required gloves to hold. Something breakable... as if I wasn't anything entirely whole in the first place.

"Do not pity me," I said, refusing to blink for fear of what it would unleash.

"Touch me and you'll find that pity is not the emotion I hold for you, Rhory."

The offer was there, but I ignored it. Reading Calix's emotions wouldn't help untie the strange knot his closeness conjured deep in my chest.

I blinked and a single tear fell from the corner of my eye. Calix reached for it before I could. The rough pad of his thumb brushed across the soft skin of cheekbone. He spread his warmth, caught my tear and drew it from my face.

"No, no crying." I sensed the command hidden beneath the soft whisper of his voice. It was reminiscent of when he called out my name only minutes before this moment. "I want to propose a deal, something for you to ponder."

I swallowed hard, sniffling. Part of me was distracted by the phantom heat of his touch, whereas the other part of me couldn't loosen that demonic tightness in my chest.

"Surely I would need something of worth to enter a deal, and I am afraid I am worthless to you."

Calix ignored me. He continued to stare deep into my eyes. "If you wish to be returned to Eamon, then I will take you. But only if you agree to one thing."

"What about your brother?" I muttered, fear kindling at the thought of Eamon but recognising it as the only outcome.

"Forget the trade, forget Silas. In truth, I would sleep better knowing you would not be in the midst of a tension you have no need of... knowing." Calix paused and took a hulking deep breath before continuing. "If you wish to go home, then I will see it done. But only when these fade."

My breath hitched as Calix brushed his thumb across the tender skin of my bruised neck. I gasped at his touch. A shiver spread across my entire body, leaving not one inch of skin without prickles. I reached up and put my fingers atop his as Calix studied the marks Eamon had left on me during our last encounter.

"Regardless if I demand to return to him now, or if you see this trade through… Eamon will paint my body in deeper bruises than these, Calix. How well would you sleep knowing the type of hands you are placing me back into?"

Calix's eyes narrowed. The colour darkened as he lowered his hand from beneath mine and returned it to his side. "Who is to say he will have hands left? I said I would return you to him; I didn't say in which state he would be in when I did so." I had never worried for Eamon before, not until this very moment. "If Eamon is smart enough to heed my warning, then all would be well. He can decide his fate, just as I wish for you to decide yours."

I stood awkwardly as Calix's threat to my husband's life sunk in. Each word settled over my consciousness like spits of ash from a spilling hearth.

"Fine," I said, breaking the tension. I fought the strange urge to raise my hand and offer it to him. Weren't deals not solidified with a shake of a hand, or the sharing of blood upon pricked fingers?

"Fine," Calix echoed.

He glanced skyward and frowned. I followed his gaze to the flashing of the near full moon that crowned the dark skies beyond the canopy of the forest. When he returned his attention to me, all concern had faded once again. "Before Millicent comes looking, I suggest we return you to your room. Her mood is always more erratic after she hunts."

Calix started away from me, and it was I that chased to follow after him.

"Millicent," I began, fumbling over roots and fighting my way back from the outstretched foliage of the forest. "Millicent said something to me…"

"Before you continue, no I will not say anymore; that is Millicent's story to share, not mine."

The conversation was dead before it even took its first breath.

Soon enough we had made it out the thickest part of the wood. The trees were thinner, allowing the starlight and moon to cast some silver across the world. Enough to see the opening of a tunnel stretched out within a mound of earth that stood thrice the size of Calix's height.

It was the entrance to the tunnels hidden beneath trailing vines that clung to the arched wall of brick and mortar.

"Shouldn't you be tying the blindfold back over my eyes?" I asked as he waved me into the dark shadows of the tunnel's gaping mouth.

"With such a proposed question, I am beginning to think you enjoy it."

Scarlet blush crest over my cheeks like a breaking wave. Calix sensed it and chuckled deeply to himself, except the sound came alive as it echoed throughout the darkness before me.

"Never mind," I grumbled as I passed him, sensing the way my stomach flipped as my shoulder brushed his firm chest.

"Trust. It is imperative when embarking into a deal," Calix said, following steps behind me. "I trust that you are not going to run away before we see it through, and I want you to trust what I have to say in return. The lack of blindfold is the first step. Again, unless you would prefer it and I would happily put it on—"

"Lead. The. Way." Each word was forced out of me with urgency.

"Pretty please," Calix replied, pouting.

I rolled my eyes. He laughed again. And Calix led me without further jibe or comment until we returned to the door to my room.

*His* room, I reminded myself once again. *His*.

It had been an entire turn of a day since I had been standing in the belly of the forest with Calix, and still I felt his touch across my neck as though it had been only minutes before. My skin was tender beneath my fingers as I inspected the bruises in the scratched mirror. The bruises had muted to pale blues and greens but were still there. I felt relief at seeing them. Even if I knew my decision to return to Eamon had not changed, part of me wished for these marks to never fade.

Although I had not long woken, I beheld a deep tiredness that told me night was upon us. Nothing was stopping me from walking out this bedroom door, through the winding tunnels and back towards the promise of fresh air in the world above. Calix wouldn't stop me. Not because he wished to keep me here against my will, but because he had kept his distance from me. I hadn't seen or heard from him since he deposited me back into this rather comfortable prison. Because that was what it was, deal or not.

Calix had provided me with the key to my own metaphoric shackles.

I stared deep into my reflection. The green of my eyes looked more vibrant compared to the dark circles beneath them. I hadn't washed in days, so much so that my poppy red hair had grown wiry and stuck up in strange angles across the back of my head; no manner of wet hands could smooth the hair and keep it down.

At least I looked the part. When Eamon would see me, I prayed he would see the state I was in and find some relief that I had returned home to him. Perhaps this forced space between us would soften his touch and remind him of a time when his language of love was not hard fists and pinching fingers.

Ever since the day he first raised a hand to me until now... I was simply waiting for the chance to save him from his darkness. Darkness I had long blamed on myself for causing. I had changed him; it was the only reason I could find for his shift in personality. Which meant this was not only my fault, but my sole responsibility to fix him.

Pushing thoughts of my husband to the far reaches of my skull, I chose to distract myself until Calix came for me. Or Millicent, except I hoped the vampire kept her distance.

I finished the plate of food that had been waiting for me when I woke. The jug of fresh mint water was now half empty. Most of the cuttings of mint were between my teeth, which I chewed all the flavour and relief from them.

Then the screaming started.

It came out of nowhere. The wall of silence that sang in the tunnels shattered as a deep, rumbling howl erupted from beyond the room.

My power burst to life and cast my hands in their golden glow. I raised them up before me, fingers shaking as another howling roar joined the echoes of the last. This one was louder. Stronger. Deeper. And it sang with pain. Agony. Hurt.

I ran towards the door which opened before I could reach for it. Millicent was waiting, her narrow yet powerful body blocking the doorway. There was no sign of panic or even a lick of concern across her stoic, red-gazed face.

"Going somewhere?" she asked just as another gargled shout sounded from down the tunnel behind her.

I looked beyond her shoulder, eyes narrowing as I tried to make sense of the location among the shadows. Millicent hadn't confirmed it, nor did I need to hear another shout to know who it came from; somewhere, deep within me, the truth lingered.

"Calix, that is Calix, isn't it?"

Millicent looked over her shoulder, an expression of boredom smoothing the creases that settled across her pale forehead. Her whip of dark hair had been collected into a single braid that hung down her spine like a snake. When she returned her attention back to me, I noticed her eyes flicker to the glow of my hands, if only for a moment.

"It is," she answered.

My blood turned to ice in every vein. "He needs help."

"Calix needs more than help."

I tried to step past her, but she moved her body in the way.

"Why aren't you going to help him!?" I gestured behind her just as another skin peeling cry sang through the dark. His pain was so raw it filled the air with a sour tang. Each inhale I took, I could taste it in the back of my throat like bile after a bout of sickness.

"Calix has asked me to keep you in your room. It's not safe for you outside it tonight."

I stepped in close to her. With the burning concern and desire to help Calix, I hardly registered the fear I once had towards the vampire. "From my impression, I didn't think you cared for my well-being."

Millicent smiled slowly. "I don't."

"Then move out of my way."

"Please?" Millicent cocked her head to the side. "Or is that word above you?"

I lifted my hands and Millicent flinched as the gold light spilled out of my skin. She reacted to my power as if I held the sun between my hands, ready to turn her dead skin to ash with one ray.

"Please," I said slowly, heart thudding in my chest. "I can feel his pain. Let me help him."

"Calix does not need your help, witch." Millicent

moved out of the doorway now, almost gesturing like gentry for me to move past her. "But you do not look like the person who is willing to take no for an answer. Go. Be the fool you are destined to be. Do not say I didn't warn you."

I should have asked her what I was to be warned against. What danger waited for me and why Calix had her stationed beyond my door like some hired guard. But when the next scream stretched out for an unnatural length of time, I found myself running. Running towards it. Running from the safety of my room.

Running towards Calix.

⚜

The golden cast of light from my hands guided me through the tunnels. I hadn't ventured in this direction before, but I felt the sense that I was losing myself. On and on, I ran. The screams echoed across the brick walls and curved ceiling. My feet splashed through puddles of stagnant water, splattering my lower legs in old dirty muck. From the corner of my eye, I saw marks etched into the walls beside me, circles and strange shapes. Some markings looked like words from a language no one old enough in this world could read.

It was clear these tunnels had been here a long time. Even the musky air smelled ancient as it burned down my throat while I continued running towards Calix.

My lungs burned. My muscles ached. Each bone rattled with the force of my footfalls. But my discomfort was nothing compared to Calix's. Whatever was happening to him, it sounded as though someone sliced every inch of skin from his body and snapped every one of his bones one by one.

I wished to claw for the red laces of my corset and free myself from the squeeze of material across my chest. There was no time to stop, let alone offer myself some comfort, not when Calix's screams of terrifying pain grew louder and louder the deeper I lost myself to the tunnels.

My light soon revealed a heavy iron door. It waited at the end of one tunnel and was locked from the outside. I came to a stop before it as Calix raged beyond. Whoever had put him inside had ensured he couldn't leave. He was locked in.

I fumbled awkwardly with the large slab of iron that rested across the width of the door. A growl of determination burst out of me as I lifted it from its confinements. The sound of the metal slamming into the stone floor joined in symphony with another of Calix's cries.

With a great tug, I pulled the door open and revealed the most horrific scene before me.

Calix was knelt in the middle of a room flooded in the glow of burning torches. Infinite chains kept him in place; he was trapped amidst the web of iron. The chains were bolted to the walls and floor. They were wrapped around his bulging arms, legs, chest, waist, neck. I could hear the very hinges scream as Calix fought against them.

He snapped his head up to me. Strands of his

shaggy brown hair were plastered to his face with sweat. Spit dribbled down his chin, mixed with blood from his pierced lips where his blunt teeth had bit into.

"Go," he roared, honey eyes burning with fire from within, "Away!"

I stepped towards him, helplessly looking from the chains to his bare skin. He only wore leather trousers that hung across his powerful hips. His chest was naked, muscles rippling like water with every howl and breath he expelled.

"Who did this…?" I mumbled. The closer I got to him, the more Calix fought the bindings of chains.

If only I could touch him, I could take his pain away. My hands still glowed, ready to do just that.

Calix tried to say something again, but he lost himself to his pain. His head threw back and his mouth split in a deafening cry. His face crumpled into itself as the contraction of agony overcame him.

Then I saw the marks. Four harsh puckered lines sliced down the right side of his proud chest. Old scars. Marks similar to that I had seen before.

On the torn, mutilated body of my mother.

It stopped me in my tracks.

Calix stopped howling and looked back to me. His wide eyes roared with panic. Silently, he begged me to help him. I pushed my dread down and went to him.

"Let me get you out of this. Then I can help with your pain."

Calix didn't fight back. He didn't refuse me. He

watched as I looped chains off from his limbs. He hissed, spitting and flinching.

"Rhory, run." He forced the words out as though it was the hardest thing for him to do. "Leave me."

"No!" I refused sharply. My knuckles grazed his scarred chest as I lifted the loop of chain from his waist and over his head. It was a puzzle to free him, but I worked quickly. Focus and determination had me solving it. His skin boiled. I had never felt such a fever in a person before.

Whatever was happening to him required more than the relief I could offer with my power. He needed St Myrinn's. Perhaps Jameson had concoctions or medicines that would ease Calix's affliction.

Once I freed him and dampened his agony, I would take Calix there myself. Millicent would have to help; I would *make* her.

I was so focused on freeing him from the web of chains that I didn't notice when his harsh breathing mutated to something entirely different.

He growled.

I stilled my hands and slowly lifted my gaze to his. At some point Calix had stopped shouting, stopped fighting.

Fear sang within me. It spiked when my eyes found his. Except it wasn't his, not the honey-tones I had grown familiar with. Now they burned a bright, molten gold with swirls of dark red dancing around his irises.

I stumbled back as the skin across his face shattered

like broken china. Flecks of skin fell away, turning to ash in the air. Beneath it, I saw fur.

Calix opened wide to reveal a mouth full of teeth which seemed to grow before my eyes.

"Go," he growled. "Nooooow." His last word drew out into the sound that didn't belong to a human. It was the song of a wolf, crying to the moon.

I scrambled away from him as his bones bent, cracked, snapped and shattered. Calix's skin fell away from him like snow captured in the wind. His face elongated and spread with dark fur.

Calix grew before my eyes. The transformation happened with fluid grace. His arms lengthened and pulled against the remaining chains. His leather trousers ripped as his legs bulged through.

I was frozen to the spot. Even my power had faded from me. All I could do was watch as the monster lifted his dripping maw and settled its unnatural eyes at me.

It was not pain I sensed without the need of touch.

This was hunger.

## ❧ 16 ❧

It seemed, when faced with a monster, one's senses betrayed them.

My ears muffled until the world sounded as though it was beneath a body of water. All I could discern was the faint *thud, thud, thud,* of my heart somewhere from deep within me. I blinked, slowly, and watched Calix stretch and mutate into a creature that was both human and wolf.

In place of skin was now washes of dark thick fur. Calix stood on two bent legs with paws the size of boulders with perfectly pointed, yellowed claws which carved grooves into the stone beneath him.

The stomach of the creature had shorter hair which outlined the sculptured mounds of humanoid muscles. His chest, thick neck, and the unnatural head of the ferocious wolf was maned like a lion and splattered with the creature's saliva.

I stared, helplessly, into the coal-red eyes of the

ALPHA OF MORTAL FLESH

monster and screamed. A part of me told myself to close my eyes, so I didn't watch as my end greeted me. But I couldn't. It was as though wooden picks held each eyelid up in its place whilst I couldn't help but study every pearly white tooth that snapped in the maw of the creature.

"Please…" I begged, tears wetting my cheeks. "Please, Calix."

The creature reacted to the name. As the final chains slipped free from him like loose trousers without a belt, the wolven beast flinched. Two pointed ears flattened back and its eyes narrowed in recognition.

Perhaps it was my desire to live that made my mind catch the subtle reaction. But I grasped onto it and shouted his name over and over, each time growing more feral and desperate. "Calix, Calix… CALIX!"

The monster bent forward until it rested on all fours. I caught the ridges of its spine ripple like water over stone as it pawed towards me. A thick tail flicked left to right out the corner of my vision. At some point I had fallen to the floor. My palms were hot where the skin had ripped against the old floor. The pain meant little as the creature came close and I scrambled backwards until I couldn't anymore. A wall trapped me at my back. I didn't dare look away from the creature, but I felt the draft of air from the open door at my side.

If I could just get out, close the door and return the iron bar back to its hold… it would give me a moment to run. To do just as Calix had commanded before the monster replaced him.

145

Hot, sickly breath washed over me and destroyed all hope for escape. Warm globs of spit dripped across my thighs as Calix leaned in close.

I turned my head to the side as the wet kiss of the wolf's nose brushed into my neck. Every muscle in my body tensed. I blinked and saw, in my mind's eyes, a maw full of pointed teeth pressing into my soft flesh.

A low rumbling growl emitted from deep within the creature's throat. It vibrated through every shadow in the room as though they were the audience for some monstrous song.

Then, to my disbelief, the creature pulled back.

There was space between us so suddenly I cried out in relief. Even if I wished to call upon my power, as though such a passive magic even had the capability to help against this beast, it had utterly left me. I couldn't sense its presence even if I wished to.

Calix uncurled to standing once again. Powerful arms ending in blackened talons flexed. Monstrous, hungry eyes widened. Strings of spittle linked every tooth as his mouth split open. When he roared, I threw my hands up before my face as though they would do something to keep the attack from coming.

The noise I made was not a word but a guttural and ancient cry of panic that filled every tunnel, cave and place within this underground world. I continued expelling the sound until my lungs burned with wildfire.

Calix roar broke into a whimper. He threw his maw from side to side, snapping teeth. Even his tail, which whipped with a mind of its own, forced itself between his elongated legs.

Then the unthinkable happened.

The creature did not feast on my flesh as I sensed it wished.

It ran. Gouging scars into the stone floor as it bolted towards the open door and ran off into the dark beyond it.

I t was Millicent who found me. Her cold touch shocked me out from the ball I had curled into on the floor. I hadn't moved since Calix had shifted into the wolven monster and fled the room. Not a muscle had dared relax ever since the last faint howl reached my ears as the creature disappeared deep into the tunnels of Darkmourn's underground.

"Get up," Millicent commanded. Her voice was careless, but her touch was gentle and guiding. Such a contrast that even in my panicked state I couldn't help but recognise it. "I need to get you back to your room before our dear Calix changes his mind and returns."

My bones ached as she drew me to standing. I was thin and average of height, but Millicent was shorter and smaller, yet could still lift me with a single hand and not break a sweat.

"He is a monster…" The words scratched at my throat as I spoke them.

"We all are monsters in someone's eyes, Rhory. Even you."

She was right. Because, for some unknown reason, that was exactly what Millicent thought I was. A monster. Her eyes flickered with hate every time she looked at me.

"What is he?"

The question hung between us. Millicent put my arm across her narrow shoulders and glanced into the shadows of the tunnel with a faint wariness.

"Quiet. He is stalking the tunnels. The further he loses himself to the wolf the more the chance that he comes searching. I've sealed him in so he can't leave out of the tunnel system, which is good news for life above ground but not for us."

Millicent started for the open door, pulling me in tow.

Her keen ears picked up in my intake of breath before I spoke. She slapped her icy fingers across my mouth and hissed, "No more speaking."

Just as Calix's eyes burned with feral warning, so did Millicent's. I swallowed my question and focused on keeping even my breathing quiet.

She moved me through the dark tunnels without need of torchlight. I found it easy to pinch my eyes closed because the natural dark threatened to drive me mad.

Millicent swore beneath her breath, picking up speed as she navigated forward. And I could hear what sped her up. The scuffling of claws against stone. The

148

growling that sang through the shadows. And the pound of heavy paws as the monster ran throughout the underground maze in search for... a feast.

By the time we reached Calix's bedchamber, Millicent pushed me through the doorway and pulled the door closed with a careless bang. Gone was her desire to keep silent. The tremendous slam would alert even the smallest of cave spiders and the hulking monster Calix had become.

Millicent backed away from the door without turning away from it.

"I can't believe he let you live," she said, hands clenched to fists at her side. "Never has he turned down meat, whatever the kind, when he has shifted. Never."

Unlike the room Calix had locked himself... no, been locked within, this one did not have chains or iron bars to keep him out, only the single bolt which Millicent had not even bothered to draw closed.

"Will he come here?" I asked, my voice small and broken.

"Even lost to the monster he is now, Calix has enough instinct to stay away," Millicent confirmed, finally facing me. If it was possible, her pale skin had grown even more ashen. Even her lips had silvered with dread. "The wood of the door is soaked in wolfsbane. Silver has been threaded through the frame and hinges. In human form Calix could enter, but in this one... Calix would keep clear for fear of what the flora and silver could do to him."

I buried my face in my shaking hands. "If you knew what he was… why did you let me go?"

"Because I can't kill you, but I thought maybe he could."

Millicent knew all along and sent me to Calix as a judge sends a criminal to the gallows for hanging.

"What's stopping you from doing it now?" I asked, dropping my empty hands to my side in defeat. "It is clear you hate me, and now it doesn't even matter as to why. You could take whatever hate you have for whatever I have done and end it. So, why don't you?"

Millicent smiled, even her eyes glowed with it. "I see in the face of death you have found your bravery. And here I was beginning to think you didn't have any."

"Answer the question," I forced out. There was no room for fear in me now, not with the wolfish beast stalking the tunnels, or the vampire who smiled at me, eyes flickering from my gaze to my neck.

"I asked you if you recognised me, and you said no. Perhaps I should get closer." Millicent did as she said, stepping into me. I didn't flinch or move away. "What if I cut my hair and tied a rope around my neck… would you recognise me then?"

Her strange comment strangled me. "I—"

"My brother died because of you," Millicent revealed, a single tear of pure blood rolling down her pale cheek. "He died because it was easier pinning the blame of your mother's murder on a creature which humans already see as evil. He…" Millicent lifted a sharp nail and pointed it directly above my heart. "He died pleading his innocence. And you watched it happen."

I did see it then. Blinking, Millicent's face morphed into that of the man who was put to death by Eamon with the crimes of killing my parents. A vampire who I knew did not kill my mother.

Years of guilt poured out of me. I gripped Millicent by her shoulders, not caring for the way she pulled her lips back from her pointed teeth and hissed in surprise.

"I pleaded with him," I spat, words rushing out of me without thought. "Eamon didn't listen. I couldn't stop him even if I wished and begged. You don't understand…"

"No," Millicent said, stiffening beneath my touch. "I do *not* understand. I watched it happen, you know. How they strung him up with a noose around his neck, knowing that would not destroy him. Your husband displayed him for all to see as the dawn's sun crept over Darkmourn and set my brother's skin ablaze. I hear his screams even now. I can taste his flesh as though his ashes coat my tongue. And whilst they all clapped and jeered at his execution, you stood and watched silently. Complicit."

I couldn't hold her hateful stare, but nor could I look away. My apology died on my lips, knowing it would not bring comfort to Millicent, or me. The words were meaningless, the same words used by Eamon after his fist struck my head, or his nails dug into my thigh beneath a table. I didn't dare speak them.

"I deserve whatever punishment you wish to hand

out."

Millicent pulled out of my hands and stepped back. "Which is exactly why you will not leave this place until the trade is done. I heard you in the forest striking a deal with Calix in a moment of his weakness. A deal to take you home. I know what waits for you there, and I want you to go back to him." She almost said it, but I knew *him* had the same meaning.

"Does Calix know?"

Millicent nodded once. "It is the reason I turned my back on my past and pledged to help Calix and Auriol in their cause. Calix knows why and how my brother was murdered, as a means to cover up the truth, to use an easy, blameable target whom no one would think twice to question for a crime. He knows everything."

"I did try to stop Eamon from killing your brother," I said again, eyes burning with hot tears which I did not deserve to shed. "He struck me hard before I could even finish my plea."

Millicent straightened and shed all emotion from her face. "You didn't try hard enough."

She was right. I didn't. Perhaps it was because a part of me wished that my mother's murderer had been found so I could have peace knowing justice was served. It was selfish of me. Regardless of Eamon and the temper he had kept hidden until the day I tried to plead the vampire's innocence, I should have fought harder. I knew he was not to blame, but I watched silently as the noose was lowered around his neck and how the rays of morning sun peeled the skin from his bones.

"His name," Millicent whispered, "was Loren."

All this time I had never known it. Never asked. I felt the weight of Loren's death push down on my shoulders and force me to my knees before his sister. She glared down at me with disgust and pity.

"When the trade is done, and you are turned back into your husband's uncaring hands… I want you to ask him why. Why he picked Loren. What it was that drove his decision. Then, and only then… will you understand it all."

Millicent turned her back to me, paced across to the chair and sat within it. There was no room for further conversation. She didn't look up at me again where I stayed, knelt in the middle of the floor.

Hours passed and the bones in my knees screamed and pleaded for me to move. But I refused. Comfort was not something I deserved.

The revelation of Calix and the beast he had become was no more than an afterthought as Loren and Millicent—and everything about what she said—occupied my mind.

Only when a firm knock sounded on the bedroom door before it opened to reveal Calix, human and dressed, did I stand.

Millicent left the room without a word.

The tension remained and only intensified as Calix finally spoke. His words pierced my chest and drove directly into my heart, aided by the heavy sorrow in his gilded but human eyes.

"You shouldn't be alive."

" **R**hory, I am *so* sorry."

We stood at opposite ends of the room, glaring at one another as his apology stormed between us. I toyed with the concept of accepting it, but in truth I didn't know the extent of what part of our story he wished to apologise for. Was it the fact he wanted to use me? Stole me from my home, my husband? Or did he wish to apologise for turning into some monstrous creature and almost killing me? It was hard to imagine what I had witnessed as reality, let alone that a monster even lurked beneath Calix's freshly repaired skin.

"What are you?" I asked, breaking the tormenting silence.

Calix took a step forward only to stop when he noticed me flinch backwards.

"There isn't exactly a name for it," he replied, studying me carefully with his gilded eyes. "Not one that would encompass what I am, and what I become."

"A wolf," I answered for him. But that wasn't entirely the truth. No wolf had the shaping of a human, with the ability to walk on its hind legs and move with mundane grace. But he wasn't human either.

"That is a part of it."

"Are you the only one?" I knew the answer before asking it.

Calix shook his head, causing chestnut hair to fall over his eyes. "Our kind is rare. Auriol, my grandmother was the first. Then her husband, but he didn't last long…"

Something Auriol had said during my first visit chose that moment to occupy my mind. "Auriol ate him. She told me that herself… I thought it was a joke."

"My grandmother is many things, but a trickster is not one of them. Yes, she killed my grandfather when it became clear his change to the *beast* gave him some power over her. So, she devoured his heart and reclaimed her rightful mantle as alpha of our pack."

"Pack?" The word fell out of my lips without restraint. "Alpha?"

"There is not a handbook on what we are. What we know comes from instinct and more so, trial and error." He gestured down at himself with two proud hands. "But what we do know is the instinctual part that sings through our blood. Auriol is the alpha."

"And what about you?"

"Would you walk with me?" Calix replied with a

question of his own. "I promise to tell you everything, but I would rather do it beneath the open sky. Last night was… torturous."

I didn't know what to say. There was a part of me that wished to refuse him, but another that thirsted for knowledge. "Is it safe?"

"With me, you mean?" I watched the lump in Calix's throat bob. "If you are wondering if I am going to turn again and hurt you, the answer is no. I am in control until the next full moon. And I promise, Rhory, I will not hurt you. I *can't* hurt you."

Before my very eyes, Calix struggled with the guilt of what had happened. I saw it in the cower of his gaze and the way he couldn't look at me for longer than a few seconds, before focusing on something unimportant like his hands or the cuff of his dark shirt.

"I know you won't," I replied. Shock creased across his face. I even caught the way his shoulders straightened, as if some weight on them had lifted.

Calix nodded. He ran his fingers through his hair and scraped it back completely from his face. The muscles in his jaw feathered as though he chewed on my words before swallowing. "Come then, I have something I wish to show you."

"Only if you promise to tell me all of it," I retorted, stepping in close to him. His scent invaded me. One deep breath and my ease had returned.

"Auriol was the first of our kind," Calix continued as we left the dark tunnels. "Her story is where this began, and it will be where it finishes as well."

It was early dawn in the world above the tunnels. Mist clung to the ground, twisting and curling around our feet as we padded through the forest. It was windy enough that the branches bent in the gusts, allowing leaves to be torn and scattered around us. I was thankful I brought my red cloak with me. It kept some warmth in and the chill of autumn out. I hugged it around myself, grateful for the comfort and the way it kept my dishevelled and dirtied appearance from view.

I had not been outside with Calix during the daytime since the first time I visited Auriol. Dawn light did little but accentuate my unwashed and messy state. Beneath Calix's attention, I felt more self-conscious than I thought possible.

"Is this some type of curse?" I asked, keeping pace at Calix's side. "Like the one the last witch put upon Lord Marius, the one that made him a vampire?"

Calix stared forward to some unseen destination he had yet to reveal. "Yes, I suppose you could say my grandmother's aliment was a result of the same witch, but not in such a direct connection. Auriol, although mortal, has been around far longer than you could comprehend. Back from times before humans returned from their walled communes. In fact, Auriol was born in Tithe, as was her brother, Arlo."

"That would make her over a hundred years of age," I said, breath fogging beyond my lips.

"One hundred and thirty-one to be exact. Although I recommend you don't mention her age. It would be unbecoming." Calix offered me a sideways smile that lasted a flicker of a second. It faded when he saw I did not hold one.

"How did it happen?"

"In the early days, after the covenant between life and death was created, my grandmother was visiting Castle Dread. Have you heard of the beasts that lurk within the castle's boundaries? Shadow wolfs, blood hounds. They have many names, all fuelled by speculation and uncertainty. But what is certain is they bite."

I had heard stories of the shadow beasts that dwelled outside of Castle Dread. They were used for stories that adults told their misbehaving children. A way to warn them from Castle Dread. And it worked. Sometimes, in the dead of night, I was certain I heard them howl.

"Auriol was attacked by… a shadow hound?"

"Attacked perhaps is not the right word," Calix replied. "Although my grandmother has not shared the details completely, and nor have I ever felt the desire to push her on the matter, but what we know is she was bitten and changed. She was the first."

*Of how many?* The question died on my lips as Calix added, "Ah, we are here."

Just beyond the border of the forest we cleared through was a lake that spanned out before us. Its surface was as still as glass and as blue as the sky. If it wasn't for the clouds above, I would have believed it connected seamlessly.

"I thought you might care to bathe," Calix said

softly. "The waters are cold, but it should help with your bruising. If not, the cold will decrease the swelling."

Considering the natural chill of autumn was as cold as an iron blade, my cheeks blossomed with heat. Noticing my embarrassment, Calix quickly added, "I won't look, and I am not suggesting you require it. Consider it an apologetic gesture; I prefer mine to be more than words. I find actions speak far louder."

"Sorry for nearly eating me?" I suggested, offering him a smile.

Calix gave me his full, undivided attention. The ring on my finger seemed to burn as I allowed his gaze to jolt my stomach. "You should be dead, Rhory. When the full moon rises, I am lost to it. I know nothing but primal instinct and hunger. I should have killed you…"

*Mood ruined.* My stomach dropped like a stone so quickly I felt sick.

He stepped in close, the toes of his boots pressing into mine. Calix had to look down at me with his added height. The sun rose across the lake behind him, his shoulders cast me in shadow.

"What stopped you?" I asked. I blinked and saw the beast that had only hours before regarded me with starving hunger.

Calix raised a hand. Slowly, he drew his fingers to a strand of my red hair and brushed it back from my brow. His finger was soft against my skin. My sharp intake of breath was not because I was scared of the claws that lurked beneath his human hand, but from the tentative care his touch held.

How could such a monster be so gentle, when the hands I was used to left bruises, not goosebumps?

"You did," Calix replied. "It was you who stopped me. In that state I know nothing but what my instincts tell me. There are no thoughts, no negotiation, no will of my own, only that of the wolf. But here you are, standing before me unscathed. Breathing."

I felt myself leaning into him when Calix withdrew his hand and returned it to his side.

I raised my hand and pressed it into his chest. Calix breathed rapidly, chest rising and falling beneath my touch. It moved my fingers up and down, causing the light of dawn to catch against the faded metal of my wedding band. For a moment I lost myself. The ring reminded me with horrifying clarity.

"Promise me you will not watch," I said, drawing the conversation down a different path.

Calix noticed my sudden change. I had to look back to the lake to stop myself from reading the disappointment that glowed in his eyes. "I would do anything you ask of me. That is the problem."

My stomach jolted again. The feeling was so divine it made me want to cry. I bit down into the insides of my lips until I could taste blood. Only when I felt I had control of myself did I speak. "About our deal... I have changed my mind."

Calix took a deep inhale, readying himself for what he believed was further disappointment. "Until your bruises fade, that was the deal."

"That was if I wished to be taken back to Eamon."

"And do you?" Calix's deep voice rose to a peak with the last word.

"I do," I said, speaking the two words just as I had when I said them to Eamon on our wedding day. "But not before you get your brother back. I think it is clear now as to why Eamon took an interest in him. Your... affliction could give him the power he clearly craves."

Calix held my stare, eyes flickering across my face, making me feel as though he drank every detail of me in. "Are you confident you wish to be in the middle of this?"

"You ask that like I have been given a choice in the first place. May I remind you, Calix, you're the one that snatched me from my bedchambers and took me for this very reason."

"Was it me? What happened last night?" he asked. "Am I the reason you changed your mind?"

I could have revealed to Calix what Millicent had not long told me, but I couldn't bear to recognise the guilt which had only just been buried down deep enough to ignore. So, I picked my answer carefully, knowing it would drive a wedge between us. A wedge that would keep my ring finger from burning my skin, even if I wished to tear it free and place my hand back upon this man's chest.

There was something so familiar about the urge.

"Yes." I turned my back on him and began fiddling with the laces of my crimson cloak. "Now, turn away. I will not be long."

Calix spoke to the back of my head. "Very few know

about us, Rhory. We are going to want to keep it that way. Our… existence puts those with power in positions of weakness. If you, or Eamon, or anyone decided to reveal our truth, then it would lead to so much death."

A violent shiver brushed over my neck as Calix took the cloak and lifted it from me. When I looked back at him, all signs of his previous gentle nature had vanished. A wall had been thrown up, and he barely looked at me. When he did, it was as though I was a stranger.

Which, I reminded myself, I was.

"I don't believe for a second that Eamon, or his Crimson Guard, would have the ability to harm you. Not after what I have witnessed."

"You are not wrong. But Lord Marius would have something to say if he discovered us. I hardly imagine he would allow such abominations to roam Darkmourn freely."

Calix read my unspoken question which glistened across my parted lips. "Why?"

"Bathe quickly," Calix said, diverting the conversation. "I should return you to the tunnels before Auriol catches wind of this. She would eat my heart next if she knew what you have learned."

He did as I asked, turned his back and walked back to the shadows of the forest's border. "Won't Millicent inform her?"

Calix's laugh rumbled through the shadows. For a moment, I caught the undertone of a growl from the beast I had met last night. "Millicent needs Auriol. She won't risk the promise of freedom for the chance to one up me. Believe it or not, her desires for a future outweigh her desire to see you pay for the death of her brother."

*He knows.* Panic surged through me. *He knows.*

"Enjoy the waters," Calix added, his voice cold as the chill that seeped from the lake's edge. "I can't promise such an offering again."

## ❧ 18 ❧

Calix stalked ahead, not once turning back to see if I followed. My hair was still drenched by the time he finally slowed, signalling our return to the tunnel's hidden entrance. My wet skin had spread stains of water across my shirt and trousers. Nothing could help against the kiss of ice the fresh lake left upon me, and the autumn breeze that seemed to want to torture me. At least I was clean. No longer did the autumn breeze remind me of how unwashed I was.

What I desired was a warm hearth and something equally warm to drink. But at least I was clean.

"Wait," Calix barked at me, breaking the competition of silence between us. His outstretched hand stopped me from passing him.

I glanced up to his profile and saw it was pinched into a deep scowl.

Something was wrong. The sense of dread nearly knocked me to the ground.

"What's the matter?" I asked. Every bone in my face ached with the cold the lake had set into it. I even had to sniff to stop my nose from running down my newly cleaned face.

Calix's nostrils flared. He tilted his head upwards and inhaled deeply. "Blood. I smell blood."

The one word set my world tilting. Suddenly, the forest seemed to cave in around us. I threw my stare around the thick wall of trees but couldn't see anything amiss.

"Stay by my side," Calix said, emanating a low growl from the pit of his chest. "Understand?"

Fear kept me rooted to the spot. My legs refused me; my arms stayed pinned to my side. I found that my mind went straight to Millicent. But daylight crowned the skies, meaning the vampire would be lurking deep in the darkness of the tunnels.

Before I could utter a word, Calix threaded his large hand into mine and captured each of my fingers between his own. His grip fought against the shaking that had set in.

Without him touching me, I didn't think I would have ever moved. It wasn't the thought of blood that scared me. Gods, I had seen enough of my own for such a thing not to bother me. It was the look on Calix's face. The way his frown aged him into something ancient and... feral.

I caught the tang of blood in the air soon enough. My sense of smell was nothing compared to Calix's, which meant I smelt it only just before I saw it.

My knees buckled and the ground raced up to great me.

Calix didn't have a chance to let go of my hand before I dropped to the forest's bed. Agony screamed through my shoulder and wrist from the great tug Calix's resistance caused.

The physical pain I felt was nothing compared to the shattering of my heart as I looked upon the body hanging from a branch before the tunnel's darkened entrance. The thick rope around the stout neck of a woman was all that kept her aloft. Her skin was burned raw from the friction as she swung like a pendulum in the breeze.

Mildred hung before me like meat in a butcher's display. It seemed her dead glassy eyes looked directly at me where I knelt. I felt the desire to scream, but I couldn't gather enough breath. The only sound that came out of me was broken and rasped.

She spun slowly, like a dancer on string. Legs and arms hanging limp. Her skin was already as grey as stone.

At some point, Calix had knelt before me. He tried to take my hands, but I swatted him away. His lips were moving but all I could hear was the creak of the giant branch that had become Mildred's gallows.

The back of her dress was split wide. Great flaps of blood-stained material gave the impression she had wings. Slow, so terribly slow, she turned until all I could see was the mutilated skin of her exposed back and the message carved upon it.

*HE IS MINE.*

Harsh, messy letters had been cut into the hunch of her back. A blade had been used. Not a pen or paper, but I recognised the handwriting immediately. The penmanship was horrifically familiar.

Sick burst out of me. Calix only just jolted back before the contents of my stomach spilled across the ground and my splayed hands. Over and over, I expelled everything possible until my stomach cramped, and my back arched in burning discomfort.

I blinked, and the world grew dark. I blinked again and the shadows refused to recede.

The third time I closed my eyes was the last. They didn't open, but the image of Mildred hanging was seared into the back of my eyelids, haunting me even in the dark.

❦

Many things had become clear since we discovered Mildred's body, yet I still felt like I had more questions, and little access to answers. Eamon knew where I was being held. His placement of Mildred was more than the message that was carved into her flesh. It was to tell me—us—that he knew. Which posed the question as to why he had not come himself to claim me? He had the entire army of Crimson Guards at his disposal. Even a small number could outnumber Calix and Millicent. Auriol was bedbound and powerless. So, what was stopping him?

All these thoughts, and more, cascaded through my mind. It was a wildfire, and no one had the power to quench such flames. I was left to burn amongst it whilst grief gripped my ankles and held me firm.

I had not long woken and my hand still ached slightly from being held by Calix. It was the first thing I felt when sleep released me. When I opened my eyes, Calix was holding my hand to his chest. His forehead was pressed atop them as well.

He must have felt me shift because he looked up and released me with urgency. It was as though he had been caught doing something he shouldn't have been doing.

I pressed my aching warm hand to my forehead to find another ache. This one was heavy and dull, located somewhere deep within my skull.

"Here." Calix shuffled in the stool perched at the bedside. "I had some tea made. It might be cold now, but the camomile should aid with the head pains."

I took the mug from him because I felt like it was the right thing to do. In truth, the thought of putting anything into my mouth conjured the urge to vomit again.

My eyes stung, signalling the arrival of my tears. Calix watched as I brought the rim of the cup to my lips as my tears cut down my cheeks. I took a small, pathetic sip and brought the mug back to my lap.

"He killed her," I uttered, voice hoarse. There was the faint taste of sick across my tongue, but the sip of tea helped bury it. "Eamon knows how important Mildred is… was to me."

I couldn't finish speaking what I wished to say aloud.

Mildred died because of me. Because I cared. If I had pushed her away, just as Eamon had urged for years now, then she would never have been used against me.

I felt guilt; it plagued me. Guilt for holding her close, for keeping her as our staff because I was not strong enough to be alone with Eamon. And now she was dead.

Calix placed a hand atop the sheets resting over my thigh. I looked down, bewildered. I didn't dare look at his eyes because I could have drowned in the sorrow within them.

"Eamon is a monster." Calix spoke slowly and carefully. There was a sense of control as each word came out after a pause, whereas I sensed his fury lurking somewhere deep. It sang to my own. "What he has done is unforgiveable. But it will happen again. As long as we have you, he will harm another."

Should I have told him that there was no one left? No one Eamon could use against me. No one I cared for, or whom cared for me.

"What has been done with her body?" I asked. The thought of her hanging... left alone for Gods knows what creature to find her. A starved vampire looking to drink the dregs of her blood, or the wildlife that sheltered within the forest.

"I have tasked Millicent to deal with the body." Calix raised a hand towards me as I jolted forward, sloshing the tea across the sheets. "Nothing will happen to Mildred's body, Rhory. I trust Millicent to do as I have asked."

"Drink her dry?" I spluttered, gagging on the thought.

"No. I have asked that she is buried immediately. If you do not trust me, then I will take you to her."

"Yes, I do… trust you. But…" I swallowed hard, staring deep into his calming gaze.

Calix took my hand in his again, gripped it firmly and said with brows raised, "Use your power and take from me what you need. Just as we did when I brought you here."

"Would that not make me a coward?" I asked, wishing to pull away from his warm, gentle touch but finding I was incapable of moving. "I should face the pain. I deserve it because I caused it. Hiding beneath someone else's stolen emotions—"

"It is not stolen when offered," Calix said, squeezing slightly. "Please, I can't bear to see you like this."

I didn't refuse him. Not again. Gold light glowed from my hand. It reflected across Calix's face, highlighting each strand of his manicured beard, to his smooth skin and masculine features. As I drank in his calm, I drank him in. From the arrow point of his straight nose to the squared lines of his jaw.

He did the same in return.

Each breath became easier as I took in his clarity. Instead of pushing my emotions into him, I buried them. At some point I would need to face it, and I couldn't expose Calix to it. I wished to keep him sheltered from my anguish.

"Is that better?" he asked.

"Much," I breathed in response, finding the weight upon my soul lessen, if only slightly.

The light dimmed to a faint shimmer. It didn't completely retreat as my power picked up a new emotion. One that I had not felt in a long time. So long that it was foreign and strange. There was no naming the feeling that Calix exuded, only the way it warmed my insides like summer sun on naked skin. It was sweet as fresh spring apples picked from an orchard. It thawed my stomach like hot soup on a winter's day. Everything about it was pleasant. Wonderful. Beautiful.

"Calix?" I whispered, his name falling out of my parted lips. My chest blossomed with this new emotion. It sang through me, filling my veins until blood no longer pumped through them but liquid bliss.

He leaned in. I didn't stop him, *couldn't* stop him. "Yes, Rhory?"

"I feel something in you," I said, finding that I leaned into him as well.

"Tell me what it is," Calix replied. "I want to hear you say it."

I pinched my eyes closed and inhaled deeply, drinking this weightless feeling in. When I opened my eyes, Calix was inches from my face. His cool breath washed over me. My eyes darted between his half-lidded eyes to the subtle part of his blush lips.

If I had the words to answer him, I would have. But

there was not a word I could find to express this emotion. There was only action.

I closed the small gap between us until our lips were pressed together. The kiss was gentle. There was no movement from either of us. Only my lips, pressed carefully into his. At first, I felt reluctance, but I was drunk on this feeling he gave me, so I didn't care.

With his spare hand, Calix lifted his fingers and danced the tips from the bottom of my neck up to my cheek. He rested it there, holding me in place. Then he pressed in deeper, forcing our lips further into one another.

I returned his urgency with my own. My spare hand gripped his shirt and crumpled the material up into my fist. He couldn't pull away even if he wanted to. And he didn't. I sensed his hunger for me dancing among other unnameable emotions. It thrummed like lightning through clouds, like wind through reeds.

The kiss changed like the seasons. It was soft at first, with slightly parted lips, and tongues entered the fray. Then the kiss was deep and wet. Vicious but tender.

It was everything.

I didn't know who broke away first, but I was breathless, and my mouth bruised raw. My jaw tickled with the memory of his coarse beard rubbing against me. No longer was he awash from the gold light of my power; our hands were not connected at all.

We stared at one another without uttering a word. Calix stood, the stool clattering to the ground. He backed away from the bedside, one hand on his hip, the other holding the lower half of his face.

"I took it too far," Calix growled. He could barely look at me. When he did, I saw disgust.

"No." The single word broke out of me. "Don't say that."

"Rhory, I'm sorry." He moved for the door. I wanted to cry out for him, but my words were caught by the sudden lump in my throat. "I'll send Millicent for you. She will take you to Mildred's body. I—I."

He looked at me a final time, brows pinched and face screwed. Then he turned and left, leaving the door wide open in his wake.

I watched the shadows of the tunnel beyond, half expecting for Calix to return. Still drunk off his borrowed emotions, it was as though the sense of what had happened had yet to hit me. I placed my fingers on my swollen lips. They were tender to the touch.

A flash of gold flickered in the corner of my eyesight. The lightness inside of me faltered as my eyes dropped to the glint of metal, to the wedding band strangling the freckled skin of my finger.

Reality returned, smashing into me all at once, allowing shame to assassinate me.

## ❧ 19 ❧

Auriol Grey stared at me from her chair, both brown and blue eyes full of judgement. I tugged the cloak around my shoulders as her gaze narrowed on my face then drifted to Calix, who sulked in the dark corner of the room. Could she sense something was wrong between us?

I fought the urge to lift a finger to my tender lips. Even hours after the incident with Calix they still felt sensitive to the touch.

"Are you certain our message has been received?" Auriol asked the moment Millicent had finished debriefing us on her quick trip to Darkmourn. She had not long returned when she had summoned me from Calix's room.

"Is that doubt I hear?" the vampire replied.

Auriol regarded Millicent with intensity. She may have been old, but even Auriol sensed the ancient presence the vampire held. Millicent's age was unknown to me, but there was something about the way she carried herself that suggested experience. Experience that came with being immortal. Most vampires I had encountered oozed the same aura, but not all of them sang with it like Millicent.

"It is no good to assume Eamon will receive it, let alone accept our terms," Auriol said.

"What did you want me to do?" Millicent retorted, arms crossed over her chest. "I hardly imagine knocking on the door and hand delivering the outline of our terms to him would help. My welcome wouldn't be warm."

I hadn't uttered a word since Millicent had brought me to this room within the underground tunnels. Keeping quiet was an easier option. I had nothing to add. Calix kept quiet too and hardly looked at me. If his gaze, framed by pinched brows, was not on Auriol or Millicent, he chose to look to an unimportant place on the wall opposite him.

Anywhere but me.

"In that case, I suppose we throw all caution to the wind. We are on the back foot. Eamon knows more than we ever wished he could. If our only chance is to go in blind, then we must," Auriol said, obviously displeased with the sudden rush to their original plan. Since Mildred had been murdered and left on their front doorstep, it was clear time no longer favoured them.

"He knows Rhory is here," Calix said finally. His voice was low and riddled with tension. "Our desire to set terms is a waste of time when Eamon could be rallying an army of his Crimson Guard to retrieve *his* —" Calix paused, swallowing back his words for a moment. "To retrieve Rhory himself."

"Except he has had all the chance to do so and has chosen to lurk in the shadows." Auriol looked so small in the chair. She was swaddled by blankets as if the cold tunnels were deadly to her. Regardless, there was something refreshed about her compared to the last time I had seen her. Auriol's voice had shed the slight gravelly tone. Her cheeks were flushed and her eyes brighter.

I couldn't imagine such a frail body breaking and splitting to make way for the monster which lurked beneath. Except when her gaze landed on me, I saw a hint of it. Something feral and old lurked within her, something that held enough power to frighten me.

"You know him better than the rest of us." Auriol glared at me once again, fixating her entire focus on me. Beneath her stare, I felt smaller than she looked. "What is stopping him from saving you, since we all know he has the power and influence to do so?"

I shrugged, unable to answer the very question I had been asking myself since we found Mildred. "Eamon is determined. His focus is sharp. If he wanted me back, he could have got me." I blinked and saw the message he had carved into Mildred's back. *HE IS MINE.* "Maybe I am just not as important to him as you first believed."

Auriol scoffed. Calix stiffened before my very eyes and Millicent exhaled a slow, long breath. They each shared a look that suggested they knew more than I did on the matter.

"You are very important to him, Rhory Coleman. I would wager that you are, perhaps, the single most important asset to him."

I opened my mouth to tell Auriol how wrong she was. There was not enough time in a day for me to go through the list of reasons to prove my theory. The bruises, the scars, the marks both visible and invisible. They spoke the truth. Alone they debunked Auriol's beliefs.

"Am I in a position to ask about this plan?" I asked, choosing to alter the conversation.

"No," Calix answered quickly. "The less you know, the safer you will be."

We stared at each other for the first time. I couldn't look away, and nor could he. The pressure of his attention snatched my breath, and burned at the skin beneath my wedding band.

"*Safe*," I repeated, tasting just how sour and wrong the word was in this situation. "We both know that is not right."

I sensed Auriol looking between us both again. The taut string of tension between Calix and I had pulled so tight I feared it would have snapped in two if it wasn't for Millicent.

"We are to meet Eamon during the witching hours tomorrow. Of course, we all know this is not a man to be trusted so I shall go ahead. It is less likely he will sense me. Us undead have a way of slipping through shadows. I will then confirm if he has answered our request and followed our clear set of instructions."

Calix continued staring at me. Even when I tore myself from him and forced myself to look at Millicent, I felt his gaze like twin daggers forged of fire, burning through my skin and into my soul.

"I want my grandson back," Auriol said. "The request we have put forward to your husband is simple. Eamon will either give Silas with the promise that you are returned to him. Or—"

"That is enough," Calix barked.

Auriol snapped her head to face her grandson. In the blur I noticed the shift in her eyes. They lost all colour, turning almost completely black besides the spark of gold glowing directly into their centres. "Do you need reminding who you give orders to, child?"

I felt the power weep from Auriol. It filled the air. Her words were so commanding I felt my own will desire to give into it. Millicent slunk back into the shadows, disappearing all but the glow of her blood-red eyes.

"D...Don't." Calix's body shook as he regarded the old woman. He winced, face twisting into a scowl. It seemed he fought against himself to speak the single word; he strained with every ounce of his being to complete it entirely.

Auriol didn't reply with words, but with a sound that rumbled from the pits of her being. Her lips pulled back from her tea-stained teeth and she snapped them together with a harsh clack.

Calix sagged backwards and... whimpered. The

sound was bizarre, to be coming out the mouth of a full-grown man; it was more akin to a puppy after being scorned by its mother.

By the time Auriol focused her attention back on me, her eyes had returned to their normal state; only the deepest wrinkles across her brow took a moment longer to smooth.

"Rhory. I wish this was different. I do. If your parents knew of the choices I have been forced to make, they would hunt me down and skin me themselves. Know that I struggle with the truth of what must be done. It is not easy for me, but this is my family. My Silas has been taken and all I want is him returned. You must understand that."

The woman speaking was no longer a wrathful crone with the beast lurking deep within her. She was broken. Tormented. And I felt the truth of her plea in my heart.

"You must do what you must," I replied, straightening myself and forcing as much confidence into my stance as I could. "If I was given the chance to return my family to me, I would do anything."

Auriol relaxed in her wheeled chair, blinking back a wave of exhaustion that drained the colour from her cheeks. All vibrance she had moments ago had faded.

"If I could ask, I wish to be taken to Mildred's resting place." I choked through a sudden sob as I said her name.

"Of course," Auriol replied. "Millicent will take you."

A cold shudder raced down my spine. I glanced into the shadows of the room where the burning sconces didn't quite reach. That was where the vampire lingered. I sensed Millicent's hesitation. She didn't voice it, because there was no need.

Calix refused on her behalf. "*I* will be the one to take him," he said, deep voice strained.

Once again, Auriol looked between us, displeased. I half expected her to force her command back to Calix, but it seemed she was lacking such energy. Instead, she waved a defeated hand. "So be it. Millicent, return me to my cottage. I wish to sleep. And, Calix, be wary."

There was no further explanation as to what, or who, Calix had to be wary of. Eamon knew we were here.

"I don't need your warning; I understand the risks. Rhory is safe with me," Calix replied, stoic and face void of emotion.

"Oh, I remember," Auriol paused briefly before looking to me, "But does he?"

## 20

Mildred's grave was no more than a mound of overturned dirt. There was no marker of stone to confirm her presence. No offering of flowers or gifts laid atop her resting place. If Calix hadn't gestured towards the ground, I would have passed it without ever knowing.

It was raining. Not heavily, but the type of rain that felt more like a mist when walked through. I was already soaked to the bone by the time we reached her burial place. My boots were covered in mud that had splattered up the shin of my trousers.

I stood there, neck aching as I looked down at the ground trying to imagine how we even got here.

"Tell me about her," Calix said, standing vigil at my side. His brown hair looked almost black now it was wet. Rivers of water ran down the side of his face, falling over the hard edges of his cheekbone and jaw. "She may be gone but speaking of the dead keeps their memory alive."

I ground my teeth together as his request burned through me. It would have been easier to refuse him. But I owed it to Mildred to spread her story.

"She was my family. We didn't share blood, but we spent so much time together. Since I was born, she worked for my parents, and then for me when they passed. She had no one else. I used to think we were unfair to her, overused her and ruined all chances of having her own life, her own family. But I once asked her about it…" I choked on my words.

"Take your time," Calix said calmly.

I swallowed hard, feeling the memory swell as a lump in my throat. "She said… how could she desire a family of her own when she has everything she ever wished for right before her."

Calix placed a firm hand on my shoulder just as the tears began. I had wondered why I had not cried since we reached her grave. There was something about speaking of Mildred aloud which made it real for me.

He didn't urge me to continue, but his touch and presence encouraged me to lighten the weight of guilt that clouded my chest.

"When my mother died, and Eamon… changed, I truly believed he would have laid Mildred off. He did move her out of our family home, but she was still allowed to return daily. I don't think I would have survived this long if it wasn't for knowing Mildred would be walking through the doors of our home. I had to be strong for her."

"Did she know?" Calix asked, voice thrumming through the smattering of rain.

He didn't need to express what he meant. I heard the true question beneath the first. *Did Mildred know how Eamon treats you?*

"No, and I never told her." I turned my body to face Calix completely. Watching rivulets of mud form across the grave was a painful reminder that once I left this place no one would ever know where to look for her. "Does that make me a coward, Calix? All these years I could have shared my burden, but instead I kept it all to myself."

Calix hesitated. I saw it in the wince of his stare and the way his hand formed a fist at his side. "You are not a coward, Rhory. I would never think such a thing, not when it comes to you."

"Then you tell me what I am." I narrowed my eyes and fixated them on his swirl of honey brown. Even if Calix didn't speak what was on his mind, I would fish the truth out of the windows to his soul. "Am I pathetic? Am I weak?"

Calix didn't so much as blink as he replied, "No. None of those."

"Adulterer?"

His brow furrowed. "Last night, that was my doing. I lured you into that. Do not add such a burden on your shoulders which you have already weighed down with the weight of the world."

I stepped in closer to him. A strand of wet hair had fallen beyond his ear. I reached up and tucked it back. Calix's breathing hitched as my finger brushed across the side of his face.

"Do you regret it?" I asked him. "Last night I mean. The kiss."

"Never," Calix said quickly. His rushed reply caught me by surprise as his face seemed to come alive with emotion. "I want to ask you the same question, but I don't think I am strong enough to face the answer."

"The only thing I regret," I said, lips coated with rain and tears, "Is that I never had the chance to meet you when this hand was free of my binding."

Calix winced as though I had slapped him. All his composure slipped, and I was certain the monster within would break free at any moment. His reaction was so powerful, I wished I could have clawed back what I had said.

"I shouldn't have… Calix, I am sorry."

He regarded my left hand and the dull light which glinted in the dawn light.

"Take it off," Calix urged.

"What?" I dropped my hand back before me and clasped it with my other.

"Take the ring off, Rhory," Calix repeated, slower. "Tonight, you will be sent back to Eamon, but until then let me show you what freedom feels like."

"I can't…" I turned my back on him and began to walk. There was not enough time to spare Mildred's grave a final look. All I knew was I had to get away from his suggestion. It was not because I didn't wish to do as he said. I longed to free my finger from the shackle Eamon had put on it. But memories of what happened the last time and the weeks of pain and broken bones that followed was still fresh in my memory.

Calix was before me. He moved with vampiric speed, but I now knew his true curse even if I didn't truly understand it. His leathers glistened with rain. His tunic was so wet it had darkened in colour and clung to every mound and curve of his torso beneath.

"Please, don't run away from me," Calix said.

"You are asking that of me, when you did the exact thing last night. You left me."

Calix held my gaze, both hands reaching out for my arms. He held them gently, and I let him. "I left you last night because I didn't wish to give you more regret to burden yourself with. If I had stayed, I need you to understand, you would have broken more vows to Eamon than you even knew existed."

The insides of my cheeks pinched as though Calix's words were an unripe fruit, and I had just taken a hard bite into its sour flesh.

"That makes you a coward," I said.

"It does. I'm not as brave as you, *Little Red.*"

I buckled at the nickname. That nickname, Calix shouldn't have known it. It was a name my father had whispered into my ear as he walked me down the aisle and handed me over to Eamon. Without Calix ever being able to know their power, those two words enraptured me.

Glancing back down to my ringed finger, I didn't notice that Calix now held it in his hands. His thumb brushed across the metal over and over, spinning it around my finger.

"The last time I took my ring off, I was punished for it." I allowed the story to come out of me; it was no good to face such a nightmare on my own when I had someone to hold the light for me. "I had sent Mildred home early because it was her birthday and I couldn't stand the idea of her standing before the sink, washing our dirtied and spoiled pots. She left, and I finished the job for her. All I had done was remove the ring and left it on the side. It was so innocent, harmless. But to Eamon, it was the end of his world…"

I took a breath, realising I had hardly allowed myself one since I started talking.

"Go on," Calix urged, holding my hand and offering his warmth. There was no need to use my power and borrow his emotions; his touch alone calmed me. "I wish to know. I want to know it all."

"Eamon put the ring back on. He was drunk and sloppy. It was like something entirely demonic had overcome him. He took the meat mallet near him and brought it down on my hand. He wanted, I believe, to smash the ring into my flesh so I could never remove it again. Just my luck, his aim was shit, and he brought it down on my hand instead. He shattered most of my bones. He hurt me all because I wanted to clean the dishes."

Calix's breathing had grown ragged. His eyes had

taken on its golden sheen. "Cunt," he growled. One word and it was cursed with so much fury even the surrounding forest seemed to bow away from Calix. "Eamon doesn't deserve you."

I didn't resist when Calix lifted my hand to his paled mouth. Wide eyed and with bated breath, I watched him. And he watched me. His rain-slicked lips pressed into my finger, covering my skin and the wedding band. Calix held my finger there for a prolonged moment. When his lips pulled back, his fingers worked with ease to remove the wedding band.

"He broke the sacred vows of your union," Calix said. He reached towards me, the ring pinched beneath his finger and thumb. A shiver spread across my skin as his knuckles brushed over my chest. I looked down the length of my nose and watched him discard the ring in the breast pocket of my shirt. It dropped like a stone, heavy and full of burdens.

*Out of sight, out of mind.*

"Eamon would never see it like that. I am his to do whatever he pleases."

Calix shook his head, eyes closed as he attempted to regain the composure that was quickly slipping away from him. "He defiles such a blessing. To have you, to be with you, should be the most coveted part of his life. He broke his promises. So, now you should shatter your promise to him."

It was unspoken, but I knew how this was going to end. I sensed it like a flame in my stomach, or fresh air in my lungs. Reading Calix's emotions was not required when his eyes glowed with his desire, his wishes.

"And how do you think I should do that?"

Calix stepped in closer. He trailed his fingers from my hands, up both arms. I shivered as he ran them over my shoulders, up my neck and to my face, where they rested on either side of it. "First, I will show you what you desire. Every place that monster has hurt you. Every scar, every bruise, every fucking mark. I wish to wash the memory of your hurt away and replace it with something else. If you would allow it of me. Tell me to release you and take you back to your room and I will do it. I would do anything for you…"

There was only one option for me. Only one thing I could say to him because, for the first time in a long time, I recognised my desire and selfishly claimed it.

"Stop talking," I said. "And show me."

Calix smiled. We were so close I could see the beautiful curve of the rain droplet that grew on the tip of his nose until it fell down into the limited space between us.

"We made a deal. I promised I would take you home when your bruises fade." Calix dove into my neck as he spoke. His scratchy beard tickled across my dampened skin. I pinched my eyes closed, lips parting in a moan as his lips greeted my tender skin. "I will kiss every one of them just to remind you of what you deserve. What *I* can offer you."

My head lolled back as Calix replaced his words with action. His lips branded my neck. His kiss was subtle to begin with. I faced the skies, rain pattering across my closed-eyed face, as Calix ran his lips, then his tongue, across my neck. He left a necklace of his saliva across it.

He guided me to the ground, all without removing his mouth from my neck. I knelt in the muddied moss-covered bed of the forest. Calix did the same before me. I found my fingers were now tangled in the wet length of his hair. My nails ran across his scalp, urging a moaning groan from deep within him.

I was disappointed when he suddenly pulled back from my neck. That feeling only lasted a moment until I found myself lost to the raging desire in his eyes.

"Rhory, I would like to take you. It would be my honour to offer you a memory to return home with. One that you can… remember this time."

I leaned into him, pressing my mouth to his as I answered, "No more talking. Take me."

Our kiss was soft and careful, whilst being desperate and rushed. We didn't require to use our eyes to know what we were doing. It had been a long time since I had laid with Eamon, but even that faded memory was easily incomparable to this feeling. Excitement bubbled in my chest, echoing the thunder in my groin.

Calix's fingers worked quickly to untie the red cloak. It slipped from my shoulders with ease. He broke away from my mouth long enough to lay the cloak out across the muddied and wet ground. "It may not be the comfort I wish to give you, but I promise you will not notice."

"For once," I said, breathless and lips raw, "I do not want you to be gentle."

"No," Calix replied, eyes narrowed. "Perhaps there would be a time for that, but this... This is something else. You mean more to me than a fuck, Rhory. Allow me to show you, if you trust me."

"But you do not know me," I said, unsure where the words came from, "Not for long."

Calix's lip curled into a snarl. "Do you trust me?" he asked, ignoring my statement as though it didn't matter. And perhaps it didn't.

"Yes, I trust you," I replied. "I am a fool, and you are a stranger, but I trust you, nonetheless."

"Good," he breathed, gilded eyes alight in the darkening storm covered sky. "Then I shall begin."

Calix took his time undressing me. It took a long time until the chill of autumn wind and rain graced my naked skin because he took breaks to kiss every part of me. His lips explored more of my body than Eamon had ever had the chance to hurt. They graced my bare shoulders, my chest, my stomach, my arms and my thighs.

I knelt on the red cloak and watched as Calix removed his own clothes. He refused my help. "I want to watch you. I want to see every thought in your eyes. I want to remember your face when you see me."

And watch him I did.

He was a god carved in flesh. Broad shoulders and a powerful, sculpted chest that gradually narrowed to his firm hips. If I had the time, I would have counted every muscle. Instead, I was hypnotised by the rivers of rain that ran over his body. I was jealous of them, wishing to touch him in the places they graced.

As Calix worked the belt of his leather trousers and plucked the buttons at his waist away one by one, I crawled across the cloak towards him. I stopped only when I knelt directly beneath him. My head was at the height of his waist. Calix didn't refuse my help now, not as my hands reached up the wet material of his trousers, over his powerful thighs to the lump of flesh that grew with every passing moment.

My palm glided over his cock. It was a monster, hidden behind material I would rip away with teeth and nails.

Calix removed his hands and placed them on the back of my head, all the while he stared down the length of his nose at me. I gazed up at him, not taking my eyes from his as I tugged down his trousers, undergarments, and freed the thick length of hard cock.

But curiosity forced my eyes further down.

My breath caught at the sheer size of him. I tried to hide my surprise, but no matter how hard I fought to steel my expression, I failed.

Calix chuckled softly at my reaction as he guided my head towards it. I offered no resistance. His hands pushed at the back of my head until my lips were inches from the glistening tip of his cock. It was as thick as my wrist was. Blessed with length, that even hard, it couldn't stand completely to attention for its weight was too great. It was crowned with dark hair that spread up to his lower stomach in a trail. My hands explored his waist, nails tickling among the coarse hair.

"Look up at me," Calix said, drawing my attention from his perfectly formed being, back to his face. "I want to see your eyes as you take me in."

He freed a hand from the back of my head. Calix took his cock in his palm, lifted it up and pressed the bell curved tip to my parted lips.

My tongue broke free. It slithered from the confines of my mouth. The moment it caressed the end of his length, I tasted his sweetness. It seeped out the eye of his cock and dribbled willingly into my mouth. The insides of my cheeks prickled with ferocious hunger that drove me forward.

I took him in, and Calix roared into the skies. I parted my lips wider as I forced as much of him into me as I could; my jaw ached and throat cramped but that didn't stop me.

I allowed him in until I couldn't physically take any more. His low chuckle encouraged me as I gagged on his cock. His fingers tensed in my hair and held me in place. I slapped both hands on his thighs for aid whilst tears gathered in my wide eyes.

"Good boy," Calix groaned, unsheathing his cock from my mouth with his hand still wrapped around its base. "Just like that. I want it all in that pretty little mouth."

I smiled with my own pride. Seeing Calix's reaction was encouraging and exciting. I stuck my tongue out, not caring for my dribble that fell onto my naked lap.

Calix bared his teeth and hissed as he slapped his thick cock onto the pad of my tongue.

One. Two. Three. Four times, he smacked it as he bit down into his lip and groaned.

"More," Calix said. "Take me again, give me your mouth."

My cock was hard too. I didn't need to touch it to know it throbbed with desire between knelt legs. I feared if I did reach for it, a single touch would race me to my end. I was not ready for this to finish. There was so much I wanted from this moment. In Calix's half-lidded eyes alone, they held promises of more to come.

I wanted it all. I wanted him.

I sucked on Calix's length until it was him who stopped me. His hand was replaced with mine as it worked up and down, following the grace of my lips. I would have gone on forever if it was not for Calix who withdrew himself suddenly. He was close to finishing for I could taste his cum within my mouth. It was different to my saliva. Thick and salty. It was a pleasure to let it coat my lips and spread its taste all throughout my mouth.

"Careful," Calix said, joining me on my knees and taking my face in his hands. "I am a selfish man. Selfish enough to know that I am not ready for this to finish. Not yet."

"Your cock tells otherwise," I replied.

Calix crashed his lips into mine. His tongue entered my mouth and twisted with my own. I wondered if he could taste himself on me.

"That pretty little mouth," Calix groaned. His fingers were in my hair. My hands groped his rock-hard chest. "I wish to bury myself in it again. Over and over until I fill you."

"Do it," I urged, not blinking as I bored through him with my gaze.

Calix's sly smile was enough to melt me into a puddle. "I have nothing to aid it, Rhory. It is not my ego speaking when I tell you my cock is far too large to take without… lubrication."

I felt a mixture of excitement and disappointment. Calix was right. His length was considerable, and its girth even more so. My ass flinched at the thought of it entering me. It was not an unpleasant thought, but I sensed there would be discomfort and Calix didn't wish to hurt me.

"But I want you," I whined, nails tracing slight red marks across the hair-covered skin of his chest. What I wished to tell him was this was our only chance. Lust was fading, giving room for reality and I sensed the wedding band in the pile of clothes to our side. It called to me. I couldn't keep my conscience buried for long.

"There are other ways I can pleasure you," Calix said, his words like a promise. "Rhory, I am going to tell you what to do, and *you* are going to do it without question."

I gasped, stomach flipping as though I had reached the peak of a steep hill and was ready to be thrown off the top of it.

"Do I make myself clear?"

Calix's brows twitched as he heard me gulp.

"Yes, crystal."

"Stand up," Calix ordered.

I had never moved so fast before. In seconds I was standing before him. Calix shuffled on his hands until his body was stretched out across my cloak. He laid on his back, gazing up at me as the rain fell over him.

"Come to me," Calix beckoned me with his hands, "Here, come and stand over my face."

My breathing was rushed and heavy. It was as if I had run from Darkmourn and back and my body suffered the consequences. Calix watched me with his soft-gold eyes as I straddled his large frame and waddled all the way up, until my feet were on either side of his shoulders.

"Turn and face the other way," Calix continued.

I listened, wishing to discover what he wanted from me.

His hands reached up for my lower legs; the hairs prickled, and my knees grew weak.

"Sit back and let me take your weight."

I looked over my shoulder and down to Calix. His entire focus was on the curve of my naked ass. He licked his lips as though he faced a delicious meal. Then I realised quickly what he wanted, and my legs almost gave out.

"Slowly," Calix drawled as I gave into his hands and the resistance of his strong arms. "Slowly."

Soon enough I was squatting over his face. I felt his

breath brush across the sensitive point of my ass, between the two cheeks he now spread.

"I want you to stroke your cock," Calix said, lips and beard tickling the skin on my ass. "If you want to cum, do it. But tell me. I want to hear you reach your bliss."

I found myself stuttering. "What… what about you?"

"Oh, my darling," Calix replied. "I've already found my bliss."

Surprised, I glanced down to his hard muscular stomach and noticed the cloudy milk-like liquid that dripped into the hair that crowned his softening cock.

Had he come as he pulled me from his mouth? How had I not noticed?

Pride swelled in my stomach. I had done that. I had caused that without even knowing and it made me feel powerful.

"Sit on my face," Calix demanded, tearing me from my thoughts, "I wish to devour you."

Calix's hands were firm as he held me in place. My knees hardly ached from the position I took. There was no room for discomfort when his tongue wreaked havoc on me. It lapped against the centre of me, twisting, licking, sucking. His teeth would come into play every now and then. When he nipped my ass, I was certain he left a mark.

I didn't care.

I wished for him to mark me. To cover me in his kisses, his bites, his sucks.

Only when Calix reminded me to stroke myself did

I do so. I was entirely hypnotised by the way he ate at me. I had never felt anything like it in my life, yet my body seemed to convince me otherwise. It was all wetness and tongue. He lapped against the centre of my ass, even going so far as to force his tongue inside of me occasionally.

When my bliss raced towards me, I couldn't form words to warn Calix as he demanded. All I could do was let out a long, breathy moan that caused birds to flock from nearby trees.

"That's it," Calix sang, voice muffled as he pulled back from my ass. His fingers dug into my cheeks and squeezed as I lost myself.

My cum joined Calix's. It splattered across his stomach. Only when the convulsions of pleasure ceased did I recognise the burn in my legs and lower back from being kept in the unique position. He could have been eating me for hours, or minutes; it was impossible to know.

I felt the need to apologise for causing such a mess as I lied down on the cloak next to him. Exhaustion overcame me. I turned my head and glanced at him to find Calix was already looking at me.

"How do you feel?" he asked, weaving his hand into mine.

"Exposed," I said, smiling.

"Then I have let you down," he replied. "You should feel powerful. Strong. Unstoppable. Those are all the things I wish for you."

I rolled onto my side. Leaning forward, I rested my

head on his chest, half expecting for him to roll away and stand. He didn't move. Instead, he encouraged me onto him. His heart thundered, thumping against the side of my head.

"I feel like I could sleep for a week…." I faltered, silencing myself quickly. We both knew we didn't have a week to waste together. Merely hours.

"Do you think, if we stay here, the world will forget about us?" I asked, not wanting to welcome the pain deep in my chest. But I was powerless to stop it from affecting me.

"Not here," Calix replied, staring up into the skies above. "But we could leave it all behind."

"You don't mean that," I said. I didn't dare focus on his words for the hope they provided could destroy me. In a strange way, as I closed my eyes and replayed his suggestion over, the words felt familiar, as though I had heard them before.

Calix faced me and his expression broke me in two. "Say the word, and I would do it. I would snatch you away and steal you for myself. There would be no Eamon. No Auriol. No brother or Crimson Guard. I know our time together has been…. sparse, but I know deep down that I could provide more for you."

"And where would we go?" I couldn't keep back the anger from my question. I hated this. I hated the way he looked at me with pleading and longing, knowing full well that what we desired, and what had to happen, were two entirely impossible things.

"To a place where we would be nameless. We would

be without a past. All we would have is what we take with us. A fresh start, a promise for a life without hurt."

"Then tell me why everything you are saying is the most painful thing I have ever felt?"

Calix sat up, his face twisting into a harsh frown. "Hope should not hurt."

"It does," I replied, sitting up beside him. I curled in on myself, hiding my naked body from the world. "To me, hope is a bait to lure me away from reality, lower my guard and destroy me."

"Then I should take you back to the tunnels," Calix said quietly. "We will have only hours until we must leave."

"Okay." It was all I could muster.

"Okay," Calix replied.

He offered me a hand, helped me stand and passed me the pile of my clothes. They were drenched and muddied, but better than being naked.

"Do you want me to turn away this time?" he asked.

"No," I replied softly.

"Good," he replied.

I turned my back on him before he could read my secret reply as it fell silently from my lips.

*Never.*

## 21

## ₃ YEARS BEFORE

D eep in the undead core of my body, I knew something was wrong. Loren hadn't returned home, and sunrise was almost upon Darkmourn. He never stayed out past the long evenings; in fact, he was always the first one home. My brother was, and had always been, introverted. When I changed him—offered him an eternal life of bloodlust and adventure—he almost did not accept it; not because he was scared of becoming one of the undead, or the idea of drinking blood unnerved him… He had said it was longer than a lifetime of speaking to people, and the thought of that displeased him.

Of course, Loren came round in the end. To my relief.

I was younger than Loren by five mortal years, but I felt maternal over him. Perhaps it was because our mother had died when we were nothing but small children, or maybe it was because our father left us when I was old enough to hold my own bottle.

Since then, we had been alone. Just me and him. We had survived together when the world first changed. Sometimes I allowed myself to think back to when Lord Marius first broke free from Castle Dread with his eternal mate, Jak Bishop. In fact, I remembered Jak from my childhood. He was like Loren, in a way. Shy and quiet, but with a dark streak lingering beneath the surface of that facade.

The difference between my brother and Jak was that Loren didn't lead to the destruction of Darkmourn. We were merely products of its obliteration. Victims.

I had been changed first. Not by choice. When the wave of the vampiric disease was freed from Castle Dread, it spread like fire to a dried wood. I remembered the hot burn of the bite to my neck, followed by the soft honey-dew liquid of blood the vampire had dribbled into my mouth.

He had wanted me as his eternal bride, admiring Lord Marius and Jak's story; he had wanted to create one of his own. Except, I had killed him before he had a chance to do any of the vile things he had whispered to me as I drank from his wrist.

Sometimes I still felt the cold slab of flesh that was his beatless heart gripped in my hand before it melted beneath my fingers and fell to the ground as ash.

When I changed Loren, it was nothing like my brutal re-birth. It was kind and soft. I would never have forced him—at least that was what I told myself. Gods only knows what I would have done if time went on and I watched my brother age, knowing he would soon die naturally and leave me in a world I did not wish to be in. Without Loren, I was nothing.

I stared out of the window of our dwelling in Old Town. Legally, it did not belong to us, but we had claimed it anyway. Our real home was down the street from this one, and I had remembered staring through the shutters of our window to this very building when I was a child. The Bishop's had lived here. I had often spied Jak as a boy looking out his own window with a look of distant pondering. Although I could not see what had caught his attention, from the direction his window faced I knew it could only have been Castle Dread he had focused on.

We had not known the Bishops were witches then, although many had speculated. It never bothered me though, I rather liked the boy even if we had never shared more than a word. Which was how I made myself feel better for taking the empty Bishop dwelling for my own and moving in with Loren as the centuries passed.

From Old Town, I had a good view into the main centre of Darkmourn. A blanket of night still fell over the world, but with the passing of time the stars winked out, readying to welcome the bastard sun.

Irritation swelled in my stomach, dampening the hunger which had returned. I should have hunted tonight, but Loren's disappearance had thrown me off. I didn't dare leave in case he returned, because I wanted to welcome him and shout until my throat was raw. He never left without telling me first. He should have warned me.

The Crimson Guard were out in full force tonight. Even Old Town—which was usually more silent than a graveyard these days—had its streets invaded with the roaches. That fact didn't help calm my nerves with Loren's lack of appearance. It only worried me more, knowing how unbalanced the town's protection force had become in the passing years. It was best for monsters like us to stay under the radar. It didn't take much for us to be snatched from the street and punished publicly for something ridiculous.

Tensions had been high since the murder of Lady Coleman, and the Crimson Guard looked for someone to blame.

Dawn was at most an hour away and Loren was still not home. I was moments from smashing our home up in frustration, which was what drove me to wear my woollen cloak and join the bustle of Darkmourn's streets.

I tucked back sheets of black hair into my hood, which I pulled down further over my eyes to hide the glow of red. It was common for vampires to frequent Darkmourn whilst the moon still ruled, but that didn't mean I wanted to catch the attention of the Crimson Guard.

Excitement thundered between the humans as I passed them. My ears picked up parts of the conversations as I slipped through the shadow of buildings around them.

*Execution. Coleman. Criminal.*

Beneath the ruby glow of the gas lamps lining the streets, I caught the movement of the living. There was never this many out at night. I could smell the sweet scent that oozed from their skin, and the promise of life nectar that lingered beneath it. As I moved further from Old Town into the residential streets, I spied empty bowls of blood left on doorsteps, and bags of coin left in thanks. The hunger within me was growing like a newborn child; if there was a bowl left, I would have taken it. Although I would not have left coin. I was old enough to remember a time where blood was free, and the demonic side of me missed it.

But I had promised Loren years ago that I would never drink from a human again—unless offered. That was a caveat in our deal I had been sure to add. Loren had never drunk blood from a human, not once. He boasted about the divine flavours of rabbit and deer. I never believed he preferred it, but his nature was far too kind to even sink teeth into the flesh of a mortal. I loved that about him. He drove me to be a better version of myself. Without him, I was nothing.

If I had a heartbeat, it would have been racing by now. I looked out across the outstretched crowd swelling in the town's centre. The Crimson Guard and humans I had passed all congregated here, joining the back of the crowd with equal excitement.

Dread cut through me. I didn't need to see what

drew their attention to know something was terribly wrong. I felt it in my bones, in every muscle and vein. The discomforting emotion thrummed through me, and it was not fucking welcome.

There was no way I could have fought through the crowd, but I longed to get a better look. I had to see for myself.

Loren's name glistened across my lips. The overwhelming desire to cry out for him took over me. He was in this crowd, he had to be. Whatever had drawn everyone here had captured his attention too. At least, that was what I attempted to convince myself.

"You," I snapped, gripping the arms of a young man to my side. His eyes threw open in surprise at my sudden presence, before his expression melted into disgust. "What is going on?"

I was far stronger than him, but that didn't mean I prevented the man from pulling out of my hold.

"I'm surprised you haven't heard," he grumbled, looking me up and down with tired hate-filled eyes. "They found the Coleman killer. They're going to hang him up so we can all watch him be brought to justice."

I looked away from the man, throwing my gaze across the sea of people as my mind put the pieces together.

"Who did it?" I asked, not wanting to know the answer.

"His name doesn't matter," the human man spat. "What matters is another one of you... monsters are slain."

I was running before I could even contemplate a reply.

Instead of moving towards the heart of the crowd, I ran around it. Darkmourn was more familiar than the lines on my palms. I knew every building, and who owned it. I had seen people come and go, die and change. Using my knowledge to my advantage, I slipped down a narrow side street as the noise of the crowd swelled behind me.

My nails tore and the skin of my palms ripped as I climbed up the side of the building. I used the old bricks as leverage beneath my feet, and my unnatural force to propel myself upwards as quick as possible. There was pain, but it didn't matter. By the time I reached my destination, I would have healed.

Towards the top of the building was an older apartment that had not been used by the humans in years. It was a hideout for vampires, a place those who needed the shadows in a time of need could use. When I threw myself over the wrought iron bannister and landed on the balcony, I caught the glint of many red eyes glaring through the darkened building within.

I was not the only vampire here today, and I would not be the last.

"Loren?" I called his name, waiting for my brother to step out of the shadows. He had to be here. With the swell of humans and Crimson Guard, he knew to use this place if he didn't feel comfortable coming home. The amount of people out this night would have sent him into the open arms of his anxiety. He knew this was a place of quiet for him.

"Brother, are you here?"

It was not my brother who replied. "He is not here." One of the vampires from the shadows spoke, voice husky and rich. They did not step forward, but that didn't prevent me from seeing as they raised their hand and pointed to somewhere behind my shoulders. "You are too late."

I refused to turn around and face what I had already known. Maybe it was our tie as siblings, or because I had been the one to sire him into this curse—my dread was justified. It was not just a misplaced feeling because he was missing, it was a feeling born from the instinctual bond between us.

"He killed the Coleman woman," the vampire from shadows spoke again.

"No," I sputtered. My knees faltered and I wobbled wildly. "He didn't—"

"We are not the ones to convince. They are…"

Tears of blood already slipped from my eyes as I turned and surveyed my living nightmare. From this height, I could see everything. Every horrific fucking detail.

The podium. The crowd. The hangman, noose and the man that stood still beneath it as the rope was lowered around his pale ivory neck.

"Loren!" I screamed, but my voice was muffled as a cold hand slapped over my mouth.

"Crying for him will not save him," the soft voice said. "Don't look, you don't need to see this."

Whoever held me tried to turn me away from the scene, but I was older and thus far stronger. I tugged free with ease, my entire body swelling with premature grief.

Standing beside my brother was a towering man with obsidian black hair. He spoke to the crowd, but I could not hear his words. The billowing cloak of red that flapped in the breeze confirmed who I already knew him to be.

Eamon Coleman, the acting Head of the Crimson Guard. And just beyond him was his husband, Rhory Coleman. The red-haired man had his arms wrapped around his thin frame, his eyes never leaving Loren. Not once. They never left my brother, not as Eamon lifted his hand and gestured downwards with a clean strike.

The sound of breaking wood broke around the entire world. My eyes flew from Rhory to Loren. The podium beneath his feet had fallen away, and my brother was left to drop. The rope stopped him from falling entirely, snapping his neck with the force and keeping him hanging.

It didn't kill him. It didn't give him the peace he deserved.

My brother was left to hang before the crowd. He gargled on his innocence, but no one listened. My dead heart broke, my soul shattered. Each one of his screams pierced me. And there was nothing I could do but watch because behind him the light of dawn crested over the world.

I was pulled back into the shadows of the building. This time I did not fight.

As the rays of light cast over Darkmourn, I watched from the safety of the room, as my brother erupted into an explosion of ash and flesh. As the crowd roared with applause, and my brother became nothing but bone—I didn't look away. I would not award myself the peace of looking elsewhere.

Unlike Rhory Coleman who didn't watch. He didn't watch as my brother died for the death of his mother, a death I did not believe my brother capable of doing. Rhory kept his gaze pinned to the ground before him whilst Loren answered for crimes he did not commit.

The crowd cheered and rumbled for hours after. I was stuck in the apartment, surrounded by vampires I did not know—as Darkmourn celebrated the death.

The death of my brother.

The death of my soul.

## ✜ 22 ✜

**M**illicent was lowering the blindfold to cover my eyes when Calix burst into the room. The slip of material fell to the floor, forgotten. It was no more than an afterthought when we both regarded the horror set into his face.

"Eamon," Calix practically roared, shaking dust from the corners of the room. "He's come."

Every ounce of warmth our last interaction gifted me vanished as though it never existed.

Millicent moved with such speed and had unsheathed two blades from her hips and gripped them in both hands within a single blink. "Fuck. Where's Auriol?"

Something darkened Calix's wide eyes. "He has her."

I moved, propelled forward by the thought of Eamon having his hands on Auriol.

"No!" Calix extended an arm to stop me. His hand

caught my shoulder, preventing me from barging into the tunnel way behind him.

"He wants me," I said, heart thundering in my chest. "Not Auriol. Me. If you let me go to him, I can stop this."

Calix glared down at me as I stared up at him. "You know I cannot let you run to him."

"Oh, just let the boy leave," Millicent snapped, gesturing towards me with one of her sharpened blades. "The human is right. Eamon wants him, not Auriol."

"This is not how this was supposed to go," Calix warned, hissing through his teeth at the vampire.

"Millicent is right." I put a hand over his chest. Beneath my touch his heart hammered, like the stampede of wild horses. It matched my own. "Eamon knows little of sense. He will not entertain your wants and desires. But he will listen to me. Let me go to him before he comes looking."

Calix didn't need to use words to answer me, because I read them clearly in his eyes. *I can't do that.*

"He *will* kill her," I added, ensuring Calix not only heard, but felt what I had to say. "You have seen what he did to Mildred, you know what he is capable of. Please, Calix. Let me go to him. Let me try."

"Then what?" Calix rushed, pressing his hand atop mine to keep it in place.

"We fail," Millicent answers. "Auriol, or Silas. That is the decision we are faced with."

"Or Rhory." Calix glowered.

"You cannot be serious." Millicent's voice pitched. "Calix, you are thinking with your cock, not your head."

Heat rose in my cheeks. Calix seemed to falter over Millicent's brazen accusation, his entire body shook beneath my palm.

"Auriol told me to keep you from him, but I disobeyed her," Millicent snapped. "I should have listened."

"You do not know what you speak of." Calix was practically vibrating with built up tension.

"I can smell it on you, fool! On both of you. Old habits die hard." Disgust twisted her face into a scowl that sharpened her features. Her eyes burned a ruby red which emanated her power. "It was a mistake ever letting you fool around with our bargaining tool. Your past blinds you. And you…" She turned her gaze at me and pinned me with it. "What do you think your dear husband will do when he finds out? Oh, perhaps abduct Auriol and punish her for the both of you? Or worse. This is on you, Calix. What comes out of this will rest on your shoulders."

Blood thundered in my ears like the rush of a tidal wave. There was nothing but Millicent's words and the knowledge of what I had to do.

"Calix, let me pass."

His hand pressed down on mine, trapping it where it rested over his chest. "Millicent, you might be right. I am selfish. I am a fool. But I am also not letting Rhory go back to him. There are other ways out of these tunnels, ways that lead away."

I caught Millicent snap her pointed teeth at Calix out the corner of my eye. She dropped her knees, readying to pounce. "Then I will take him to Eamon myself."

"There will be no need for that," I said. Gold light emitted from beneath Calix's large hand. It spilled out as though he held a star between his fingers. The glow cast shadows across the bottom of his face, highlighting the realisation that struck him. "I can take myself."

I pulled the exhaustion from deep within my bones and forced it into Calix. The rush of sharing the emotion was violent. It came out of me willingly, without resistance or care. The more I pushed into Calix I felt revigorated. Alert.

His golden eyes grew heavy. His mouth slackened and the colour drained from his face.

I pulled my power back only when Calix's body had fallen to the ground. His breathing was even, his eyes closed.

"What did you do?" Millicent asked, wariness etched in her voice.

"I put him to sleep," I said, staring down at his large frame.

The vampire stepped to my side and peered down at Calix. "You made the right choice, for everyone."

"This is the only choice."

When Millicent looked at me, it was not with her usual disdain. The lines around her red eyes had softened. Even the scowl she wore with pride had faded, allowing room for a slight smile. "Then we should go before the *beast* awakens. Or, before you change your mind."

❦

The further we ventured out of the tunnels, the thicker my panic became. It was as dense as a cloud. I waded through it as if it was smoke stinging at my eyes and clogging my throat.

Millicent was unbothered, forging ahead only to stop when we neared the exit. Daylight spilled into the tunnels. Millicent regarded it with horror, hissing like a cat drenched in cold water.

"This is all you from here," Millicent said. "He will kill me for this."

She couldn't leave the tunnels with me, but I felt lighter knowing she had planned to.

I was numb, the only thought passing through my mind was of Auriol and her safety.

"It is fine," I said, finding myself reaching out for Millicent. Her strong arm was made of pure muscle. She did not flinch as I took it in my hand. "Go back to Calix. If Eamon comes for him, keep Calix safe. For me."

Millicent swore under her breath for a final time. "Calix will never forgive me for this. Good luck, Rhory."

I offered her a smile, one that pulled awkwardly at my face. "Millicent, for what it is worth, I never believed your brother was the one who killed my mother. His death has never left me, nor did it satisfy me to know he was cast the blame. I did try to stop him… Eamon made sure I never did again."

Millicent stared daggers through me. I felt her gaze burn at the far back of my skull. Part of me wished for her to say something, but she chose the path of silence. I let go of her arm. She turned, without a word, and ran back into the dark tunnel. Perhaps I should have told her that I was sorry, but I imagined those words were as meaningless to Millicent as they were to me.

Eamon waited for me beyond the tunnel's exit.

My eyes fell on him where he stood, unable to focus on anything else. His crimson cloak draped perfectly over his shoulders, tugged gently by the breeze flirting through the forest. Eamon held both hands before him, clasped with only his thumb drumming with impatience. At first glance it seemed he was alone. Then my eyes adjusted. For every tree in the clearing, there was a further two of the Crimson Guard waiting. And not a single one was without a weapon. All but Eamon, who was empty handed.

"I trust you received my message," Eamon said, unclasping his hands and letting them drop to his sides.

Each step towards him was difficult. I felt the resistance my mind placed on my body. It was like walking through knee-high mud.

"The one you had carved into Mildred's back?" I asked, surprised by my fury that overwhelmed me. Eamon didn't so much as flinch at my accusation. It was clear he had nothing to hide from his Crimson Guard. "How could you have that done… to her?"

"Oh, my darling, you know me better than to think I had someone else do that for me."

"You disgust me." My heart thundered in my chest, filling my ears with the rush of blood. "Only you have such capacity for evil."

Eamon pouted, stretched up on his tiptoes and made a spectacle of looking behind me. "Where is the mutt? From the strongly worded letter he had posted through our front door, I would have thought I was to be greeted by the big bad wolf himself."

"Where is Auriol?" I countered his question.

"Auriol Grey." Eamon raised his hands up as though to show he didn't have her hiding in his palms. "She is on her way to the reunion she has petitioned so tirelessly for."

"Silas," I echoed Calix's brother's name.

"See, I am not a monster." Eamon narrowed his eyes on me. In four large strides, he closed the gap between us. His closeness caused a shiver of disgust to roll over my skin. "And I don't like the way you are looking at me, dear husband. You should feel relief that I have come to save you. So why do you snarl like a feral creature? It would seem your captors have rubbed off on you."

He leaned in close as he whispered. I could smell last night's overindulgence of wine. It was sharp, lacing his mouth with a scent that revolted me yet still the sickly smell of lavender lingered beneath it all.

I opened my mouth to say something. To spill all the

hateful thoughts I had harboured for him. The audience of his Crimson Guard would at least prolong the physical pain which waited for me, so speaking my mind would make no difference. But Eamon silenced me with what he said next.

"I saw you both," Eamon hissed into my ear. Flecks of spit hit the side of my face. I didn't dare move to wipe it clear. "Last night. You have betrayed me. Dishonoured me. Til death do us part, do you remember chanting those words? Because I certainly do."

"How could I ever forget?" I replied, filling each word with burning fire.

"You make me *sick*."

Eamon trembled with rage. I glanced out the corner of my eye to see the whites of his almost entirely red. He looked exhausted this close up. Dark shadows hung beneath his eyes, giving his face the gaunt expression of a skinless skull.

"I *will* kill him. Your mutt. I'll be the one to put him down."

"Calix was not the one to speak the vows. It was me. I am the one who deserves punishment," I hissed, jaw aching from clamping my teeth shut. Heat flooded my cheeks as some of the Crimson Guard began to quietly laugh among themselves. Eamon showed no sign of sharing their humour.

"You had him in your mouth." Eamon lost his control for a moment. It was long enough that he snapped his hand back and sent the back of it into my cheek. I blinked and saw stars. I tasted blood. It filled my cheeks as I unsheathed my teeth from the soft flesh of my tongue.

"That mouth is mine. You will do well to remember that." He pulled away slowly, righting himself and smoothing the fury from his expression. "We are leaving."

I flinched back a step. Eamon struck out like a viper and wrapped his fingers around my forearm. His nails pinched my skin through the layering of my shirt, uncaring and familiar.

"*If*," he sneered, "You wish for Auriol to stay alive long enough to be reunited with her grandson, then I suggest you do as I say."

Tears filled my eyes. I didn't dare blink for fear they would show Eamon just how much power he had over me.

"Come," Eamon commanded, pulling at my arm. "It seems we have much catching up to do."

I couldn't refuse him as he tugged me from the tunnel's exit. As we moved away, the Crimson Guard filed in towards it, silver blades raised at the waiting dark.

"What…" I foresaw what was going to happen. "No, stop!"

I dug my heels into the ground, forcing my weight against Eamon. His grasp on me tightened, but it was useless as I was blinded by the desire to act. In the dark of my mind, I saw Calix slumped out across the ground, forced into his lured sleep. Millicent was alone.

Although I had no doubt she was powerful, I hardly imagined the sea of countless and unending Crimson Guards would struggle to cut her down. Cut them both down.

"That beast deserves to die," Eamon shouted. My shoulder blade screamed louder with agony. "He has defiled my husband. He stole you from our home and ruined you. I am owed his head for what ghastly deeds he has made you do. And you should be thanking me!"

It was no good fighting against Eamon. He was too strong, his body accustomed to years of training and endurance, whereas mine was more used to bruises and scars.

I changed tactics, fuelled by my urge to stop the bloodshed that would soon spill within the tunnels.

Spinning on my husband, I tried to reach for any skin I could find. He had once warned me what he would do to me if I ever used my power against him. But there was no promise of pain that was as severe as murderous agony which would ensue if Calix was harmed.

The sudden lack of resistance set Eamon off-kilter. He lurched backwards as I threw my weight towards him. Eamon's eyes widened as my free hand reached for his face. My nails were inches from the skin of his cheek as he used my momentum, spun me around and held my back to his chest, arm pinned between us.

"Watch them do it," Eamon spoke into my ear. His lips brushed my skin, turning my stomach inside out. "Watch as my guards hunt for the wolf. Did you know that silver burns the monster's flesh? I didn't, not until I found out."

I was certain my shoulder had dislocated. The pain blinded me, but I wouldn't close my eyes. I couldn't.

"I'm sorry, I'm sorry! It wasn't him… please, Eamon. If you love me then leave him."

Eamon pressed a dry-lipped kiss to the side of my face. I recoiled as much as I could, but he had me trapped before him. My skin burned in the place where his lips had touched. "I love you enough to protect you from harm. Which is why I must hunt the wolf and see that its skin hangs from our walls. Perhaps I could make you a rug, or a blanket? Hush now…" He stroked my hair with his free hand. "If you listen you might just hear his howls. It's a magical noise, one you will never forget."

"Bastard," I spat.

Eamon tugged at my arm, sending a terrible pain across my shoulder and back. If he wasn't holding me up, I would have fallen to my knees. "Am I? For killing the creature that pillaged you? I have seen men hung at the gallows for less."

"Calix didn't… it wasn't—"

"Enough," Eamon snapped a final time. "That is quite enough."

I could do little but watch and wait as the Crimson Guard flooded into the waiting dark. They filed in, one by one, in search for their prey. For Calix. And Eamon was right. It didn't take long before the screams started. Except they were not the screams he desired to listen for.

The loosening of his hold on me confirmed that. As did the wave of men and women who ran out of the tunnels they had just entered.

"What...?" Eamon breathed but was quickly silenced by the screams of his guards.

A growl echoed from the shadows of the tunnel, following every human that left them. It rumbled through the earth until I felt the power behind it vibrate through my bones.

The howl of a wolf sounded from deep within the tunnels. It was a song. A song of hunger, anger, and most of all...

*Hate.*

Calix prowled from the shadows, thick paws padding heavily across the ground. I felt each one echo through the dewy bed of the forest and up my stiffened legs. In his mouth he held a torn and bloodied arm. As he moved, the fingers wiggled as though they waved. Which was impossible, because the arm was not attached to anything. Severed.

"Take him down!" Eamon screamed so loudly my ears felt as though they would bleed. "Stop running, you *fucking* cowards, and take that bastard down."

The Crimson Guard had mostly scattered, but it seemed they feared Eamon more than the monster moving towards them. Silver blades raised, the Crimson Guard did not so much as move towards Calix, but they didn't run away from him either. Instead, they held their ground, each one quaking like a leaf in wind.

"Calix," I breathed his name. His dark, pointed ears twitched. Slowly, he lifted his eyes towards me.

The whites were completely black, all beside the star of gold in their centre. Power emanated from him, thundering and as demanding as the growl deep in his throat.

As before, Calix was part wolf and part man. His body had grown in size and width. Muscles had grown in places impossible to the mundane.

He had left the dark tunnels on all fours but uncurled himself when he saw me. Calix towered far taller than anyone else as he stood on his bowed, back legs. He snatched the severed limb from between his jaws and discarded it on the ground before him with a wet smack.

"Master Grey," Eamon said, demanding the creature's attention.

Calix snapped his monstrous stare from me, to the man who held me pinned before him. His maw pulled back into a snarl, exposing teeth coated in human blood and flesh. The growl Calix emitted sent a handful of Crimson Guards from their station as they fled into the forest.

A noise rumbled from deep in Calix's thick fur-coated neck and sounded like a word. *Eamon.*

My husband laughed, recognising his name as I had. "If you care for the safety of your grandmother, your brother, then I suggest you turn back into your tunnels and leave with your tail between your legs."

Calix took a giant step forward. It was clear Eamon's threat was unimportant to him.

I yelped in pain as Eamon tugged on my dislocated

arm. One slight pull and it felt like my skin had been set ablaze.

Calix faltered. Eamon laughed again. "Oh, I see. Has family become an afterthought for you now? Perhaps I must alter my warning if my intentions are not clear. Another move and Rhory here will suffer the consequences." Eamon leaned into my ear. He traced a finger down the side of my face. Although his touch was soft, I felt the bite of his nail leave a red mark across my skin. "Tell him, dear husband of mine, warn the creature what will happen to you if he doesn't listen."

A wave of defiance crested over me like a wave. As it crashed down, my will was torn from me and hurtled violently from my control. Perhaps it was the knowledge that if Calix heeded Eamon's warning, I would suffer regardless. Pain would wait for me at home as it always did. Punishment for my actions, no matter how just it may have been, would greet me.

I pushed against Eamon's hand until my head was straight. My eyes settled on the monster named Calix. I levelled my chin and my eyes focused on the monster. When I spoke, it was clear and without panic, "Do it. Kill them all."

Eamon didn't have the chance to release me before Calix threw his head back to the skies and howled. Then the monster was running. On all fours, Calix tore at the ground. As he came to the line of cowering guards, he threw himself into the air. Powerful limbs forced him into the sky as he leapt over the wall of flesh and silver which kept us separated.

The force of his landing caused the ground to shake. But Calix didn't stop. Didn't falter. He ran fast, scratching marks deep into the dirt with his blade-like claws.

Only when the flash of silver reflected across the creature's face did he stop.

Eamon held a knife to my throat. The sharp bite of metal sliced into my skin, enough to sting. It was cold at first, until the warmth of blood began to trickle from the nick the blade had gifted me.

"Down!" Eamon snarled, "Dog."

Calix snapped his teeth at Eamon but didn't dare move another inch towards us. Already the Crimson Guard was gathering at Calix's back, creating a circle around the three of us with the points of blades held inward.

"Rhory is mine," Eamon growled, pressing the blade into my skin. I swallowed and felt my skin split even more. "Do you understand? He is mine."

The heckles across Calix's large back lifted.

"Leash the beast," Eamon shouted for his guards. "Remember, the silver will protect you."

Tension was thick in the air within the forest's clearing. It clogged in my throat and threatened to choke me to death. Behind Calix a band of guards were holding a thick chain which ended in a belt-like collar. It gleamed, entirely laced with silver. It was the type of collar the elite of Darkmourn tied around their pedigree dogs, as though to prove even the pets they owned benefit from more wealth than most of the city's population.

Except this was made for one creature alone: Calix.

"When we peel the pelt from your back, Calix, remember we gave you the choice. I gave you the choice all those years ago." Eamon spat as he spoke, his teeth equally bared as the jaws of the wolf before him. "I would have let you scuttle back into the dark place you have called home. Even after what you have done to my husband. I deserve your head, your hands, for what you did. I may even slice that devil tongue from your maw and hang it on my wall as a reminder to Rhory what happens to those who break the eternal vows of our union. Yes," Eamon barked a deranged laugh. "Yes! That is exactly what I'll—"

Calix pounced towards us, silencing my husband. Eamon shouted out like a child grasped in fear. The blade swiped from my neck and lifted towards Calix. I dropped just as the pointed jaw of the wolf lifted towards me.

I cowered on the ground as hot blood rain down across my head. It drenched me, mixing with the ruby red of my hair until it was entirely soaked.

Eamon's scream lit the forest. It was drawn out and breathless. A part of me wished to clap my good hand over my ear, but intrigue won. I glanced up to see Eamon clutching his handless arm. He had fallen back to the ground, holding his wound to his chest as blood spluttered like a fountain. My husband's skin had turned an ivory white as the colour bled from him and over me.

Calix pawed towards him. The wolf was chewing on something as he moved. A gag crawled up my throat as

I saw the glint of a wedding band around a finger which was still attached to a hand. A hand that was more pulp, flesh and snapped bone as Calix devoured it.

The wolf prowled forward, ready to feast on more of Eamon's flesh. Until something stopped him. Calix yelped in pain, jerking his massive paw from the ground. I looked down and saw the silver knife Eamon had held to my throat not that long ago. It had pricked Calix's paw.

It was so small, so pathetic in comparison to the wolf, but the pain it caused him was overwhelming. Agony sang in the wolf's howl as he thrashed and cried. Eamon screamed too, with incoherent words. His Crimson Guard watched in horror and confusion as to what to do. Without an order, they were useless.

Whereas the forest seemed bathed in chaos, I felt oddly calm. I reached for the silver knife, covered in both mine and Eamon's blood. I snatched it from the ground. Calix flinched away from me, whimpering.

I turned towards Eamon. He was ashen and his eyelids heavy. He could hardly look at me as I towered over him, the knife held in my good arm.

"Look at me," I said, hand shaking as I pointed the blade at him. Eamon didn't listen. He was focused on the blood and exposed bone that once was a hand. "I said look at me!" I screamed over his caws.

He did. Eamon lifted his paling eyes from his wound up to me. They had glazed with pain and delusion, and he looked through me rather than at me. Slowly, he regarded the knife and then me, and smiled.

"What... what are you going... to do with that, darling?" he asked, struggling to speak as the agony of his severed hand clogged his throat.

I could kill him. Finish this. All I could think about was burying the blade in Eamon's skull so I could watch the light drain from his eyes.

And I would have done it. I would have killed him then and there if it wasn't for Calix.

The wolf swept me from my feet and held me to his powerful chest. He was all warmth and strength. It was as though a statue held me, one coated in fur and flesh. I resisted at first, but quickly gave in to my desires. Burying my head into the coarse fur which enveloped me, I blocked out my fear.

A rumbling echoed across the side of my face. It came from deep within Calix, and although it was word-less, it was not meaningless.

*No.*

Then, we were moving. I was vaguely aware of our direction, but I pinched my eyes closed as the blurring of the world made me feel sick. All that mattered was Calix had me, and I had him.

Wind ripped past my ears and slapped at my face. Even with my eyes closed I was aware that the light had vanished, and we were bathed in darkness. Calix never stopped running. He moved awkwardly on his hind legs, shifting us from side to side violently. It was painfully clear that he moved better on all fours, but that didn't matter. He was still faster than any human in this form.

He ran and ran until the air became thick with dust

and age. All I heard was the scratch of his claws against stone and the thunderous roar of his breathing as it echoed around us.

Calix slowed to a stop. The world was spinning even after he placed me carefully on the floor and released me. The lack of his touch drove a shard of panic into my heart. I threw open my eyes, but it was pointless. There was no light here. Not natural, or fire blessed. It was pure darkness. Complete and unending shadow. I closed my eyes again, fearing that the dark would make me mad.

"Calix?" I asked the darkness, and it replied with my own echo. *Calix, Calix, Calix.*

The pain caught up with me as I waited for a reply. My shoulder burned with fire. The skin on my neck prickled from the slight cut Eamon and his knife had left on me. Even my fist ached. I relaxed my hand and the silver-bladed knife clattered to the dark ground. I hadn't even realised I still held it until it was no longer in my hand. The lack of its presence was not comforting.

In this dark place, there was no good trying to find it again.

"Ca-lix?" I asked the dark again. My voice broke this time. In the echo I could hear how pathetic and scared I sounded.

Had the wolf discarded me and left me here? I knew we had entered back into the tunnels, but it was clear we had ventured further into them than I had before.

"Calix!" I shouted this time, cringing at the loud screech of my plea. "Don't leave me."

Something soft shuffled across the floor before me. I searched the dark, but it was pointless. Still there was only gloom.

"I am here," the dark said. No, Calix. It was Calix.

Arms reached out from the shadows and folded around me. I felt the naked press of skin. Human skin. It was warm and welcoming so I scrambled into it and sobbed, not caring for anything but knowing I was not alone.

"Rhory," Calix said, his voice thick and rasped. A shiver burned up my spine as I felt the press of his chin rest upon the crown of my head. There was the familiar tickle of a beard, and the long exhale of relief which sang to my very soul. Although I could not see what I touched, I knew with complete certainty it was Calix. His skin was moist beneath the palms of my reaching hands which grasped his powerful naked back and held on firm.

"Don't leave me," I cried. "Don't go."

"I've got you," he said, brushing the back of my head with his hand. "I'm here."

## ⚜ 24 ⚜

**M**illicent found us before the Crimson Guard had much of a chance. It could have been hours or minutes, I didn't know. In the dark, time didn't seem to exist. Neither Calix nor I heard her coming. She was a wraith, moving on soundless feet with the grace of air. It was the fire she held in the glass lantern which gave her away.

"Both of you," she snapped as firelight flickered over her stern face, "Get up."

How long had we been sat on the ground in the dark, grasping one another as though our lives depended on it? Long enough that my muscles stiffened, and my skin seemed to stitch with his.

"Eamon is alive." Her voice melted across me, finally pulling me out of the trance of Calix's embrace and the dread which had overcome me. Millicent's pale skin glowed as though a dying star was captured beneath it, reflecting the light of the lantern she held out towards us.

"I should have finished him—" I began, until Millicent shot her hand towards me, gripped my forearm, and pulled.

"You left the bastard without a hand. Do you know how serious this is?"

My bones creaked as Millicent pulled me away from Calix. I was aware he was without clothes, but beneath the exposing glow of fire, we both could see how entirely naked he was. And he didn't care, showing no effort to cover his modesty as he peered up at Millicent. What I also didn't account for was Calix still had the smudging of blood across his mouth and jaw. Eamon's blood was more a stain of black across the lower half of his face.

"It would not be wise to waste time worrying about the past," Calix replied coolly.

"What were you thinking?" she hissed, teeth flashing. "Auriol has been taken by the man you have mutilated. If you thought her treatment would have been kind before, it will be hell for her now! If she is even still alive."

Calix didn't utter a word. Nor did I.

Even though we had not said anything to one another, I knew we both shared the guilt. And even before Millicent confirmed Eamon survived Calix's attack, I knew he was not dead. I still felt the leash like tether binding us together, even if Calix had torn his hand clean off, taking the wedding band Eamon wore with it.

"Get up, Calix," Millicent snapped, glaring with ruby red eyes at him. "We don't have the luxury of sitting and doing nothing."

"And go where?" Calix's voice rumbled through the dark, blending with the inky blackness.

"There is only one direction we can go. If the path back is not possible, we must therefore venture forward. Calix, get your sorry ass off the ground and get moving."

Millicent had not once let go of me. Her skin was ice cold to the touch that it stung slightly. She was careful not to pull at my dislocated arm, which I clutched to my chest.

"Try not to scream," Millicent said to me, distracting me from Calix as he stood.

"Wait—" I couldn't finish my question before Millicent reached for my arm. I gulped just as her nails caught my skin. With a great jolt, she twisted it at an awkward angle. The sharp snap of pain lasted but a second, then relief settled in. The pop of my bone fixing into its socket echoed throughout the dark.

"Fuck me," I gasped out as a rush passed through my head.

"Better?" Millicent's smile elongated above the flickering lamp.

Slowly, I moved my arm around, testing for pain or lack of use. It was uncomfortable at most, but manageable.

"Thank you," I replied, rolling my shoulder backwards.

"I can do little for the cut on your neck," Millicent muttered to me, tongue tracing her lip as she surveyed the blood which had dried beneath the wound. "Your arm will feel sore for a day at most."

Millicent steadied her gaze to Calix. I watched her red eyes trail him from bare foot to blood-coated chin.

Calix turned his head away in silent refusal. "Take Rhory and get him somewhere safe. I need to—"

"Need to *what*, you sorry fool!" Millicent withdrew her hand from me kicked his foot with a firm boot. "Auriol has been captured, Silas has not been returned, and not only have you shaken the hornets' nest, but you also kicked, pissed, and set the bastard on fire. Now, if you wish for the chance to save them, I suggest you get moving. We have a way to walk. Then you can sit all you want and mope about your actions and their consequences."

Calix unfurled even taller than before, stretching his long naked limbs until he towered over us both. Millicent kept her eyes upwards with ease, whereas I felt as though I struggled to hold Calix's stare. I pulled the torn, bloodied red cloak from my shoulders and handed it to Calix.

His fingers brushed my hand as he took it with a smile that sang with thanks, although it never reached his eyes. Those golden orbs seemed lost to the moment, dazed almost.

"Wouldn't want to scare the shadows," I said, forcing a fake smile.

Calix wrapped the material around his waist. The red matched the dried blood that was smeared around his chest, his neck, the lower part of his face. He caught my stare. I found that I looked away, embarrassed he had caught me regarding the evidence of the death he had recently caused.

Should it have repulsed me? Because it didn't.

He didn't.

"It is not the shadows that you should fear," Millicent warned, her voice edged with unwavering seriousness. "Quick, follow me before the real demons reveal themselves."

I would have thought Millicent was playing some joke on us, but the stoic expression on Calix's face, and the way he placed a reassuring hand on the small of my back to urge me forward, proved otherwise.

As we navigated the dark tunnels, Millicent leading the way with her lantern held high, I kept looking behind me as though someone—or something—unseen followed.

I didn't know where our destination was, but as we climbed in single file up the iron-handled ladder and through the wooden latch far above us, I would never have expected this.

"What is this place?" I asked, rubbing at the ache of my shoulder. The climb up and into this room had reminded me it had been hanging out of its socket not so long ago.

Calix followed in last, closing the hatch that gave way to the sheer drop into the dark tunnels below. "Somewhere familiar, no doubt. Millicent, your scent is everywhere."

"What did you expect of me?" Millicent said, smiling as she looked around. There was a softness to her expression. "That I would rest in the dark corners of the tunnels whilst you stayed in your warm bed? Or that my life began only when I came to you? Because both concepts are ridiculous."

"This… is your home?" I stepped forward just as Millicent blew out the flame that danced within the lantern. Without it, we were covered in darkness. Shapes of furniture draped in dust-ridden sheets looked more like hunched crones spectating from the corners of the room. Where I trod, my footsteps left marks in the dust settled across the floor.

"Careful, *witch*. I am merely a squatter demanding my rights. This place does not and will not belong to me. However, its original tenant has found more… opulent dwellings. We will not be disturbed here."

Calix began talking to Millicent in hushed tones. Whatever they were discussing, it was not for me to hear. Perhaps I should have demanded to know what they spoke of, but I was transfixed by the beam of silver light which cut through the pitch-black room.

I paced across the space, aware of the old creaking

floorboards. Each step caused the ground to scream. Before me was a window, or it should have been a window if it was not for the thick planks which had been nailed across it from the outside. There was only enough of a gap for me to see outside. As soon as my eyes settled on the darkened street, and the wall of buildings which leaned on one another for support, I knew without question where the tunnels had led us.

"We are in Old Town." I turned my back on the window, interrupting Calix and Millicent's somewhat secret conversation.

"Directly in its heart," Millicent confirmed.

"Which is exactly why we are returning to the tunnels and looking for somewhere else to stay. Somewhere far from Darkmourn." Calix stormed towards me, the muscles across his exposed chest and stomach etched into his body like stone. "Come, Rhory. We must leave."

"No," Millicent added, following behind me. "That is exactly why we are staying. Eamon will never know to look for us here. No one will. Even if they searched the tunnels, they would come out from many other exits before this one."

"I... I think Millicent is right." I felt the desire to look back out the window.

"Rhory," Calix breathed, reaching for my hand. I let him take it, glad for the comforting steadiness his touch provided me. His eyes were wide, pleading. "Old Town is a stone's throw from your home. From Castle Dread. We are directly in the line of sight of all who would wish to see us dead. I have put you in this position, which means I have taken on the responsibility to keep you safe. Please… let me do that. Let me keep you out of harm's way."

The silver beam of moonlight that sliced into the room from the window at my back illuminated Calix's state. He was covered in blood, naked and barely concealed beneath my cloak, with the weight of so much on his shoulders. He needed to wash, and rest. We all did.

I tore my eyes from Calix and looked to Millicent who hovered over his shoulder. "What is important is righting the wrongs of Eamon. I know my husband." The word soured in my mouth like spoiled milk. "He is as resilient as he is crazed. Something is driving him to act in such a manner, and he will not stop until he gets what he wants. I suppose it has been for a very long time. If we are to see Auriol and Silas returned in one piece, then we must find out what he wants from them."

"What good will that do?" Calix asked, his low voice causing shivers across my skin.

"It is how we are going to stop him. By finding out what he desires and tearing it from beneath him until all he can do is fall."

Millicent's laugh was as light and shrill as a bird. "Who is this man who has crawled out of the dark? I barely recognise him."

I gritted my teeth, tensing my jaw as Millicent pinned me beneath her ruby eyes. "He is someone who has been buried away, against his will, for a long time.

Someone who is ready to shed the bindings put upon them and do the right thing."

"Survived," Calix said, squeezing my hand. "He is someone who has survived."

I nodded, swallowing hard as the lump persisted in my throat. "And I am someone who wishes to thrive. His control over me must end."

"Then I should give you some house rules," Millicent said, gesturing around her. "No one must know we are here. When it is dark, we keep it that way. During the day, we stay quiet. We cannot draw any attention to ourselves. Well, you both can't. I am still an unseen player on the board, and I wish to keep it that way. You'll find a bedroom upstairs. The one at the end of the corridor is mine, keep out. I trust you both will not complain if you are forced to share the other. It is that or one of you can flip a coin to decide who has the floor."

Even after everything that had conspired, I found my chest warmed and stomach flipped at the thought of sharing a bed with Calix. It was better than a dirt covered ground in the middle of a forest. Even Calix reacted silently to the suggestion. His was subtle, but clear from the way the lines across his forehead smoothed and the tension around his mouth eased.

"The bed," Calix said, unable to take his eyes off me. "Will be sufficient."

I found myself nodding like an overenthusiastic child. "More than fine."

"Good, because the rooms can be cursed with a

nasty draft. The views are not the only breathtaking thing in this building."

"Seems like you read my mind," Calix added softly.

"Calix, you stink." Millicent's nose flared as she passed us. "And for someone who rather enjoys the delicacy of blood, you are spoiling it for me. You need to wash. The roof has an issue with leaks, as well as other things. This house is ancient, so the water supply is sparse. Use the gathered rainwater in the jugs and vases I have laid out to clean yourself. Come morning, I will see you both have something to eat and drink. Then, we discuss how three unlikely creatures are going to stop a raging mortal from tearing more families apart."

## 25

The old wooden box seat beneath the window in our bedroom creaked with aggravation as I sat upon it. Once the material atop it would have been a vibrant red, but time had sapped the colour from it. And the comfort. Moths and other unwanted guests had devoured the cushion's stuffing until it was left flat and lacklustre.

This window, like the rest in the house, had been boarded up; enough to stop prying eyes looking in, but not looking out. Through a narrow slit, I was transfixed by the breath-taking view of Castle Dread. It seemed this place was built for the very purpose of this view.

The waning moon hung far above its tallest peak, washing the castle's dark stone walls in silver light. The castle was alive from within. Golden warm firelight spilled out of the multitude of stained-glass windows. A shiver of comfort purred across my skin at the thought of luxury. There was nothing of the sort in this house.

"See something you like?" Calix asked as he entered the room, two cracked jugs full of water in either hand.

For once, I didn't feel the urge to look at him. Instead, I trailed my eyes down the castle's grandeur, imagining rooms teeming with halflings Jak Bishop collected, as someone would with shells on the seafront. I looked from the narrow street just outside this house, which opened up to the bridge separating the castle from town. It was as quiet as the dead, which was befitting for the vampire lord and his lover who silently ruled from the castle.

"I wonder why they called it Castle Dread," I said, finding that I whispered because I didn't wish to shatter the stillness of this place. "That is the name given to a place people fear, or harbour discomfort towards. I can't help but see it in a different light."

"Auriol told me of a time when Marius, The Lord of Eternal Night, was trapped as punishment inside the castle's walls…"

"And the last witch, Jak, was sent to kill him but failed, and unleashed an age of death across Darkmourn. We all know the story. I'm surprised it hasn't been etched into our bones or carved beneath our skin, from the number of times it has been told to us. What I want to know is: why? Why the name? It would seem that Darkmourn and its people find it easy to remember the bad side of our history, but no one talks about the time before it. Strange that."

There was the clink of china against wood. I tore my

eyes from the view to a new one. Calix covered in dried blood that now looked as brown as dirt or smeared mud. He had exchanged my red cloak with a spare pair of trousers Millicent provided; they must have belonged to her brother. The rest of him was unclothed. Until he was cleaned, he didn't want to spoil the only spare clothing accessible to him, and the jugs and bowls of water he had carried down from the house's attic was going to fix that.

"You are the only one of us who would ever have the chance to find the answers you seek," Calix said. He snatched a cloth that hung from the belt of his leather trousers. I watched as he wrung it in his hands, giving himself something to do as I drank him in. "If you wanted to walk up to the castle's doors and ask for entry, it would be given to you."

"Because of what I am," I answered for him.

"A witch, you can say it."

I pushed myself from the box seat, cringing at the loud cry of relief the wood gave. "I promised my mother that I would never go."

Calix's smooth face changed at the mention of my mother. It was a reaction I had seen before, as though he was disgusted by it. "With all due respect, Rhory, Ana is no longer alive. It is hard to keep the promises of the dead. Trust me. You could walk up to the castle now and put this all behind you. Eamon. Your pain. *Me.* We wouldn't matter when you are kept safely behind those walls."

I felt both pained and comforted by Calix's brash

words. He was right, my mother was dead, but he was also wrong. Promises were immortal.

"What good would that do for my parent's legacy if I was to give Eamon what he wanted all along? My home, the Crimson Guard. Haven't I given him enough? My life, my happiness, my love. See what he has done with that and you will get a glimpse of what would become of Eamon if I walked into the den of vipers, never to look back."

Calix's face pinched in confusion. "The Crimson Guard is already his, no?"

I laughed. Of course, he would think that. But I knew the truth. It had been read out to me the night of my father's death. I have long believed it was the reason Eamon raised his hand to me the first time. Out of frustration and anger. Defeat.

"As long as I am alive, the Crimson Guard falls into Eamon's control. I die, and he loses it. It was my father's dying wish, literally; a change made to his will only days before my marriage to Eamon."

I practically witnessed the pieces of a puzzle fall into place within Calix's mind. His stare fell to the ground, his eyes flickering and mouth parted as he worked it all out.

The sorrow he regarded me with almost brought me to my knees. "All this time, you stayed with him because you had a death wish."

I nodded, not feeling anything but a deep, echoing numbness inside of me. "I am a coward. I couldn't end myself, but I knew Eamon might. His fits of rage grew the more he became used to hurting me. I knew it would only be a matter of time when his fist hit me too hard, or he strangled me long enough to kill me. Part of the reason I stayed with him is because I couldn't bring myself to do it. The other part of me—the sadistic and hateful side he created—stayed because I longed for him to do it, only for him to suffer the realisation that his actions are the reason he lost everything he ever wanted."

Calix discarded the cloth without thought, and took me in his hands. I felt so incredibly small when I stood before him. It was the way his neck craned down when he looked at me, or how his hands were so large that it made my arms feel as brittle and narrow as a twig.

"I'm sorry to disappoint you, but I am never going to let that happen."

I folded against Calix's chest, uncaring if my cheek pressed into the dried blood of the Crimson Guard. Calix ran his hand across my head over and over, soothing me with his touch and the beat of his heart that slammed within his ribcage. I felt every beat. Every single powerful pump as though it kicked against the side of my head.

My hands trembled as I traced my fingers up his hard stomach to the four, puckered red scars across his chest. I hadn't dared ask him about them for fear of what he would say. All this time I had allowed myself the bliss of not knowing. I couldn't hide from it anymore.

"These marks…" I began but stopped myself as my

fingers brushed over the puckered lumps. It was the familiarity of the touch that silenced me. If I closed my eyes, it was as though I had been in this very position before with the question lingering across my tongue.

"What is the matter?" Calix asked softly, holding me close.

"I just… how is it I hardly know you, yet my body tells me otherwise?"

Calix's breathing hitched. His reaction stopped me and drew my hand away from the scars on his chest. His lips paled, and parted, but nothing but a choked gasp came out.

"Is it pathetic to admit?" I said, pulling free of Calix. My legs felt like they might have given way at any moment, so I took the chance to sit on the edge of the bed. Calix stayed standing, unmoving, as though something I had said rooted him to the spot.

"Your mind and your body are two separate entities, both carrying different memories."

"And why would my body hold a memory for you?" I asked, feeling my mouth become dry as I spoke. There was something in his gaze, an ominous shadow passing over the glow of the sun and blocking it out completely.

"Because it should. It remembers what you do not."

A nervous laugh burst out of me. It was the heavy weight of Calix's stare that unnerved me, because I sensed there was something hiding behind it. I recognised the emotion for what it was. Even without my power, his feelings sang in the air, thick and suffocating. *Sadness. Regret.* But there was something else. I had sensed guilt on Calix once before, but this was stronger. More prevalent.

"Auriol told me to leave it, but I.... I don't think I can, Rhory. I am selfish, I told you this. But all I want is for you to remember."

"Remember what?" I asked, unable to move as I glanced up at him.

"No, I shouldn't have said anything." Calix turned his back on me. I watched the rise and fall of his broad back as he struggled to calm himself.

Before he could take a single step away, I snapped, "Don't you dare, Calix."

He regarded me over his shoulder with thick brows pinched over his sorrowful gaze. The weight behind his stare was so powerful it almost knocked me backwards. "It has been a long day," Calix said softly. "I would feel better talking about this tomorrow."

"What should I remember?" I pushed on, refusing to give this up.

The question hung between us, a storm cloud of wonder which thundered in the silence as I waited for my answer.

Calix came and took a seat next to me. The old mattress lifted with the balance of our weight.

"Look at me," Calix commanded. "Look at me in my eyes and tell me you do not remember. I know the truth, but I need to hear it from you... One last time."

I did as he asked, frustration shimmering through me. The pressure was so strong; I was moments from bursting. It had not been the first time I had heard such a comment to my memory, or me remembering. My mind worked through the remarks Auriol and Calix had made, even something Eamon had said to Calix when he first came and took me from my home.

"What, Calix? Please, don't talk to me in riddles."

He raised his stare to me. There was something mesmerising about how his golden eyes glowed, even in such a dark place. But now, they were rimmed with sudden tears that snatched my breath away and conjured a harsh cramping in my chest. That one look, and the emotion behind it, made it hard for me to think.

"Me," Calix said, refusing to look away. "You should remember me."

## 26

"Rhory, you should remember me," Calix repeated. He stared at me, hopeful, his gilded eyes rimmed with sadness. The honesty in his gaze was so boiling, it scalded me.

Calix sagged forward and rested his blood-coated chin on his muscular chest. Whereas I couldn't take my eyes off of him, he refused to look at me.

A high-pitched whirling bounded through my skull. For a moment, the room and the world around beyond it faded out of view. There was only Calix, and his words which stabbed deep into me sharper than any knife could.

"Why should I?" I asked, and as I spoke, it was as though I was buried beneath a body of water, unable to hear anything clearly. Even though deep down I knew the answer, my mind still searched for Calix, but I couldn't find him in my memories.

"Yes, you should. But there has been a block placed upon your mind, a barrier keeping you from the truth. Trust me, I would never have told you if I didn't think—"

"I don't know what you are talking about!" Frustration riled out of me. I felt like a dog chasing a bone I could never reach. "Just shut up, please! This is unfair."

"Rhory, we have met one another before." Calix looked at me. "Many times, in fact. Auriol and me, when we requested for you to come to the cottage, it was a test. I opened the door and saw you standing there, staring blankly at me, and I knew. I knew, from the look in those beautiful eyes, you didn't remember."

My tongue felt swollen in my dry mouth. "Remember... what?"

Calix paused before replying. His eyes narrowed, flickering between my wide eyes and parted lips. He dropped his attention to his hands which were fist-sized boulders on his lap.

"In the forest," Calix said. "That was not the first time Eamon found us together. The night before your engagement, I was there with you. And that was the last time I saw you."

"I don't understand what you are saying, Calix!" I shouted now, uncaring for the vow of silence I promised Millicent. Her rules didn't matter when my brain felt like it would implode with what Calix was telling me.

"Our families had been friends for a long time.

Auriol and your father's parents were alive during a time when the world was rebuilding and the living and the dead were learning to live together in harmony. My grandmother was there at the creation of the Crimson Guard. She hoped to protect the mortals in a world where the immortals thrived. She put your ancestors in charge because she knew they held the same morals and beliefs. Me and you. We..." Calix spluttered on the words. He looked down at his hands, as did I; his knuckles were white with tension.

I placed a hand over his and gold light spilled forth, and I eased his emotions enough for him to continue. With my power, I also searched for truth. And he had it in abundance. Everything Calix was saying was real, but why could my mind not believe it?

He looked at me as the lines of tension melted from his face.

"Continue," I breathed. "Please, I need to know."

Calix nodded, the muscles in his jaw flexing. "Eamon wormed his way into your family like an infection. He worked beneath your father, idolised him, we all thought. Then he turned his sights on you, and he was not prepared to stop at getting you, or what you could give him. My family tried to warn yours, and they were shunned for it. At the time Auriol didn't know about me and you. No one did. But Eamon... He knew because he found us, in your home, in your bed."

My head ached as I tried to make sense of what Calix revealed. No matter how much honesty I felt from within Calix, I couldn't find the memory of what he was saying. It was blank. My past was clear and colourful, and there was not one scene of him in it.

"These scars." Calix lifted my hand to his chest and pressed my cold fingers to his skin. He was warm as a hearth in winter. "Just as I told you the first time you asked, were given to me by my brother. He did it, the night he killed my parent's murderers. I tried to stop him from chasing revenge but failed. I failed him, just as I failed you. And I can see that telling you was a mistake. It was indulgent and has caused you pain."

"Why?" The word was more a command than a question. "Why do I not remember?"

"Eamon knew of a witch." Calix refused to look me in the eye as he spoke. "Someone with the power to tamper with your mind and make you remember what he wanted you to remember, whilst removing what he didn't wish for you to know."

As Calix spoke, I raised my spare hand and pushed my fingers into the soft skin of my temple.

"We heard of your engagement to Eamon the following day. I came back to see you. I didn't know what I expected to find, but you were happy. Smiling and celebrating an engagement you would never have even entertained the night prior. For a long time, I thought it had all been a game to you. Until you turned up at the cottage and looked at me as though I was a stranger. I knew then. What we had, what we shared… only a curse of a mind could bury that."

"Why didn't you tell me before…?" I asked, feeling tears cutting down my cheeks. Deep inside, I felt empty. Half made. Something was lost to me, and even knowing it gave me little comfort.

"Because I, like you, made a promise. Auriol commanded me to keep my silence. I tried to do as she wished, but I knew I was to break that promise the moment I laid eyes on you. I am a weak man for it, I know."

I retrieved my hand from him and called back my power. The room was bathed in darkness once again, except this time everything felt different. Nervous energy buzzed beneath my skin. It itched and ached, needing an escape that I couldn't give it.

"After everything you have said, I feel like I am drowning in questions more so than before."

Calix exhaled a laboured breath. "I wish I could make you remember."

I cringed at the thought of a witch tampering with my mind. Never had Eamon suggested he knew of someone with power. In fact, he always promoted the concept of those with magic being herded into Castle Dread like cattle.

"I need a moment," I said, standing from the bed and leaving Calix behind me as I paced towards the door. There was nowhere for me to go, but I couldn't sit down and let the knowledge of a past I could not remember scolded me. I had to move, I had to get away.

"Rhory," Calix called out for me. All this time he

had spoken so calmly, but when he spoke my name, it froze me to the spot. "I'm sorry if I have hurt you with what I've explained. Know it has never been my intention."

"That's just it," I replied, looking back at him over my shoulder, "There is nothing more debilitating than the truth. Even a truth I cannot remember."

"No," Calix replied, eyes cutting into me. "You are wrong. The truth is freeing if you let it be."

I held his stare, searching a feeling that told me it was familiar. I clawed through my mind, searching for a flash of a memory of him. Of Calix. And there was nothing. Just Eamon and my life, and the happiness before there was gloom.

"I don't remember you," I said with finality.

Calix flinched slightly before straightening and replacing the armour he usually wore across his face. "I know, but, Rhory, I remember you. My heart has known pain. Pain I wouldn't even wish upon Eamon. And I have ached for you. Longed for you. But I know, I know it will never be the same. You will never know the feelings I harbour for you, feelings that we once shared. And I am sorry about that. But if it is any consolation, I have held the same flame for you I did all those years ago. A flame not even Eamon could extinguish. I missed you with such terrible, boiling agony. Just the thought of you could undo me. Your mind might not remember, but your body does. You said as such…"

Fury crawled up my throat and came out as a vicious scream. It was not fury at him, but at the frustration that my mind was not my own. My memory, although belonging to me, had been taken from me. Eamon had infected my body, my will and now my mind and I felt wrath at that truth.

"But I don't remember you! Fuck my body. It matters little! I don't remember... I don't... remember."

Calix was there, kneeling on the ground before me. He moved with such speed that the still surface of the water in the jugs and bowls rippled as though a stone had been thrown within them. "I can't give you back the memories that have been taken from you, Rhory. But if you let me, I will replace them."

My entire body trembled with so many conflicting emotions, I felt as though I would burst if handled with uncaring hands. But there was nothing uncaring about Calix, not the way he held me now or looked at me. But it was the last thing I desired in this moment.

As I stared down at him, I finally understood the guilt and hurt which cursed him when I was near. It seemed my presence caused him pain, but his presence for me did the opposite.

"I want to remember you," I said, tears falling between us. Even Calix's eyes glistened, but he had enough control to keep them back. "I want nothing more than to look at you the way you look at me."

Calix's shoulders sagged inward. He exhaled a long, tempered breath before he replied, "And you will. Eamon is the only one with the knowledge of how to undo this."

"He won't do it freely," I said.

A shadow passed over Calix's face. His eyes narrowed, and the gold seemed to glow from within. Then he whispered words that had as much power in them as if he would have screamed it at the top of his lungs, "Oh, he will. If that is what you desire, I will ensure it happens."

## 27

## ₃ YEARS BEFORE

Rhory Coleman was the most beautiful creature I had ever seen. I couldn't take my eyes off him. Although, if I closed my eyes or looked away, the image of him would have been engraved in the dark of my mind.

His hair was as red as poppies. No, it was deeper. Richer. A colour that would have made the flower jealous. I was transfixed by the deep gleam of his green eyes. I lost myself in them, just as I did with the forest. They were never-ending pools, welcoming me in and refusing to let me go.

Rhory Coleman had thirteen freckles which spanned across the bridge of his nose and fell over his cheeks. Each one was as perfect as the next. If there was not a table between us, I would likely have reached out and placed my finger upon each one in turn.

Conversation rang around the room, but I cared little for it. Even Ana Coleman—Rhory's mother—

attempted to spark chatter with me, but it was useless. My focus was on her son. It was solely on him.

This was not the first time I had seen him. But before, it was always from afar. Even then, he captured my attention and held it hostage until he was out of sight. Then it was my mind he occupied.

Tonight would be different. It was the first time the Grey's had been invited for supper. It was the end of autumn feast. Across the table before me was plates piled high with pumpkin seeded bread, meats, bowls of spiced soup, an array of different flavoured cheese, seasoned and roasted potatoes with streams of steam which danced in the air above them. Glasses of wine never went empty, always refilled by one of the many housemaids the Coleman's hired.

All but my glass. I had not touched it since I had sat down. Nor did I reach out to spoon food onto my plate. I couldn't do anything but look at him. And he knew it. Rhory sensed my attention and glowed beneath it, his cheeks blossoming with a scarlet blush

Rhory's father was seated at the head of the table. To Michal's side was my grandmother, Auriol, and on the other was his shadow, Eamon, a young man who had climbed the ranks of the Crimson Guard in the past few years. It amazed me how bored he looked. Perhaps Eamon's mood was affected by my brother who practically chewed his ear off with one-sided conversation. Silas always was one to talk. Since we were children my younger brother was always better in crowds. Where he thrived, I wanted to slip into the shadows where I could prowl and watch.

Until now. Now, I wanted to be in the light so Rhory could see me.

And see me he did.

"Would you like some?"

I snapped out of my trance when I realised it was Rhory who held a plate of thinly sliced beef over the table towards me. My eyes fell from his, to the spreading of red across his cheeks and then down to his hand. He held the plate firmly and the way he did so gave me view to the dusting of freckles across his knuckles. I wondered just how far they went as I followed their constellation into the shadows of his sleeve.

"Thank you," I replied, realising quickly that Rhory was still holding the plate and some awkward seconds had passed.

"You're welcome," he replied quietly.

I took the plate. As I did, it was Rhory's opportunity for his gaze to wander. A warmth spread across my chest as I felt his eyes trail over me. Then they fell to his knife and fork, severing his attention.

It was disappointment that urged me to speak again. I wanted his eyes on me, not anything or anyone else. "All these years, and I am surprised this is the first time we have met."

Rhory looked back up, smiling. "Is it really?"

I nodded, feeling suddenly embarrassed I had not put more effort into my appearance before I came. My beard was unkept and my hair fell loosely around my face. It felt silly to keep having to tuck the unruly strands behind my ear, but it seemed to make Rhory smile at least.

"I believe so," I replied, taking the glass in my hand just to give it something to do. "I would have remembered if we had."

"And why is that?" Rhory asked, looking at me through his lashes.

Something uncoiled in the pit of my stomach. The suggestive gleam in his eyes was enough to undo me. How could a stranger have such an ability to disable me?

"Because you are rather memorable," I said, my voice edged with confidence.

The apples of his cheeks blossomed a deeper scarlet. Matching that of the cloaks Michal Coleman, Eamon, and the handful of other Crimson Guard's wore around the table. Rhory's eyes fell, once again, to his plate. Guilt twisted through me.

"I didn't mean to embarrass you." I couldn't stop myself from blurting out. Thank the Gods I held the glass of wine, otherwise I might have smacked my palm against my forehead.

"You haven't at all," Rhory said.

We didn't say anything again after that. I wanted to add something else in, but I feared my mouth would get me into further bother.

Ana Coleman had turned to Auriol and was speaking on how well Michal's health had seemed to steady. All of Darkmourn had known of Michal Coleman's mental decline over the past years, and even I had been shocked to have seen such a strong man being wheeled into the dining room. I was glad her attention was diverted, but I couldn't help but sense the way her eyes fell back over to me and her son. As well as Eamon. He watched, even as Silas leaned in and whispered something into his ear.

If Rhory had not filled my mind, I may have wondered further as to my brother's comfort with the Crimson Guard. He acted familiarly around him, which shouldn't have surprised me as Silas was always the more social of the two of us.

Since our parents' murder, he had come more out of his shell whereas I sulked further into mine. I almost refused to come tonight, but with Rhory so close before me, I didn't regret joining one slight bit.

I decided to join in and eat something. If anything, it gave me something else to focus on. No matter if I wanted to, I couldn't sit here and just watch Rhory. It was odd and would likely scare him off. And that was the opposite of how I desired to make him feel.

The evening moved on quickly. The savoury food was swapped out for a display of desserts. Not even the sweet smells of cinnamon, nutmeg and clove could distract me from Rhory. His attention had soured as the evening progressed, which caused an uncomfortable pang to fill my chest. Rhory watched his father every now and then. His smile had faded completely when his mother had to go and help Michal with his food. He had only so much energy to feed himself so Ana had to swap places with Auriol just so she could sit beside him and help him with each mouthful.

I couldn't bear to see Rhory in such a way. The sorrow didn't suit his face. He had the type of expression that deserved to smile. His face was made for it, not sadness.

Rhory was more focused on his parents than his dessert. He, like me, hardly touched his plate.

I had to distract him. I had to do something to make his smile return. In hindsight, it was a childish act but that was how he made me feel. He made me feel small and juvenile. So, I stretched my leg out beneath the table and knocked my foot into his.

Rhory looked back to me, surprise passing across his handsome face.

"I was hoping," I said, now I had his attention again, "Would you care to give me a tour?"

"A tour?" Rhory replied. "Of what?"

"Anything," I breathed, not caring. I just wanted to get him out of the room, alone.

Rhory held my gaze. I was prepared for him to refuse me, because of course my request was ridiculous. Then, my heart jolted as Rhory's chair screeched back and he stood.

The entire room fell silent.

"What is it darling?" Ana called out, lowering the spoon from her husband's mouth. He had food down the side of his lips. If it was not for the napkin she had tucked into his collar, his shirt would have been covered in caramel sauce.

"I am going to show Calix Grey our library, if you do not mind."

How did he know my name? Had I told him? I racked my brain, trying to remember when I had said it. But I knew, deep down, I had never revealed it.

Which meant he knew it before. And I longed for him to say it again.

Ana Coleman looked to me, her gaze narrowing slightly. "But we are having dessert. Mildred made your favourite—"

"And I am sure there will be some spare," Rhory interrupted. I got the impression he often got what he wanted.

"Let them go," Auriol said from beside me. My grandmother was half a bowl into the trifle. For such an old woman, she could certainly put away her food, especially if it was of the sugary variety.

I stood too, before anyone else could object. But nothing came. Ana agreed, allowing us to leave. Which was strange, because never in my thirty-two years of life had I needed to ask permission to leave a table. It only added to how young I felt around Rhory. I almost had the urge to giggle as he gestured for me to follow him.

We left the dining room quickly, moving into the warmth of the fire-lit foyer beyond. Sweeping stairs stretched out before us, disappearing up into the floor above.

"So," Rhory said, turning around to face me, "You've got me away from them all."

I opened my mouth to reply, but he promptly added, "And don't play coy, I rather enjoy honesty."

I exhaled through a smile, feeling my cheeks ache with the expression. Rhory was far shorter than me, but beneath his gaze he made me feel small. "And here I thought you were desperate to show me the library."

Rhory leaned his weight on one leg, popping his hip out and crossing his arms. "Are you much of a reader?"

I couldn't lie to him. "Not really."

"So, you wouldn't be bothered to see it."

"Is it empty?" I asked.

Rhory narrowed his jade green eyes. "All this just to get me alone. Is that it?"

I straightened my back, refusing to back down. "I must practice on my ability to be subtle."

Rhory pouted his pink-blush lips. "Yes, you should. It needs improving"

I prepared myself for him to tell me to go back to the dining room, but that was not the command that came out of his mouth. Instead, he turned his back on me and faced the stairs.

"But I must admit that I admire your effort," Rhory said, walking away from me. I was left, standing like a fool, in the middle of his foyer when he called back over his shoulder, "Come then. You've got me alone until dessert is over. If I was you, I wouldn't waste another moment."

T here was not much talking between us when we reached Michal's office. Before I could even admire the wall of bookshelves and the grand oak carved desk placed in the middle of the room, Rhory was on me.

His mouth crashed into mine before the door clicked shut completely at our backs. The suddenness of it took my breath away, but I didn't shy away from it. My back was shoved into the door, spine pressed into it with the weight of Rhory before me.

His hands were on my face, his fingers running through my beard and up my cheeks. His skin was warm, but I held back the urge to hold him in return. I feared it would shatter this illusion, if I dared move a muscle it would ruin this moment.

Noticing my lack of response, Rhory pulled back. He practically leaned on me, on his tiptoes, until he pulled away, wiping his mouth with the back of his sleeve.

"Perhaps I got the wrong end of the stick," he said. Even in the dull glow of the silver moon beyond the room, I could still make out the embarrassment creeping over his face. My eyesight was far better than most, but it was my ability to hear the beating of his heart which transfixed me. It thundered wildly, skipping every time he caught my gaze.

"No, you certainly are not wrong." I pushed from the door and closed the space between us in two strides. Rhory's chin was smooth to the touch as I slipped my two fingers beneath it and lifted upwards until he was looking at me again. "I just thought we might have had a conversation first, although I am not going to pretend I'm disappointed we haven't."

"Who are you?" Rhory asked, the question knocking me off guard. "And how dare they keep you from me. The feasts Mother and Father put on would have been more bearable if you had joined them."

"So, you are telling me you don't bring random men into dark rooms and kiss them?" I replied, still holding Rhory's chin in my grasp. Excitement bubbled in my chest, making it harder for me to take in a decent breath. "Because I warn you, if you say you do, I will be painfully disappointed."

"No," Rhory whispered, blinking his doe-wide eyes. "Never."

"Then I consider myself lucky," I murmured. "And if it helps curve the embarrassment you feel… I want to know you."

"Is that why you have always looked at me?" Rhory asked. "I've seen you do it for years."

"Does my attention make you feel uncomfortable?" I replied.

Rhory shook his head. A curl of poppy-red hair fell over his eye. I took my fingers from his chin and brought them up to the pesky strand. As I brushed it back in place, I felt Rhory's skin shiver beneath my touch. His heart pounded proudly in his chest, singing to me and my soul.

Knowing I had such a power over him almost brought me to my knees.

"You interest me," I said, feeling the words rush out of me. "Rhory Coleman."

"Is that a compliment?" he asked, gaze flickering over me as though he drank me in.

"It is if you wish it to be. I want to see you again," I said, tilting my head. "If you would care to."

"At the next gathering, or before?"

"No." I swallowed hard. "I want to see you tomorrow, and the day after and the day after."

"Is that obsession, or healthy infatuation?" Rhory narrowed his eyes as his smile cut wider across his beautiful face.

I couldn't hold myself back anymore. There was something about the gleam in his eyes which was as irresistible as a siren's call. I lowered my mouth to his, stopping only when our lips were a hairsbreadth away from each other. "Maybe a helping of both. I *want* to know you. Everything. Your mind, your soul. I want to know what makes you tick. What gets you out of bed in the morning. I want to know that smile, how it looks and feels. I want it all."

Rhory closed his eyes slowly. "Mother would not like it. She doesn't really like your family, you know."

"Ah, now it makes sense. The refusing son, are you using me to upset her?"

"Yes," Rhory said, matter-of-factly. "But it doesn't mean I don't wish you to use me in return."

"Tell me then, if I am going to willingly let you use me… What is it you want?"

"A comfortable life," Rhory said, still keeping his eyes closed. "One of my choosing." As he replied, his lips brushed mine. The touch clawed a ragged moan from deep within me.

"I could give you that, and more."

Rhory leaned into me, just as I pulled away. His eyes snapped open wide as I allowed myself to create distance between us. Each step was hard to complete, but I did it because I had to.

"Prove it to me," I said, wanting nothing more than to snatch him back in my arms.

"How would I do that?" Rhory asked breathlessly.

I glanced outside, regarding the slither of the moon. It had been two days since I had turned last and I still felt the violent night beneath the tunnels and the chains Auriol and Silas had wrapped around my body. Rhory was safe with me until the moon was full again. I was in control, and I wanted him.

"Tomorrow morning," I said finally. "I will come for you then."

"Mother will not like it," Rhory repeated.

"I get the impression you do not care what she approves of or not."

The corners of Rhory's mouth lifted. The smile was becoming and overcame his entire face until his eyes glowed with it.

"Tomorrow it is then," Rhory said. "But I don't know if I have the patience to wait that long."

A laugh bubbled out of me, echoing the lightness that filled my chest. "Believe me, Rhory, I have waited a long time for this. I think you can wait until tomorrow morning. I'm not the type of man to steal you away in the night."

"That is a shame." Rhory pouted, flexing his fingers at his sides as though he didn't know what to do with himself. "And what type of man are you, Calix Grey?"

"Meet me tomorrow, and you will find out."

"I," Rhory swept towards me, snatching control of the moment with the press of his chest into the firmness of my stomach, "Very much look forward to it."

I knew, with complete certainty, Rhory spoke with honesty as my ears focused on the steady hum of his heart. He didn't refuse me as I lifted my stable hand and pressed it over his chest. It beat beneath my soft touch, and I knew then that it was the most precious thing to me in this world and the next. And I would do anything to protect it. *Anything.*

## ❦ 28 ❦

I woke to the muffled murmurings of Calix and Millicent, far beneath the bedroom. The gaps in the floorboards did little to silence their conversation. At first, the sound was comforting and kind, for my mind was still gripped in the bliss of rest. But that bliss quickly vanished. Straining my ears, I could pick out words here and there through the groggy tiredness that lingered in my mind. But then the events of the night prior came flooding back in full destructive force.

My first mistake was to stretch my arms out of the cocoon of warmth the quilt provided me. I was instantly scolded by the cold chill that seeped in through the broken glass windows and thin old walls. My second mistake came quickly after as I chose to face the memories from last night and the new understanding that my mind was not, in fact, mine at all.

Calix and I had hardly spoken after he revealed our shared history. History I could not remember, no matter how hard I tried. It would have been easier to believe he had lied about it all. But that didn't feel right, not when one touch of his skin revealed to me the truth. He was not lying.

The headache I had fallen asleep to was back in full force.

Throwing my legs out of the bed, I stood beside the mound of a pillows and tangled sheets where Calix had slept on the floor beside me. I should have offered for him to stay in the bed with me. Gods know there was enough room. But selfishly, I needed space. Not that it helped. My mind told me that was what I required, but my heart longed for his touch, his closeness. Instead, I afforded myself escape only when his breathing slowed, signalling he had found sleep. I followed soon after, lulled into rest by the symphony of his inhales and exhales.

By the time I made it down the rickety stairs, Calix and Millicent came to an abrupt halt in whatever they discussed. Although I had heard enough. My name was mixed in with the low murmurings about Eamon.

"Good afternoon," Millicent said from her seat. She was placed far in the shadowy corners of the room, far from the little light of late day which infected the shadowed space. Although there were wooden boards across the windows which kept the majority of the daylight out, Millicent was taking no chances.

Calix smiled weakly at me but didn't speak a word. He could hardly hold my stare before dropping it back to his hands which toyed with one another on his lap.

I took my seat between them. The legs of the chair were uneven, causing it to rock as I put my full weight down on it.

"Have I interrupted?" I asked, voice light with caution.

"Not at all," Millicent said, muffling Calix's quiet answer. She extended a rolled parchment across to me. I plucked it from between her fingers, already recognising the wax seal and the emblem it bore. "We were discussing this. Here. Feast your eyes on your husband's new attempt to get you back."

Dread filled my stomach and coiled itself down my legs. "Where did you get it?"

"They are practically blowing with the breeze through the streets," Millicent added. "The devil works hard, but Eamon works harder. He has put the notice up across town. But this one, this I found back at Auriol's cottage last night. It was nailed to the door like an eviction notice."

I spared Calix a glance before unrolling the parchment; he never met my gaze. His knee was bobbing with nervous energy, and the skin around his thumb had been picked raw. I resisted the urge to reach out for him and take his hand, knowing how natural that would have been but also knowing I didn't have it in me to hold him.

"At least, this time, the message has not been carved into someone's skin," Calix said as my eyes trailed the wording across the parchment. "Although, give him time and Eamon will grow desperate when this attempt fails and he is forced to find another."

My name had been scrawled in untidy and thick penmanship beneath the word **Missing**. It was a short notice which detailed the incorrect account that I had been missing for days and whoever found me would be awarded a trunk of coins.

"...to be paid in abundance by the Crimson Guard for the return of Rhory Coleman," I read it aloud, twice.

"So much money that, if I needed such a thing, it would have me turning on you," Millicent added, grinning over the lip of a mug. Her lips were stained a deeper red than usual. Even her teeth looked darker, until her tongue cleared the liquid away. It quickly dawned on me that she was drinking blood, although it took a moment for the scent to reach me and invade my nose. As though noticing my shock, Millicent smiled. The harsh tang of copper flooded the air, as though she sucked on the very coins Eamon had promised Darkmourn as payment for my return.

"Smart, I will give it to Eamon," she continued. "He has placed more of the notices in the poorer areas of Darkmourn. Because he knows they will give tooth and nail to get that money. And atop that, he has practically tripled his force of Crimson Guards overnight with the promise of reward."

"But it also tells us something else," Calix added as he took the parchment from my hands and rolled it up in his. I hadn't realised I had started to shake until my fingers were without something to hold. "He knows we are in Darkmourn and it will only be a matter of time before he gains entry into every home, establishment, and dwelling to find you."

"Are we are going to sit and wait until he does?" I asked, because it was the only question I could fathom.

"That is one option, one of many," Millicent said. "I have a few other suggestions—"

Calix stood abruptly, the notice no more than a crumpled ball of paper in his fist. His breathing was ragged. Even his eyes were wide and unblinking, the whites almost entirely bloodshot.

"Steady boy," Millicent said, but there was no humour in her voice. She feared him or feared what he'd be as he was moments from losing control and shifting. "It will do none of us well if you let out the wolf now."

"Calix." I was beside him, my hand around his wrist. "It is going to be okay. Look at me."

He did, just as my power slipped from my skin and snatched his uncontrolled rage and replaced it with something easier to breathe through.

The force of his emotions slammed into me. It was boiling, so hot my skin prickled raw, as though I had been an inch away from a roaring inferno. When I couldn't take any more of his fury, I released him and slumped back into my chair.

"Thank gods for that," Millicent cooed from her chair. "I rather like this house; I wouldn't want it destroyed."

"Sorry," Calix fussed, running a hand through the length of his brown hair. "I can't bear the feeling of being forced into a corner. Eamon took something very dear from me, and I will not let it happen again."

Millicent leaned forward. "We will save Silas. And Auriol."

Calix didn't tell Millicent that they were not who he spoke of, but one subtle glance my way proved my suspicions. He spoke of me.

"Eamon is painting a picture for the public." The words came out of me without thought. "To combat it, we should paint one of our own."

"What do you mean to do?" Calix asked.

"I never was one for art," Millicent mumbled.

"Millicent, I know you said you were not one for money either," I said, the idea coming to me quickly. "But if you give me to Eamon and claim the prize, he will never expect the truth behind it."

"No, absolutely not." Calix slapped his palm on the table. The glasses and china mugs clattered against one another violently.

Millicent leaned forward, smiling with a glint in her ruby eyes. "Keep going."

"Eamon needs me alive if he wishes to keep control of the Crimson Guard. He may hurt me, but he cannot kill me. Take me back to him. He knows not of Millicent's involvement, and will never blink twice at a vampire trading in a human for their own benefit."

"Did you not just hear what I said?" Calix whispered. "Rhory, you can't possibly think we will let you do this."

"We?" Millicent echoed. I was never more thankful for her thinly veiled and blatant untethered disloyalty to me. "Unless you can come up with another idea that doesn't involve eating the limbs of the man who is literally tying the noose around your family's neck, then I suggest we listen to Rhory. The boy is finally speaking sense."

"Let me do this," I said, ready to fall to my knees before Calix and beg. "He is my husband and the Crimson Guard is my father's legacy. Allow me to right his wrongs, return your family back to you and prevent this from happening again. Calix, I am no longer scared of him. I can only stop him if I am close enough, and if Darkmourn knows that I have been returned home, all eyes will be on me and my welfare. It will be harder for Eamon to hide with so many eyes on us."

It took a moment for Calix to answer me. It was not another refusal, because he likely saw it was pointless to try. Defiance and determination danced within the blood in my veins, and if I felt it, he surely could see it.

"What has changed?" he asked, gold eyes softening at their edges.

"I finally have something to fight for."

"Rhory has a point," Millicent said over the rim of her cup. This time she didn't add any sarcastic comments. "He can get into the nest and get the information needed about Auriol and Silas's whereabouts."

"Best to strike the monster whilst he is down," I said,

eyeing them both. "Eamon has been wounded. He is weak. Darkmourn's attention is on him. One wrong move and he fucks everything up."

"If you go to him, Rhory, I cannot protect you." Calix's words settled over me.

"It is time I protect myself," I replied, feeling a swell within my chest at the notion. My hand uncurled before me, fingers peeling away like the petals of a flower until my power glowed between them. "It is time this ends."

It quickly became apparent that this house once belonged to witches. Strange marks had been carved into doorframes, dust coated candles had been piled within old cabinets full of curiosities. But the most obvious evidence was the worn-leather book I found beneath the bed I had slept in.

I had not exactly gone looking for it, but the distraction came at a perfect time. Millicent had faded back into the tunnels, and I had left Calix pacing in the room downstairs. He had hardly looked at me since our conversation earlier that afternoon, and I had to distract myself from his silence.

As much as I desired his company, it only reminded me of what I was missing: my memories.

A part of me felt wrong for even touching the book, but the moment it was in my hands, I felt some desire to lose myself to it. Growing up with my mother and her wishes to keep our powers hidden, I never had the chance to contemplate what it meant to be a witch. There was nothing in our home that could reveal our truth. No books or objects that would incriminate us. If it did, we would have both been shipped to Castle Dread, never to be seen again. And Mother would have done anything to stop that from ever happening.

Finding this book, and the untold secrets within, made me feel as though I was doing something entirely wrong yet entirely right.

A star had been worn into the leather-bound cover, the grooves painted with gold leaf which had survived the ages. As I opened it carefully, pages cracked. They were stained brown with age and worn at the corners from the many fingers which had touched it. The spine was delicate, I had to lay it out across my lap carefully just to ensure I didn't crack it.

There was a name scrawled onto the first page, nothing else.

"Bishop," I read it aloud. Dread uncurled deep within me as I repeated the name aloud. If there was one witch family that was infamous among Darkmourn, it was the Bishops. The book confirmed that this house belonged to Jak Bishop, Lord Marius's eternal mate.

I flicked through the pages, in awe that I held something that once had been touched by a Bishop witch. Some pages held no writing at all, but drawings and marks much like the ones around the doorframes and carved into the stone slabs at every entrance point. I even recognised some symbols and shapes identical to those I had seen etched onto the walls within tunnels beneath Darkmourn.

Other pages were crammed full of writings. Words and poems, which I knew in my heart of hearts to be spells. I had the urge to read a few aloud, but bit down on my tongue for fear of what would happen.

"Found anything of interest?" a voice asked from the room's entrance.

I looked up, surprised at Calix's sudden appearance. He leaned against the doorframe, studying me just as I studied the book. A cloud of dust exploded as I slammed it shut, feeling embarrassed I had been caught, although unsure why.

"It was under the bed," I said quickly, as though I had to come up with some excuse. "I couldn't bear the idea of sitting still and doing nothing. At least a book is good company."

Calix pushed himself from the doorframe and paced towards me. "Care to tell me what it is about?"

I placed it behind me, childishly hiding it from view. "Some erotic love story. You wouldn't like it."

"Wouldn't I?" Calix asked, one thick brow raising in jest. "And suddenly you know everything about my likes and dislikes?"

"Well," I snapped, "You seem to know all of mine. Doesn't seem fair to me."

His sarcastic gleam faded as my words slapped into him. He knew what I referred to. The untouched conversation we had left from the night prior was still taut between us, the tension so thick it was like wading through a frozen lake.

Calix took a seat next to me and sighed. "I shouldn't have told you. It was not fair to play with your mind like that."

"What isn't fair is my mind is not my own. My memories should be mine, but they are not. I do not know what has been tampered with and what hasn't."

"I wish I could answer that for you, Rhory, I really do."

I wished to recite all the warm memories I held onto. The ones of me and Eamon in love. My mind was full of scenes, replaying over and over as though I tried to search for missing details and reasons to prove to myself that they were not real. There was the one of Eamon and me leaving a feast and scampering up into Father's library where Eamon had kissed me for the first time. No, I had kissed him. There were others. So many vivid visions of us together, courting and moving from Dark-mourn as though we were the only two in the entire world. How could all those memories, colourful and real that I could almost taste, almost smell them now, be fake? If it wasn't for the truth that scorched from Calix as I read his emotions with my power, I would have dismissed what he said as a lie. It would have been easier.

"I could tell you everything. Gods knows I wish to share the burden of these memories I have with some-one. Perhaps then it would make everything feel real, and not some made-up scenarios which I have been made to feel they are. Since it happened, since you were taken from me, I have driven myself mad. What good is the truth if you are the only one who bears it?"

My answer came out quick. "No. Calix, I don't want to hear it. I can't—"

I buried my face in my hands, sensing the pang of a headache beginning.

Calix couldn't hide the hurt in his reaction; when he replied, his voice was low and tired. "Understood. I may want many things, but to burden you with something unwanted is not one of them. I should leave you to your—"

Before he could leave, I gripped his wrist and held on desperately.

"Show me," I pleaded, addressing my innermost desires. "I don't want you to tell me about the past. I want you to show it to me. Show me what it was like. My mind cannot remember, but my body... I think it remembers. It remembers you, where I cannot."

His lips parted slowly. I thought he would say something; instead, he exhaled a long breath whilst lifting a finger towards my face. A shiver spread down my spine as his fingertip trailed from my temple, across the rise of my cheekbone and down to my jaw. He was an artist. His hand was his tool as he painted my face in a scarlet blush.

"Are you sure this is what you want from me?" he asked, voice dropping to a low whisper.

I nodded, unable to remove my eyes from his. "I am certain."

Calix guided me without words. He took my hand, urged me slowly from my seat and pulled me on to his lap. The bed creaked loudly beneath us. It made his expression break into a smile. I smiled back, not because of the sound, but the knowledge of how badly I wanted this. Neither of us spoke of what was to happen. We both knew it. We both *wanted* it with equal measure.

A distraction. From memories and illusions. Something to take our minds off a world I could not understand, at no fault of my own.

In a blink, I was straddling him. My knees were on either side of his hips, pressing into the warmth of his legs. His hands gripped on my thighs desperately. I felt the pinch of his nails through the cotton of my trousers.

There was something about the way Calix touched me that made thinking of anything but the now impossible. Our past didn't matter, and nor did the events that would come in the future. All I could focus on was him, whilst he was solely focused on me.

Calix wove his hand up my arched back and spread his fingers through my hair. He tugged on the roots, ensuring his grip was firm before he brought my face to his.

I kissed his smile. It was feather soft and lingering. He held me to him, exhaling through his nose and tickling the blushed skin of my face as his lips melded with mine. Both my hands found either side of his face. The hairs of his short beard scratched my soft palms, sending a new shiver up my arms, across my shoulders and down to my ass.

"Does your body remember?" he asked, breaking away momentarily from our kiss. "Only you can answer that."

I rocked on him, our kiss intensifying from gentle to hungry. By the time our tongues danced together, Calix was as hard as stone beneath me.

There was a thrill coming from the knowledge that I had such power over him. I didn't need to pay attention to his cock to make it stand to its desperate attention. He groaned into my mouth as I swayed my hips back and forth. I enjoyed the ache his hardness gave me as it pressed into my ass cheeks.

Pulling back slightly, I marvelled at Calix's lips; how pink and swollen they were.

"From the moment I saw you, my body craved your touch. I believed it to be sinful thoughts, but now I know otherwise. There is nothing sinful about you," Calix whispered.

He dropped his hands from my face and let them linger on my shoulders. Calix's fingers moved, easing the tension from my taut muscles, as I stared directly into his golden-glazed eyes.

"I like the idea of being someone's sin," Calix continued, speaking softly.

"Then be mine,' I said as warmth unfurled in my chest. 'Entirely."

Calix's lips twitched upwards, but it was his eyes which shone with his glee. "It would be my pleasure. This—what is to happen—will not be like it was in the woods."

"By that," I said, biting my lip, "Do you mean you are not going to finish so... prematurely?"

His brows furrowed, giving his expression one of danger and desire. "That wasn't exactly what I was suggesting, but yes. If you care to know, I am going to hold back until I am buried inside of you. Only when I ride your tight hole until you beg for me to finish will I plant my seed."

My stomach flipped; my mouth burst with saliva. "And what if Millicent returns?"

"She won't." His answer was clear and final.

A new spreading of warmth cursed my cheeks. "Does she know?"

"That we are going to fuck in her house? Perhaps not."

"Fuck?" I barked a laugh. "Were you always so vulgar?"

Calix lowered his forehead and pressed it to mine. I pinched my eyes closed, gasping as his cool breath washed over me. "Believe it or not, but you were rarely in the mood for making love. Although when we did so, from the moment I entered you, you would *beg* for me to fuck you."

"Did I?" My mind reeled at the thought. This time, it was not painful to hear of something I could not remember.

"Indeed," Calix growled through an exhale, "You did."

I opened my eyes slowly, holding back a childish giggle as I found his intense stare boring straight through me into the back of my skull. Beneath it, I felt naked. Exposed. Even with my clothes still clinging to my body.

"Would you like to play a game?"

Calix tilted his head in amusement, his golden eyes glinting with intrigue. "Well, that depends on the game."

I pushed off him, feeling his fingers lingering on me as long as they could, until I was standing out of reach. "I am going to ask you a question about the *before*."

"Before?"

I nodded. "For every answer you give me, I will remove a piece of clothing. Care to play?"

Calix reached for the hard mound of flesh pressing through the cloth of his trousers. His hand gripped it and held on, thumb moving slowly as he watched me. His touch alone had the power to fix me, undo me and fix me again. "Ask away, *Little Red*."

"That name," I started, exchanging what would have been my first question for this. "You used it before, but I couldn't understand why you would know my parents' nickname for me."

Calix pouted. "Well, that is not a question. If you are asking why I used it, it was because I secretly hoped it would spark some memory back to life in you. It didn't work. And it was not a nickname your parents gave you. It was mine. Perhaps, when your memory was tampered with, it took those memories and morphed them into something new. Little Red, it belongs to me. Like you did."

"Belong to you? Is that so?"

"It is, and I belonged to you."

My cheeks warmed with a blush beneath his intense gaze and equally intense words.

"Next question. That one was just a warmup." I began unbuttoning the shirt whilst Calix massaged his cock through his trousers. He hardly blinked as he watched me. Slowly, I lifted the material over my head and dumped it on the floor beside me. The movement had ruffled my hair; it took effort not to lift a hand and smooth it back down.

"Hurry, before I grow tired of waiting and decide to rip your clothing off you myself."

I breathed out a laugh, one that smoothed the serious lines of Calix's face. His beauty was heart-breaking and breathtaking.

"Did I know what you were before?"

Calix's hand movements faltered. "No. I was going to tell you, but Auriol forbade it. It is dangerous to tell others, even those you trust most. It was what led to my parents…"

Calix faltered as a look of pure sadness spread across his expression. I couldn't bear to see such a look spoil his eyes, so I lifted my hand and brushed it down the side of his face. As though Calix was hypnotised by me, his unexpected turn in emotions faded like smoke and his hungry desire returned as I popped the single thread button at the top of my trousers; a simple wiggle made them fall to my ankles.

"Only one more question," Calix said, gesturing to my undershorts, entirely distracted by my nakedness.

"I didn't say it was going to be a long game." I thumbed the elastic band of my undershorts, nail brushing slowly across the skin coated with fine ginger hair. Calix moved from the bed, got on his knees before me and took the position of a man in prayer.

I looked down at him. "What are you doing, you fool?"

"Ask me the last question," Calix said, staring up at me from the floor. "And when I answer it, I want to be the one to remove... these." He flicked his hand towards the remaining piece of clothing.

My final question took a moment to locate. When it came down to it, I was uncertain if it was out of jealousy or perhaps hope. "Since..."

"Spit it out," Calix said, smiling mischievously at me. "Or swallow it, your choice."

Every hair on my arms and legs stood to attention. "Have you been with anyone else since... our before?"

Calix smiled proudly, lifted his chin and released a low hum before answering. He raised his large, powerful hands and hooked his fingers into the band of my undershorts. I lifted my hands out of the way, cheeks pinching with excitement.

"Not a soul," Calix answered. "Perhaps it is the curse that floods my blood, but like the wolf... when I have found a *mate*, no one else compares. Ever."

Calix removed my undershorts, his eyes fixated on my cock which slipped free and stood proud and hard between my parted legs. "Hello again," he moaned, eyeing it with an intensity that made my mouth prick with saliva.

I parted my lips to reply, but soon gasped as Calix opened his mouth, extended his wet tongue, and brought it to my tip. Bliss exploded through me as Calix took me into his mouth. My knees threatened to give way as the pleasure of his warm soft suck overcame me. I closed my eyes and gave into the feeling. Part of it was from fear that if I watched him take me, I would be the one to reach a premature finish this time.

From the tip to the base of my shaft, where curls of short ginger hair covered me, Calix devoured me. He didn't use his hands, but moved his tongue in beautiful circles, ensuring every inch of me was glistening with his spit.

My eyes shot open when the feeling stopped suddenly. I hardly cared for the dribble of his saliva that slithered down the base of my cock, onto my balls, where it elongated into a drip and splashed on the floor between my separated feet. Disappointment wracked through me. Calix rocked back on his knees, staring up at me. His cock was free of his trousers and in his hand. He worked it slowly, allowing a bud of spit to fall from his lips onto the curve of his cock.

"You taste just how I remembered," Calix said. "Sweet as summer berries."

As he spoke, I felt a seeping of cum slip from the head of my cock, followed by a knee-buckling shiver which spread from my length across my entire body and soul.

"Fuck me," I said quickly. Desperately. Without thinking, simply speaking my deepest desire into existence. It was the way he looked at me, drank me in, and the way his large hand rubbed his cock, which conjured such sudden starvation from me.

"There it is," Calix said, standing from his knelt place on the floor. For a moment, I forgot how tall he was. When he uncurled to full height, it was he who now looked down at me. "I am not even inside of you yet, and you already want me to fuck you."

"Perhaps my body does remember then," I said, voice barely a whisper.

"Hmm. We will see."

I walked around Calix. He was rooted to the spot, whilst his rich eyes tracked me until he was forced to turn around to continue watching me.

"Where do you think you are going?" he asked, voice rumbling like far off thunder.

I sat on the bed, pushed myself into its middle and laid down on my back. "To bed. Care to join me?"

"I want nothing more," Calix groaned, stepping in until the wooden frame of the bed pressed into his shins. His trousers, like mine, fell with ease to his ankles, which he had stepped out of on his way to the bed. "You always did enjoy this position; however, you were partial to riding me as though I was a throne, and you the king who ruled from it."

I lifted my knees up, cocked my legs, and spread

them. There was something thrilling about being so exposed before him. How his eyes flickered to the centre of my ass, then back to my face.

"I want you so bad," I beckoned him, "Let me watch your face when you enter inside of me."

Calix joined me on the bed, crawling over me. His long cock flopped down, heavy; I felt it crash into the inside of my thigh as he brought himself atop me.

"I will be careful with you," he said, reading the moment of fear that washed over me. His thick length was far greater than Eamon's cock. It'd be a miracle if it would enter me without hurting. Eamon was not as blessed as Calix, but still caused me discomfort. It was something else he never apologised for.

Before my mind could move away from this moment to darker thoughts, Calix lowered himself down and kissed me. I was vaguely aware of his bulging arms flexing as they held up his weight. Soon enough, there was no room for thoughts of Eamon. Only Calix, his cock, and the way he was about to fuck me... just how I wanted it. Just how he *knew* to give it to me.

"Spit for me," Calix said. He brought his hand to my mouth.

I did as he asked. My neck strained as I pressed my lips to his fingers, gathered the spit in my mouth and forced it out. Once I was done, and he had lathered his cock with it, he brought his hand back to my mouth, slipping a finger to my lips and parting them.

"More," he demanded.

I was pleased to give him what he wanted.

Calix did the same. Three times he took the saliva from his mouth and stroked it across his cock. Every time, his moan of pleasure grew. He bit down into his lower lip by the last time, straining against his urge to continue working his wet cock with his hand.

Nerves bubbled in my chest. Calix must have heard the skip of my heart as he turned his attention back to me. "Are you nervous?"

I looked to his spit-glittered fingers. "Is that enough... to, you know?"

A sly grin etched across his handsome face. He playfully glowered at me through his thick brows and spoke, "Reach into my jacket pocket."

I did as he asked. His jacket was on floor beside the bed. The cold brush of wind toyed with my bare hole as I bent over, plucked the jacket up and wove my hand into the inner pocket. The tips of my fingers met the kiss of glass.

I pulled free a small vial, no bigger than the palm of my hand. Clear liquid sloshed inside, stopped only from spilling by the cork stuffed in the top. I held it out to Calix, as though displaying evidence. "You've come prepared."

A blush crept over his face. "It wasn't that I expected this but..."

I stifled Calix's excuse by popping the cork and tipping the contents atop his already wet cock. It dribbled out of the vial, thick as honey but as clear as spring water. My hand soon became lathered with the lubrication, which I promptly brought to my hole and spread it around.

Calix didn't say a word as he watched me. The vial smashed on the floor beside the bed, signalling its uselessness now that it was empty.

"Then I suppose you should stock up," I said, lowering my legs back over his waist until I straddled his cock.

"Oh, I will. Tell me when it is too much," Calix said, guiding his length and pressing the hard, curved tip of it to my ass.

"Okay," I breathed, bracing myself for the pain.

But it didn't happen. The burn was not scalding, but warm and welcoming. Calix used a hand and lifted my lower back up, creating a natural arch. His touch relaxed me, which eased his entrance. He completely focused on ensuring I was not harmed. All the while, I sensed his desire to bury his cock in me.

I didn't know I was moaning until I felt the press of his hips. He was in. Completely, with not a single inch spared. The knowledge had me gripping my cock whilst I rolled my hips, familiarising myself with the swell of his length inside of me.

"You…" Calix breathed as his eyes became glassy with desire. "You are so tight. So… good."

He pulled himself out of me, unsheathing his length from my ass. He did so slowly, ensuring my hole grew used to his presence before he ruined me. Calix had been so careful and gentle, but it was not what I desired now. Urgency had me thrusting myself back and forth, enjoying the slide of his cock in me. His thick and demanding presence stretched and pleased me.

"Fuck me, Calix. I want you to take me, fuck me, devour me."

Calix lowered himself back down over me. I kept my knees raised skyward. He folded my legs between us, placing my shin to his chest and keeping me trapped. "Oh, I am going to do all that and more. Again, and again. This… this is something no magic can ever make you forget. I will make sure of that."

Calix, of course, was correct. I could never have ever forgotten this. He fucked me just as I begged him to. In fact, over and over I said those words.

*Fuck me. Fuck me. Fuck me.*

He always delivered.

Each time I spoke the words, whether aloud or screamed in my mind, his thrusts got harder, faster, to where each slam of his hips caused the words to jolt out of me.

Gone was the warning of keeping quiet in this house. It was a miracle if all of Old Town didn't hear my screams of pleasure.

"Open your mouth," Calix commanded. As I did, he took his middle finger and slipped it between my lips. "Suck it."

I kept my gaze fixated on his as I sucked his finger, just as he'd sucked my cock. He thrusted into me, grunting each time he was buried completely in my tight warmth. My tongue wrapped around his finger and my lips pinched down on it.

"Good boy," Calix groaned. "You are such a good boy."

Thank the Gods I had something in my mouth to stop me from crying out, because Calix reached for my cock and began stroking it in rhythm with his thrusts.

Sweat beaded on his temples, running down the line of his face like rain on a glass window. His length of hair was wild and untamed. Everything about him was a *beast*. Which was why when Calix howled, it didn't scare or shock me. It was natural, although the sound was anything but.

His howl rocked the very walls of the house. It sang of his pleasure and I knew he was racing towards the edge of it, ready to throw himself off the precipice. My ass tightened as I knew he reached his climax, just as his hand worked me to the edge of mine. Breathless, I sucked harder on his finger whilst moaning in tune with his howl.

Calix came inside of me. His cock throbbed as it expelled its milky seed deep within. I raced to my climax as Calix jerked my cock with his fist. The world became sensitive and soft. The rub of his hand became too much to bear. He let go, as though he read my body's reaction. Everything he did, *everything*, was thought-out and familiar, as if he knew my likes and dislikes like the lines on his palms.

Which, in fact, he did.

Calix flopped on the bed beside me after he eased himself free of my hold. There no care for clean-up. Nor did I mind, as I felt a little of his seed seep out from my ass and spread across the sweat-damp sheets of the bed. All there was room for was the enjoyment of his lingering feeling of pleasure that stormed through me.

He rolled his head to the side and faced me. I did the same. Calix smiled at me with heavy eyes. "If Millicent didn't know about us before, I am sure she does now."

"It doesn't matter," I replied breathlessly, even though I had done little of the hard work. It seemed I was rather inept at lying on my back. "Hell, even if Lord Marius himself heard your howl, it was worth it."

Calix brought his hand to my finger and brushed his thumb over my lip. A kiss followed. It was brief before he flopped back down on the bed, exhausted but smiling with closed eyes.

I stared up at the ceiling, still reeling from the joy his sex had given me. "It was worth it. All of it."

"And it will not be the last time."

I smiled to myself. "How are you so confident in that?"

"Because it is in my nature. Threaded through my very being. You are part of my pack. You always have been. And I will be damned if I ever let you stray far again. No matter the consequence."

"Does that make you my alpha?" I asked into the dark.

"If that is what you wish to submit yourself to."

"How does it work?"

Calix sighed as he gazed up into the darkening

ceiling. "In a pack of wolves, there is always an alpha. It is instinctual. However, any leader can be contested."

"Auriol," I said softly, finding it odd to speak of her when her grandson had just been buried within me. "She's your alpha?"

"She is. Until I contest her title."

"It is that easy for you to take it?"

Calix rolled over to face me. The bed creaked with the weight of his movement. "I would need to kill her and devour her heart if I wished to become the true alpha. Just as she did with my grandfather after she turned him with her bite, and he *turned* on her."

Part of me was repulsed, where another part of me felt excited intrigue.

"You wouldn't do that though," I said.

"No, not unless the moment called for it."

His words settled over me, draining the warmth from my body at the thought of such a vile act. I felt the atmosphere we had created in this room slip away like ice in the first thaw of spring.

"Then you better keep your heart safe from me," I said, stretching my hand over his chest and resting it over the solid beat of his heart. "Otherwise, I might be forced to contest my alpha and eat it."

"You can have it," Calix said. "It is yours. It has always been yours; it always will be. No matter what happened or what happens... It belongs to you."

His words took my breath away. They solely returned the warmth to my body, sparking heat in the kindling of my soul until every limb, finger, and vein hummed with *him*.

"Get some rest," I said. "I am going to need you back to full strength come morning. Before I have to—"

"No, no, no." Calix grabbed me, brought me into his side, and nestled me into the crook of his arm and chest. "No talk of tomorrow. One night, just one more night, and I want to pretend we have nothing to face outside this room."

I pressed a kiss into the damp, sweat-slicked skin of his hard chest before granting him a reply. He knew what was to come when the sun set tomorrow. Our plan would start its first stages, and Calix would be forced to leave my side.

"One more night," I repeated his sentiment. "Until we can claim another, my alpha."

## 🌱 30 🌱

In the hours which passed, Calix and I didn't remove ourselves from one another. If our fingers were not entwined, or my hands draped carefully on his scarred chest, we were kissing and dancing with naked limbs and a burning thirst for one another. We slept too, a little. Only brief breaks between the exhausting yet thrilling entanglement we had entered. The night passed into day and day into night. Time slipped away from us, replacing our enjoyment for one another with the feeling of impending doom.

Our bliss was short-lived when Millicent came knocking on our closed door.

Her red eyes surveyed the state of the room the moment she pushed it open. Millicent didn't wait for us to answer her knock, nor did she require to. This was her home; we were merely visitors. Calix hardly stirred at her presence. Instead, he pulled me in closer to his chest with a muscled arm scooped under my neck, and rested it on my upper arm.

"If you are done defiling my brother's room, we should make haste and get this over with," she said, nose flaring as she smelled the air and the tang of sex the hours had poisoned it with. "May I suggest you wash before I return you back to your husband. I wouldn't want him smelling another man's scent all over you."

I slipped from Calix's hold, pulling the crumpled sheets with me. "There is no need. Eamon saw me and Calix in the forest, he would likely expect nothing less."

"And let him," Calix growled.

Millicent grinned like a cat seeing milk. "Very well. Both of you, meet me downstairs to discuss the next steps. If I am to walk Rhory to his front door and deposit him, it should be with a believable story. A solid one, which explains how and why I found him."

The vampire turned on her heel and departed into the shadows of the hallway beyond the room. Her quick visit had shattered the aura of peace we had conjured, allowing room for the impending anxiety to overcome me.

I sat on the edge of the bed, gaze stuck to a spot on the wall. A warm hand trailed up my back and slipped over my neck. Where Calix placed his fingers, he finished with a brief kiss.

"Tell me how you feel?" His question was as dark as the skies beyond the house. "Voice it aloud, it may help."

"Frightened," I replied. It was the easiest answer to

give. "But determined. There is nothing Eamon can do to me which he hasn't done before. He may hurt me, punish me. This time, I know what it is for."

"I will remind you, you don't need to do this," Calix said, lips purring into the skin of my neck. "If you told me you had changed your mind, I would not care. You mean more to me than I could put into words."

"You also care for your family, and I will see that they are returned to you. I know what it is like to lose everything you ever loved; I cannot see you go through that."

"And what will you do when it is over? When it is you that I desire the most?"

"Find a way." Tears filled my eyes, but I refused to let them fall. I was in control of my emotions, just as I could be with others. And now, I was the master of them all. "Calix, listen to me. I *will* find a way to remember you. Eamon has the key to many things, and if he refuses to give it to me willingly, I will break the damn lock myself."

"There he is," Calix exhaled, as though some weight had been lifted from his shoulders. "The man I love. He is returning. Seeing you as the broken shell I found standing outside my door was never who I had been forced to leave. Knowing you leave me with a slither of your past self gives me the confidence that you'll see this through. I'm rooting for you. We all are."

Our plan was simple. Millicent would say she found me roaming the streets of Old Town after fleeing Calix. Eamon was not to know that I was aware of our past, and I would lean into that. It would be easy to perform the unknowing fool, since it had been the part I had been playing for years. Of course, Millicent would have to make it look unsuspecting.

"Is this really necessary?" Calix asked, soul brimming with distress. The thin leather cord he used to tie his hair back from his face did wonders to show every line and crease of concern as he looked between his hand and my face.

"If we want Eamon to believe Rhory fled you, it would be more credible if he was returned…marked," Millicent replied, "By you."

"It's fine," I said, lifting Calix's chin with my finger so he would focus on me, and not the dark claws that had replaced his fingers. The shift from human to the wolf had only reached up to the crook of his arm. Not a single scrap of skin was left; in its place was dark fur and yellow talons. "I will be okay."

"If you can't see it through…" Millicent began, but Calix stopped her with one look.

"No one else is to lay a hand on Rhory. No one."

I marvelled at the warmth that spilled from Calix's fur-coated arm as I took it by the elbow and lifted it to my exposed chest. There was slight resistance, but Calix allowed me to guide his claws up until they pressed firmly into my skin. "You can't hurt me."

His gold eyes brimmed, and thick brows quivered. "I can."

I knew Calix could not draw his claws across my chest without encouragement, so I did it for him. We held one another's stare as I pierced my skin with his claws. I pushed only enough to draw beads of blood. Then, with great effort, I guided his powerful touch downwards.

Pain lashed through my chest, cramping every muscle in my body. I offered Calix a smile, whilst concealing the discomfort I was in. If it wasn't for the insides of my cheeks which I bit down on, I would have hissed out in agony.

"That is enough." Calix drew back.

"Yes, that is more than convincing. Rhory, take this." Millicent thrust her hand towards me, whilst keeping her gaze the other way. Pinched between her painted nails was a square of cloth with embroidered frills sown around its outside. "Clean yourself up before I forget myself."

As I dabbed away the dribbles of blood that oozed from my new cuts, I watched as Calix's fur melted from his arm like ash caught in the wind, revealing pink flesh beneath. By the time I had wiped away most of the gore, his arm was mundane once again.

"I hate myself for hurting you." Calix leaned forward, taking the blood-stained cloth and dabbing it across the bloodied marks.

"You could never hurt me," I whispered, not wishing for him to know how the stinging of the wound felt more like fire blossoming across my skin. "Never."

Calix studied my lips as though he attempted to understand my words.

"It is highly imperative to our plan. So, let us leave whilst the blood still weeps." Millicent stood quickly, still averting her eyes from me. As she referred to the blood, it seemed she strained at the word. "Rhory, say your farewells and meet me by the door for the next part of our ridiculous plan."

Calix took me into his arms before Millicent's footsteps faded into the darkness of the Bishop's house. I pressed my face into his chest, closing my eyes and inhaling the moment so I would never forget it. No longer did I care for the stinging of my fresh wound, not when he held me.

"This is not a goodbye," Calix whispered, his lips tracing the words on the top of my head.

"Then why does it feel like it is?" I asked, not daring to move. All I cared for was the smoothing circles his hands made on my back, and the way his earthy scent filled my nose with each breath in.

"I will not be far," Calix said. "If you need me, I will come for you."

He had given me the option to call this all off if I required it. Part of me wished he had never told me. It made giving up easy, knowing something so simple was the only thing from preventing him from coming to save me. All it would take was setting a lit candle by my window, and Calix would come bursting through the door to my home to claim me, as he had before. The thought was tempting. I feared I was not strong enough to ignore it when the time came.

"Let's hope it does not get to that." I pulled back, feeling Calix's reluctance to let me go. His touch fell down the length of my arms and took my hands in his. He squeezed them, and I squeezed back.

We stared at one another in silence. His eyes flickered across my entire face, drinking me in. Every second I stayed with him was another closer to me giving up before I had even stepped out of the door.

"I will remember you," I said, watching Calix's proud face break with every word of my promise.

"That doesn't matter to me," Calix pleaded, pulling me to him a final time. "What matters is that you come back to me safe and sound."

"But it matters to me. Eamon has taken from me, and it is time I claim it back."

Calix took my face in his hands and lifted it until we were looking at one another again. We were inches apart. No longer did he bother to control his tears, which he let fall freely from each corner of his pinched eyes.

"Just come back to me," Calix whispered through quivering lips. "That is all I wish for you to promise."

I reached up and brushed a single tear from his cheek. He leaned into my hand, closed his eyes and exhaled a long and taut breath.

"Calix, look at me."

As he did, gold light spilled gently from my hands.

My use of power was not to take his emotions from him nor provide him with replacements. It was different this time. I simply wished for him to feel my burning honesty as I answered him.

"I cannot explain it yet, but I do not think we could ever be separated. Not forever. It seems we will always find a way back to one another."

The lines around his eyes lessened. The tension around his mouth relaxed. In the glow of his handsome, honey-pure eyes, I knew he felt the truth I spoke. It eased his tension, smothering it like a flame within the eye of a storm.

"Two days," Calix said calmly. "We will give you two days. Eamon has had you long enough. No matter your success, or failure, I will come for you. That is my promise to you."

I guided his face down to mine. He followed willingly.

"What are you going to do this time?" I asked, stopping him only when his lips were a hairbreadth away from mine. "Break into my house, throw me over your shoulder and take me away into the night?"

"Well, it would not be the first time. Why would it matter if I did it again?"

My stomach flipped. "Something to look forward to then."

"Indeed, it is," Calix purred. Slowly, he brought his lips down to mine and kissed me as though it were our first and last time. The gentle caress of his mouth against mine, and the memory it left on my lips, carried me from the house in Old Town, all the way back to Eamon.

To my husband. To my monster.

This time, it would be different. I would no longer allow Eamon to hold any power over me. It would be my turn to force power on him until he was completely suffocated beneath it.

## ❧ 31 ❧

My throat burned as I expelled my feral screams. The noise shattered the night. My lungs constricted as I shouted over and over until I felt the strain of breathlessness force me to my knees. Millicent had told us to keep quiet. But that rule no longer mattered. Not as I shouted into the night with all the frustration and determination of my promise to Calix.

This was the first part of our plan. A fine pencil sketch on a canvas, which would soon become the picture we would paint to combat Eamon's story of a missing man.

Millicent reached me before the patrons of the Darkmourn, dead or alive, had much of a chance. She claimed me publicly, as windows were thrown open and people came rushing out to see what caused the ruckus. Of course, it was planned. For me to run through Darkmourn screaming bloody murder with a torn crimson cloak, claw marks down my chest. It was all to paint the very public picture that I was a victim of something horrific. Something unseen and terrible.

I was a survivor, and all of Darkmourn would find out before Eamon. Just that alone made me scream harder, shout louder.

Our plan was well thought out. *Manipulative*, Millicent had said. I gave props to the vampire where it was due because she played her part well. She had her arm draped over my shoulder, tugging me in close to her side as we navigated the dark streets of the town whilst they filled with an audience.

"Keep it up," Millicent had whispered as we moved closer towards my home. She had to flash her teeth at others who attempted to step in our way. I could see their starved desire to take me from Millicent and return me to Eamon so they could be the one to claim the prize. But when they saw the points of her teeth, and the deep flashing of blood-red eyes, they all backed away.

No one crossed Millicent. Not even the Crimson Guards, who came rushing over to see what the fuss was about. One of them looked at me. That was all it took. They all recognised me instantly.

I half expected them to take me from Millicent, but they didn't dare. The posters they had spread around Darkmourn made it clear, and if they went against the promise of money, it would not have done well for their imperfectly laid illusion.

Instead of taking me from Millicent, they formed a

wall around us as we moved through the streets, bathed in the red glow of streetlamps. With the sketch of my face plastered upon buildings we passed, there was no denying I was Rhory Coleman, and I had been found.

Eamon was waiting for me. I saw him through the crowd of heads the moment we turned onto our street. He stood within the doorframe of our home, high-lighted by the warmth of fire and light behind him. My heart quickened its pace as I regarded him. Millicent sensed it and held on tighter. She didn't offer me words of comfort, nor did she need to.

With the Crimson Guards around us, and the street full of nosey townsfolk following at our back, this was exactly the show we wished to put on. I was not surprised when I had to fight the urge to smile.

"Rhory?" Eamon called out. There was a slight rasp to his voice, a congested tone that suggested he was not well. The exasperation in his voice did well to show him as the broken man who'd had his love taken from him. I hated how genuine his sorrow looked, and the way he leaned against the doorframe, as if one look at me would bring him to his knees.

As we grew closer and Eamon's outline became more defined, I could see exactly the cause of his weak-ness. Eamon's arm was bandaged. He had his arm lifted in a sling across his chest. Where his hand should have been was now a stump of wrapped bandages. The urge to smile at the memory of his pain was almost too powerful to ignore.

I was stopped before the pathway that led to our

front door. Bathed in the glow of firelight from the many windows before me, I was illuminated for everyone to see.

"Tell me this is not some cruel trick." Eamon mumbled, clutching his chest with his remaining hand. "Or have you truly come back to me?"

The surrounding crowd was silent. All I could hear was the thundering of their following footsteps, and the symphony my heartbeat played in pace with them. My dearest husband was playing his doting part well, but I would play it better.

"My love," I cried out, pulling free of Millicent and stumbling up the stone path to our front door. As I reached him, I fell to my knees. I sensed Eamon's shock within his reluctance to catch me. Not that he could help with a missing hand and a body riddled in pain.

The clapping began as Eamon lowered himself to me with a hiss of pain. Once again, I fought the urge to smile. Knowing he was suffering at the hands of Calix was thrilling. Regardless, he had to believe my reaction, just as the crowd did. If we were to be successful, Eamon had to believe Calix had harmed me, and I escaped. It all mattered to my manipulation of him, and the crowd who watched.

"I'm home," I cried out loud enough for all to hear. "I found my way back to you."

I cringed into Eamon's cold chest as he pulled me into him. Choosing not to shy away, I threw my hands over his shoulders and placed a hard and rushed kiss onto his unsuspecting mouth. Our faces clashed into one another, and I felt the nip of my lip against his teeth.

His entire demeanour was tense and uncomfortable. Knowing that only urged me to kiss him deeper. The crowd ate it up just as Millicent said they would. The cry they gave out was like the strike of lightning in a storm. It was Eamon who pulled back first. I would have continued kissing him until his mouth was bruised and bloodied.

"What has *he* done to you?" Eamon asked through gritted teeth as he took in the torn cloak and my dishevelled nature. His blue eyes studied the wounds on my chest, but his gaze showed no care or compassion. It was as though he was surveying something new, something he was unfamiliar with.

I couldn't answer truthfully, although the urge to lean into Eamon's ear and whisper to him how Calix had fucked me so hard that I still felt the echo of his cock even as he held me now. Instead, I forced my face into a fearful frown as I took Eamon's hand in mine and brought his fingers to the clawed marks on my chest. His touch was cold and as soft as silk. My skin itched and stung, but I made certain to press his hand into the wound, until it was smeared with blood.

"He did this," I forced out, blinking out the fake tears I had conjured. "Please, I just want to be home…"

"You're ruined," Eamon hissed into my ear as he guided me to standing. I inhaled sharply, feeling my lungs swell with dread as my husband faced the doting crowd. He righted his tone and spoke more to the crowd than to me. "Rhory, you are safe. I won't let anything happen to you again."

I couldn't focus on the lack of his emotions as he spoke, not when he steered me towards the door and ushered me inside our home. The Crimson Guard followed swiftly; I caught their movement out of the corner of my eye. In their midst was Millicent, who couldn't break away from them even if she desired to. By the time the door closed, shutting off the chaos of the streets, Eamon called an end to the grand show we had all put on. The second we were out of sight, he released me, almost pushing me away with a shove that hurt him more than it did me.

We stood in the foyer's centre, with Millicent and a handful of Crimson Guards lingering on the opposite side.

I continued my act, forcing tears out of my burning eyes as I tried to press myself back into Eamon's hold. He refused me again.

"Do not touch me," Eamon snarled, teeth clashing like a rabid dog. He looked me up and down, then spat at the ground before my feet. "You are unclean. Spoiled."

"But, husband—"

"I'll take my prize and be on my way," Millicent called out, interrupting the tension between us. "I wouldn't want to ruin such a precious moment with my presence."

Eamon ignored Millicent, showing no sign he even recognised her presence. My skin burned beneath his scrutinizing gaze. There was a darkness behind his eyes. A silent promise of hateful thoughts. It was as though he searched for proof; proof Calix had, in fact, ruined me.

Eamon's nose flared slightly as disgust rolled over his face.

"One of you, see that the bath is filled," Eamon said whilst beholding me, but his words were directed to his Crimson Guard. What he said next was for me, and only me. "You are covered in his stink. Before we discuss anything, I want to see him scrubbed from you."

Hate swelled within me. I felt protective of the knowledge that Calix lingered on me. It took great effort not to refuse Eamon.

"Yes," I forced out. "Just don't leave me." I cringed at my own pleading. More so when it didn't conjure the reaction I'd hoped from him. Eamon's lack of physical touch was not proving well for my act.

"About that prize—"

"Silence yourself," Eamon barked, finally turning his attention to Millicent. "*Vampire.*"

The Crimson Guard swelled around her, closing in on her from all sides.

"My apologies, but did I misunderstand the notice?" Millicent held her ground as rough hands reached towards her from all sides. "You promised coin for his return."

Eamon spat at Millicent's feet, just as he had mine. The splash of phlegm crashed into the wooden panelled flooring at her feet, some droplets hitting into her boots. Loathing deepened his face into a mask that mirrored

something of a beast. "Oh, you shall get your thanks."
Eamon looked back at me, ushering with his remaining
hand for me to step towards the stairs. "Come, *husband*.
Let us clean you up."

I couldn't refuse him. But I didn't want to leave
Millicent. Something felt terribly wrong, and from the
panic that set into her face, Millicent sensed it too. I
could hardly see her through the swell of red cloaks,
who closed in on her from all sides.

"She saved me," I pleaded. Eamon kept his gaze on
the stairs, urging me forward with a push to my lower
back.

"*She* is a vampire," he answered coolly. "Money
matters little to her kind."

Millicent was struggling, hissing curses at those who
grabbed her.

"Stop it." I pulled back enough from Eamon to step
back towards Millicent. But Eamon's strength surprised
me. His hand gripped the back of my neck and
squeezed, yanking me backwards with a harsh tug.

"Oh, my darling," he said; although his words
sounded as though they should have been filled with
compassion, his expression was distant. "Vampires do
not deserve to be rewarded. Don't you see? They are the
problem with this world. They always have been."

"But you—"

"Do not concern yourself with it," he snapped. "It
was her misfortune she found you, and my fortune she
did. Now, are you going to continue to struggle, or

would you prefer I ask a few of my guards to help you up the stairs?"

I struggled beneath his grip. How could someone pale and sickly from his wound hold such strength in one hand? I knew his touch well. But this... this was different.

"Darkmourn knows she is here," I said, urgently reminding Eamon that many people had witnessed Millicent come into the home. If they didn't see her leave, there would be questions. And Eamon hated questions.

His hand squeezed harder until the skin beneath his pinch felt as though it was on fire. "Then it will be a lesson to Darkmourn. I no longer care for their approval; it matters little to me now. Now I have what I want most."

Millicent's vulgar shouts and struggles followed me all the way from the ground floor of our home up to my bathroom. I didn't dare say another word for fear of what would become of her. Eamon didn't know Millicent had anything to do with Calix, but his reaction to her had been birthed from something entirely different.

I trusted the Crimson Guard would not act out of turn. Their entire purpose was to see the protection of all kinds, both the living and the undead. That was what they were created for: balance and peace.

Eamon was muttering something beneath his breath, but I couldn't make it out, not as the hallway we passed suddenly filled with bodies. Men and women spilled from the many closed doors, exiting rooms which

316

had not been used in years. Faces I didn't recognise surrounded us, all human, and all watching.

Our home had gone from a place for only the both of us to the opposite; even before they revealed themselves behind the closed doors there was a sense of fullness to our home.

"I was lonely without you," Eamon said, pulling me the final stretch towards the door that spilled with steam from beneath the small opening; the air grew heavy with it.

We walked into the cloud of warm air and into the bathroom. There was heat everywhere. It choked me.

"Who are those people in our house?"

"My people," Eamon said before correcting himself, "My warriors."

It didn't make sense, nor could I work it out as I struggled to navigate the steam filled room.

Eamon finally let go of my neck, allowing me to crash to the floor. I could see the outline of his dark frame move through the steam. He closed the door with a slam. The click conjured a jolt of childish fear to slip around my soul.

"Remove your clothes," Eamon commanded, watching me from a distance. He was no more than a dark shape through the thick cloud of steam and moisture.

"No…" I said, pulling the strength to resist from deep within me.

Eamon flinched, then expelled a breathy laugh. "Don't make me ask again, Rhory. You will not like it."

He was right. There was no point in fighting him. At least not yet. I focused on the reason for my being here and used it to lift my fingers to the buttons of my shirt. Eamon watched me undress. He didn't offer to help, although I felt his gaze follow every subtle move as I removed each piece of blood-coated clothing. It had been a long time since I was last naked before him. Being so now felt demoralising and wrong. Discomfort flooded through me, thickening in my veins.

"Do you know how I feel?" Eamon asked, brow creased with deep lines. He stepped in close, the mist peeled away from his features until he was fully corporeal again. "You belong to me, but you gave yourself away to another. Every inch of your skin should be mine, but it doesn't feel like it is. Looking at you *sickens* me."

His words conjured a shiver to spread across every inch of skin his eyes surveyed. I felt completely and utterly exposed. My hands shook as I clutched at my length, hiding it from the scrutiny of his tormented stare.

"I… I came back for you." I forced the words out. "Everything that I have done… everything that has happened, it has been a mistake."

"Do not lie to me!" Eamon shouted, body trembling with fury. "Do not dare utter another fucking lie out of that mouth or I swear…"

He raised his hand up suddenly. I flinched backwards, almost tripping over the pile of clothes I felt on the floor, as I raised my arms protectively before me. But there was no pain which followed. No slap of a palm, or smack of a fist. When I peered back through my shield of my arms, I saw Eamon smiling.

"Get in the bath."

I couldn't move, even if I wanted to.

"Get *in*," Eamon commanded again, voice steady. His words echoed throughout the room. It disrupted the steam that oozed from the water's surface.

"I'm sorry—"

"In!"

I skipped forward, no longer caring for my nakedness. My mind screamed for me to obey. Doing so would protect me from him.

My toes burned as they slipped beneath the tub of water. It was hot, but not scalding. The temperature was warm enough that my skin prickled with discomfort. I fought the urge to itch. Giving myself over to the pain gave me a sense of clarity. It reminded me of what I was here to do. Giving in, I slipped beneath the water until only my head was above it. Eamon stepped to the tub's side, parting the thick steam. With his remaining hand, he pulled up a three-legged stool and perched himself upon it. From somewhere unseen, he produced a dried sponge.

"Lean forward," he said, flicking his hand in dismissal. I did as he asked, not wishing to show any resistance. "As it seems your back is your preferred place to lay, I will start by cleaning it."

His insult stung, but that didn't prevent the sly smile that spoiled my lips as I leaned forward and curved my back for him. Where the water was so warm, it made the air of the bathroom have a terrible chill. I couldn't help but shiver, which Eamon soon noticed as he began pressing the sponge to my back and moving it methodically.

"No, no. This will not do," he said. I felt him withdraw the sponge. The skin he had rubbed stung from fresh scratches. "I cannot have my husband cold."

There was the shuffling of feet, soon followed by the splash of water against water.

"Fuck!" I screamed out, lurching forward. I gripped the side of the tub, trying to pull myself away from the splattering of boiling water Eamon poured into the tub.

"I must purge *him* from your skin," Eamon said over the cascading water. "Do you think I want to do this? Do you truly believe I enjoy hurting you? If you would just do as you must and behave, you would not force my hand."

I cowered in a ball at the furthest point of the tub I could move towards. My back hissed with agony from the splashes of boiled water which splattered upon my skin. There was no denying I would be greeted with punishment upon my return. Perhaps I deserved it for breaking our vows. But as I leaned back into the scalding water I reminded myself just how little the vows of our marriage meant. They were spoken from lies. Whatever Eamon had done to my mind, whatever tinkering and altering he had seen done to my memory, had led me blindly into our union.

*It means nothing,* I reminded myself, *it all means nothing.*

I repeated the statements over and over as my body acclimatised to the hotter water. As I eased back into it, thankful as the boiling water diluted to a bearable point, I didn't stop internally screaming the sentiments on repeat.

"No one is making you do this…" I hissed as he returned to scrubbing my back with the sponge. He pressed harder now. The coarse edges of it scratched the hot water into my skin. I didn't need to see my back to know it was covered in cuts.

"I love you," Eamon said, as though that was a justified answer. "Everything I do is because I love you."

I hated hearing those words from him. He spoiled them. Tore all meaning from them and ruined them. Between the pain he caused me physically, and the mental disgust his declaration of love cursed me with, I couldn't help but forget myself.

My lips grew slick. Words came out of me without so much as a thought to them, or what reaction they would conjure. "It is not me you love. It never has been. You love me because I am the leash connecting you to the Crimson Guard. That is what you love—"

Eamon cracked his fist into the back of my head. I blinked and saw stars. Blood burst across my tongue as my tooth cut into the inside of my lip.

"Never think as though you can speak on my behalf, Rhory. I fear you forget yourself. And it would seem that it is not only your body that requires cleaning, but your mind." Before I could react, Eamon had discarded the sponge and reached down for another jug of boiling water.

Except, this time, when he poured the scalding water into the tub, he aimed it at my lap.

I felt red. I saw red. I tasted red. The world was bathed in it, but the pain was delayed.

I took a deep inhale, and then it came so sudden and sharp, I almost lost control and gave into the darkness of peace. My cheeks filled with spit and blood as I did everything in my power not to scream.

His remaining hand gripped my neck. Nails bit into the tender flesh and squeezed. Eamon was leaning over the tub, holding me in his vice-grip so I could not squirm away from him. He brought his lips to my ear and hissed, "Another word and I will—"

He didn't finish. He *couldn't* finish. I slapped my hand around his wrist and streams of gold billowed out with such force the entire world exploded in light. With every ounce of my desperation and rage, I thrust the pain from my body and poisoned Eamon with it.

One moment, it stormed through me. The next, it had vanished.

Eamon's blue eyes bulged. His face cracked into a mask of terror. Then he erupted in a scream of pure agonising pain. I grinned at him, my teeth stained with my blood.

"It would do you well to remember," I said, each word coming out with ease, "You, my kind husband, need me more than I need you."

I released his wrist, and the power blinked out.

Eamon fell backwards, howling viciously into the darkened room. The sound of his suffering was the most beautiful thing I had ever heard. He whimpered and cried as he scuttled away from me. He had landed awkwardly on the bathroom's flagstone floor and pulled his body with one hand as far from the tub as he could manage, all whilst I never took my eyes off of him.

Slowly, the pain returned, but it was not as bad as it had been. It was worth it, in a way. As though I bathed in warmed milk, I eased myself back in whilst Eamon whimpered like a scorned dog. I ensured I left the majority of my agony inside of him, as both a reminder and a warning.

"I wish to bathe alone," I called out, languishing in the sickly calm which soothed my burned back. I knew, in time, it would stop me from moving. But for now, I relished in knowing that Eamon would suffer from the pain he had caused me. "Leave me."

Eamon couldn't form words as the agony sunk its talons into him and refused to let go. I lolled my head to the side and watched as he picked himself up from the floor and dragged his body towards the door. He didn't spare me a glance as he left. He wouldn't. I would make sure that every time he laid his eyes on me it would hurt.

That was my promise to him.

## 3 YEARS BEFORE

"Can I ask you something?" As Rhory spoke, his voice vibrated through my body. He had laid his head upon the hardening muscles of my chest, whilst tracing his finger over the mounds across my abdomen. I felt the press of his ear as he enjoyed the song that was the beat of my heart. And gods how it thundered when he touched me.

The cold breeze of early winter filtered in through the open window of his bedroom. Not only did it provide fresh air to the room, but it was an attempt to remove the scent of sex we had left. If Ana or Michal were to find us, it would have shattered the illusion we had crafted in the months that'd passed. A world where there was only us. Together. An illusion which would only last as long as we allowed it.

"Anything," I said to him, tracing my fingertips across his back. As much as I enjoyed our silence, when there was only his breathing and the song of hearts beating proudly in my skull, hearing Rhory's voice was one of the wonders of the world.

He shifted himself so he could peer up at me. I adored the swell of his lips after we kissed. How I painted his face in a smile with my touch. It made me feel powerful.

"Why don't you ever speak about your parents?" he asked.

The question caught me off guard.

Rhory must have noticed my reaction, because he quickly pushed himself off me as he fumbled over his apology. "I shouldn't have asked, forget it—"

"No," I said, urging him back down onto me. I hated how quickly the cold affected me when his warmth was removed. "It is okay, Rhory. I have nothing to hide from you." As I spoke my lie, it sent a shockwave of pain through my chest. Even if I dared to contemplate it, I always lied to Rhory. I lied to him about what I was, what my history consisted of. There was always a mistruth as I exposed my past to him, knowing I could never tell him about what I was—even if it was all my soul told me to do.

Auriol would never allow it.

"My parents were murdered," I said aloud. I found that every time I spoke the words, it hurt less and less each time. "It is not that I do not honour their memory by refusing to speak about them. You see, my brother and grandmother took their passing badly. I have grown used to tiptoeing around the conversation of my parents because I do not wish to hurt my family."

"My father said it was a vampire who killed them." A heavy sadness filled Rhory's eyes. I hated seeing such an emotion on him.

"It was, but it was also their friend. Michal is right, it was."

I felt the question lingering on Rhory's lips, but it seemed he didn't dare speak it aloud.

*Why?*

Part of me waited for him to ask it, knowing I could never reveal the entire truth. When he didn't speak the word out loud, I was relieved. It was one less lie I had to tell him.

What was known about my parent's murderer was it was done by a rogue vampire, which was not uncommon in Darkmourn. What Darkmourn didn't know was the vampire killed my parents because of the threat they posed to him.

Auriol warned us not to tell others about our affliction. Our curse. My parents didn't listen. They believed they could trust someone, and it only ended in their demise.

"It must hurt," Rhory said, drawing me out of the terrible memories. He always had a way of clawing me out of the dark.

"Terribly," I said. "It seems those who pose the most danger to you are the ones closest."

"That is not true, Calix. I wouldn't hurt you," Rhory said quickly. There was an urgency to his words which I felt deep within me. "Not ever."

In the pause that followed, I wished I could promise

Rhory the same. But I couldn't. It was not a lie I was willing to offer him.

"You underestimate the power you have over me," I said.

A dark cloud passed behind Rhory's eyes, darkening them. He glanced away from me, proving I had said something wrong.

"It's getting late," Rhory said, filling the silence. "Father will be back from his check up at St Myrinn's soon and…"

"And I should leave, before they find me in bed with their darling son." I brought my mouth down and pressed a kiss into his forehead. As I did, I inhaled deeply, drawing in his scent so it would last me until we next stole a moment together. My body and soul warmed by the way his heart skipped a beat when I touched him. If only he could hear mine. He would know it did the same.

"I hate this," Rhory said as I pulled back. "It does not feel right hiding… what we have."

It had been almost three months since that first night we had spoken. And a glorious month it had been. Stolen moments. Hours lost to one another.

"One day," I said, offering him a promise I was unsure I could keep.

"When?" Rhory asked, frowning deeply up at me.

"If I am to court you, I want to do it properly. With your father's permission."

Rhory took his hand and ran it across my stomach. Beneath where his touch trailed, my muscles hardened in anticipation, as did the proud muscle which waited beneath the sheets.

"It is not my father's permission you should be worrying about. It is Mother's. And if you do not speak with her soon, then she might end up forcing me with someone of her own choosing. Someone she thinks would be best for me. The more Father's health declines, the more her urgency to see me cared for intensifies."

The thought of Rhory being with anyone else woke the monster within me. The feeling was swift and over-whelming.

"There is no one else," I said, pressing down the force within me.

"No?" Rhory teased, not knowing the command he had over me—over the wolf. "What about one of the Crimson Guard? I am sure Mother would love to see me with—"

"No. One. Else."

Rhory exhaled through a sly grin. He narrowed his eyes at me whilst continuing to draw his hand down the mounds of my stomach, towards the thin slip of bedsheet that covered my cock. The wolf within me was not the only thing to awaken. The growing lump just shy of Rhory's hand was a physical result of his touch.

"Then be quick about it," Rhory said, fingers disap-pearing beneath the sheets. "Because you are right. There is no one else. There is you and only you. I want you and if all of Darkmourn doesn't know, then it is pointless."

"What did I say, Little Red?" A shiver passed across

Rhory's skin as I used the nickname I had given him all those nights ago. "Those closest to you are the most dangerous. Get too close to me and you might regret it."

"What are you going to do?" Rhory sang. "Bite me?"

My stomach jolted as Rhory's hand found my cock. His fingers wrapped around it, urging it to harden like stone. "If you so desire."

"Well," Rhory said, slipping down the length of his bed. He never once took his eyes off of me, not as he gripped my cock firmly, pulled the sheet back to reveal it, and placed himself beneath it so he looked up my length towards me. "Stay with me tonight."

"I—I can't."

Rhory lifted my cock and pressed the tip to his parted mouth. I gasped at the tickle of his soft lips, knowing full well what was to follow.

"Then I will make you."

"And how do you propose you are going to do that?"

Rhory finally diverted his stare from my eyes and settled on the curved head of my cock. It looked larger in his small nimble hands. With the length lifted to his face, it swelled me with pride.

"I have my ways," Rhory said.

"Auriol would not be pleased if I do not return home."

Rhory's fingers tightened, drawing a moan from deep within me. "Are you really going to make me get on my knees and beg?"

"As much as that would be a pretty sight, no. You do not need to beg."

Rhory's eyes lit up as he read the suggestive look I painted across my face.

"Does that mean you will stay?" Rhory murmured, looking up at me with doe-wide eyes. "Tonight?"

I nodded and reached down, running my fingers through his poppy-red hair. "How could I refuse you, Rhory Coleman?"

"You will not regret it," Rhory said, allowing my hand to guide his face closer to my cock. "I promise."

His heartbeat quickened in sync with mine. My gaze looked towards the closed door just as Rhory wrapped his little wet mouth around my cock. Then there was only darkness and pleasure. As much as I wished to watch him take me in, I had to tilt my head to the side and bite my teeth down on the pillow. If I didn't, the howl which brewed deep within me would have burst free.

Rhory's tongue had magic all of its own. It twisted and caressed my cock, whilst his fist moved gently up and down. He was my undoing. My destruction. He was bliss in physical form. My everything. Our time together had been short, but it had been equally full.

Even with the wedge of my mistruths between us, I had never felt closer to anyone. He took my mind off my world and created a new one where we existed solely in it, together. There was no wolf. There was no Crimson Guard. No death and responsibility. If only we could keep the door to this room shut forever, never to leave again. But one glance across the room to the dark night beyond the window was enough of a reminder that our time was limited. The moon hung heavy and almost full. In a matter of days, my control over the lurking wolf within would be torn from me. Instead of Rhory being draped across my body, it would be silver chains and bolts.

It was a reminder of what I was, and the danger I posed to Rhory.

And as he sucked my length, taking it all in until I felt the soft warmth of the back of his throat, I knew this would never last. Not like this, not in Darkmourn. Our responsibilities would forever keep us apart. Until the day I was brave enough to tell him. Brave enough to leave Darkmourn, together.

*One day,* I told myself as Rhory fought a spit-riddled gag, *One day soon.*

Our perfectly crafted illusion would become our reality. Even if we both had sacrifices to make before that could happen.

My chest warmed as I looked down and studied Rhory taking me into his mouth. He too glanced up at me, through long lashes, with eyes that screamed with desire. I couldn't continue watching him without the threat of exploding entirely in his soft throat.

I gripped Rhory's jaw and withdrew him from me.

"Something wrong?" he asked, lips glistening with his spit and my pre-cum.

"Sit on me," I said, unable to hold the command

from my tone. Rhory's eyes widened and glistened with excitement. "Now."

Rhory didn't hesitate. As he slithered up my body and positioned his legs over my hips, I reached for the vial of natural oils which would aid my cock into him. There was never a vial far from me; one always knocked about in the inner breast pocket of my jacket, in easy reach. With Rhory's insatiable appetite, I had to be prepared.

"I'll do it," Rhory said, snatching the vial and tipping the clear oil into his waiting palm. Without taking his eyes off me, he rubbed his hands together and reached behind his ass. I couldn't see his hands grip my cock, but by the gods I felt it. A shiver burst across my length and spread like wildfire across every inch of skin.

His soft hands were a pleasure in their own right. I melted beneath them and he ensured every inch was coated in the oil. Although, if he was not careful, I would spread my seed before I could grace his tight, glorious hole.

I had to put my hands behind my head or they would wander across Rhory's bare torso. It was selfish, I recognised, but all I longed to do was touch him. So, when I closed my eyes, I could recount Rhory's body without the need to see it. I desired to learn every brush of soft skin and hard corner of bone and muscle. I wanted it all.

Rhory eased himself onto my cock, expelling the longest and loudest moan I could imagine. I joined in,

unable to contain my enjoyment as his tight hole strangled the length of my cock.

It was a miracle the entirety of Darkmourn could
not hear.

Rhory gripped my tensed chest, his thumb and fore-
finger spreading the oil across my nipples which he
twisted between his touch.

The bedsheets crumpled around us as he took me in
and bounced himself up and down. He continued
fucking my cock until his knees ached. Then I took over.
I retrieved my hands from behind my head, happy to
give them something to do. I gripped Rhory's legs,
where his small ass met his thighs. I held him up and
thrust myself skyward, knowing from the roll of his eyes
that my tip pressed firmly into his prostate; the shivers
which coated his freckled arms revealed as much.

We were both lost to one another that neither knew
the door to his room had opened. My ears betrayed me,
focused solely on the thumping of Rhory's intoxicating
heart, that when the second joined in it was too late.

I pulled Rhory down on top of me as though it
would shield his modesty from view. Rhory gasped out,
the sound accompanied by the wet pop of my cock
escaping him.

Eamon stood in the doorway, his wide blue eyes
surveying the room.

If Rhory didn't have his hand on me, I would have
broken free from the bed and devoured the intruder. My
instincts burned for me to do it, to explode from the

sheets and destroy Eamon before he could leave and reveal what he had seen.

Silence bathed the room. There was only room for our heavy breathing and the slow, steady beat of Eamon's heart.

"Pardon me," Eamon said finally, bowing his head but not before his smile cut across his face. "I should have knocked."

It was Rhory that replied, for words failed me. It was the wolf who lingered within me, and I knew if I opened my mouth, it would only be to howl in threat.

"Get out," Rhory said, quietly at first.

Eamon didn't move.

"I said get out!"

When Eamon lifted his stare back towards us, his smile was nothing more than a memory. Although his paled lips were straight, I still recognised the glint of it in his bright eyes.

"Ana sent me back earlier," Eamon said. "She wished for me to check on you. But I can see you are being… well cared for—"

"OUT!"

Eamon didn't dare speak again. Instead, he walked backwards out of the room and closed the door with a soft click.

How could such a quiet sound be so wholly world-shattering?

## ✵ 33 ✵

My body felt as though it had been ridden over by a stampede of wild horses. Every small move and my skin ached. It was tight from the burns, and raw as sun-bleached hide. No matter if it was clothing or bedsheets which rubbed, the discomfort was agony. Whereas my mind was exhausted, the pain encapsulated in my body refused sleep and rest. What little time I got was soon interrupted by the brush of silk across my burns. Just a simple touch, and it restarted the wildfire of torture across my back.

I had stared at the burns in the mirror of my bedroom. Although it felt like my entire back was on fire, it was only a lashing diagonally across my shoulder blades which caused my pain. I knew from my time at St Myrinn's that the burns were not the worst, but enough to blister and scab in the coming days.

Between my body's discomfort, and my mind's reeling, it was the noise of a full house that kept me awake into the early hours, until the dark of night eased into the lighter tones of dawn.

I had found it easier to sleep on the cushioned ledge beneath my grand window, where the cold breeze beyond flirted with my back. I had watched the night pass, searching the street for Calix or Millicent, in the hooded faces that passed below me. The game of seeking was the catalyst to my eyes growing heavy and sleep finally claiming me.

By the time the obnoxious knock on my bedroom's door came, I felt as though I had only found rest for a broken hour or two, at most.

"Eamon wishes to have your company during breakfast," a light voiced woman said from my door. She had not waited for me to allow her to enter. When she stepped into the room, it was with a smirk plastered across her freckled face.

"And if I say no?" I asked, shifting to a sitting position, my back screaming from the movement.

"Eamon doesn't like that word," she sneered, grinning through thin, freckled lips. "It would best you come with me before he comes to retrieve you, don't you think?"

This stranger was right, of course. And the glint in her gaze told me she knew what Eamon did to me behind closed doors. But her smile confirmed she was unbothered by it—in fact, she seemed rather pleased by the fact.

I gathered myself, steeled my expression, and walked past her. This was my home. It belonged to me. And I would not let anyone make me feel otherwise.

Our dining room had not been so full in years. Since my parent's respective deaths, there had only ever been two seats occupied. Today, there was not a single space free. In fact, chairs and stools from other rooms within my home had been brought to the table, creating more places for the men and women of the Crimson Guard to take a seat.

They had disrobed from their red cloaks. If it was not for their conversations, I would have not known they were Crimson Guards at all. Instead of the heavy red material that confirmed their station, they were each dressed in leathers that hugged their athletic builds. Most had blades at their hips, whereas others had placed them heavily on the table. One stout man with a proud beard and a face marked in scars used his short blade to cut into his eggs.

Conversation bloomed throughout the room. Yet I was not the only one who didn't speak. Eamon sat at the head of the table, opposite to me, and watched me the entire time. His food was left untouched, as was mine. Although the eggs looked fluffy and white, with a yolk which popped and spread beautifully over charred bread, I couldn't face a mouthful.

Eamon was my enemy, and I was not about to break bread with him.

I allowed my mind to slip to that of Calix. It felt good to let him occupy my mind whilst in Eamon's company. The betrayal of it gave me a sense of confidence I would need to get me through this. I had just over a day to get the answers I required before Calix came for me. It was my fuel. I refused to leave Eamon again without knowing where Auriol and Silas were being kept.

Perhaps a part of Eamon's vindictive nature had slipped into me as a tithe for the pain I had given him in the bathroom last night. Whatever had dampened my fear of him was welcomed.

The chair screamed across the floor as I stood abruptly from the table. All around me, the conversation faded into silence. Every head turned to look at me, each expression one of dislike. I picked up my glass of freshly pressed apple juice and lifted it. "If I may, I would like for us to each raise our glasses in a toast."

My smile faltered when not a single one of the Crimson Guard followed my request. Instead, they glared at me as though I was the stranger in their home.

Swallowing hard, I continued, "It has been many years since I have seen so many faces in this room. My father would smile down on us now if he knew the Crimson Guard shared our—"

The laughing began before I could even finish my sentence. Not a single person around the table kept their composure. Even Eamon roared with a bark that shook the chandelier above us.

Slowly, my husband stood, clapping his hands with

an uncomfortably prolonged rhythm. "Sit down, Rhory, before you make yourself look even more a fool."

My knees wobbled, but I locked them in place. I refused to be shunned in my own home, before the very people that belonged to me. Not him, me. Although my cheeks burned, and my face likely turned a red richer than the cloaks these men and women wore, I stood firm.

"I have not finished," I snapped, grasping onto the confidence which burned through me, not wishing to let it go.

The pale liquid in my glass shook with my hand, but I refused to lower it.

Then Eamon lifted his glass.

"Then allow me to offer a toast of my own," Eamon responded, staring directly through me. His lip curled into a faint snarl as his eyes sang with the memory of the night before. The pain I had forced into him had faded. In fact, he looked more rejuvenated than he had when I saw him waiting for me on the front step of this house.

"I am confident Rhory needs no introduction." Eamon leaned down to the woman close at his side and shared a smile that screamed of secrets. She was the same person who collected me from my room. Her hair was as red as mine, her face as equally freckled. It seemed Eamon had a type, which made me wonder if Calix's suggestion that something had occurred between Silas and Eamon was true. "What do you think? Should I include Rhory in on our little secret?"

My blood turned cold as he looked back at me.

"Can he be trusted, sire?" The woman tilted her head, brown eyes glowing with an emotion that stung at my chest.

"Does it matter if he cannot?" Eamon replied. "He isn't going anywhere, and if he does it will be over far before then."

The room laughed again, each nodding in agreement with Eamon's comment.

I lifted my chin, trying to force some confidence into my expression. Eamon acknowledged the silent thoughts that passed through my mind.

"Rhory, there are no Crimson Guards in this house."

I looked across the table, gesturing to the crowd who watched with faces of glee and humour. "Then who sits at my father's table, if not his people?" I asked, voice faltering enough for Eamon to notice.

It was as if the entire room faded away, and it was only Eamon and I left.

"My people," Eamon corrected. "These are mine."

"What are you saying, *husband*?" I spat the title, using it as a weapon, much like he had used it against me.

Eamon tutted, smacking his tongue to the roof of his mouth. He moved from around the table with steady grace and walked the length of the room towards me. "Something you said to me last night… it stuck with me. I need you. It was true, at first. I needed you, but that is no longer true. Not in the sense which I imagine you believe, or have been *told* to believe."

I sat down as his proximity overwhelmed me. Eamon stopped prowling as he reached the back of my chair. His hand gripped the wood and squeezed, causing it to creak beneath his strong hold.

"The Crimson Guard belong to you because *I* belong to you," I hissed through gritted teeth. "Without me, you have nothing. Am I wrong?"

"Oh, no. You are not wrong." He swept his hands to his sides as though he were an actor, and the room was his stage. The men and women audibly reacted, playing their part as his doting crowd. "The Crimson Guard are mine as long as you are alive. But I no longer have a need for the Crimson Guard. I have something better, something stronger. Which means you, darling husband, have lost your importance to me."

Horror cut through me. Eamon brought his head down to my ear and sniffed. The sound shocked me into a trancelike state.

As though reading my mind, he whispered something into my ear, "Do not worry, I won't kill you. You are safe from that at least…"

There was something unfinished about his comment.

I stood again, forcing Eamon back with my sudden movement. The raw skin of my back screamed with agony as I stepped from my chair and tried to move towards the room's door. But I was stopped when two bodies pressed in behind me. I'd turned too late; two men blocked me from reaching the door.

"If I am safe, then you will let me leave this room."

Eamon pouted, his sharp brows pulling down over his vivid eyes. "Do you not want me to introduce you to our new family?"

I wished to wrap my fingers around Eamon and pour all my dark emotions into him. "What I wish is to return to my room."

"You were not always so spoiled, brat."

"I would say the same for you, but I cannot remember what you were—"

"Ah, so you know." Eamon smiled broadly. "But how much did he tell you?"

I tried to step in close to Eamon but was stopped by rough hands on my shoulders.

"What you are looking at, Rhory, are the saviours the Crimson Guard had hoped to be," Eamon said. "I couldn't have them, not completely, so I've made a new legion of my own. One that will do as I bid, one who shares my vision of a world we deserve. And together," Eamon raised his glass higher, enjoying himself as he watched his followers cause me pain before him, "We will purify the world and return it to the way it should have always been." He believed every word he said aloud. His eyes were alive as he preached his sermon to the room and his followers reacted by slamming their fists down on the table whilst stomping feet beneath it.

"And how do you believe you'll accomplish that?"

His expression hardened. Eamon's smile dropped until his lips were pinched into a thin, taut line. "What I care about is the lives of mortals. The living has suffered beneath the rule of the dead for long enough. It is time we take back what was ours to begin with."

"Then release Auriol and Silas. If you care for the living, you will not hold them hostage."

"Hostage?" Eamon repeated, eyes wide in shock. The room murmured in quiet words and giggles. "What other poisonous lies has he fed you?"

"Calix," I said his name aloud. It was clear the act I had returned home with was useless. If Eamon had bought it at first, that was long gone. There was no need to keep up pretences now.

"He told me the truth." I leaned in as close to Eamon as the rough hands allowed and whispered the final words into his ear. "He told me everything."

"Is that so?" he replied. "Then, if you know everything as you say, you know the truth of what became of your mother?"

"What truth is this?"

"How Calix slaughtered Ana in his madness and jealousy?"

"You lying cunt..." I breathed, laughing at the absurdity of his words. "Are you so desperate to keep me beneath your thumb that you would allude to such..."

Eamon's expression did not crack or waver. "Oh, so he didn't tell you everything."

The ground fell away from me. A haze passed over the room, shrouding my vision and deafening my ears. It was as though a sea had washed over me. Violent hands dragged me down into the dark depths of Eamon's words.

"Here," Eamon said, offering his remaining hand to me. "If you care to find the truth, let me repeat it to you again so you can feel it."

I glanced at his hand as though it were a strange thing. Blinking back tears, I couldn't move my arm even if I wished to. I knew Eamon offered for me to use my powers on him, but I didn't dare. He lowered his hand to his side and sighed, as though it pained him to tell me. Although his voice was heavy with sadness, his eyes glowed with enjoyment.

He loved every moment of this.

"If you do not believe the truth from me, then perhaps you will believe it from someone else." Eamon shot a look at the room and every single person in it stood. Soon enough, the walls echoed with heavy footfalls as it emptied, all but the nameless woman Eamon had shared his prolonged look with.

"If you do not wish to believe the words from my mouth, then perhaps you would like to hear it from Auriol?" Eamon asked, gesturing for the open door. "I am sure she will gladly share the truth with you."

"Auriol," I mouthed her name. "She is here?"

Eamon's brows pinched downwards in the centre. His frown was the most genuine thing about him. "Where else would she be?"

I couldn't answer him.

Eamon offered me a final, pitiful smile and then turned his back on me. He left the room, and the two men holding me made sure I followed. Without them, I wouldn't have moved an inch.

There was nothing I could think about as I was led out of the dining room and up the stairs towards the left side of our home, an area Eamon had banned me from entering, the part of the house which had once belonged to my father. Suddenly, we stood before a door I had not seen open since Eamon had Father moved to St Myrinn's Infirmary.

"Protecting you from the truth has been a great struggle," Eamon said as he retrieved a brass key out of his breast pocket. "I should have given up long ago."

"I don't believe you," I murmured. A numb wave rolled through my body, leaving no inch spared. "I won't. All you have done, all you do, is lie."

"Don't, or can't?" Eamon asked as he slipped the key into the ancient brass lock and turned. The dull click reverberated through me as the door was pushed open.

"I will let you discover the truth yourself," Eamon said, leaning in and pressing a cold kiss to my cheek. I didn't have the energy to cringe away, not as I faced the room I had not seen for a long time. My eyes fell first on the ancient woman slumped in a wheeled chair in the centre, her frail body draped in woollen blankets and thick silver chains. "When you are finished, I will wait here to welcome you back."

I couldn't move a muscle, not because I was weak, but because I feared what I would discover once I stepped into the room before me.

"He wouldn't do it to me…" I murmured, mind fixed solely on Calix. Even the thought of him murdering my mother was a ridiculous concept. It was laughable to even suggest it as the truth.

"Sometimes," Eamon said, "The truth is not always the freedom you believe it will be. Go claim it. See that you will not find the solace you expect. Rhory, I know you see me as a monster, but I am merely a product of what the world has made me. We—even those you loved most—are monsters. We all are."

T he door clicked shut at my back. It was not a loud sound, but I flinched regardless. Anxiety stabbed its talons into the top of my spine and dragged itself downwards as I took in the situation before me.

It was the stale smell that slammed into me first. The musk was so thick in the air that I fought the urge to gag as it wormed its way down my throat. It was the scent that came with a room being refused fresh air for years. Dust had claimed Father's study. Unable to remove my eyes from the slumped form of Auriol, I waited for the turn of a key and the click of a lock. It didn't come. I held my breath as I listened out for Eamon's muffled voice. He was whispering to the woman, and I couldn't make out a word. Soon enough, they had both faded away into the house, leaving me in the almost quiet.

Auriol showed no signs that she recognised my

arrival. Her head had lolled to the side, resting upon her shoulder at an ungodly angle. The sour tang of her breath came out of her parted mouth, and her lips were crusted with dried spit.

She was illuminated by a single bright strip of daylight that cut through the gap within the heavy curtains. It fell perfectly upon her, ensuring her terrible state was proudly put on display; without it, I would have believed her dead. Only as I stepped towards her, tiptoeing cautiously across creaking floorboards, could I see the slight rise and fall of her chest. Relief flooded through me, regardless of the horrible rattling sound that spluttered from within her chest.

"Auriol," I mumbled. My hands shook with the desire to tug the chains from her until I saw they had been bolted into the wooden planked floor beneath her chair. It reminded me of when I found Calix, locked within a room in a web of chains. This was no different, except her chains were layered with blankets across her ancient and frail body.

Her mouth moved. She said a single word through a rasped exhale. At first, I didn't make it out, until she said it again. "Arlo…"

I knelt before her and reached out for her hand which waited upon her lap. Her skin was sickly warm.

"It's Rhory," I corrected. "I'm here."

It was a natural response for my power to rear its presence in moments like this. I couldn't count how many times I had spent with the old and suffering. Even during father's last days, I took away his discomfort and replaced it with something softer. Lighter.

As the golden glow of my gift shone across her wrinkled face, I caught the flutter of her eyes. Auriol was not in pain. Not exactly. The feeling I took from her was one of deep exhaustion, the type that worked its way into one's bones like woodlice to walls. Except there was nothing natural about this feeling. It was forced. As I took it in, easing the feeling from the old woman, I couldn't help but feel poisoned by it. Drugged or drunk. My mind felt as soft as cotton.

"Let go of me," Auriol demanded. Thin fingers gripped my wrist and pushed me away. As we broke contact there was a faint ringing in my ears.

Auriol was alert now. Her mismatched eyes were wide with the wisps of silver brows furrowed over them. I fell back from her chair and landed hard on my ass. A dull ache thrummed around my head. I lifted my fingers to my temple and exhaled a long groan.

"Wolfsbane," Auriol confirmed, her voice rough as though something filled her throat. "No matter the food they present me, or the drink they force down my throat, it's laced with the herb."

It took a few deep breaths for the heavy sensation to fade; all the while I held her stare, as she held mine.

"Rhory, I am disappointed to see you before me," Auriol said, her voice no longer sounding as if two people spoke at slight intervals from each other. Her words were clear as they were honest.

"As am I," I replied, sensing the drunk sensation

fading slowly from my body. As it did, I was reminded with the single burning question I had to ask her. But, no matter how my mind replayed what Eamon had said, I couldn't find the words to speak it aloud.

"Auriol," I said quietly, "Tell me it is not true."

Her mismatched eyes darkened. If it was not for the chains across her lap, she might have leaned forward and grasped my face in a motherly way.

"Dearest," she murmured, her voice strained and tired. "I am going to need a more specific question if you are hoping for me to answer you."

"Did…" I gathered myself with a breath. "Is my mother dead because Calix killed her?"

Auriol hardly flinched, let alone blinked. Instead, her eyes widened, and the corners of her thin lips pulled downwards. My heart dropped too as she lowered her gaze from mine, unable to hold it any longer.

"No," I breathed, my skin itching with disbelief as I read the answer in her widening eyes.

"I do not know," Auriol said quickly. "Eamon has a sure way of getting into someone's head. Do you know, even when your father's mind was being gripped by his debilitating sickness, he had his suspicions about Eamon?"

My body ached as I pushed myself to standing. Skin still raw from the night prior, I was glad for the discomfort; it helped me focus. "What do you mean? Please, Auriol. You must tell me the truth. I need to know, hell I deserve to know!"

"I cannot." When Auriol looked at me, it was not

with her usual frown. Sadness aged her face. It caused her eyes to droop and her wrinkles to deepen. "I wish I could be the one to vouch for my grandson's innocence, or guilt, but I cannot."

"Why!?" I said, practically begging. "Eamon told me Calix killed her. The marks... the damage her body endured." As I inhaled sharply, my mind was full of the memories. Torn limbs. Deep marks etched into flesh. Shattered bones. I didn't dare close my eyes again for fear of being lost to the horror forever. "I saw her. There were marks left on her body, the same as what Calix has on his chest. We both know no human would have the strength to cause such damage, and no vampire would leave so much blood..."

Auriol tempted to reach for me, but the chains restrained her from only being able to lift her hand an inch from her lap. Frustration whipped across her face with a snarl. "There are only two people who know the truth of that night," she said. "In the years since your mother's murder, I questioned Calix. He has never given me an answer."

"And who is the other?"

Auriol winced as she said the name, "Silas."

The world went oddly still.

"Could he have done it?" A strange, warped sense of hope filled me. Was it someone else who broke my world apart?

She shook her head, not in refusal, but because she didn't have the answers I sought.

I dropped my chin to my chest, feeling a wave of exhaustion rush over me.

"It happened the night of your wedding to Eamon," Auriol said suddenly, telling me something I already knew. "We had each been invited. Some twisted joke Eamon played on Calix, knowing your history. The Grey's and the Coleman's have been allies for many years, so it was not strange for us to be invited, but Calix understood the message behind it. It was that night when Silas was taken from us. I refused the invite, not wishing to see a union between you and Eamon, knowing your father's lack of confidence in it. Perhaps if I had, I would have been able to prevent whatever had happened that night."

I buried my face in my hands, head thumping as though thunder ruled within it. Everyone knew my past but me. Understanding that fact caused me such vicious pain.

"Who did this to me!?" I cried out, slapping my hand against the side of my head as though it would loosen the buried memories and return them to me.

"Rhory," Auriol sang, her tone motherly and soft. "Rhory. Tell me why you are here and not leagues away."

"I came back to find you, and Silas."

"You should have left us," Auriol said, matter-of-factly. "What of Calix? Does Eamon have him?"

"No," I replied, head raw from my own self destruction.

Auriol exhaled, sagging forward in her chair with

relief. "Good. That is good. And it is important he does not come."

"He will…" I hissed. "Calix will come for me by tomorrow evening, that's if I don't summon him with a candle in my window before then."

Auriol's face opened up in fury, eyes widening and mouth gasping. If the chains were not binding her, she would have thrown her body out of the chair just to stifle me. "That cannot happen. Do you hear me, Rhory? Calix must stay far away. There is nothing good waiting for him here."

Even without touching her, Auriol's panic almost floored me. "It is not safe. For you. For him."

"Eamon is going to kill me," I said, breathless. "He said as much, in his way. He no longer needs me."

Lightning coursed over my body, raising every hair across my arms.

"I hope not." It was all she said. Even I could recognise that there was no comfort in her words. "Do you know it was in this very room your father altered his will? I was here as witness as he wrote in the covenant, tying your life to Eamon's command of the Crimson Guard. It happened days before your wedding to Eamon. An engagement most did not expect, but to your father, you seemed joyful and in your right mind. Which, of course, you were. But by then, your mind was an altered version, one to benefit your sudden union with Eamon. Your father had his concerns over Eamon's intentions, but you were the happiest he had seen you. He didn't wish to think the worst, but he was always a careful and well thought out man… even when his own mind had deteriorated over the years. He may not have known himself, but he knew you."

My eyes pricked with tears, and the dull thud in my skull worsened. As Auriol spoke, I pressed the heels of my hands into my eyes and focused on steadying my breathing. In the dark, I could almost make out the scenes she described, played out in colour and sound.

"You knew," I said. "You knew about Calix and I."

"I did," Auriol replied. Hearing her say it aloud was strange. It confirmed what I was trying to convince myself was the truth. But in turn, it frustrated me more.

"Did you not think to tell my father what had happened to me? That my mind had been tampered with, poisoned with witchcraft, so my reality was actually not mine at all?" When I dropped my palms from my eyes, they came back slick with tears, silent droplets that were without sobs. They poured from my eyes as though the heavens had opened and unleashed a storm.

"At that point, it was not clear as to what had been done to you."

"And when did it become clear? When did you work out what Eamon had done to me, just to get close enough to marry me and take the Crimson Guard as his own?" I couldn't hide the fury from my voice. Likely, the entire building and its occupants could hear me shout. Not that I cared. Let them hear. Let Eamon hear me, for it was only a matter of moments before I found him and demanded to be fixed, no matter the cost.

"I understand you are in pain, but the answers you

think you seek will only hurt further. What matters now is that Eamon no longer requires the Crimson Guard. Which means he no longer requires you. It is only by the grace of his humanity that he's kept you alive long enough for you to talk to me."

"And what grace would that be?" I asked, gazing at the old woman through a blur of tears.

"I am afraid I cannot answer that either." The chains across Auriol's lap shuffled as she tried to right herself. "Rhory, I need to ask this of you. Forget about this, all of it. Get out of this house, find Calix, and convince him to do the same. Leave Darkmourn."

I blinked, confusion riling through me. "Do you truly believe we can forget about this? How can I possibly move on, knowing the hurt and danger Eamon poses to you, to Silas? To everyone?"

"But you could," she said, wincing slightly at the weight pressed across her. "Do not be ashamed to admit it."

"If you have given up, what about Silas? All of this is because you wanted him back. Surely we cannot just turn our back on—"

It was not Auriol's words which interrupted me but the look on her face. Her mask of age deepened before me; even her eyes seemed to glaze with a feral sadness that aged her by years.

"I was wrong," Auriol muttered, voice broken. "So very wrong."

I reached forward for her. "About what?"

Slowly, she found my eyes again. The whites of hers

had stained a scarlet red and she seemed to shake as though a cold chill flooded the room. "He is…"

A knock sounded at the door behind us. Three loud raps of knuckles to wood, each with prolonged gaps of time between one another.

Silence followed. My eyes locked on the brass knob of the door, waiting for it to turn and open. It didn't. When the knock came again, it was more a ferocious bang. It made me jump to my feet and call out in reply, "Yes?"

There was nothing, no reply but the string of tense silence.

"I'm tired," Auriol groaned from behind me, "Let him in so I can be put to rest."

There was no ignoring her exhaustion as she spoke. Unable to follow my body's urge to keep still, I paced across the room and reached for the door just as another knock came again. It was louder and faster. Impatient. Urged by it, I pulled the door open.

Shock blazed across my mind. It kept me immobile as I regarded the man before me.

"Have you finished with my grandmother?" the man said with a forced smile.

I blinked hard, unable to make sense of what I had witnessed. It was as if Calix stood before me. Bright honey eyes full of life, a proud square jaw with bones chiselled from stone. His hair was shaved close to the scalp, not swept and lustrous as I last saw it. He wore a burnt brown cloak pinned across his neck, the colour of spoiled blood and rust.

But this couldn't be Calix…

He was thinner and taller. This person's skin did not have a glow but looked as pale and colourless as a corpse. Drained. The dark circles beneath his gaunt eyes looked more like old bruises than tiredness.

"Excuse me," he hissed through gritted yellowed teeth.

My body moved without thinking. I stepped aside as the man strode past me, focused solely on the old woman trapped in her chair. He had a slight limp in his gait. It caused the china pot and cup on the tray to clink together as he crossed the room.

I shifted my attention from the man to Auriol. Her face had morphed into a snarl. She bared her teeth, wide eyes not daring to blink as she studied the man setting the tray down and pulling up a stool beside her.

It was as though he just remembered I still watched from the doorway because he snapped his attention to me and barked, "Get out."

No matter the fear his command gave me, I still could not move. It was not until Auriol spoke, her voice as soft as it had been the first time I had met her, "Rhory, would you be so kind to leave me with my grandson? Silas and I have much to catch up on."

*Silas.* His name repeated in my mind, as though it was both familiar and unfamiliar. How could he possibly be here, before me? It made little sense. Eamon's supposed captive, walking freely in my home. But, Silas *was* here, in this room, dressed and somewhat well. And very much alive.

He glared at me like a starved feral hound would while it guarded a bowl of rich cooked meat. Unable to hold his attention, I scampered from the room, wishing to put distance between us and the hateful gaze he regarded me with.

## ❧ 35 ❧

I had to find Eamon. It was all I could think of as I left Auriol and Silas, closing the door on the impossible scene. Never had I felt the desire to run towards my husband, until now. Now I needed him with a burning need which only he could quench.

My mind still reeled on having seen Silas. So much so, I didn't fully contemplate why the house was so... empty. Whereas the rooms and hallways had been filled with men and women, I couldn't find a single soul.

It was not until I made it down into the foyer, through the dining hall, and into the kitchen that I heard the horrifying sounds. I stopped, shocked at first, as I surveyed the empty rooms whilst my hearing stretched out for the sound. It took a moment to register what I heard, were muffled by layers of stone and mortar, but loud enough for me to hear. Screams. Blood-curdling screams which set my soul aflame. So powerful that the ground beneath my feet vibrated with them.

I followed the shrieks into the pantry and down the curving steps towards the dank room beneath. Mildred used to refer to the cellar as her castle of curiosities. Once filled with hanging meats, vegetables in towering crates and a wall of bottled wine and liquor, it was now full of a sea of humans.

Silas was not the only one to wear a cloak of russet brown. They all did. I looked across the room stuffed full of humans and found they were all adorned with an identical cloak. It had a similar design to the red cloaks I had grown used to the Crimson Guard wearing, except the noticeable difference was its colour. These were the shade of dried, old blood.

I pushed my way through the wall of bodies. Grunts and displeased mumbles followed me, but I didn't care. Nothing mattered beside the skull-piercing screams which lit the room in a blaze far greater than any burning sconces could reach.

My mind revealed to me who it was that cried out. I refused to believe it, but there was something so familiar which sickened me.

Eamon was in the centre of the crowd. I caught a flash of his bright, sky-blue eyes staring down at someone on the floor before him. They were wide. Feral. It wasn't until I forced myself to the front of the mob, and the large open space in the heart of it opened up, that my worst fear was confirmed as truth.

"Millicent!" I shouted so loud my throat burned

with her name. Desperation to reach her fuelled me. It dampened the pain in my back and the confusion rioting in my mind.

The vampire was sprawled out on the ground. Her shirt had been torn, exposing the raw skin of her back. It was smeared with blood, but I couldn't see any marks. Her wounds had healed, but the evidence was there. And the sharp tipped whip Eamon had curled in his fist explained the blood. There was an abundance of it.

No one stopped me as I threw myself towards her. She didn't seem to notice my arrival either, not at first.

"I've got you," I cried out, covering her body with mine. She felt so small beneath me. If it was not for the violent shivering that overcame her, I would have believed she was already dead.

"Get away from it," Eamon growled, towering above me. His face screwed in a scowl. Sweat dripped down the side of his jaw and plastered the dark-black hair across his forehead. As I regarded him, I was repulsed by the splash of blood on his cheek. It was the same dark gore that smudged my chest; it covered the silver-tipped end of the whip and coated Eamon's knuckles.

"You're a monster!" I screamed, spitting and hissing like a cat. "She doesn't deserve this."

Eamon didn't look surprised at my reaction. Instead, he pulled a face, one a displeased parent gave a child who bothered them. I too was vaguely aware of his crowd watching, equally pissed off that I had ruined their show.

Eamon simply replied, "She is a vampire." As though that was a good enough reason for such a crime.

"No, Eamon. This is not what you stand for! You have sworn yourself to protect all. That was your pledge to the Crimson Guard and your promise to the people of Darkmourn. What crimes are you punishing her for… Eamon, tell me!"

He inhaled deeply, lips quivering as they parted, and he answered, "Existing."

Millicent groaned beneath me. I felt her weight shift, but I refused to move off of her. If I did, I couldn't bear the thought of him bringing down the whip on her. I would rather have taken it.

"I won't let you do this," I said, tears of fury and sorrow cutting down my face.

I flinched as Eamon lifted the whip. He smiled, releasing a sharp tutting sound from his tongue. "How noble. You truly do take after your father. Shame, I always preferred your mother's company."

The sharp lash of the whip never came. I refused to look away. Holding Eamon's gaze in contest was my form of defiance. To my surprise, he handed over the weapon to someone in the crowd.

Once his only hand was free, Eamon brushed it down over his dark trousers, smudging Millicent's blood from his fingers.

"Perhaps we shall take this conversation elsewhere?" he asked as he knelt before me, pity tugging down his face.

My jaw ached from the tension. It was a surprise my

teeth did not completely shatter beneath the force as I gritted them together.

"I am not leaving her," I spat.

"No?" Eamon muttered, looking over my head to his throng of watching humans. "Then we will have this conversation with an audience."

"There is nothing I have to say," I said, ready to reach out and grab him. If I could just grasp a slither of his skin, I could immobilise him with some haunting emotions. Gods knows I harboured enough of them. Millicent had warned me never to take her emotions, but I felt her pain, even without the use of my power. I could transfer it into Eamon, and ruin him with it. But what of the crowd? There was thirty, perhaps close to forty, of Eamon's brown-cloaked followers watching. I could never fight my way out, but I would be damned to try.

"Eamon, you do not want to do this."

He sighed. "Believe me, it is all I have ever wanted to do. There is not an ounce of compassion I have for such monsters. Rhory, I don't have the energy to convince you as to why this is the right thing to do…"

"Torturing her is not the right thing to do," I growled as my body boiled over with hate for this man.

Eamon leaned in close until the waft of lavender with the undertones of blood washed over me. "You have no idea what these monsters took from me. No idea what I was forced to watch, all because the monsters require blood to survive."

A tension thrummed through the crowd. It was a ripple of muted voices, each in agreement with Eamon.

"Is that why you kept Silas alive all this time? Does your hate only extend to vampires?"

"Kept Silas alive?" Eamon repeated. "What did you expect to find? His supposed abduction is just another lie Calix fed you. You see, Rhory, being with me will reveal all sorts of truths."

Millicent whimpered beneath me. She sounded like a child, calling out for a mother who was long dead.

"If you wish to be in the deal of truths, then do so," I said. "Tell me, all of it."

Eamon reached out his blood-stained fingers and drew them towards my face. I pulled away before he could touch me. His hand hovered in the air for a moment before he lowered it, defeated. It was the first time he had done that before. If he had wanted to touch me, he would have. Something had changed.

"Rhory, I am going to save the world." His words shocked me to the very core.

"You are delusional."

"Perhaps I am, but that doesn't take away from what I am going to do."

"Save it from what?" I asked, spitting. "Because the only monster I see is you. Eamon, the hate that feds you will be your demise."

Eamon's eyes flickered to the hunched form I separated him from. As he looked at me, his scowl twisted into something feral. "Those creatures have taken enough from us."

"Yet you are sworn to protect them," I snapped before the crowd erupted in laughter that drowned me out.

"I have sworn many things, partaken in many vows, except there is only one that matters to me. The vow I made myself as I was forced to hide beneath the floorboards of my childhood home while my parent's blood splashed across my face, drenching me from head to foot. Days, that is how long your precious Crimson Guard took to save me. Days. And those monsters were given the time to luxuriate in my parent's blood, feast and escape without punishment. Every vampire I slay is another vampire closer to those who destroyed my life. It is worth it."

I had never seen Eamon cry before. Never did I believe he even had such a capability of that emotion. Until now. Now, his eyes filled with defiant tears as he spoke. I watched his restraint as he refused to blink and release them.

"You told me your parents died from a sickness," I said, unpacking yet another mistruth from him.

"And they did." Eamon jabbed a finger towards Millicent. I lowered myself over her further, feeling the press of her cold, still body as a constant beneath me. "They are a sickness. A disease that started and spread. It ruined our world for years, broke families apart and sent the humans to live behind walls. Suddenly, we were expected to live beside them. To break bread and share wine, never knowing if they will turn on us just for the need to feed."

I saw hate in his eyes, it oozed from him. And the sentiment behind each word… the crowd who watched agreed wholeheartedly.

"Why did you join the Crimson Guard?" I asked. "Why go through all those lengths to join a force that is supposed to protect all kinds? Living and dead, when you only ever favoured one?"

"Because they failed me. Do you know what the Crimson Guard, what your father did, when they found me covered in my parent's blood, hiding beneath floorboards, days after vampires broke into my home and destroyed my life?" Eamon's entire body trembled as he spoke. "Tell me!"

I flinched back at his sudden display of anger.

"Nothing," he answered for me. "The Crimson Guard did nothing. Your father did nothing. They let my parent's murderers roam free and closed the investigation when the perpetrators were not found. So, I knew I had to save myself if no one else would. No matter what it would take, I would get penance for what *they* took from me. Tell me, dear husband, does that make me a terrible person? To hunt the *monsters* of this world, to right their wrongs?"

I took my time to answer, mostly because I couldn't find the right words. The man before me was broken and twisted. He was a monster created by his experiences. "What makes a monster? Is it their actions that justify such a title? Because, if so, you would see one every time you look in a mirror, *husband*."

Eamon regarded me with honest disappointment.

He exhaled a breath, rocked back on his heels and stood. Still, I refused to move from Millicent who had gone so terribly still beneath me.

"I *am* going to save this world," Eamon repeated his earlier statement, as though saying it again would convince me.

"And how do you suppose you are going to do that?" I asked.

"I am going to destroy them," Eamon said. "All of them. It is about time Darkmourn returns to its former glory. Where the living rule, and the dead are no more than forgotten bodies buried beneath the ground."

It was my turn to laugh. It came out of me, echoing across the crowd.

Eamon winced, as though my reaction stabbed him in the chest. He soon righted himself, steeling his expression and glaring down at me. "Do not underestimate a desperate man. He would do anything to get what he wants. *Anything.*"

We both knew what he referred to.

"Does that include having a witch alter my mind to forget my past just so you could marry into my family and steal the Crimson Guard from beneath me?"

Eamon's frown broke into a smile. He flashed teeth as he grinned, looking down at me with the flickering of fire casting monstrous shadows across his face. "Ah, I suppose it does."

"Give. It. Back." The three words broke out of me.

Eamon leaned forward, washing his breath over me. "I'm afraid I do not have the capabilities for that."

I jolted towards him, fuelled by my own desperation and hate. My nails missed his face by inches. Someone from the crowd broke forward and grabbed me with harsh hands, yanking me back. I was torn from Millicent and shoved into a wall of waiting hands who pinched and squeezed until I was completely entrapped in a web of them.

"Return him to his room," Eamon commanded. He flicked his wrist, gesturing for me to be swept away.

"Millicent," I growled. "Millicent, get up!"

The vampire pressed two hands on the ground either side of her and raised herself up enough for me to see her face. Her eyes were burning ruby, her fangs overlapping paled lips. Spittle burst from her mouth as she snarled towards Eamon, who hardly flinched in response.

"Fight," I cried, putting everything I had in my resistance to Eamon's followers. "Fight them, Millicent!"

"Get out of here," she managed, tears of blood tracing down her eyes. "Foolish boy."

Millicent's fight lasted only a moment. Eamon brought down his boot onto her back, knocking her to the ground. The crack of her skull reverberated across the room, followed by her broken cry.

"I would have allowed you to stay and watch," Eamon called out to me as the hands of his followers dragged me back towards the stairs. "To see what becomes of a vampire when bitten by a wolf. But you ruined it, as you always do."

It took a moment for what Eamon had said to register in my mind.

"All these years, and it took Calix to give me what I desired, when Silas refused me. Imagine how deeply Silas hates his brother—especially after the one thing he kept from me was handed to me by Calix, the same man who never wished to save his brother."

Eamon was just about to slip from view when his words finally made sense. My eyes shot from Millicent's unconscious body to Eamon, then around the crowd of his followers who seemed to flood towards her.

"I'm sure I will have the chance to thank Calix myself," Eamon said as the outline of his body shivered. "It was a fair price to pay, my hand for power."

Before my very eyes, Eamon's skin shattered, bursting apart like ash. Shadows coiled outward, dark as a winter's night. My blood ran cold, my mind reeling from the impossibility of what I witnessed. Then, from among the cloud of shadow which engulfed him, came a howl. Then another. And another. Just before the cellar disappeared from view, I watched as the remaining men and women in the room burst into plumes of shadow, replacing their human form for another.

*Wolves.*

They were all wolves.

### ❧ 36 ❧

I listened to their howls, each one clear as day all the way up in my bedroom. The sound rocked the walls, seemingly never-ending. Every soul in Dark-mourn, living and dead, would have heard them. But why would they come looking? Why send for the Crimson Guard, when they were standing sentry before my home stopping anyone from interfering? I was left alone, with nothing but the truth to keep me company. All I could do was sit on my bed and listen to Eamon's wolves as the reality of what it meant settled over me like burning ash.

Eamon had changed. He had become a wolf. When Calix had bitten him, it had mutated him, just as the shadow-hound had with Auriol. I could only make assumptions about how the change occurred, but it certainly explained Millicent's reaction. What I knew as a solid fact was Eamon had truly become the beast he was supposed to hunt.

I picked through the facts, trying to make sense of what was happening. Eamon's wolf form did not look the same as Calix's. Whereas Calix presented like a monster, with long limbs and the remnants of a human shape, Eamon was more similar to a large wolf, one I would have found lurking in the woods beyond Darkmourn.

It was the same with the rest of his followers. *His pack.*

The streets of Darkmourn heard it all. I could see them from my window, looking towards the house with confusion or fear, scuttling off as though the house itself was cursed, and they had to flee it. Beyond my home, the Crimson Guard loitered, but they never came to investigate. Instead, those red cloaked protectors stopped inquisitive beings from coming up to our door.

They were complicit. And whatever Eamon was doing, he no longer cared to hide.

Millicent had stopped screaming, but I couldn't tell if it was hours or mere seconds when the cries of anguish silenced. Her cries of pain and terror echoed in my ears. Although I felt her suffering in every cry, at least I knew she was still alive. Now, I was not so sure. Her silence spoke volumes. I couldn't bear it. I longed to hear her cry out, just to know if she still lived.

My knuckles were bloody, as were my torn palms and bruised fingers. The wooden door to my room was scarred from where I smashed into it, trying to break myself free. Shattered remains of a chair were scattered across the floor before it. Everything I could use to break myself free didn't work. All it did was conjure muffled laughter from those Eamon had stationed on the other side.

I was left staring at the candle in my hands. My last option. Night had fallen upon Darkmourn and all it would take was for me to light it and place it in my window, and Calix would come. For me. He would save me, save Millicent. But then there was the problem of Silas, Eamon, and the wolves. Calix wouldn't stand a chance. Calling for him would only put him in grave danger. No matter how I longed for him, I didn't dare put him in that situation.

There had to be a way out of this. Something I could do to work myself free. It only took one look back to the door and the smashed furniture before it to dwindle my hopes.

I soon heard the familiar rattling of wheels and the stamping of hooves upon the street beyond. Picking myself up, I discarded the candle on the bed and moved for a better look. Beyond the house, lining the streets, were carriages; a row of them stretched for as far as I could see. Crimson Guards moved among the coaches, opening the doors and lowering the steps to allow for someone to exit, or enter them, with ease.

The wall beneath my palm shook as our front door burst open. I jolted back, pulling the velvet curtain over me, enough to obscure me from view, but not completely so I could still watch what was happening.

I recognised Eamon first. The top of his head caught the red glow of the streetlamps. From this viewpoint I could see his black hair had thinned, revealing bald skin beneath. Behind him followed the same red-haired woman that seemed to always be close to his side. I felt nothing as I watched Eamon stop and offer her a hand as he hoisted her into the carriage with him.

Then the rest of his followers joined them. No longer were they in their wolf forms but dressed in finery befitting royalty. Except, unlike the Crimson Guards, who welcomed them and helped them into the carriages, they wore cloaks of russet brown.

My breath caught in my throat as I watched Auriol exit my home. She was being helped down the path by two of Eamon's followers. Her head was bowed, and her legs hardly moved. She was practically dragged into a carriage. I longed to call out for her, but I stopped myself when I caught the flash of silver beneath the blanket across her shoulders. She still wore chains of silver as though it was armour. It was clear Auriol's limping body was riddled with wolfsbane.

Movement from Eamon's carriage snatched my attention. He climbed out and paused. His gaze shifted from the front door as it closed with a bang—the tremor vibrating in the wall beside me—and lifted his chin to my window. His sky-blue eyes pierced through me. I gasped, breath fogging on the glass between us. The red glow of the streetlamps bathed his face in the colour of blood. Eamon smiled up at me, his lips parting in a word which I could make out even without sound.

*Goodbye.*

"Are you enjoying the view?"

My blood ran cold at the voice behind me. I had not heard the door open, but the visitor was not discreet when it was slammed shut again.

Silas stood in my room, his hands clasped over his waist with his head bent slightly at an angle. As I had the first time I'd seen him, it took me a moment to discern him from Calix. They looked so similar, except Calix glowed with health and vitality. Silas looked sickly and pained, as though standing was enough to hurt him. His skin was a strange colour, as though he had not been blessed with sunlight for years. Even the whites of his eyes had a yellow tinge, which matched perfectly with the stains across his teeth. He wore a cloak matching that of Eamon and his followers. It made Silas look smaller as it fell over his narrow shoulders. His shirt and trousers hung around him like a tent, clasped together by a scruffy belt decorated with a bone-carved wolf in the hilt of a blade. Beside it, looped around his belt, was a twine of rope.

"Did... did Eamon deem you unimportant enough to leave you behind tonight?" I asked, hearing the clatter of hooves and the screech of wheels against stone. If I looked over my shoulder, I would have seen the carriages move away.

Silas noted the shift of my eyes to the door he stood before. He clicked his tongue, shaking his head like a displeased parent. "Eamon has asked that I see you to bed. Then I will join him for the evening's celebration."

I swallowed my discomfort and stared directly into his eyes. Calix's eyes glowed like molten gold. Silas's eyes seemed more comparative to the colour of piss. "And do you enjoy obeying the commands of someone who has kept you captive for years?"

"No," Silas replied calmly. "No, I don't." Hope burst in my chest like a breath of fresh air. It was soon suffocated when Silas's smile widened, and he continued, "However, we both know just how… forceful he can be. So, for both our sakes, would you get into bed?"

I couldn't move even if I wanted to. "Why are you helping him?"

Silas pondered the question for a moment, wringing his hands together. "It is not that I am helping him, Rhory, but merely helping myself." He put a finger to his lips as though he didn't want anyone to hear.

"So, this has nothing to do with the fact you are in love with him."

My words hit their mark. Silas rocked back a step, widening his unblinking eyes until every red vein was visible. "Love is fickle. It means little."

"I don't mean to offend you," I said. "Eamon has a way of infecting a person's mind and blinding them. What he has done to you, he did to me. You don't need to do this."

"Yes," Silas snapped. He jolted forward, nostrils flaring. "In fact, I do."

"Calix could save us—" Before I could finish, Silas's entire demeanour cracked. He sprung forward, gripping my upper arm with his hand. I tried to pull back, but he was quicker than me. With a fast tug, I crashed hard into his chest.

"Bed," he hissed, nails breaking into the skin of my arms. "Now."

With a push, I was sent sprawling to the ground. Pain shot up my back from the fall, jarring every bone in my spine.

"Do not think for a moment that Calix would ever wish to save me."

I scrambled back from Silas as he prowled towards me. He never seemed to blink. His eyes were always wide and watching. *Let him watch*; the thought was as hot as it was sharp. Just as Silas leaned down over me, I raised my hands, ready for him. The only bare skin was his hands, neck, and face. It didn't matter what I reached for as long as I touched him.

Light spluttered to life at the tips of my fingers. Silas regarded them with a frown before stepping back.

"Touch me again," I sneered, spit flying out of my lips, "See what happens."

"I am not your enemy, Rhory."

My power brightened. "Then what are you?"

"Someone who would like to see you in bed so he can enjoy his evening. Please, do as I ask." Although his words were calm, I saw a flash of the monster pass behind his eyes. It was brief, but enough to take my breath away.

We regarded one another for a moment. Silas with his hands held before him, and me on the floor with the glow of gold bursting from my palms.

"Stubborn as ever," Silas said, eyes tracing over every inch of me.

"You have no idea," I replied.

"Oh, I do. In fact, I know there is no way you are going to do as I ask. So, if you are willing to get into bed all on your own, I will offer you something you cannot resist."

"There is nothing—*nothing*—you could give me."

"No?" Silas said, narrowing his eyes. "Not even the name of the witch, the very one who fucked around with your mind?"

"You're lying."

"Am I? Get into bed and see."

My body moved with little thought. Silas smiled, knowing he had bested me.

Without completely withdrawing my power, it faded to a faint shimmer. Still, Silas kept back as I stood from the floor. I stepped towards the bed until its frame pressed into the back of my legs. He watched me with such interest as I took a seat on the sheets and shuffled back.

"I don't remember me, but I remember you," Silas said.

I shook my head. "Good for you."

"It is." Disappointment curved his thin pale lips. "The curse is as strong as the witch who cast it. I was rather hoping you would be freed from it when she died, but I gather such power has a life of its own, beyond its caster."

His words immobilised me, enough that I hardly cared as he unlooped the rope from his belt and walked to the foot of the bed.

"She is dead? The one who did this?"

Silas smiled, but it didn't quiet reach his eyes. They looked almost... sad. "Of course, she is. And I am surprised you haven't figured it out yet."

"Name," I said. "I'm on the bed, so tell me her name."

Silas's hands were already on my ankle before I could pull away. He traced his fingertips over my foot so gently it almost tickled. Then, in one swift motion, he looped the rope around my feet, binding them together and tethering them to the frame of the bed.

I pulled hard against it, but the rope pulled tighter. The rub of it over my skin burned. "No... stop!"

"Quiet. You know what happens when we don't listen, and I do not want the evening's festivities to be spoiled by Eamon's wrath if he knows I didn't do as he asked."

I sat up and reached down for the rope to free myself. In a blink, Silas had moved to the head of the bed. His hands gripped my shoulders. With one harsh push, he slammed me back down on the bed, the force so harsh my skull shook with the impact. The mattress was soft, but the slam of my body into it still drove the wind out of me.

There was no chance to fight against Silas as he withdrew another length of rope and tied it around both of my wrists. Before I could have had so much as a chance to scream out, he stretched my arms back and knotted the rope to the bedframe.

"That's better," Silas said, his lips brushing close to

my ear. "So much better. And how the tables turn. It was your darling husband who last tied me to a bed, but I expected a much… happier ending. Instead, he left me tied up for three years, begging me to change him. I refused, because it was the right thing to do, but as always Calix came in and gave him exactly what he wanted. I can't say you'll last as long as I did, but you will appreciate how I felt, even if it is for a brief time."

I pinched my eyes closed, turning my head as far away from him as I could. Struggling only pinched the ropes further into my skin, but I couldn't calm myself. The guttural urge to fight for my life overtook me. When Silas brought his face over mine, all wide eyes and glistening lips grinning, I thrust my skull upwards and into his nose. Bone cracked. I felt the splash of warm blood fall across my face before Silas jolted back with a howl of agony.

"You little cunt!" Silas roared. He had his hand clutched to his face. Blood spilled between his fingers and down his chin, splashing across his brown cloak.

"Go on," I screamed over his cries of pain. "Run back to your master like the good little pup you are!"

I could taste his blood in my mouth. It didn't disgust me as I thought it would. Not even the dull ache across my skull from the impact bothered me. I revelled in watching him suffer.

Silas paced the room, thrashing himself around as though he was in the grips of a tantrum. I felt the feral urge to laugh at him. But my adrenaline quickly faded from a roar to a dull whisper.

"Do you know?" Silas said, his teeth stained red with blood. "I was going to defy Eamon tonight. For the first time, I was going to refuse him something. Now, I am not so sure."

Silas jolted forward. His hand shot towards me, but no impact came. Where I thought he was going to strike me, he didn't. Instead, he picked up the candle I had forgotten I'd left on the bed.

"I heard you," Silas said, returning to his pacing. "I heard what you said to my grandmother."

He moved towards a wall lamp and lifted the candle to the flame. The wick caught instantly. Silas didn't bother looking at me again. His gaze was focused back on the windows.

"How quick do you think my brother will be?" Silas asked, still refusing to look at me while all I could do was look at him.

I continued my struggle until my wrists and ankles rubbed raw against the rope. The pain mattered little. All I focused on was getting free, whilst I watched Silas with unwavering intent.

"Do not trust his word, Rhory. Anything that comes out of Calix's mouth is fabricated. He lies with ease. Calix has known, all these years, where Eamon had kept me. Yet all this time, he has played into Auriol's wishes to save me. Except he lied to her. He pretended like he had no clue where I was when he did."

Silas moved across the room, his broken nose already drying.

"Lies," I spat. "Calix has only ever wanted to see you returned home. He would do anything to—"

"For the sake of your life," Silas growled, snapping his head towards me. He stood before the window, burning candle in hand. I knew in that moment what he had heard me reveal to Auriol. That if I placed a candle in the window, Calix would come for me. "I suggest you stop. Stop preaching lies for I have no patience to listen to them."

Silas lowered the candle and placed it on the floor. It was just out of view from the window. At first, I felt relief, then disappointment. Calix would never see the light from the candle's position on the floor.

"You know my power," I said. "If anyone can know the difference between a lie and truth, it is me. I have felt Calix, and I know what he has wanted, and it has always been to save you."

Silas exhaled a long breath from his nose. The lacklustre yellow of his eyes stood out against the rust brown of his drying blood. "Okay, then do something for me. When he comes for you, and he will, I want you to ask him a question." Silas drew the curtain closed, covering the window completely. Straining my neck up as far as the bindings allowed, I saw the bottom of the material flirt with the open flame of the candle. There was hardly any space between both.

Silas moved for the door, not taking his eyes off me as he spoke. "Touch him, look into his eyes, feel his truth when you ask him what the reason was behind him leaving me with Eamon. Was it because he didn't know where I was being held? Or…"

I could hardly breathe as Silas opened the door.

"Or was it because I am the only one who knew that he had your mother murdered? That he killed her."

The world seemed to fall away from me. "No… I don't believe you."

"Did you hope I did it? Not that it would matter if you did. It is clear you would only care to hear the answer from Calix himself. So, do it… when he comes, ask him yourself. Ask him why he murdered your mother in cold blood. He never wanted to save me; he simply hoped his dark secret would die with me."

"Fuck you!" I screamed. The volume of my cry was muffled beneath the noise in my head.

"What a mouth you have," Silas said, amusement brightening his face. He glanced a final time towards the candle beneath the curtains and smiled. "You know, Eamon wanted your death to look natural. An accident. A candle misplaced. No questions asked. Except Eamon does not account for fighters, he never has. And I think you are a fighter, Rhory. We will just need to see if Calix comes and saves you, or if you are ready to save yourself for once."

## ❧ 37 ❧

The fire caught quickly. I watched, the muscles in my neck screaming, as the flame sparked on the hem of the curtains and licked upwards until the window was ablaze in flame. I was transfixed by the hunger of the fire, so much so that the ceiling of the room was thick with dark clouds of smoke before I even attempted to break free.

My wrists burned as I yanked hard against the rope. Circlets of bloody skin wrapped around my ankles, making my foot slick and wet. But no matter how hard I fought the bindings only seemed to tighten.

"Help!" I screamed, my frustration as hot as the fire that scorched the room.

The glass of the windows cracked against the heat. Wood spat and hissed as the flames soon spread across the wall, charring everything black in its wake.

I kicked out at the wooden frame of the bed, hoping the force would break it so I could work myself free. My

383

attempts were useless. Pointless. My eyes streamed with tears, stinging from the smoke that desired to choke me. Its opaque fingers infiltrated my nose and mouth until I felt the smoke with every inhale.

If the fire didn't kill me, the smoke would.

I fought until my wrists and ankles were bloody, and pain no longer mattered. Something Silas had said about me saving myself was all that I could focus on. If I didn't swear as I screamed, I would have called for Calix. But I didn't know him anymore. Perhaps I never did. I feared he would come, and I would be forced to face what Silas had suggested. That Calix had killed my mother. He was the monster that tore her into pieces and left her for dead.

Quickly, the fire ate away towards me. Snakes of it slithered across the floor, spreading up reading chairs and melting the portraits on my walls.

"Rhory!"

My name was so clear that it dwarfed the noise of the fire's roar of starvation.

"Rhory!"

It was closer now.

I turned my head towards the door just as it burst open. It was not knocked in but ripped from the hinges on the other side and thrown into the hallway beyond.

Calix stood in the doorway, the crook of his arm held over his nose. It was hard to see him as my eyes blurred with tears, nor could I focus as the coughing begun. The hacks rocked my chest, each as powerful as the one before. My lungs bellowed in agony. I couldn't help but take in the breaths my lungs cried out for, but each time only encouraged more of the smoke to enter. I welcomed it in, to drown me from the inside out.

"I've got you," Calix said, his voice closer now. "Little Red, I have you."

I hadn't realised I had closed my eyes until the closeness of his voice surprised me. Part of me believed the darkness was because the smoke had finally overcome me, but when I opened my eyes, it was to watch Calix reaching up to my hands. I didn't feel his touch; I tried to, but felt nothing.

Calix quickly moved from my hands to the bottom of the bed. Still, I could not feel what he was doing, but I could see. His hands took the bedframe. I blinked, noticing his arms bulge as he pulled it towards him. With a violent snap, the wood came away in pieces.

My ankles were still bound with rope, but that was no longer connected to anything. Before I could so much as wiggle a toe, I was out of the bed. Calix carried me, pressing my face into his shirt and holding it there. When I breathed in, it was not smoke and heat I smelled, it was forest and open skies—it was Calix.

I was vaguely aware as the cold kiss of fresh air graced the back of my sticky neck. A shiver spread across my skin, passing across my arms and shoulders as though I had wings of my own. I parted my lips and breathed in a mouthful of air. Fresh air.

Each inhale was both painful and beautiful. I must have been crying because Calix's hand was running across the back of my head as he whispered words of encouragement into my ear.

"It is okay, Rhory. You are going to be okay. I should never have left you."

When I was brave enough to open my eyes, it was to see the wash of red across a busy street. I pushed back from Calix, still held in his arms, and surveyed the world around me. The street was full of people. Their faces were on me or looking up at the blaze that had overcome my room above them. The fire cast a vicious glow across the street, making people wince and pull away in shouts of fear.

At some point my windows had burst outward, shattering the glass across the street beneath it. Black smoke billowed out into the night, blending seamlessly with the darkened sky.

"He must go to St. Myrinn's," a voice said from beside me. I couldn't see the speaker but could hear the honest concern in it. It was as thick as the smoke that spread above us. Smoke that still clung to my lungs, no matter how hard I fought to clear them.

"He will be fine," Calix said, dismissing the person.

"Where is the Crimson Guard?" another voice cried out. "This is Eamon Coleman's husband; someone must alert Eamon to this!"

"There is no need…" Calix began. Hearing his voice awoke me from the hypnotic trance the fire had lulled me into. I slammed my hands into Calix's chest as hard as I could. As I did so, I thought I heard one onlooker call out *rope* as they saw my bindings.

*His hands have been tied.*

*Can you see his ankles?*

On and on, I fought. I had to break free. I had to get away from him.

"Rhory, stop," Calix said, forced to put me on the ground by my erratic movements. I thrashed and kicked, remembering everything that had been revealed to me.

"Let him go!" someone called as cold hands tried to help me away from Calix. I glanced towards the woman who assisted me. For a moment I thought it was Mildred, with her nest of silver hair and eyes magnified by round spectacles. The trick of my mind almost broke me, because of course she was not Mildred. Mildred was dead, just as I should have been.

As the woman coddled me and tried to lead me from the path beyond my house, I didn't once take my eyes off of Calix. "We must get you to see a healer, dear boy. Then we will find your husband—"

"No," I broke free from her with ease, "No, I don't want him. He did this!"

The crowd murmured into silence. For the first time, I saw just how many people watched on. Vampires with eyes glowing red and humans dressed in their night-clothes. Not a single person looked elsewhere, all eyes were on me.

"Eamon did this!" I raised my arms until the frayed rope dangled for everyone to see. Blood and rope-burned skin were illuminated. There was no hiding from it anymore. No excuses and lies to keep up Eamon's illusion of the kind and loving man everyone believed him to be. It was time they knew him for his truth. "And this… this is only a glimpse of what he is capable of."

No one spoke. No one but Calix, who was suddenly at my back, hand resting on my shoulder. "It is over. No more lying for him."

My arms shook as I kept them aloft. I scanned my eyes over the crowd, which seemed to grow with each passing second. I heard their whispers, felt their judging stares. It didn't matter if they believed me or not. I knew it was the truth, and for once, I would not conceal it.

"Lying," I laughed, mouth slick with smoke and ash. My stomach cramped, threatening to overcome me and make me sick. "It seems everyone is adequate at such a skill, even you."

Calix fell back a step as I turned on him. My mind told me to look at him with hate, but my heart sang another tune. The conflict within me was overwhelming that I didn't know whether to run from him or run to him.

I glanced back at the open door to my home. It looked more like the gaping mouth of a burning devil. Then my heart dropped like a stone in my chest.

"Millicent," I breathed, forgetting about Calix. About all of it. "She is still in there!"

Calix snapped his head back to the house. "I thought she…"

There was no time to tell Calix about what had happened. How Millicent had returned me home, expecting a prize but getting pain and torture in the cellar instead. It was the fire which spread across the upper floor of the house that screamed, but if I closed my eyes, I was certain I heard Millicent above it all.

I moved passed Calix, only to be stopped by his hand. He held my arm, urging me to stop. "I will go."

It was easy to pull out of his hand. "No."

That single word looked as though it broke Calix into pieces. He let go of me, his hand falling back to his side, fingers flexing as though they didn't know what to do with themselves. His wide gaze spoke a thousand silent words; it seemed he was choosing which to say.

"I do not need you to save me, nor anyone else," I whispered.

Calix's jaw hardened, then he nodded. "I will be right behind you."

We found Millicent in the cellar. The fire had not yet reached down here, but one look up the stairs from the foyer and it was clear the fire was enjoying its feast. There was no coming back from this. As I ran through the dining room, to the kitchen and down the cellar's stairs, I couldn't help but think the same thing over and over.

*Let it burn. Let it all burn.*

Millicent's clothes were torn and bloody. Her skin was covered in bite marks, huge puckered scars which had refused to heal completely. Whatever they had done to her, she should have healed by now. But she hadn't.

Her body was a storybook of the horror she had faced down here. One look and I could read it all.

"We need to get you out!" I yelled in a panic.

She was lying on her back, staring up at the dark ceiling with wide, unblinking eyes. I fell to my knees beside her, hearing Calix swear beneath his breath behind us. Vampires were cold to the touch, but when I grasped her hand, her skin was like ice. She shook as though a fever had overcome her. Dark circles haunted beneath her reddened eyes. Her lips were moving as she mumbled to herself in the dark.

"*She* needs blood to heal," Calix said, rushing to her other side. He stared at me over her body, sorrow drawing his face into a mask of distress. "If she doesn't drink, she will die slowly and painfully. Our bite is deadly to a vampire."

"I…" Millicent croaked, a tear of blood rolling down the side of her face and falling into her greasy hairline. "I am already dead, you fool."

"Millie," Calix said, brushing a hand across her head. He winced, as though the touch burned him. "I thought you left. You didn't come back… and I thought you finally decided it was easier to turn your back on all of this."

Millicent laughed, but soon broke into sobs of pain. "And I should have. It would have saved me a lot of discomfort."

"You need to drink," Calix said again, frantically glaring across her.

Millicent turned her head away from him, pinching

her face as though the thought alone was disgusting. "Tell him… Rhory, tell Calix to leave me in peace. Let me go, both of you."

I looked between them both. "Not today. You need to heal. We don't have long until the fire reaches down here."

"Fire?" Millicent asked as her eyes pinched closed. She spoke slowly, as though it was painful to do so. "Oh, I always wondered what it would feel like to… to burn. It would be better than having those beasts bite and chew at my body. I am certain… certain of that."

"Eamon is a wolf," I said, looking back at Calix. He looked across Millicent's marked body as though he couldn't understand what he was seeing. "Him and all of his followers. They are all…"

"Mutts," Millicent spat. "Fucking mutts."

"I did it." It was the only word Calix could manage. "Didn't I? This is my doing."

If I told Calix about his brother, it would open up the other conversations we needed to have. But it didn't feel right accusing him of the murder of my mother when Millicent was suffering on the ground between us. That time would come.

"Don't say I didn't warn you," Millicent moaned.

She opened her eyes again and looked directly at me. If it was not for the red and the flash of sharp teeth, she looked almost human. A human who suffered with pain they wouldn't survive.

"I begged him to kill me," she said, laughing and crying at the same time. "But he refused. Every time he bit into my body, or his wolves tore into my skin, I begged, pleaded for him to finish me. When he was done, and I was left to die, do you know what he told me? Why he never finished the job he so desperately wanted to do?"

I pressed my hand to her face. With burning desperation, I wished to provide Millicent comfort but didn't know how. She had made me promise not to use my power on her, and I couldn't break it.

"He cannot hurt you anymore," I said.

"Oh, Rhory," Millicent pinched her eyes closed, and another tear of blood dribbled down the side of her face, "He means to kill all vampires… Tonight."

"What do you mean?" I asked.

"No more talking. We need to get you both out of here!" Calix said, voice breaking as he pleaded. "Before the fire reaches us."

Millicent pursed her lips and hushed Calix. "Eamon has gone to the place it all started. In his words, he wishes to rip the head of the viper who rules the nest. Do you know what happens when you kill a vampire, Rhory?"

I blinked and saw the execution of Millicent's brother in the dark of my mind. The scene of him hanging would haunt me, but the way the sunlight peeled his flesh clean from his bones as he bellowed in agony felt so real; I could almost hear him now.

"Millicent, we need to—" I started, but she snapped at me with pointed teeth.

"Listen to me!" Millicent said, wheezing. "I have

endured this because of you, so you listen to me." Her words pierced through me, cutting deep into my soul; they stung far greater than anything I had faced. "When a vampire sires another, it binds them. By killing one, you kill them all. Eamon knows this. And he means to enter the nest this evening, with his newfound power, and use it to purify Darkmourn. To destroy Lord Marius is to destroy us all."

I held Calix's stare across Millicent's ruined body as she broke into a fit of laughter. Blood bubbled out of her mouth, staining the pale skin around it.

"Then we must stop him," I said, voice shaking. Whether we saved Millicent now, she would soon perish if what she revealed was true. If Eamon succeeded in his plans, all vampires would perish. This was not what the Crimson Guard stood for. It was not what *I* stood for.

Eamon had torn too many people apart with his thirst for revenge. And I felt responsible for stopping him.

"Is… is the offer of blood still on the table?" Millicent broke the tension between us.

I raised my arm above Millicent. Rolling back the sleeve, I exposed my skin and the blue veins that webbed beneath it. Millicent was hesitant as she regarded my offering.

"Well, well," she sang, tongue lapping up at her paling lips. "I would be lying if I said I hadn't fantasised about what you tasted like, Rhory."

I brought my arm down and guided it until the skin

tickled across her mouth. "Drink your fill. Then we will stop my fucking husband."

"Do it gently," Calix warned quickly. "Millie, I don't want him to feel any pain."

Millicent's reply was muffled as she pressed her lips to my arm and inhaled through her nose. "Oh, he will enjoy it. They always do."

Millicent's teeth sank into my skin with ease. I didn't feel any discomfort, only the lap of her tongue against my skin and the pressure of her suck as she drew the blood out. All the while, I gritted my teeth and stared at Calix.

I looked through his eyes, deep into his skull, searching for the truth.

There had been a time when I had felt guilt lurking within Calix. The emotion was sour and left an after-taste in me the last time I had used my power on him. It had never crossed my mind that it would be because he killed my mother. But, as I looked at him now, regarding his furrowed brows and sorrow-filled eyes, I felt as though I knew my answer without asking it.

What I didn't know was why. Why he had done it? What happened that night, when I was celebrating my union with Eamon, believing the day to be the happiest of my life?

"Tell me," I said to Calix as Millicent drew blood from my arm and my home burned above. "Why did you do it? Why did you kill my mother?"

Calix bowed his head, glaring to his hands as though they were deadly weapons resting on his thighs. Then he opened his mouth and told me the truth—all of it, no matter how dark and deadly it was. There was no detail spared as Millicent drank from me, and Calix offloaded the burden he had hidden from me…

He told me *everything*.

## ❧  38  ❧

## 3 YEARS BEFORE

*This is a mistake. I should not have come.*

The thought overwhelmed me as I stood, dumfounded, before the door to Rhory's home. A place I had vowed to myself never to return to. Yet here I stood because I was pathetic. Weak.

A flurry of snow fell around me, casting Darkmourn in a blanket of pure endless white. It was late afternoon, but the fresh layer of winter kept the world brighter than it should have been at such an hour. Flakes soaked through my heavy jacket, making the leather smell damp. I was certainly not dressed for a wedding, one I had never intended to attend… until the invite arrived.

And yet here I was, waiting before the door like a fool.

The invite was no more than a crumpled ball of parchment within my fist. I should have thrown it out the moment Silas brought it to me. And I would have. Except my brother was adamant he was going to attend.

And Auriol commanded me to retrieve him. I couldn't refuse her. Her control over me was powerful enough to move my limbs even against my better judgement.

I convinced myself I had only come here for Silas, not because I longed to see Rhory again. Which was a lie, but perhaps if I kept repeating it to myself, I would wish it into existence. If I saw Rhory, it would destroy those last surviving parts of me.

Rhory and Eamon's ceremony shouldn't have finished by now, but the house was dark. Quiet. I would have taken the emptiness as a sign to turn away and forget this. Silas could find his own way home, likely drunk and merry from the enjoyment of my sorrow and pain. He always thrived in my pity, but what little brothers didn't enjoy the downfall of their elders?

Except the house wasn't silent. Not completely. I could hear the heartbeats; the regular thumps thundered in my head as though they demanded my attention.

Auriol's command just raged within me. The siren song of her request had me raising my fist to the door. I knocked, two loud raps that disturbed the peace inside. The sound of my knuckles against wood interrupted the beating hearts, causing one of them to skip. In all my years, I had memorised Silas's heart-song. And he was here. I heard him above the rest. And I needed to get him out. Once I did, I would never return here again.

*Never.*

The door was thrown open, and Ana Coleman stood before me. Her sudden presence surprised me—

enough to take a step back from the doorstep—as did the vicious smile that spread across her beautiful face.

"I was beginning to think you had ignored my invitation, Calix Grey. Please, come inside before you catch your death. This weather is… wicked."

"My apologies," I replied, bowing my head from her intense gaze. "But I have only come to retrieve my brother."

I could hear Silas from inside the foyer, talking loudly to another with a deep voice. Ana soon stepped aside, revealing who my brother spoke with, although I would have recognised the deep tones of the man's voice even in the darkest of rooms.

Eamon. Now, Eamon Coleman.

Fury sparked deep in my chest as I regarded him, until Ana blocked him from view. The deep maroon dress Ana wore slid across the polished floor of her home, giving the impression she floated more than walked. Her waves of dark brown hair had been pinned up and off her face, all except a single strand that fell perfectly before her azure eyes.

"We are not strangers, Calix. Please, come in and enjoy one drink with us. It is a momentous day," Ana said.

"Momentous indeed. It is not every day I get to marry the love of your life." Eamon stood, dressed in a fine suit of obsidian material, with the clasp of a crimson cloak draped from his shoulders. He held a glass in his hand and raised it to my brother, who held its twin.

"Eamon, I believe you have misspoken," I said, glaring as both men turned and looked at me. Neither one smiled.

"No, not at all," Eamon replied with a cruel smile.

A rage swept over me as I watched my brother toasting to the man who stole my heart and kept it for himself. It took great effort to stay standing on the step. What I desired was to run through the foyer and tear Eamon to shreds. To make him feel every scrap of agony he caused me when he took Rhory from me.

I might have, if Ana hadn't had leaned forward. "Calix, dear, one drink."

"Silas, come." The command snapped out of me.

Disgust crawled over Silas's face as he swept his gaze across me. "I don't bow to your requests, brother."

I swept past Ana and into the warmth of her home. Silas rocked back a step, whilst Eamon held firm. Ana closed the door. The slam of it almost made me lose my composure. I stiffened when she slipped up behind me, her nails tickling up my back and over my shoulder like a spider.

"Allow me to fetch you something to drink. A toast is without merit if you do not have something strong to raise."

Eamon nodded his head to Ana, smiling his thanks as she slipped from the foyer into the darkened dining hall beyond. The same place I had first shared a conversation with Rhory. It was hard not to forget myself in the forest of memories we had shared in this home. Our history together was stained across every room. I felt the intoxicating call of them wishing to drag me away in its current.

"Master Grey." Eamon offered me a handsome smile, the very same he had when he opened the door to Rhory's bedroom and found us, entangled, together in it. I didn't see how Rhory could have fallen in love with him. He was everything Rhory despised. He was perfect, from the brush of his midnight hair across his head to the bright sky-blue eyes. Even the way he carried himself, straight-backed and always displaying his charming smile. This was the type of man that would make Rhory shiver. At least that was what I believed. I was wrong, of course, because my eyes caught the glint of a wedding band around Eamon's finger, confirming my greatest fear.

Eamon caught the shift of my attention and lifted his finger up before him, showing off the polished metal for all to see. "Silver. Pretty metal, isn't it?"

"Silas," I snapped. "I will not ask you again. It's time to go home."

My brother stepped forward, half positioning himself between Eamon and me. "And I will not remind you again, brother. I am not some dog you can bark orders at."

He was right. I was not the alpha. Not yet. Auriol could have given him a single command to leave, and he would have raced out of this house before dropping the glass from his hand. That power was not mine to claim.

"You're drunk," I said, disgust creeping across my face. I couldn't hide my emotions, nor did I desire to.

"Oh, come on, Calix. Do not spoil the mood of the day." Ana danced back into the foyer, glass in hand. I kept my arms folded across my chest, refusing her offer. I was not here to toast to my heartbreak.

"Shouldn't you be with your guests?" I asked, no longer caring for anyone but Eamon. "What would Rhory say if he discovered his newly wed was raising glasses with his previous lover?"

Ana smacked my shoulder. "Oh, Calix, please do not say such vile accusations. I can't bear to hear them."

Eamon smiled at that and raised his glass again. Silas followed suit, quietly amused by the tension that thrummed between us all. I snatched the glass from Ana, praying that something strong was promised. A rush of spirits would help me walk out of this place without blood on my hands.

Eamon placed his arm over my brother's shoulders and pulled him close to his side. Their proximity disgusted me. It was not an emotion Silas shared, as he seemed completely entranced by Eamon's touch.

"Now," Eamon said, pulling a face of forced confusion. "Whatever should we toast to?"

Silas looked directly at me as he replied, "To love, perhaps."

"Very good," Eamon purred, sharing a quick look at Ana. I couldn't make out what it spoke of. By the time I glanced at Rhory's mother, she was hiding a snicker behind her painted nails.

"To love then," Eamon said, raising his glass higher to the sky. "And to remembering it."

I was the first to drink, draining the glass of the wine and thrusting it back towards Ana, who carefully took it from me. Silas was next. He laughed as a dribble of the red liquid spread down his chin. It was Eamon who plucked the pocket square and brought it to my brother's face, tentatively clearing him of the spillage.

"If we are done here," I said, enjoying the ease of the wine as it slipped down my throat and numbed my chest. Sweeping my hand towards the door, I focused on my brother. "Silas."

Silas frowned, took a reluctant step towards me, and stumbled. Confusion pinched his dark brows down, creasing his face. It was a moment of embarrassment, as though he didn't understand how he had lost his footing.

"Careful," Eamon sang, but refused to step forward and help.

Silas opened his mouth to say something. Perhaps to make some childish joke about the wine and his head, but the words that came out of him made little sense. The glass slipped from his fingers and shattered at his feet, coating the floor in shards of glass.

Instinct took over. I shifted my weight to step towards him, but I didn't move. I fell over myself as the world tilted on its axis. The ground raced up to greet me. I couldn't even raise my arms to soften the fall. My face crashed into the cold panels of the floor, bone and wood clashing together in a jarring crack. Pain split my skull. Claws pierced my brain and pinched down hard, attempting to tear it into multiple parts.

I blinked as the dull light of the room grew too

harsh. When I opened my eyes again, it was to watch feet moving towards me. Then a voice spoke through the haze.

"Wolfsbane," Eamon said, tutting down at me.

I tried to shift my face around so I could see him, but everything was blurry. I was only vaguely aware that Silas too was on the floor, hands gripping his stomach as he moaned and wailed.

"Such a pesky weed to locate. Did you know it grows in abundance beyond Castle Dread? I didn't, not until Silas revealed it all to me. The weed grows from the blood of a dead wolf. Hence the name, a wolf's bane, tragic but almost poetic. I wouldn't hold it against him, of course. His youth and, well… how do I say this without sounding as though I am gloating? Silas's obsession with me has led him to have rather loose lips."

Eamon squatted over me. A smile broke out across his face, twisting it into a mask of horror. "Do you find it strange to know that I have not only fucked Rhory, but I have also fucked your brother?"

Ana clicked her tongue from somewhere out of sight. "Eamon, how crude."

My mouth seemed to have been sewn together. I couldn't speak even if I wished to. The wolfsbane was spreading through me like wildfire. It turned my muscles to stone, and my marrow to honey. It was a feeling I was familiar with, from years of Auriol testing our resistance to the plant, but the dosage Eamon had provided was far greater than anything I had devoured before.

I must have been crying, because Eamon lifted a

hand to the side of my face and brushed something cool away from my cheek.

"Now, now," he sang. "I will not kill you. You, Calix Grey, are not my enemy. In fact, you are the means for me to see my enemies destroyed. Once and for all. What I am going to do is offer you peace, as thanks for everything you are going to give me."

*Peace?* I scoffed at such a ridiculous concept while my wolf stirred with hungry vengeance. *You are my enemy. And one day I will destroy you.*

"Let this be a warning," Eamon said, pointing his finger in my face. "If you come back for Rhory, if you so much as go near him, it will be his pretty little skin I mark."

"Oh, Eamon, do not speak in such ways. Or do I need to remind you of our deal?" Ana moved into view above me, the tap of her heels teetering across the floor. Her outline rippled as the drug took hold. Her features were blurred and warped, but her grin was as clear as the sun breaking through the clouds of a storm.

A name formed on my lips. It may not have made sense as I spoke it aloud, but to me, it rang true.

*Rhory.*

"You are going to forget all about him, just as he forgot about you."

The pain dulled, lightening if only a little.

"Ana," Eamon said, standing and making room for Rhory's mother. "I trust I can leave you to work your magic whilst I deal with Silas?"

Ana lifted her dress up, enough for her to have room

to kneel before me. With each blink, the wolfsbane was fading. My gaze sharpened first, followed swiftly by my other senses.

"You," I managed as Ana leaned over me, hands outstretched.

"I have only ever wanted what was best for my son. My first and only child. And you, Master Grey, are not worthy."

Her power burned to life like fire blossoming across her hands. The glow was a cold white. It filled the protruding veins in her fingers, lighting her skin up from the inside.

"What… what have you done to him?" Each word was hard to force out, but I did so with every ounce of effort I could muster.

She scowled down at me, face ageing before my eyes. "I made him forget you. Every part of his mind you occupied, I changed, altered. I filled it with Eamon, placing him in all the slots you once invaded. He is a far greater match. Where you would have only been dangerous for him… Eamon would be his saviour."

"W—Why?" I fumbled over the words.

Ana glanced over her shoulder. I followed her attention, seeing that Silas and Eamon were no longer with us. I could hear the creak of boards above us, and the drag of a heavy body against the floor.

Satisfied no one else could hear, Ana leaned over me and whispered her answer into my ear. "Because Eamon gave me a choice. What Rhory is, what I am. Eamon knows. I did it to keep Rhory from being dragged to

Castle Dread and being disposed of like the other halflings and witches discovered in this godforsaken town. Your proximity to my son puts him in danger, which I cannot allow. Be thankful Eamon simply wishes for me to alter your mind and not kill you, because I certainly argued that ending you would be the easier of options."

She pulled back, hands swirling with white light.

"Michal… would not—"

"Michal doesn't even know his own name, let alone what is best for Rhory. His mind is mine, just as Rhory's and yours will be. Now, careful… otherwise, the outcome may leave you… ruined, as my dear husband is now. He is the perfect example of what happens when you resist me."

"You are a monster," I hissed through clenched teeth. My jaw ached as I fought the wolfsbane and the beast within me. It longed to be freed.

"No," Ana said, face lit from beneath by the glow of her magic. "I am a mother. And I will do everything to see my family thrive."

"Rhory… will… remember."

"This will hurt," she said, lifting her hands towards my face. "As all good things do. And I would sooner die than break the curse. Rhory will never remember you…"

Perhaps it was the fury at what had been revealed, or the desire to never allow myself to forget Rhory, but my desperation blew through the cobwebs the wolfsbane settled over me. The change happened before she could lower her fingers to my head.

My skin split in two. My bones shattered like glass.

Without hesitation, the wolf within me burst beyond its cage of flesh, past my better judgement. There was no more thinking. No more Calix. Silas. Eamon. There was only flesh and blood as the wolf tore into Rhory's mother, snuffing out her power. Her life. As the monster's jaws bit down into her neck and severed it from her shoulders with the ease of melted butter, Ana hardly had the chance to scream. When she did, it was a song of gargled blood and death.

## 39

Calix had killed my mother. He was the murderer, the monster. That fact alone was hard to bear, as was the knowledge that Ana Coleman was the name I had longed to uncover, the witch who altered my mind. My *own mother* was the one responsible for tearing into my memories. She ripped them apart and, in turn, stole everything away from me. Because of her, I was married to a monster. Since her death, I have faced pain both physically and mentally. Because of her desire to see me safe, she handed me over to the man who stripped the last remaining scraps of my life away with his bare hands. And what I couldn't fathom atop it all was that was not her only devilish sin. Not only did she play with my memories as though they were hers to own, but she also tampered with Father's mind, destroying him slowly from the inside.

She killed him.

She did this to me.

Her power tore our family apart. Her actions led to this very moment as I walked out of our house, bathed in smoke and ash from the fire, towards the battle which waited for me within Castle Dread.

It should have pained me hearing what Calix had kept from me. The events which happened the hours before I found my mother's body torn to shreds. Instead, I drowned in fury; not because Calix had done it, but furious I would never have the chance to confront her. By killing my mother, Calix had taken any chance from me of ever asking her the only question that seemed to poison my mind.

*Mother, was it worth it?*

I couldn't form words as we travelled to Castle Dread. No one spoke to me. Not Millicent, who slowly, but surely, healed from her wounds. Or Calix. Even though he was not in my viewpoint, I felt him look at me. There was an expectant shimmer in his eyes. He trod carefully around me, as though he walked on glass. I couldn't fathom the chance of catching his gaze for fear it would be the final straw that broke me. All I could do was face forward as we moved through Darkmourn towards our final destination.

Millicent led the way. Although the scarred teeth marks had not completely faded, my blood had given her enough vitality to walk herself out of my burning home without aid. Each step seemed to provide her with more strength. Soon enough, her gait evened, and her shoulders rolled back until she was once again a picture of health.

I did what I did best and buried everything. All my thoughts and feelings, I forced them deep inside of me until I felt only the physical echo of pain. Now was not the time to focus on self-pity, not with the real threat which still hung over Darkmourn, like the axe held aloft by an executioner.

If Eamon succeeded in killing Lord Marius, it would lead to Millicent's demise, as well as every other vampire sired from him. I kept my focus on the back of her straight black hair, waiting with bated breath for her to stop and crumble to ash before my eyes. As long as she was moving, we had time.

The walk was torture, as was the silence that occupied it. All I could think about was what Calix had revealed. No matter how hard I tried to fill my mind with other concerns, it always led back to my mother. How Eamon seemed to have enamoured Silas, leading to his eventual imprisonment. What Mother had done to me, and her warped reasonings. And mostly, what would have happened if she had made Calix forget about me? Above it all, knowing that was almost a possibility drove daggers into my heart.

Even after everything he had done, and everything I could not remember, Calix was my tether, whether or not I wished to admit it.

I found myself stifling the urge to laugh. The feeling came over me so suddenly as Castle Dread loomed ahead. After everything Mother had done to ensure I never set foot near this place, here I was walking across the bridge directly into the harsh shadows the monstrous building cast across Old Town.

The presence of the castle had our party of three slowing. I was so used to the silence and the patter of our boots against cobbled stone that when Millicent spoke it jolted surprise through my soul.

"I'm all for going in knifes out and poised for blood, but this may be one moment when a plan would be a good idea." Millicent glanced between the glowing windows of Castle Dread, to Calix and then to me.

Before us stretched the ancient stone bridge that connected the castle to Old Town. It was weathered from years, and the stones stained a dusty black. There was no light here, beside that of the fire-lit windows and the waning moon far above. Even the stars seemed to disappear. Perhaps they too sensed the darkness in this place.

From our vantage point, the face of the castle looked more like a grinning face with hungry eyes, promising damnation inside it.

"Just keep to the path," Calix said, striding past us. "You both know what waits in the shadows if you leave it."

*Wolves.*

"And I have had just about enough company with wolves for a lifetime," Millicent muttered, unsheathing the twin daggers Calix had returned to her. "No offence."

Calix continued walking, ready for the shadows to swallow him whole.

"Wait," I called out, "Calix."

He stopped in his tracks as my voice echoed. Nerves overcame me as I waited for him to turn back to look at me. Calix hesitated, likely caused by the fact my calling his name was the first thing I had said to him since he revealed his crime.

My breath hitched when he finally looked my way. His gold eyes glowed through the darkness between us, casting me in a warmth and chill of equal measure.

"We don't have the time, Little Red."

His use of the nickname weakened my knees. It would have been easier to fall to them and sob, to unleash the storm of emotions which riled throughout me.

"You do not have to do this," he said, as though that was what immobilised me.

I shook my head. "It is not myself I am worried about. Not this time."

How could I tell him what I truly feared? Speaking it into existence would only make it seem more of a possibility. Because when Marius discovered the danger Calix's kind was to him, what was stopping the vampire lord from destroying every single one of them?

I walked towards Calix, carefully stepping from one stone slab to the next. He stiffened as I closed in on him, but soon melted when I reached up with my hands and graced my cold-tipped fingers against the warmth of his face.

My lover. My heart. My mother's killer.

"I'm so sorry, Rhory." Calix broke the moment my touch graced him. He dropped his chin to his chest and loosed a weighted breath, one I imagined he held in for a long time.

"Not now," I said, jaw clenched. "You do not get to say that to me now. Not yet."

"I never wanted for any of this," he replied as the grim expression furrowed his brows and rimmed his bright eyes with a devious glint.

"Nor did I. But here we are and eventually we have the truth to face. Together."

I glanced behind me, but Millicent was nowhere to be seen. Calix didn't seem alarmed, nor surprised.

"What I deserve for the pain I have caused you... I deserve to—"

"Together, did you hear me? Calix, look at me."

Calix took my face in his hands, holding me in place with gentled ease. "I should have told you sooner."

"And why didn't you?" I said, breathless. "Tell me that, at least."

Calix paused. He took a moment to gather himself whilst his eyes roamed across my face, my body, leaving no inch unattended. "Because I have taken so much from you. And what I didn't wish to be responsible for was ruining the image you held for your mother."

"Knowing the truth would have freed me."

Calix shook his head. "No. You are the only one who can free yourself. I thought, by upholding the lies, I would shield you from more agony. If I told you the truth of what she did, I feared it would break you."

"You are right," I replied, mesmerised by the glow of his eyes in the dark, and the way his breath blew out in clouds of silver beyond his lips. "It *has* broken me, but you are the only one who can see that I am put back together. Which is why I do not want you to do this."

"Do what?"

"Expose yourself," I snapped. "Doing so will reveal what you are. And I need you, Calix; I need you to survive this night so you can help me put together the mess in my mind. You owe me that, at least. And if something happens to you, our *before* dies with you."

"Oh, Little Red. But that is exactly why I must," Calix said. "Rhory, let me fight for you."

"There will be nothing left to fight for if you are dead, Calix. Lord Marius will not allow you to live if he knows what you are… the threat your life is to his and to his kin. If you die, you take the truth with you. I cannot remember what happened between us and my mother is not alive to fix it, which means you are the only one with the knowledge of our truth. If you die, you take it with you, and I can never be whole. I will never be fixed."

"When will you learn?" Calix whispered, using his leverage and guiding my face to his. The winds whipped at his hair, casting it across his face. "You need no one but yourself. There will come a time when you'll understand that others do not have the power to fix you. We can help you hold the parts together, but only you can truly patch them together. You do not need me for that."

"I do," I forced out. My throat seemed to squeeze in on itself. "I need you, and I want you."

"Then I am the luckiest man alive," he said, brushing the tear from my face. "And that is why I am going to see this through. My brother must be reasoned with, and Eamon dealt with. I can only pray to whoever listens that Lord Marius finds it in his cold still heart to pardon me if we save him."

"Promise me," I said.

"I promise. Which means little unless I seal it with a kiss."

I closed my eyes, providing no resistance as Calix lowered his lips to mine.

"I have killed six of them… no, maybe five. It is easy to lose count when the sound of breaking necks is all so similar."

Reluctantly, we pulled away from each other to see Millicent standing in a cloak of shadows. Her hands were covered in blood, as were the sharp blades which she cleaned methodically on her trousers. Only when the blood had been cleared from each side did she force them back into the sheathes at her hips.

"Crimson Guards?" I asked, noting the deep red of blood.

Millicent pulled a face, with one brow raised far above the other. "Rhory, I am not sure that is the name they are using anymore."

"Eamon's pack," Calix corrected, his voice thick with darkness.

"Yes, and it was definitely six of them I killed.

Enjoyed every single moment." After what they did to her in the cellar, I couldn't fault Millicent for the wide smile she displayed as she spoke.

"Eamon has the outskirts of the castle surrounded or did. I know, from experience, there are far more than only six of the fuckers. He'll have the rest of them inside with him, no doubt."

Adrenaline buzzed through me. It started at the ground, working its way upwards until I was filled with a fresh sense of confidence. "Let's get on with it. I have something I wish to say to my husband."

Millicent giggled maniacally and unsheathed one of her blades, extending it to me handle first. "Here, this might help with that conversation."

I felt the weight of the blade the moment it was passed to me. Holding such a weapon gave me a new sense of power, which both frightened and thrilled me.

"You know how to use that, don't you?" Calix slipped in behind me, put his arms around my waist and brought his lips so close to my ear it sent shivers across my back.

"Stab him with the sharp end," I replied, feeling my heart swell in my chest at the thought.

"Precisely," Calix replied. "Just like that."

A howl sliced through the night. It demanded our attention, forcing us to look towards the source of the noise. Toward Castle Dread, and the sound which came from within its old stone walls.

"Auriol," Calix said, releasing me and moving towards the sound. "It is her. She calls to her pack."

By the time the next long pained howl reached us, we were running towards it. I could only focus on following Millicent and Calix as they moved with unnatural speed and urgency.

I caught something out of the corner of my eye as we moved, unusual enough for me to look properly. What I saw was something no story could have warned me about. Shadows in the shape of hounds ran amongst the darkness within the castle's grounds beside us. They too heard Auriol's cry. A pack of cursed wolves listened as their creation cried out for help.

We all prepared to heed it.

## 40

There was not a single one of Eamon's pack to greet us within the main entrance of Castle Dread. Where we expected his followers to fill the space, there were only ghosts and the echoes of far-off voices. The only evidence of life where the scattered remains of those Millicent had left in the castle grounds for the shadow hounds to feast upon.

Calix stormed ahead, his speed increasing every time Auriol howled. His hands were balled into fists, which he used to propel himself through the foyer, up the grand stairs that stretched out directly before us then around the balcony atop it. Millicent stuck by my side, her hand on my arm in some protective manner.

My lungs burned, as did my legs. My body was a patchwork of pain, from Millicent's bite mark on my arm, to the burns across my back and the raw skin at my wrists and ankles. I used every ounce of agony to keep me going. It fuelled me, and reminded me it was nothing compared to what I felt inside.

Every muscle felt strained as we followed in pursuit of Calix. Even my fingers ached as they grew used to holding onto the dagger Millicent had gifted me. In an ideal world, I would have had the time to grow used to its weight and balance. Instead, I could only grip on harder and hope it would provide me some comfort with whatever we were about to face.

It wasn't until we had taken another flight of stairs upwards, and rounded multiple corridors lined with closed black doors and walls decorated with hanging paintings in gilded frames, that I recognised something was missing. *Witches*. This place should have been teeming with them. For years, Lord Marius and his beloved Jak had collected those with powers like rare items to be studied. Except the castle felt empty. It was the quiet that made me question if Mother had been right all along. If the witches were not here, then what became of them?

Before I could allow a new dread to enter me, Calix stopped beyond a door which looked no different to the many others we had passed.

"How many are there?" Millicent asked.

"Enough to cause us a problem," Calix whispered, the side of his face pressing into the wood of the door as he listened to something beyond it.

I strained my ears but couldn't pick anything up but the thundering beat of my heart; Calix must have heard it too, because he turned his full attention on me and winced.

"I should not have brought you here," Calix said, lips drawing back into a tight line as he inhaled. "It's not safe. There are too many of them."

"Which is exactly why I am here." I stepped from Millicent, who finally released my arm. The tingle of her grip didn't leave me, as though her fingers had left an imprint on my skin.

Calix's eyes searched my face for something, then glanced down at the dagger in my hands. Did he see the way I shook?

"You have another weapon in your arsenal," Calix muttered. "Do not be afraid to use it when the time comes."

I wanted to share my concern about the missing witches, but there was no time. Auriol howled again, making Calix recoil backwards.

"Go," Millicent hissed, her eyes glowing red and teeth bared, "Now."

Calix offered me a final look before opening the door and slipping inside. I took a step to follow him, but the door closed, and Millicent had returned her fingers back to my arm.

"He can't go alone!" I choked out, unable to pull free.

"Give Calix a chance," Millicent replied. 'Do this for him, as he is doing this for you.'

I stopped resisting at her comment for it had the power to immobilise me.

*Do this for him, as he is doing this for you.*

With a swift tug, we were moving away from the door, back in the direction we had come. My chest panged with a bitter shock that sang similarly to betrayal or jealousy.

"Millicent, we need to go back to him," I spat as we raced down the corridor, my feet slapping the ground as I tried to keep up.

"And we will," Millicent replied. "But first we must create a distraction, something to allow time for Calix to have even the slightest chance against Eamon and his pack."

I almost tripped as Millicent pulled me down one set of stairs after another. Soon enough, we were back at the main entrance. It was not the front door we moved for. Hidden in the shadows beyond the grand staircase was another corridor. It was narrow, and likely used as a place for servants or maids to slip through unseen.

"Millicent," I snarled, trying once again to pull away. "Tell me what we need to do!"

"I'm sorry," she said quietly, her voice buried beneath my heavy footfalls. "Know that I will let nothing happen to you."

Panic clawed up my throat. I opened my mouth to scream out for Calix, but the terror did well to silence and strangle me.

Auriol howled once again, and this time the noise was so close it rocked through the dark space and echoed across the stone walls beside us. I felt like being back in the tunnels beneath Darkmourn, the way the sound grew the more it shattered the dark.

"I have always wanted to make a grand entrance," Millicent said, unbothered by the fast pace of our running, or my struggling. "Books suggest it would have been better received if I was dressed in a ball gown that looked more like the decoration on top of a cake. I never understood the appeal. I prefer my entrance to be more… memorable than that." After she finished speaking, she added as an afterthought, "Hide your dagger."

There was no arguing with the look in her eyes. I slipped it into the belt of my trousers and folded my tunic over the hilt. The cold press of the blade against my back was a welcome relief.

"Am I a fool to trust you?"

Millicent giggled lightly. Even in the dark, I conjured an image of her deadly smile. "We are all fools, Rhory. Some more deadly than others."

The hallway stopped at a smaller door than the others we had seen. The paint on this was worn and scratched. It almost shattered completely when Millicent raised a boot and kicked into it.

Light flooded the narrow corridor, spilling out from the room beyond. For a moment I was blinded by it, enough that I couldn't make anything out as Millicent pulled me into the light.

"Eamon Coleman," Millicent cried out. The name alone turned my body to stone, as well as the realisation of exactly what distraction Millicent had alluded to. "I believe I have something that belongs to you."

I blinked, and the world steadied.

We had entered a monstrous room overspilling with grandeur. Golden sconces burned across the walls, each one glowing with roses of ruby flame. The light reflected off the stone walls, bathing shadows across the ceiling far above, making it seem endless.

To one side of the room stood a man who glowed as bright as a star. His skin was pale as death, and his hair so white even winter's first snow would be jealous of its colour. Blood-red eyes picked up the glow of fire and seemed to swallow the light and reflect it from within— and they looked directly at me.

Marius, Lord of the Eternal Night. Father of the Dead. Sire of the vampires.

He stood alone atop a raised dais, his entire body trembling with fury.

It was the whimper that drew my attention from the vampire lord to the middle of the room. Covered almost entirely in a blanket of webbed silver chains was a wolf. Auriol. She was splayed beneath the net like a creature captured in the woods by hunters. She was both human and wolf, like Calix had been. Her limbs were long and drawn out, covered in patches of grey fur that showed a leathered skin beneath.

Seeing her blew away the trancelike state which gripped me. Her name formed on the tip of my tongue. As if sensing it, she opened eyes of swirling honey and looked at me. It was brief. Then she closed them and whimpered softly like an animal welcoming death.

"Rhory?" My name broke out in question. All I had

to do was look to the opposite side of the room to see its speaker.

Eamon stood within a halo of his followers. Once the Crimson Guard, they were each dressed in cloaks of russet brown that looked like aged, dried blood instead of the new lifeblood they were sworn to protect. Just beyond Eamon's shoulder was Silas, sulking behind him with his head down, but eyes raised up and looking through his long lashes.

"What is the meaning of this?" Boomed the voice of Lord Marius. It was demanding and powerful but did little to sway me from the confusion that crossed my husband's face.

As the corners of Eamon's lips tugged downward, mine seemed to rise.

"My apologies, sire," Millicent sang loud for all to hear. The grip of her fingers released me. She leaned into my ear and whispered, "Go to him, Little Red. Run to him."

The use of my nickname was a gift, one which over-spilled with newfound confidence.

With a shove, I was moving. Running, just as Milli-cent said, towards Eamon. As I had when Millicent last returned me to my husband, I put on the show of my lifetime. Throwing myself down the final steps, I crashed into his chest and wrapped my arms around his waist. He didn't lower his arm over me, which rather lucky because if he did, he would have found the dagger hiding in the waistband of my trousers.

"Are you surprised?" I whispered, feeling Eamon

stiffen beneath my arms. Part of me wondered if he could smell the remnants of our burning home on me, whilst the other part was focused on how we were to save Auriol and Lord Marius.

"Enough of this," Eamon growled, shrugging me away into another set of arms. It was Silas who withdrew me into the throng of the crowd, placing me behind Eamon who regarded Lord Marius once again.

Millicent paced into the room, her short blade drawn. "Lord Marius," Millicent called out, "Would you do me the honour of following me out of this room before those men and women attempt to kill you?"

The bark of the vampire lord's laugh was sharp, whipping the room and everyone in it. "You have broken into my home and interrupted a meeting with my Crimson Guard. Whatever spectacle you believe to achieve here, I would stop whilst you are ahead."

I was surprised when Eamon called for his followers to restrain Millicent at Lord Marius's order. Silas slapped a hand over my mouth as I cried out, ready to break my act and admit that Millicent was right.

"Not. Yet," Silas whispered through gritted teeth. Then he said, "So, you are a fighter."

My body stilled as Silas ensured I watched the wave of Eamon's followers overcome Millicent. I expected her to put up a fight, but she didn't. She took a pathetic swing towards the first woman that reached her, but it was poorly timed. The blade was knocked from Millicent's grasp and she was taken by multiple hands.

She could have fought them off if she wanted, but

Millicent behaved. It was the knowing glint in her eyes that calmed me. This was all part of the plan she had not revealed to me, a plan that had seemed to change as the minutes went on.

"Pardon my suggestion, Lord Marius, but this would be a better time than any to prove to you the danger these creatures pose to you." Eamon gestured towards Auriol, and then Millicent, who stood as still as a statue in the grasp of the five strangers who held her.

Lord Marius's face was expressive. No matter the emotion he held, he showed it across his handsome face in dramatic flairs. And Eamon's suggestion had displeased him.

"You forget yourself," Lord Marius said, taking a step down from his dais. Both his hands were clasped behind his back, putting a strain on the decorative jacket he wore. It seemed to have been crafted from the richest of velvets that rippled like the surface of a lake as it reflected the firelight. "I am not in the sport of watching my chosen protectors of Darkmourn suggest a display of murder, all to prove a point." He nodded his head slightly towards Auriol, looking almost pained to see her suffering beneath the weight of the silver. "This is not a creature I am familiar with, but I hear her heartbeat and recognise she is a living being. Which begs me to ask you why you cause her to suffer. Is this what the Crimson Guard have become? A group inclined for the dramatics? Now, I will not ask you again. Remove these chains so I can discuss directly with Ms Grey the details of this…" Marius tilted his head. "…Issue."

426

"I'm afraid I cannot do that." As Eamon spoke, his remaining followers fanned out across the room, russet cloaks brushing the floor. Marius watched, eyes following each one of them. It was then he brought his hands before him, flashing the sharp points of polished nails.

"May I remind you, you stand in my home," Marius spoke carefully. "I have extended my invitation to you, and now I revoke it. Do not make me remove you myself, and that cloak you are wearing."

"Do you mean this cloak?" Eamon was the only one wearing the original red cloak that confirmed his station. He reached for the clasp with his free hand and unclipped it. He drew the material from his shoulders, extended his arm, then dropped it. "Oh, you can have the fucking cloak."

Darkness swelled beyond Marius as though wings of pure night burst from his back. His eyes burned as he split his mouth and bared a jaw full of teeth sharper than any forged blade. "Get out of my home. All of you."

"No," Eamon replied, speaking the word as though it brewed in the fires of his chest. "Marius, there was once a time your monsters invaded my home without invitation. They left only when they desired. And I wish to do the same here, tonight."

"I sense my brother is close," Silas whispered into my ear beneath Eamon's speech. "Waiting for the right moment to come and save the day."

My lips and teeth brushed Silas's palm as I tried to

bite him. He emitted a low chuckle at my attempts and held down firmer. I clawed my hands into it as much as he allowed. No matter how I tried to pull his hand away, it didn't budge.

Marius was surrounded within seconds.

"Eamon Coleman," Marius growled. "What have you done?"

"I remembered what it means to value life over death," Eamon replied.

For a moment, I saw fear pinch across Marius's deep stare. He looked to his side, almost expectant that someone was there with him, except the space was empty.

"Take this man and remove him," Marius called out his command to Eamon's pack. No one listened. Marius repeated himself, this time his words laced with viperous danger. "Remove Eamon Coleman from this room now, or you will all face the same punishment."

"They do not take orders from you," Eamon sang, pacing freely up and down the space where Auriol lay. "These fearless humans are loyal to me, not the Crimson Guard. Not you. They are mine."

Silas's chest rattled as he chuckled to himself. "Hmm. Are they?"

Marius bowed his knees and lowered himself. His fingers curved into claw-like points and he hissed to the men and women who slowly closed in on him. Ancient determination boiled in his blood-red eyes as he prepared to defend himself.

I looked at Millicent, waiting for some sort of signal.

Her eyes were focused upwards, towards the shadows above. I followed her attention as much as Silas's hold allowed, looking up to see a narrow walkway that hid in the shadows. Millicent saw something out of my line of sight. When she looked back at me, I caught the subtle shake of her head.

*Not yet*, her actions said. *Not yet.*

My power lurked far beneath my skin. I felt its presence rear its head and prepare. Calix was right. I had a weapon. Something not forged by steel, yet still as deadly. And I would use it when the time was right.

"Your rule must end," Eamon shouted, almost hysteric as his voice cracked. "It is time I right the world you destroyed. To balance the scales back in favour of the living."

"Do you think you are the first to try?" Marius spat, more beast than man. "Fool, to think you have a chance against me. I have slaughtered more numbers than those you have brought with you. This is no threat, simply an annoyance."

"Oh?" Eamon said, scanning his eyes across his followers. They seemed to glisten with tears of pride. "I can see what made you think such a thing. But, Marius, I tried to warn you. What Auriol has become poses a great threat to the vampire kind. *We* are the threat. I think it may sink in just how deadly if I show you."

"Strange what trauma can do to one's mind," Silas said, mouth so close to the side of my face I could smell the harsh rotting of his teeth. "It either empowers you or blinds you. Which one will it be for Eamon?"

"Now!" Millicent was released suddenly as those holding her melted into clouds of shadow. From within, the rumbling growls of wolves called out.

As I unleashed my power on Silas with lightning precision, I could not tell if he underestimated me, or knew this would happen and simply waited patiently for the inevitable. Gold light erupted across his hand as though my fingers cast flame upon his skin.

His hold on me relaxed as I pushed an avalanche of feelings into his body. I fed him fear and panic, exhaustion and pain. Every negative emotion I harboured released out of me and into him. The force was sudden and vigorous.

Breaking free of him, I reached my hand into the back of my trousers and pulled the blade out. My legs pumped hard, and I seemed to forget to breathe. All I could focus on was Eamon's back as I closed in on him, dagger poised and ready to strike.

Somewhere I heard Marius expel a battle cry as wolves leaped out of the clouds of shadow. Millicent was calling my name. Eamon was too focused on his grand revelation. He was lost to watching Marius's reaction that he didn't see me coming.

I lifted the blade above my head and thrust it downward with the full momentum of my body. Then the ground fell away from me with such force the blade went flying from my hand. Commotion lit the room as it was suddenly filled with wolves far larger than normal, although not humanoid like Calix and Auriol.

"Did you truly believe such emotions would work to

destroy me?" Silas hissed into my ear. He tore me backwards. I couldn't do anything to stop him from dragging me away from Eamon—who, all the while, still had not noticed how close he came to death.

"I have lived with those emotions for years." Silas gripped the back of my neck, his nails breaking skin as he pulled me away. "They are meaningless. I am numb to them."

I searched the room to find Millicent now standing at Lord Marius's side, dagger raised and teeth flashing. She held my gaze for only a moment before tracking the large brown wolf that pawed the stone floor before her, as though it sized up its prey.

"I want you to understand," Eamon called out, "Your death is for all those families your creations have destroyed. For the children who lost parents, and the parents who lost children, all because you had no control over the undead. When my pack tears into you, limb from limb, I wish for you to recognise that you caused this. This is your doing, let that be your last thought. Just as your monsters ripped into my family and killed them as I watched, my monsters will do the same to you."

The wolves throughout the room buzzed with a feral energy. Each one yipped and whined, hardly able to contain themselves.

"Take my word for it," Lord Marius shouted out a final time. "Revenge does not fill the void. It simply whets its appetite and fuels its hunger. It never satisfies."

"Thank you for your wise words, but I think I will

decide that for myself." Eamon dismissed him, lifted a finger and pointed directly at Lord Marius. Then he called out his command which echoed across the room's sudden silence before it exploded into chaos.

"Feast. Kill Lord Marius. End it. *Now*."

## 41

E amon's pack of wolves broke the line and pounced towards Marius, unsuspecting of any danger which awaited them. Their jaws were split wide, flashing teeth far larger and sharper than the vampire lord had.

Marius hissed, readied himself, and the shadows at his back flared as though they came alive when a new howl lit the room. My head shot skyward—up towards the shadowed ceiling—as a shape emerged from the walkway above me. Blinking, I hardly could watch as it moved with unnatural speed. From the balcony, it threw itself over and fell towards the ground. It was nothing but a blur of fleshy mass, dark limbs, claws and bared teeth. The first of Eamon's wolves who leaped towards Marius never would have had the chance to survive.

It was Calix who fell from above, faint wisps of shadow still spreading from his newly changed form. He landed atop the leaping wolf, using its body to soften his fall. I felt the crack of bones reverberate in my body as the wolf was thrust to the ground beneath Calix's large paws. It exploded beneath the force; limbs and gore splattered outward in a circlet of destruction.

Blood misted the air, filling it with a sickening copper coating that seemed to lather the back of my throat. It was everywhere. Leaking around the ground, spreading like rivers through the grout between the slabs.

Eamon's wolves closest to the impact zone broke apart from their formation, some completely covered in chunks of their kin. Droplets had sprayed across Marius's face too. Compared to the glow of his ice-pale skin, the wolf's gore looked black.

Calix uncurled his monstrous form, taloned feet digging into the mess of flesh, blood and shattered bone beneath him. He towered before Marius and Millicent; his large form blocked them both from view.

Calix flicked his golden eyes away from the wolves and settled his attention on Eamon for a brief moment before looking at me. Silas's grip on me tightened. Calix's maw creased into a mask of pure fury, and he threw his head skyward, bellowing a howl that shook the foundations of the castle itself.

"I was hoping you would show yourself," Eamon said, silencing Calix's roar as he spoke. His voice oozed confidence, as did his posture, which he kept straight with shoulders rolled back. "I have been meaning to thank you."

Calix fell forward, landing on all fours. The thick tail at his back swished side to side, just beyond the mountainous curve of his strong back.

"You took my hand, but you gave me something far more useful. Power. Which is why I am going to give you a chance. You've earned it." Eamon didn't flinch as Calix prowled towards him. The wolves around Calix scattered, whimpering and yipping, but Eamon held firm. "Step aside, and I will allow you to take Rhory from this room, unharmed. He will be yours." Eamon looked back at me briefly, flashing me a smile. "It is what you have always wanted, isn't it? And you can have it. If, that is, you turn away and allow me to finish this."

Calix bowed his head, peeled his lips away from his teeth, and erupted in a growl of refusal. Although the sound was far from human, the meaning behind it was clear to all.

Eamon shrugged. "Then my *pack* will rip through you and everything in this room to see the vampires destroyed."

At his words, the wolves throughout the room continued to fuss. Eamon was far too focused on his wish to destroy Lord Marius that he didn't seem to notice his pack lacked confidence as they faced down a true monster before them.

I had stopped fighting against Silas whilst I watched the man I love contest the man who attempted to see me destroyed. All I could think about was how I burned with longing to see Eamon murdered. If I was not the one burying a dagger in his back, it hardly mattered; as long as his blood spread across this floor, that was all I wished for.

"Would you care to see what you made me?" Eamon asked, raising arms to his sides. One hand flexed with fingers, the other was simply a mound of bandages from where Calix had torn it off.

Drool leaked from between Calix's serrated teeth as he studied Eamon. I wanted to shout out and demand he finished this, but a part of me kept as silent as Marius, who watched on with blood drying on his face.

"Dear me!" Eamon laughed out. "It is a wonder what Rhory ever saw in you. You are a terrible conversationalist."

Calix snapped his jaws. Eamon thumped backwards as his skin burst into shadowed ash. As the cloud of it took over him, he disappeared for a moment and re-emerged as a wolf. His fur was as white as snow, and his eyes were so blue it made the sky look dull in comparison. He was larger than the rest of his pack, but still did not compare against a monstrous form like Calix.

The pack of wolves reformed as Eamon padded into their line. His presence re-fuelled them. Eamon howled and barked, throwing his head around frantically. It was a wonder his mouth did not froth.

Millicent raised her short blade and pointed it directly at Eamon. Her straight black hair was caught in the unseen wind of Marius's shadows. Her dark eyes peered down the sharp length of her blade as she spoke.

"When you fail, and you will, know that I will

proudly wear your pelt in memory of what you took from me," Millicent vowed.

Eamon snapped his teeth. He likely did not know what Millicent spoke of, but I did. And I knew the dark promise of death that lingered in her vow.

*I only hoped she was right.*

The line of wolves fussed, snapping teeth at one another as they burned with an uncontrolled energy. *Hunger.*

"Everything Eamon has done to get to this very moment," Silas whispered from behind me, "And what was it for?"

I tried again to pull back, but his nails dug deeper into me and my mouth was covered firmly by his hand.

"Eamon is a bad man," Silas murmured, suddenly withdrawing his hold.

"Then stop him," I pleaded, unable to stifle the shaking of my voice. Without Silas's hand, I longed to call out for Calix but feared my distraction would be his demise.

When Silas replied in a loud shout, my entire body stilled; I tried to inhale but choked on air as his command strangled me, invaded my conscience and undid me from the inside out. "*Attack.*"

The tension in the room changed. It cracked like lightning, splitting the wolves apart until every single one of them shifted and faced a new threat.

They each faced Eamon.

My husband's eyes burst wide, and his pointed ears

flattened to his head. He couldn't do so much as whimper before the pack of wolves flooded over him in a wave of exposed teeth and claws.

I didn't so much as cry out as I watched Eamon being ripped apart.

My stomach cramped with pain, and the burn of bile crept up the back of my throat. No matter how sick it made me, I couldn't turn away.

Eamon's snow-white fur stained black with his blood. I listened to every tear of skin as the pack ripped apart his limbs with their teeth and claws. The cracks of bone breaking beneath powerful jaws revolted me, as did the bellowing laughs that came out of Silas who watched on, his eyes glowing as bright as a dying star. Limb from limb, I felt the wet tear of skin and snapping breaks of bone deep from within me. Growls of hungry torment devoured the room. Blood sprayed until the majority of it was coated across the wolves who feasted upon Eamon.

When the pack pulled away, jaws smeared with

blood and skin, the corpse they left behind was unrecognisable.

"Brother." Silas turned his attention on Calix as the pack gathered around him. "It has been such a long time since I last saw you. I would ask if you missed me, but I regret to admit I already know the answer."

My entire body trembled. I looked to the mess that could no longer be described with any other word, and searched deep within me for the relief I expected to find. There was nothing. Eamon's death was unexpected, but it should have made me feel lighter. Free, perhaps. But the shackles did not lift. Grief sunk its talons into my stomach and squeezed.

"You… killed him." The words broke out of me. As I finally looked away from the pile of blood-coated flesh and fur, Silas became my focus.

"Is that not what you wanted? What you asked of me?" Silas asked, peering over his shoulder whilst Calix still prowled in his monstrous form before the vampire lord and Millicent. "You asked me to stop him, and I did."

"Why would you…" I failed to finish, gaze flicking to the dagger that waited a stretch away on the floor. The tension had not evaporated with Eamon's death, but grew heavier and more potent. Millicent hissed at the wolves closest to her, sensing the same strange emotion in the air as I did.

"You were not the only victim of Eamon's narrowed focus on revenge. He used me for what I was, and when I didn't give him what he desired, he broke me down bit by bit until my choice was taken from me. And then you... brother, you had to bite him, didn't you?" Silas focused solely on Calix again. As though reading some silent cue, three wolves separated from the pack around him and faced me. Teeth bared and covered in Eamon's blood, they narrowed their ferocious gaze upon me.

"You *turned* Eamon," Silas spat. "You revealed to him it was possible. I hid it from him for years, and you ruined it. Do you know what he did to me when he discovered what your bite did to him? What it made him?"

Calix's wolven face seemed to soften as his brother spoke, ears flicked backwards, and a light whimper broke at the back of his throat.

"I thought I knew pain, but that night when Eamon first turned..." Silas looked downward, choking on his words. "He tore into me over and over until I broke and gave him what he desired. A pack. A group of loyal men and women he could use to take down Lord Marius and complete his lifelong search for vengeance. A source powerful enough to resist the undead. To end them."

Millicent slipped from Lord Marius's side, dagger still in hand and fangs on display. Carefully she paced down from the dais like a cat on silent paws. Each step was well timed and precise, and not once did she remove her ruby stare from Silas.

"It is over," Millicent said. "Eamon is dead. Lord Marius is safe. Why don't we take this family matter elsewhere?"

441

Lord Marius straightened, his voice booming out across the room. "No one is to leave."

"The vampire is right," Silas sang. "You see, what first drew me to Eamon was his desires and aspirations. Eamon was not the only one who lost parents because of a vampire. I'm surprised Calix can even bear your company... bitch."

Millicent stopped only when Silas spat at her feet. Disgust wrinkled across her face as she regarded it.

"You don't want to do this," I called out, stepping towards Silas. "I know better than anyone what hurt follows Eamon in his wake. Whatever has happened, we can get through this."

"Together?" Silas spun wildly on me, a look of feral humour creasing his face. "Get your head out of the clouds, Rhory."

"And how will it end? With more bloodshed? More families torn in two?" I snapped, unable to catch a breath as the presence of my anxiety swelled in my chest.

Silas trailed me with his sickly gaze, all the while the room was filled with the growls of wolves. Beneath it all, a small whimper sounded. Auriol.

"There is nothing you can say to sympathise with me. If it is humanity you are looking for, then my dearest brother should have saved me all those years ago before Eamon tore it from me."

Auriol gasped out again. The silver chains holding her down hissed into flesh and clattered against stone.

"What about her?" I said, gesturing to Auriol. "Auriol loves you. She played no part in this."

Silas glanced to his grandmother, and for a moment his face pinched in a painful sadness.

"Her suffering will end," Silas said, his voice detached as his gaze was lost to us all. "Soon."

Millicent edged slowly towards Auriol. Her movements were slight and soundless that Silas didn't notice as his focus was fixed on me.

"Silas, please. End this. I know there is a part of you left. A part Eamon could never reach. Grasp it—"

"Enough!" Silas screamed, his voice catching in his throat. "I don't wish to hear this anymore."

Calix shot forward, ready to leave Marius's side to help me.

I raised a hand and looked the monster dead in his gilded eyes. "Stay."

He couldn't refuse me, even if he wanted to. Calix's tail folded between his legs. He stopped his pursuit, falling back into line with the vampire lord who hissed like a feral cat at the wolves who prowled around him.

"Well." Silas clapped, the sound echoing around us like thunder. "Would you look at that. My brother, the man Auriol believes worthy enough to snatch the mantle as alpha, yet here he is... whimpering under the command of some worthless weak man. I pity you, brother, truly I do."

Calix flashed teeth, spittle dripping down his thick maw. Millicent was only a stretch away from Auriol now. Silas was focused on his brother and the humour of watching him follow my command that he didn't notice as she reached her.

If she could free Auriol, only she would have the power to command Silas to stand down. She could end this.

"They killed our parents, Calix. Eamon was many things, but he was right in his want to purify the world. And we, we have the power to do it. We are the key. You can either stand in my way and be torn down or stand beside me whilst we fix this world. No more hiding in the shadows, brother. No more tunnels. We can be free."

I couldn't swallow without feeling the swell of my heart in my throat. How could Eamon have died, yet his words still lived on so vividly?

"Killing me will not solve your torment," Marius called out.

"It may not," Silas said. "But I will still enjoy every moment."

The clink of chains falling upon stone silenced the room. All heads turned towards it, to see Millicent helping Auriol from the ground, the tatters of her clothes around her human frame barely covering her modesty. Her skin was a patchwork of burns and marks. Without Millicent holding her up, the old woman would never have had a chance to stand.

"No," Silas breathed, understanding what was to come.

Auriol's shadowed eyes flickered open. Her eyelids were heavy, her skin almost tinged with purple from the poisoning of wolfsbane. Limp silver hair fell over her shoulders, obscuring the sagging of skin which clung to her old bones like wax to a candle.

Millicent's lips tipped upwards in a sneer as Silas began moving towards them. In one arm she held the only person powerful enough to control the pack, Calix and Silas. In the other, she held the twin blade to the one she had given me.

I held my breath, waiting for Auriol to do something. Her mouth parted, exposing a paled tongue between clenched teeth. My mind screamed with the desperation for Auriol to end this, to call out and finish this war of blood and family.

Calix howled with fury, unmoving from his place beside Marius just as I commanded him. I was not his alpha, but he followed my words without hesitation. Silas shouted out, hoping to smother his grandmother's pending command.

"Come on," Millicent mouthed, her grin fading the closer Silas got. "*Do* something."

The whites of Auriol's eyes where bloodshot with violent veins of red and purple. She could barely keep them open. I began to move. Power swirled around my hands, coating my skin in curling flames of gold light, as I chased after Silas.

Silas changed too. Shadow burst from his skin, peeling it away in ash and dust, to reveal the arm of a monster beneath. Yellow curved claws dragged beside him as he reached his grandmother.

Millicent released Auriol, forcing the woman behind her, just as Silas met them. She clattered to the floor with a thud, no more a flesh filled bag of brittle bones.

Silas couldn't stop himself. He thrust his clawed arm forward as the rest of his body broke apart to reveal the wolf beneath. Millicent met him, shielding Auriol with her body.

I would never forget the sound of Silas's claws ripping deep into Millicent's stomach. It seemed every other sound faded into the room, allowing the slow wet tear to sing through the silence. Millicent's red eyes bulged wide as her face broke into a snarl. Silas hoisted her from the ground, holding her up with only the claws he'd embedded deep into her. Gravity tugged her downward, encouraging the claws to continue their pursuit through her stomach and up to her chest.

A noise tore out of me. It was feral and pained and boiled with my emotions. Millicent's name rushed out of the incoherent sounds, leaving its own scarred mark in the flesh of my throat. I couldn't take my eyes off her. Not once did Millicent scream out in pain. Beside her paled taut lips and wide red eyes, her face was not a mask of agony… but a mask of determination.

She raised the dagger aloft before the monster and brought it down with a warrior's cry.

Silas couldn't pull away completely, not when his claws had trapped him close to her. The dagger missed the intended mark of his forehead. Instead, it sliced down the side of his face, clean through his eye.

The blade fell from Millicent's hand as Silas threw his large, wolven head from side to side. Blood sprayed

446

across Millicent, casting her in droplets of gore as dark as her obsidian hair. She smiled through it all, catching Silas's blood in her mouth and across her teeth.

Every being in the room watched as Millicent's smile faded. It was cleared from existence as Silas gathered himself enough to wrap his large powerful jaw around her neck. With a sickening wet snap, Silas tore Millicent from his claws with the force of his mouth and threw her, as though she was nothing but a discarded bone.

I didn't dare blink. There was nothing I could do but watch, vaguely aware of the muffled sounds of chaos as the room exploded in it. All I could do was study the strange scene as Millicent's body crashed against the floor, smearing blood in its wake, until she came to a perfect stop directly before me.

Millicent bled out in my arms, her blood staining my clothes and skin. To the touch, she was as cold as fresh winter snow, so cold it almost burned as my fingers graced her skin, brushing hair from her face until they came back completely slick and wet.

"Please," I begged her, tears rolling down my nose and falling upon her upturned face like rain. She could hardly keep her eyes open. They fluttered shut, and each time it took longer for her to find the strength to open them again.

"Did I hurt him?" she gasped, flashing pointed teeth covered in her blood. Millicent coughed, forcing blood to pump out of the jagged tears across the skin of her neck.

I could hear Silas's thunderous roars above the howls of his pack. Calix was fighting them back from Marius, throwing his powerful limbs wide to knock those who attempted to attack out of the way. Bodies of wolves skittered across the floor like skipping stones on a lake, but they didn't sink. They got back up and raced towards him with more desperation and fury.

"You did," I replied, swallowing the bile that burned at the back of my throat.

Silas could hardly calm himself. He clutched at his gouged eye, pressing the pad of his monstrous claws to the now empty socket as he roared in agony and fury.

Millicent smiled weakly before breaking into another fit of coughs. I placed my hand atop the wounds on her neck. Flaps of flesh moved beneath my palm. Silas's teeth had cut so deep it prevented her from healing.

"But I didn't kill him, did I?"

I shook my head, more tears falling. "No, you didn't."

Although his eye was shattered beneath the force of her dagger, and he was momentarily blinded, Silas could still fight. He would fight, as soon as he gathered himself.

"The fucker... he really hurt me," Millicent hissed, skin turning ashen before me. Cracks formed across her blood-soaked skin. Time was finally catching up with her. I blinked and her youthful face sank in on itself. Even the lustrous obsidian of her hair faded, leaving grey and silver in its place.

"Tell me what to do," I pleaded, not willing to let her go.

Whilst I cried over her ageing body, Millicent smiled up at me, looking skyward at something she only seemed to see. "I am going to see my brother again. Don't cry for me, Rhory… I have lived more lives than you could imagine. And I'm ready… I'm ready for this curse to end."

Her eyes fluttered as she looked back at me. Her skin peeled away in clouds of ash beneath my fingers, making it hard to hold on to her.

"And just as I was beginning to rather like you, Rhory Coleman."

I traced my hand over her face, feeling her skin come away beneath it.

"I'm sorry," I sobbed, heart breaking in my chest. "I'm sorry for everything I have caused you and the loss you have endured because of me."

Millicent raised her hand up to my face. Her arm shook and trembled like a leaf stuck in a storm. Her hand was aged and bent with crooked bones that belonged on a corpse. I didn't pull away from her. Selfishly wishing to prolong this moment, I closed my eyes and leaned into her freezing touch, wishing to memorise it for a lifetime.

"Be quiet, you sappy fool. I do not wish to hear it."

I placed my hand on hers and held it there. Now was not the time to honour past promises or heed old threats. Millicent was dying, and she could do little to stop me from using my power to sooth her. It was the easiest choice I had ever made.

Gold light slipped outward from my hand. It blossomed to life, enveloping her crooked fingers in a halo of pure, painless emotion. As I had many times before, I drew in all her discomfort and buried it deep inside of me. In her final moments, I would ensure she felt nothing but the kiss of peace and serenity. That was the very least I could do for her.

Millicent's mouth parted. She exhaled a long gasp as her eyes rolled back into her head. A single, blood-red tear ran down the side of her face. All the while, her smile never faded. When she reached her end, it was with her smile proudly cut across her face.

"Goodbye, Rhory," she whispered, her lips coming apart and melting in ash. "Thank you for…"

Beneath my hand, hers crumbled to nothing. Where her body had been was now a pile of ash and dust buried among blood-stained clothes.

Grief stabbed its talons into my heart and refused to let go. I levelled my stare from her remains to Silas who threw his wolven head back and forth. All I could think about was his death. I focused on the boiling fury that sparked deep within me. It burned hot, but regardless, I reached down and grasped it.

I got up, allowing Millicent's ash to fall from my legs in a cloud of death around me. My power raged around my hands, gold and brilliant. One hand was fisted, the other held tight onto the dagger Millicent had used to tear out Silas's eye. The leather-bound handle still held Millicent's frozen touch, and that also fuelled me.

Emotions swarmed around me. Pain, anger, hunger, desperation, hate. Each step from Millicent's remains felt as though I waded through mud. My legs fought against the resistance of emotions, kicking through it as I navigated towards Silas.

Silas calmed suddenly. He must have sensed me coming because he snapped his large head towards me and bored through me with his one remaining eye. Where the other golden orb had been was now an empty socket of dripping blood that oozed down his black fur and smeared freely into his parted jaw.

Then I felt another presence behind me. Strong talon-tipped claws sliced at the stone floor as Calix loomed over me at my side. I risked a glance and stared deep into his glowing eyes. He had left Lord Marius to fight for himself against the onslaught of Silas's pack. I longed to tell Calix to leave, but his presence stilled the frantic clash of my heart. Lord Marius cried out in anguish as he fought tooth and sharp nail against the beasts that were commanded to kill him.

"Your first mistake was not killing me when you had the chance," I spat, pointing the silver-bladed dagger at Silas. He dropped on all fours, claws scratching against stone and jaws snapping vigorously. "It ends. Now."

I stepped back, allowing Calix to prowl forward. As much as I longed to draw the silver across Silas's body, I would be dead within moments. Winning a fight was knowing one's strength. And this was not my fight, no matter how I wished it damned was.

Silas regarded his brother, tilted his head knowingly, and I was certain his elongated jaw peaked upwards into a smile. Calix exploded in a howl, matched by the rumbling growl his brother made. Silas leaped skyward first, and Calix joined in. As both bodies crashed, I felt the boom rattle my bones.

Lord Marius cried out as I watched, slightly dazed by the vicious grace the monstrous wolves attacked each other. It was the second cry from the vampire that had me turning to face him. A wolf was on him, jaw clamped around his outstretched arm.

I blinked and saw Millicent in the waiting dark, screaming out in pain as Eamon and his pack tore into her in the cellar of my home. It was enough to steel my mind. Energy buzzed through me, brightening my power and forcing my body forward. Silver blade slicing out before me, I ran for the vampire lord. Lord Marius wailed on the floor, clutching his blood-soaked arm. The pain of the wolf's bite was like liquid fire, I felt it sing as my power picked it up. It was so powerful, I didn't need to touch him to sense it.

I swung the blade fast and hard, bringing it into the neck of the wolf. It yelped, releasing Marius and skirting back from me. The silver was enough to disable the creature. It gave me the spare moment to raise up a glowing hand before it could completely escape.

As my fingers graced its fur-coated skin, I forced my exhaustion into it whilst stealing its strength as payment. My mind sparked, rejuvenated with the wolf's energy, whilst the creature slumped in a heap before us. I kicked hard, forcing the limp body down the steps of the dais when it knocked down the wolf who attacked next.

On I fought, muscles burning and mind alive. Time mattered little. Nothing mattered but surviving. If we failed, Millicent's death would be pointless. I couldn't allow that.

I snarled back at the wolves that were brave enough to come for me. I cut through so many that the silver of the blade was buried beneath dark blood.

With each death, I drew on my past self. The part of me who had been stolen. The part Calix had gifted back to me with his return to my life.

I was blindsided as a wolf pounced on me out of nowhere. Its jaw snapped inches before my face, but I knew from the agony I felt pouring off its skin that my blade had buried itself deep into its soft underbelly. I drew it upwards with everything I had. Its skin separated with ease until the ropes of its innards spilled over my chest and legs.

Pushing the wolf off, I ensured he felt the pain tenfold as I used my power to intensify what it experienced.

Three wolves were left, howling in chorus with Marius's cries and the roars of the brothers caught in their battle. I sensed the remaining creature's trepidation as they regarded me. One of them raced forward but lost its confidence as I swung the blade towards its face. He tumbled down the dais steps, reeling onto its side with a sharp whimper.

"Come on then!" I screamed, waving the blade around as though it was a sword of great myth. I saw the golden glow of my power reflected in the wolf's eyes as they looked from the death I had caused, and the promise of more death leaking with light from my hands.

The wolf who had fallen did not stay down for long. When it got up from the floor, it whimpered, barked its jaws at me, and ran towards the door at the far end of the room. The final two who remained followed it, nipping and yipping at its heels.

"Witch," Marius hissed, fingers coated in his own blood as he held his arm close to his chest. The sound snapped my attention back to him. The dais was awash with blood. It coated the stone floor, pooling it in the vision of a dark lake. As was Marius, whose skin glistened with the obsidian gore of his lifeforce.

"Help," he gasped, blood gargling in his throat, "Me."

There was no room to think. I almost tripped over the intestines of the wolf I had sliced open as I threw myself towards the screeching vampire lord. He reached out towards me with blood-slick nails, and gripped on with the last bit of strength he had.

"I can take your pain away," I said, breathless as I brought myself to Marius's side.

He glanced up at me, broken and weak. With my power glowing around my hands like fire, I felt the whispers of his agony. It was enough to make someone beg for death.

"But I cannot save you." That was beyond my capabilities. I was the puppeteer of emotions, not life.

"Jak!" Marius cried out for his love, spit flying out from his mouth. There was a glassy haze to his dark red eyes. It passed over like a cloud, sending the man into a maze of deliria. "Jak. Jak! I do not want to die."

I clasped Marius's hand and forced my will into him. He was in no mind to accept or refuse, so I acted as I knew I must. The vampire lord's eyes burst open as though breaking free from the trance his pain had trapped him in. I felt his fear. The fear of death. Fear of being forced to leave someone behind without saying goodbye. And I took it. Snatched it alongside any other feral or vile emotion I could find.

Lord Marius blinked up at me with his moon-wide eyes, as though seeing me for the first time. I sensed he tried to pull himself away, but I held on firm. I would not let go until every ounce of his pain was mine to claim.

"You need to help Calix," I cried out, grasping the burning fire of the wolf's bite until it became so real to me that my arm burned as though I had been bitten. I felt the skin rip and blood leak out, although there was no wound to see on me. Regardless, the agony was real.

The dull light of the room had become too much. My head throbbed, and I felt death lingering, but it wasn't my death. This was Marius's impending doom. And, if he didn't heal, the poison of the bite would claim him.

"I cannot—"

I released his hand, withdrawing my power. His pain dulled almost instantly, flooding back into the vampire in a tidal wave. He was knocked backwards by its return, so much so that the vampire lord could not fight me as I brought my wrist to his mouth, sliced it across his exposed fangs, and let my blood spill freely into his throat.

My head spun from the release. It was the second time I had given blood today, and my body knew it. Weakness crept in at the sides of my vision, but I refused to pull away. At first, Marius did not flinch. He gargled on my life's essence as it dribbled down his throat. Then his lips closed down on my wrist and I felt his tongue lap at my cut skin like a dog to water.

Pleasure rolled down my spine. It was all consuming, I forgot about the world as it crest over me in a wave of pure force. Cocking my head back, I groaned skyward, with my eyes drawing closed.

Marius attempted to pull back after a while, but he had not drunk enough. I held the back of his head and forced his mouth to my wrist harder.

As the vampire lord drank my blood from me, sucking my veins dry and making the room feel distant and strange, I watched the wolves fight as though I observed them through a muted lens.

Calix and Silas threw themselves around the great room in a bundle of claws and teeth. Walls cracked as they crashed into them. The ground thundered with their force. Even the air seemed to hum with their howls and cries. Both were covered in blood. There was so much. My eyes couldn't track their movements long enough to discern whose blood it was, not as they both moved with such speed and strength. It didn't matter. All that mattered was the sucking and nipping of Marius's mouth on my wrist and the feeling of warmth that spread across my chest.

I gasped out in disappointment when Marius finally withdrew his teeth from my skin. This time, it was me who was far too weak to refuse him.

Marius was no longer lying on the floor. He knelt before me, lowering me to the wet ground until it was I lying down. His lips were painted red, some blood stained his chin and neck.

A sorrowful pain creased his forehead and passed behind his bright, alert eyes.

"Thank you," Marius said softly as he released me. My head pressed against the floor, making the world look as though it was on an axis. Marius brushed the red curls from my head, his cold hand welcome against the burning temperature which gripped my body.

"Calix." The name broke out of me, taking the final dregs of my strength. If I could have raised my hand and pointed, I would have. But my body was numb, and my mind detached.

Marius nodded. The grimace caught across his face, twisting it into a mask of something deadly. Then, in a blink, he moved. His body was a blur as he joined the fight between brothers.

Calix was on the ground whilst Silas towered over him. Darkness swelled in at the corners of my eyes, making it harder to keep them open. I could do nothing but watch as Silas brought down his split jaws towards Calix's exposed neck.

I didn't wish to look away, but my heavy eyes

betrayed me. I fought hard to open them. When I managed only a slither of a parting it was to find that Silas no longer pinned my love down. Marius had his arm wrapped around the Silas's neck, distracting him long enough for Calix to get off the floor. The vampire clung to the beast's back like a child whilst he brought his teeth down into Silas's thick neck. Over and over, Marius bit. Flesh tore away and gore burst from the fresh wound. Silas roared, claws reaching up for Marius to tear him free.

Calix was there. He grasped his brother's jaw with one large talon-tipped paw. Marius continued to feast on Silas, who could no longer howl in pain, not with Calix grasping the lower part of his jaw as though it belonged to him. Silas's single eye remained wide and knowing as he sensed what was to come. He kept it open the entire time, refusing to look away as Calix growled inches from his face.

Then Calix's growl exploded in a howl.

He jolted his muscular arm and ripped Silas's face into two parts. Silas's jaw came away with little resistance. Marius leapt from his back before the limp body fell to the ground with a shuddering thump.

Calix discarded the dripping mass of bone and flesh. I winced as the wet slap of the jaw was thrown to the ground where it slid to a stop at the bottom of the dais before me. Teeth and bone flashed through slick meaty flesh as it dribbled blood, wetting the stone beneath it.

Sickness stormed deep in my stomach, but I couldn't move, couldn't look away. If I closed my eyes, I understood the shadows would be waiting. But it was growing harder to fight them. My body was no longer my own. Nor was my mind.

Soon enough, the darkness closed in, shielding me from the horror of the lump of Silas's useless meat. It finally claimed me. Somewhere beyond it, I heard my name, but I couldn't be sure. I would have opened my eyes to see if someone spoke it, but I was married to the darkness. And, like Eamon, it refused to let me go.

The only thing I was certain of was the pain across my wrist. The echo of Marius's kiss lingered as a reminder of why I was fading.

"It is over, my love." A voice from the darkness sang. It was familiar and warm. It was home.

Again, I fought with every last scrap of strength I had, but I couldn't open my eyes. Not even a little.

When the voice spoke again, it was intimate as it was distant—far off, as though it spoke through miles of darkened tunnels. Three words, that was the last I heard; I focused on them as they echoed, growing quieter with each recurrence until there was only silence.

"I've got you."

## ❧ 44 ❧

I woke to the caress of lips against my mouth. The touch was gentle yet commanding, enough to discard the shadows and draw me back out into the light. My eyes fluttered open, adjusting to the warm amber glow that coaxed me out of sleep. As my body came alive, I was vaguely aware of the pressure of bedsheets strewn across my lower half. Pinpricks of needles tickled across my legs and feet, causing them to dance beneath the silken sheets.

Disappointment purred through my confused mind as the lips finally drew back and left me. I longed to call out, to demand they return, but my body did not yet feel like my own. Not entirely.

The familiar brush of a finger pressed to my forehead. Beneath its sudden presence a cascade of shivers spread over my skin. The single touch was the stone that was thrown into the still lake, creating gargantuan waves of disturbance. I opened my eyes enough to make out

461

the shape of a man hovering above me. He was haloed in golden light.

The owner of the tender touch drew a finger across my forehead, down past my temple and along the curve of my jaw. "For a moment there... you had me thinking I lost you, Little Red."

My heart burst in my chest as the blurred figure came into focus. Calix leaned down close, blocking out the light so all I could focus on was him. He wore a smile that had the power to break my heart and remake it. His light brown hair had been gathered in a bun held together by a tie of leather string. A single strand fell over his face as he leaned in once again and brought his lips to mine.

"Calix," I exhaled his name, the word muffled by the press of our mouths.

My body arched upwards, desperate to eradicate every inch between us. I lifted both arms and linked them around the back of his neck. This time, Calix would not pull away from my kiss until I desired.

"Careful," he moaned as my tongue met his.

"Don't let me go," I managed, voice rough as stone.

"I will never let you go," Calix replied before diving back into my kiss. "Never."

Slowly, my mind woke alongside my body. Flashes of the bloodied room and the death that haunted it flooded my mind, replacing the warmth Calix gifted me with a terrifying chill. Questions overwhelmed me, distracting me from the man in my arms. I found my eyes drawn to the wrapping of white bandages across my wrist and the faint pink stain of blood that seeped from beneath it.

Calix felt my body stiffen beneath his hold. It was his signal to draw away.

"Where am I?" I asked, trying to get a better look around me but my neck ached and the light was suddenly too bright to bear. Calix lowered me slowly back to the cloud of pillows that supported my neck. As he stepped back, I could make out grand stone walls, elaborate sconces burning with pillar candles that reflected light off gilded frames with time-worn paintings. The room was somewhat moderate but adorned with rich coloured rugs and dark-wood furniture.

"Lord Marius insisted you stayed here until you healed," Calix said, his face creasing with obvious concern. A shadow passed behind his eyes as he spoke. I wondered if the same shadow mirrored in my gaze—we both could no longer hide from what had happened.

"And where is here?" I repeated, knowing I was certainly not being seen in St Myrinn's. Beside the narrow bed I lay in and the dark wood cabinet at the bed's side, there was little other furniture in the room. It was the perfect blend of plain, whilst also feeling as though I had stepped back in time. Even the air was thick with age. With each rasped inhale I felt the history of this stone room seep within me.

"Castle Dread," Calix confirmed.

Alarm clawed my body. My sore muscles spasmed at my physical recoiling and I gasped out, "I need to get out of here…"

"You are safe," Calix said quickly. "You are safe, Rhory. I will let nothing happen to you."

I looked to the closed door at the end of the room, half expecting someone to barge in and take me for being a witch.

"You need to drink something," Calix offered, fussing with a chalice on the bedside cabinet. "It has been three nights and you have hardly had anything to eat or drink besides what little water I have encouraged you to take. Finish a glass, and then we can talk. About it all."

*Three days.* I could hardly comprehend the time I had missed, so much so that I didn't refuse Calix as he brought the cold metal to my mouth, held the back of my neck with his hand and tipped the chalice. The cold rush of water was divine and I groaned as it soothed my dry throat. I had not realised just how thirsty I was until my eyes stared at the empty bottom of the chalice.

"More," I gasped as water dribbled down my chin and the burning in my throat soothed.

Calix poured another. The sound of water filling the chalice was the most beautiful song. I finished the second offering quicker than the first, gulping each mouthful down as though it was my last.

Dribbles of water slipped beyond my lips and fell into my hairline. Calix took his thumb and gathered the stray droplets with it. "I cannot express the relief I have for seeing you with your eyes open. Rhory..." Calix's voice faltered. It faded into a long sigh.

I had not yet noticed the exhaustion that painted

Calix's face. His eyes were ringed with dark shadows, his skin pale as though the castle had drained the colour from him. Across his neck, I could see the faint red marks from newly healed wounds. I longed to reach up and touch them, to kiss them just as he did with the marks Eamon had left on my body.

My eyes drank him in with the same thirst my body had for the water. I trailed him from head to foot, recognising the shirt he wore was far too tight on his torso. It was clear he had not washed, nor was he dressed in his own attire.

His fist was pressed into the side of my bed. I crept my fingers across the sheets and wove them around his balled-up hand until it unravelled like a flower to sunlight.

"Take me home," I asked, staring deep into his eyes.

Calix held my gaze for a moment, then dropped his stare to the floor.

"What is wrong?"

Calix exhaled. It was long and slow. His sigh alone told tales of the tension he harboured inside of him. "My invitation to stay here has expired. Lord Marius has given me instructions to leave."

"Then we will go," I said, trying to push myself up, but fire burned at my wrist as I leaned on it. I hissed out through clenched teeth as my mind spun from the sudden rush of discomfort.

"Careful," Calix fussed, a deep growl emanating from deep in his throat. "The bite marks will take time to heal. If you tear open the fresh skin, the wounds will persist."

I could still feel the haunting pleasure of Lord Marius's bite. How his tongue lapped at my skin and sucked hard. But I also remembered how it was Calix's face in the dark of my mind. It was him I had imagined when the world faded.

"I'm fine, Calix. I am. Come on, help me up and we will leave…"

Calix's eyes screamed with refusal. "Rhory, I cannot take you with me."

"Yes!" I snapped with urgency. "Yes, you can."

Calix shook his head, returning his hand to the side of my face. He held it tenderly. I leaned into him, never wishing for him to pull away.

"Lord Marius has bid me a pardon. He allows me to keep my life, but I must leave Darkmourn as part of our arrangement."

I couldn't bear the broken gleam in his eyes. "Arrangement?" I echoed, the word tasting strange in my mouth.

Calix winced but didn't look away; I could see the pain that statement gifted him. "They know the danger I pose. Marius will not take any further risks."

"You killed Silas. You killed your own brother to save Marius! What more do you need to sacrifice to prove you would be no threat?" I didn't dare to blink, fearing of seeing the bloodshed. In my mind's eye, I could still see the torn half-formed jaw of Silas on the floor before me. Discarded. Useless. No one could survive that. Then another death flooded over me. Millicent. And all at once, I felt debilitated by the memory. If I wasn't in this bed, I would have been knocked down by the force of my grief.

"I may have helped save him, but that does not change what I am."

"This is wrong," I said, almost shouting.

"It is done."

"Then I will talk to him!" I said, fumbling over my words. "I saved his fucking life. If I didn't give him my blood, he would have died to the wolf's bite. Just like…"

I couldn't speak her name. It lodged in my throat like a thorn.

Calix smiled down at me, although the upturn of his mouth did little to conceal the sadness in his eyes. "Millicent got what she always wanted," Calix said. "It was what she asked Auriol for when she first found us."

Suddenly, the light of the burning sconces grew too harsh. I pinched my eyes closed, trying to unscramble Calix's words.

"She always wanted to be released from her…"

"Curse," I answered for him, echoing what Millicent had said when she perished in the cradle of my arms.

I opened my eyes to find Calix staring through me with his. The gold sheen of his irises glowed as tears pooled within them. There was something so heartbreaking and beautiful to see such a man cry.

"How could you leave me?" I complained as the sharp stabbing pain exploded behind my eyes. "After everything."

"I told you, I could never leave you."

"That makes no sense!" I shouted now, wanting to grasp Calix's shirt so I could prevent him from ever moving away.

Calix didn't answer. Instead, he brushed the hair away from my forehead and brought a kiss to my sticky skin. "I am so proud of you, Rhory."

"As am I," another voice sang from the doorway. Neither of us had noticed it had opened, nor that someone had entered.

Lord Marius stood before us, skin glowing bright as a star. His posture was pin-straight, with shoulders rolled back and hands held behind him. I felt Calix tense; he moved and stood at the end of the bed, blocking the vampire lord from view.

"Am I not permitted to say my farewells?" Calix asked, voice laced with something feral.

I could not see Marius's expression as Calix shielded me, but I could certainly hear the slight edge of fear in his voice as he chose his next words carefully. "Of course. I simply wanted to check on our patient, to ensure he is improving."

"Rhory is fine."

I shouldn't have enjoyed another man speaking for me, but when Calix did, my entire body buzzed with adrenaline. It was an emotion which seemed entirely misplaced in such a situation.

"Then my offer of blood would not be required?" Marius asked.

"As it hasn't been required for the past three nights," Calix replied, stone cold.

"Even if my blood could have healed Rhory sooner?"

The thought of ingesting the blood of a vampire displeased me. It was strange to hear it so blatantly offered, when Lord Marius himself was the one to outlaw such a thing.

"I am sure it would," Calix said, glancing back at me. "But Rhory is strong. He does not require your aid. He needs no one."

That was a lie. I wished to shout at Calix, to remind him just how wrong he was. I needed someone. He was the one who I needed the most.

"Indeed, he is strong." Marius stepped aside so I could see him. I caught the flash as his tongue traced his lower lip. A contemplative glint passed over his ruby eyes as he regarded me. "As he had just so beautifully put it, he *fucking* saved my life. I am in debt to him."

I cringed with embarrassment for being overheard but refused to lower my stare from the vampire.

"And because of your bravery, I am forever in your debt," Marius said. "I also have someone who is *dying* to meet you and thank you himself."

I wanted to spit at him, to show just how little I cared for his gift of thanks. The only gift I wanted stood before me and was moments from being banished from Darkmourn entirely.

"There is only one thing I want," I spat.

Marius regarded me for a moment before turning

his eyes back to Calix. My proud protector, who had hardly moved an inch since the vampire lord stepped into the room.

"Master Grey," Marius said. "Your grandmother has awoken too if you would like to visit her. Then, I am afraid, it will be time for you to take your leave."

"Auriol, is she alive?" My question broke out of me, demanding both of their attention. I had almost convinced myself that she had died. In fact, it pained me to admit, but I hardly paid her any mind after Silas murdered Millicent.

"Of course, she is," Marius said, dark brows pinching over his brow. "If there is one thing about my friend Auriol… she is stubborn in the face of death. She is an example of the defiance of the mortals she so cares to protect. And she is a long-standing friend, and I treasure friends. The years we have known one another have made us family, although she wouldn't care to admit it. Auriol's wellbeing is of my utmost importance."

Calix scoffed to himself, granting him a sideways glance from the vampire lord.

"Will you be banishing her then? Is that how you treat friends, or just those who kill their own family to save you?" I asked.

"Auriol," Marius said carefully, her name rolling over his silver tongue, "Will stay here with me until her brother, Arlo, returns to care for her. I am sure he would be highly interested in what she has become during his absence—as am I."

"A weapon who can destroy you, that is what you

mean. That is why you are sending Calix away, even after he proved he is no threat to you," I spat, anger boiling at his decision to care for Auriol, but to discard Calix as though he was nothing.

"Yes, exactly, however I think your annoyance should not be aimed at me entirely," Marius confirmed, bringing a sharp nailed finger to his jaw and scratching at it. "Calix, have you informed your dearest that the decision for you to leave Darkmourn was, in fact, your own suggestion?"

My heart stilled, quivered, then felt as though it would shatter entirely.

Calix turned his head sideways so I could witness his profile draw down into a frown. "I had not."

Marius tutted, pulling a face with wide eyes and raised brows. "Oh, well. Perhaps I will wait beyond the door as you say your final goodbyes."

I couldn't utter a word as Marius swept from the room, leaving the destruction his revelation had left in it.

"Tell me he is lying," I said.

"Rhory, I am sorry."

"What was the other option?" My voice was stoic, and as empty of emotion as I felt.

Calix tensed, his eyes flashing a molten gold as he looked away from me. "It doesn't matter——"

"What was the fucking option, Calix!?" I screamed, not caring for the cramping of pain that seized across my chest.

Calix slowly looked up at me. Even without my power, I could read the guilt that oozed from him. "I am a monster. The big bad wolf that killed your mother, my brother, Millicent, and almost you. I am dangerous. If a rabid dog attacked someone, it would be put down."

"Death?" I said, hating how the word sounded when it came out of my mouth. "That is no option."

"No," Calix corrected. "Marius is a fair man. He would not have killed me."

"Spit it out then," I said, anger and love coiling inside of me in an inferno. "For once, take your chance and be honest with me."

My words struck Calix and he stumbled back. It took a moment for him to right himself. When he did, he paced towards the side of the bed, his hand racing across the sheets tentatively. He knelt beside it, forcing me to turn my head on the pillow to see him. Wide-eyed and face sheet white, he leaned in and pressed a lingering kiss to my forehead.

"Sometimes we make sacrifices for the better," Calix said softly. "Just know I am proud of my decision, as I am proud of you."

Exhaustion kept me from fighting him. I felt the finality in his words and didn't wish to spend our last moments arguing over something that would not change. If he desired to leave me, I would not give into my pity and wallow in it.

"Tell me where to go… where to find you?" I asked, unable to hide the quiver in my voice.

"The world is a large place." Calix brought his lips from my forehead to my mouth and kissed me again. His lips lingered far longer than the one on my head. I refused to kiss him back. Refused to show him I cared, when internally I felt as though I was being torn into pieces. "Someone dear to me once told me that Darkmourn is merely a small part of a large world. Who knows what else is out there."

"The world is not a big enough place to stop me from finding you," I said, determination burning in my eyes. "Calix, I will find you."

He leaned in, eyes racing over my face as though he drank me in for a final time. "I am counting on it."

"I am serious," I said, tears cutting down my face. "No one can stop me. Not Marius. Not Darkmourn. Not anything. I lost you once and found you. Do you hear what I am saying to you, Calix? I *will* find you again."

Calix steeled his expression but couldn't hide the tears that lingered in his eyes. "You are free, Rhory. Free from Eamon, from me. You can decide the path you take. I do not deserve your promises."

"The only path I wish to take is the one with you standing beside me," I said, choking on the truth of the words. "Because I love you."

"I know," Calix replied, smiling through the palpable sadness.

"Is that it? Is that all you can say?"

"The last time I told you I loved you, you never came back to me. I pondered if I had never said it in the first place, you would have come to me that night we were to run away. The night before your mother cursed your mind to forget me. If I don't say it now, then you really will be forced to find me."

"You are cruel," I said as I urged his mouth back to mine. My fingers knotted in his hair, keeping him in place.

"Well," Calix said. "I am the big bad wolf. Being cruel seems like a fitting title for me."

"Okay, if that is what you wish to be… Then I will hunt you down. Hunt you down and slaughter you myself for leaving."

A shiver ran across my entire body as Calix's lips moved to my ear and whispered, "Is that a promise?"

I grasped his hand and let my power spill out of me. It lit the room with a glow of gold light that mirrored the stunning tones of Calix's eyes. When I replied, I wanted Calix to feel my honesty. To recognise the burning truth in my words deep in his soul. I let my emotions pour into his being as I replied.

"I promise."

## ❧ 45 ❧

J ak Bishop waited for me in the library, just as
Marius had said he would have. The vampire lord
patted a hand on my shoulder as he left me
beyond the door, bidding me farewell with a final
thanks for saving his life. I couldn't respond to him.
Words failed me, as all I felt was numb. *Empty*. Empty
without Calix, who had been forced to leave hours
before this. Knowing it was Calix's choice to go not only
drove the knife of pain into my chest but twisted it
thoroughly.

He had left me.

There was certainly nothing beastly about Marius.
All the stories my mother had told me, all her warnings
to keep my power hidden, seemed almost misplaced as I
stood before the door to Jak Bishop's haven.

I raised my hand, ready to bring my knuckles down
to knock, when a silken voice rang out from within.

"No need for formalities," Jak said, his voice barely

muffled by the thick wooden door. "You can enter, Rhory Coleman. My home is open to the likes of you."

The brass handle of the door was freezing to the touch as I grasped, turned, and pushed it open. Warmth welcomed me, as did light. The glow of freshly lit fires bathed the library in gold and amber. I had not noticed just how cold the rest of Castle Dread seemed until I was engulfed in the room's embrace.

The door shut with a final click at my back. There was no going back now. Now I faced the very thing I had hidden from. The very being my mother had betrayed me and my father to keep me from.

Jak sat on a large red cushioned chair with his legs drawn up and a big leather-bound book open across his lap. From my vantage point at the door I could see only the side of his face. Dark curls fell over his forehead, gently brushing just shy of his perfectly shaped brows. He was a beauty, just as the stories told. With large all-seeing eyes and smooth skin stretched across the proud bone structure of his face. The fire lit him from a certain angle that made the hollows of his cheek deep, and the red vampiric glow of his eyes like the freshest of blood.

He closed the book with a thud and hugged it to his chest. As he beckoned me over to him, I caught the silver foiling of lettering across the spine. For a moment, I thought the swirling calligraphy spelled out his name.

"So, you are the witch who saved my husband," Jak said calmly, eyeing me up and down as I sat in the thick-cushioned chair before him. "In doing so, saving me and all those we have sired since Darkmourn first fell."

"I did what I had to do," I replied.

"Then it is only just that I personally thank you."

"It was the right thing to do," I said, voice void of emotion; Jak furrowed his perfectly sleek brows downward as he noticed. "But it was Calix who saved your husband. Not me. Perhaps your thanks would be better off given to him, for it would be wasted on the likes of me."

"Keeping him alive is our thanks. We have yet to understand what he is, but it is clear how deadly he can be." Jak lowered his eyes, fingers picking at the leather bindings of the book.

"So, the tales are true. You *are* unkind."

Jak smiled, welcoming my backhanded comment. "Oh, is that what they say about me? Seems rather tame, considering..."

My body trembled. I gripped the edges of the chair and picked at the thinning velvet with my nails. The cool kiss of Jak's red vampiric eyes fell to my wrists, and the freshly tied bandages which had not long been replaced.

"I know your story, Rhory. I know what you have lost to be sitting in that very seat." The caring nature of his voice surprised me, as did the softening of his eyes as he glanced back at my face.

"We all have made sacrifices," I replied. "Some more than others."

"Millicent." A sorrowful glint darkened the ruby of his eyes. I pondered what colour they had been before Marius changed him. "That is a name I will not forget.

She fought beside Marius, and for that he will ensure her story is written to last an age and the next."

Pain stabbed through my chest. I felt it pierce slowly into my heart, inch by inch, until the thud of the hilt was all that was left. It seemed I was rather accustomed to the pain and I pondered if I would never be without it now.

"I'll never forget her either," I said, turning my attention to the licking flames in the fire at my side. The warmth tickled the skin of my face but did little to prevent the tears from pricking in my eyes at the thought of her.

"Tell me, because I admit I am curious. How is it I have not known of you before?" Jak asked. It was a question I knew was on Marius's lips when he saw me use my power against Silas. Before Calix ripped his jaw in two. "You are a witch, and yet you have been kept from me all this time."

There was no hiding anymore. Not that I cared to. Jak could take me, lock me away and it wouldn't matter. I had nothing left, nothing to fight for.

"My mother warned me about you," I said, levelling my eyes with Jak once again. "She told me you collect witches. And they are never seen again. She didn't wish for me to become another name on the list, so she became the very devil to ensure that never happened."

"Well." Jak smiled. "She should have tried harder."

There was nothing for me to say.

"Humour me. What is it you have been taught to believe happens to the witches I take?" Jak asked, tilting his head and narrowing his eyes at me. The fire beside me flared unnaturally, the flames turning a cold, cobalt blue in my peripheral.

"The answers are endless," I said before answering his question with one of my own, "What I know is Castle Dread is empty of them. Beside you, and Marius, there is not another living soul here. So, you humour me, Jak. Where are they?"

Jak's pink blush lips turned up into a grin. "Safe."

"My mother didn't trust you," I said.

Jak's smile faltered as honest hurt pinched across his brow. "Is this from the same woman who used her hidden power to alter your mind, poison it, and marry you off to a man who hurt you?"

My mouth parted, but no sound came out.

"Auriol told us everything," Jak confirmed. My first reaction was to ask if she was well. I had not seen her since she was carried out from the room in Marius's arms. But Jak continued before I could even draw a breath.

"It is why I wished to speak to you. Alone. Rhory, you and I are not as different as you may think. We are both products of the poison of our mothers. The Darkmourn we all know today is built on the backs of parents who use their children to settle old scores. Look at those parents now, they are all dead. Six feet under, so to say. Mine. Yours. You survived her, whereas I helped destroy the world to seek revenge on mine. It is all in here." Jak tapped the plain cover of the book. The leather looked almost wet as the unnaturally blue flames reflected across it. "If you stay with me, you will learn it all."

"No," I said. "For all I know you kill the witches."

"Of course, I don't. I train them. Ready them."

"For what?" I asked, chest filling with a strange, unwanted worry at Jak's dark expression.

Jak uncurled his legs, placed them on the ground, and stood. He was no taller than me in height, but as he towered before my chair, bathed in his cobalt firelight, he looked like a giant from old tales.

"The world requires balance. Who knows what new threats will come—just as Calix and Auriol have proved... they can be lurking anywhere."

It didn't exactly answer my question, but I sensed from Jak's demeanour that he didn't want to elaborate.

"Do you know I was once foretold to return magic to the world? I may not have done it as my mother wished, but I am now doing it in my own way. I never take the witches against their will. They are invited to join me. To train and learn about their powers in a world who would prefer to scrub all mention of witches from existence. It was my fault the hate and discrimination against the witches started, and it will be my legacy to fix it."

"Did you ask me to see you to thank me, or extend that same invitation?"

Jak didn't reply at first. He lifted the heavy tome, slotted it into a gap on the shelf and pushed it in. The sound of the book sliding against the wooden shelf sent a comfortable shiver across my skin. *Who knew such a noise was so pleasant?*

"It would not feel right to offer such an invitation because I know you would answer from a mind that is still not your own."

When Jak looked back at me, the force of his attention nearly knocked me out of the chair. I raised a hand and tapped my fingers to my temple, knowing exactly what Jak alluded to.

"My answer would be the same, no matter the state of my mind."

"Let us test that theory, shall we? Rhory, I would like to offer you a gift. A thanks for what you have done for my family."

"I want nothing," I said, voice breaking as I scrambled for an excuse to give him. "There is nothing you could give me, nothing I desire."

"Strange," Jak said, screwing up his face as he regarded me with a mischievous smile. "When I last spoke with Master Grey, he warned me you would say that. So, he made me a deal."

The world seemed to quiet at Jak's words, as though his voice had the power to still everything around us.

"Oh, I know all about his deal," I replied, feeling the numb agony that had settled on me since Calix left, intensify.

"Then I trust Calix told you what he asked of us? What he wanted in return for him leaving Darkmourn?"

The question hung between us. My silence was enough confirmation that I didn't know what was offered as part of the deal. Calix had a way of keeping secrets from me, it seemed.

"Calix left Darkmourn under one condition. In fact, I seem to remember him being rather passionate about what he wished for."

"What did he ask for?"

"I was simply going to give you wealth and an abundance of comfort as thanks for saving Marius's life, but Calix had a better idea. He promised to stay out of Darkmourn as long as I was the one to break the curse put upon your mind. Calix made a deal to stay away, as long as your mind is freed. He wanted you to remember... he said he wished for you to remember your *before*."

I choked on my breath as my words flew out of me. "Is it possible?"

Jak laughed, the light sound like the fluttering of bird's wings. "Anything is possible in Darkmourn."

A smile of disbelief creased across my face.

Jak grinned in return. It was breathtaking and wonderful, captured on a youthful face which his immortality had frozen upon him. Jak Bishop was older than I could imagine, but he looked slightly younger than me. It was the tone he spoke in and the way he carried himself which truly revealed the many years he had on me.

"With the power us witches hold anything is possible. If you wished to learn it all, I would teach you. If you decided that was not the path you wish to take, then I would not question it."

I leaned forward in my chair, my body moving closer towards Jak. All I could think about was the possibility that Jak could fix me. I longed for my mother's influence to release me, so I could not torment myself with knowing what I remembered was real or conjured.

I longed to remember with every ounce of my being and it was possible because of Calix.

"Do it," I begged, tears streaming down my face and slipping over my smile. "Please."

Jak bent down towards the lit hearth, scooping his hand into the blue flames. He brought out a bud of fire which twisted an inch above the skin of his palm. It hovered silently, not burning or maiming him. He turned his attention to me and closed the space until he stood carefully between my separated legs. A wash of his scent brushed over me. It was as light as spring air, with the underbite of spiced cinnamon.

"Be free, Rhory Coleman. Reclaim your mind. Your life. For it starts, anew, today."

I pinched my eyes closed as Jak Bishop brought the flame towards my temple and pressed it against my cool skin. At his touch, a rigid breath of power rushed through my skull. In the dark of my mind, I felt his magic penetrate through barriers; the force knocked them down, crumbling the mental walls one after the other.

. . .

There was pain, but I didn't shy away from it. I welcomed it, embraced it. And in the dark, slowly emerging through the heavy fog which had been forced over my mind, was a face. A face I knew from now, but slowly remembered from before.

Calix Grey stepped free, and with the phantom of him came the monstrous wave of our story careening towards me. I surrendered willingly to it with nothing but the swell of bliss within me.

## 3 YEARS BEFORE

*We will run away, Little Red. Together. Come to me, come to the cottage. I will wait for you, and then we will both be free from secrets. We will be free, together. I love you.*

Calix's promise repeated over in my mind as I clambered around my bedroom, stuffing clothes into a bag until its seams stretched. I was fuelled with desperation and urgency. My mind was so lost to it I hardly paid attention to what I packed. I was completely focused on the darkening sky beyond my room, and the knowledge that Calix would be waiting for me. In my mind's eye, I could see him waiting at Auriol's cottage, prepared to flee Darkmourn and all its shackles the moment I arrived.

I wondered if he felt the same swell of excitement as I did. Had the same feeling clogged his throat and quickened the pace of his heart until his ribs ached? As I stuffed another shirt into my pack, I smiled. I hadn't stopped smiling since this morning when I had seen him last and he presented this idea of us leaving Darkmourn, together.

Since then, it was all I could ponder, which was not a new concept because Calix always filled my mind.

Snatching up the pack, I didn't bother to glance back at the room as I left it. Knowing it was the last time I would pass through its door filled me with renewed excitement. Yes, I had memories made within its walls which I would always think back to with a full heart, but those memories involved Calix. And we were about to step out of our boundaries and create far more than I could ever imagine possible.

The house was silent as I passed through it. It was not uncommon for me to be alone here, and this time I almost felt sad knowing I was to leave it. Mother and Father were still at St Myrinn's for Father's weekly health check. Mildred had likely left for the day, after ensuring the rooms were full of the smells of cooking and freshly washed bedding.

I would miss Mildred. If I thought about her long enough, I might have stopped in my tracks. Of course, I would miss my parents as well; there was no denying that. But watching Father's health deteriorate was painful, and Mother had locked me up in my cage long enough. Father had always longed for me to see the world, but Mother kept the key to my cage on her at all times. She had grown complacent that I would never leave. Perhaps she believed the years of drumming in the horrors of the world would prevent me from even opening the door to my cage a fraction. Now, I would kick it down.

I had to leave before Eamon revealed to Mother what he had seen the night prior. Fear clawed up my throat as I thought back to him. All it had taken was the Crimson Guard to slip his head around the door to my room, to find me sat above Calix, bare for all to see. That one moment had ruined everything, or had it freed me?

Eamon was loyal to my father, and I had no doubt he would expose our secret in time. Which was why I had to leave tonight before Mother found some way to keep me from Calix, just as she always had.

It had been her fear of our truth ever being exposed which had kept me smothered. Until Calix, I had not cared to mind. Now, knowing what freedom and the fresh air felt like, I longed for it.

My feet smacked against the freshly oiled wood floors. As I took the last step down into the foyer, I nearly slipped. Catching myself on the banister, I took a moment to calm down—whereas my mind willed for me to leave and I would, my body reacted to the guilt I should be feeling.

"Careful."

A gasp broke out of me as I glanced up to see Eamon standing sentry at my front door. My breath lodged in my throat, blocking the string of curses that wished to spill from my mouth.

"Good evening, Eamon," I said, grasping my pack of clothes tight to my side. His bright azure eyes glanced towards it for a brief moment before returning to me.

"Rhory," Eamon replied, bluntly. "Are you planning on going somewhere?"

I lifted my chin, steeling my gaze as I regarded him. "What does it matter to you?"

"Your wellbeing matters to me," he replied quickly, watching me as though I was his prey. I refused to allow it to deter me. I continued moving towards the door, towards him. Only when the tips of my boots were close to him did I stop.

"Excuse me," I said, gesturing with a flick of my eyes for him to move out of my way.

Eamon hardly moved, only so much as to lift his arms and cross them over his broad chest. I hated the way he looked at me, how his eyes traced across my body, his sly grin lengthening at its corners.

I fought the urge to shiver, knowing exactly what thoughts plagued his mind.

"It is good to see you dressed more... appropriately," Eamon said. "Or, just dressed—"

"Didn't you hear me?" I snapped as my skin crawled in response to his comment. I squared my shoulders, but my small frame was unimportant compared to Eamon's. "I said, excuse me."

"Oh, I heard. But I am afraid I am under strict instructions to keep you from leaving tonight."

For the first time, I was unable to keep the panic from infecting me. I felt its chill spread across my chest, travelling with numbing speed down my arms and legs, until I was entirely numb. There was something sinister about the glint in Eamon's bright eyes. How he found this entire interaction... amusing.

"By whose orders?" I asked.

"*Mine.*"

Eamon didn't shift his gaze to the new voice, but I did. Before I even turned and looked, I knew it was Mother who had slipped into the room behind me. She always had a way of moving with silent grace—some people admired that about her, whereas it made me uneasy.

Ana Coleman danced across the foyer towards me. I couldn't see her heels beneath the long skirt of her maroon dress, but I could certainly hear the click of them. The swish of material around her ankles gave my mother the impression of floating.

"Allow me to take this from you," Mother said, reaching out for the pack I held.

My knuckles tensed on the strap, turning white beneath my grip. Mother kept her hand extended, but soon realised I was not going to give it to her. Her nails curled inward, likely pinching the skin of her palm as she fisted her hand and returned it to her side. There was no concealing the flash of displeasure that creased across her beautiful face.

"I thought you were out for the evening," I said, finally locating the courage to speak.

Mother pouted and drew her eyebrows down until her forehead pinched in wrinkled lines. "Jameson thought it best for your father to stay over at St. Myrinn's for observation this evening."

"And you left him?" I said, accusation lacing my tongue. Mother never left Father's side. Never. Where he was, she was there, hovering beyond his shoulder like a second shadow.

"Well, I would have stayed with him, dear, but how could I knowing my only son was home attempting to betray us behind our backs?"

I stumbled back a step beneath the force of her blatant, unapologetic accusation.

Unluckily, Eamon was there to stop me with a firm hand to my shoulder. His touch shocked me, as did the way his fingers curled over my shoulder bone and held firm. I tried to pull away, but his grip was iron.

"Rhory, how could you do this to me?" Mother breathed through her obvious hurt.

I couldn't fight Eamon off whilst holding the pack to my side. Mother took her moment and snatched it from beneath my arm. I called out to stop her, but one look scolded me into forced silence.

"Leaving me, leaving your father, all when you know just how dangerous the world can be for people like us."

My blood chilled, knowing Eamon was behind me and Mother had alluded to the very secret she fought to keep hidden. *Did Eamon know?*

"I am going, Mother."

She paused, eyes widening more than I believed natural.

"Pardon me—"

Eamon couldn't stop me from jolting forward, not as I threw my elbow back into his ribs and then slammed my hip into his groin. I marvelled at the way the wind was driven from him, enough to loosen his hold for me to break out of it.

My skin burned beneath his fingers as I pulled free of him. Mother was far too shocked at my refusal of her that she put up no fight when I reached for the pack and yanked it from her.

"Please," I snapped, breathless as adrenaline flooded through me. "Don't try and stop me."

Mother glanced over my shoulder to Eamon, snarling at his moans of discomfort. When she looked back to me, the lines of her face only deepened. "Calix Grey isn't suitable for you," she said, finally broaching the very topic I wondered if she knew about. "He is dangerous."

I almost laughed. How could Mother accuse another of being dangerous when she was the one who kept me under lock and key?

"You don't know him," I said. "Mother, I know you love me, but your need to smother me has driven us to this very moment. Please, you need to let me go."

She took a step forward, her arms raised out before her as though she didn't know what to do with them. "But, Rhory... everything I do is to keep you safe. There are sacrifices I have made, ones you could not even comprehend. I cannot just let you go when my only task in life is to keep you safe."

"Calix has my best interests at heart," I said, calmly.

If Mother cared for me, and truly understood I was safe with him, then she would let me go. If she loved me enough, she would do it. She would do it, for me.

She took another tentative step towards me, continuing to hold out her arms as though I would run into them. Except, I wasn't a child anymore. I hadn't been a child for a long time. And it was high time Mother recognised that.

"Why didn't you tell me about him?" she asked. "Do you know how painful it was to find out from…" Her eyes flickered to Eamon once again, who kept silent and sentry before the door. I still felt his phantom touch on my shoulder; my skin ached from both disgust and tension from where his fingers had gripped me.

"Would it have mattered if I had?" I retorted. "If you knew, you would still not have approved. Even if I am the happiest around him. Even when he makes me feel loved and safe and…"

"He is a monster," she snapped, reaching forward and grasping me by the upper arms. Her face was twisted into a mask of desperation, with wide eyes and lips which paled with tension.

"Anyone else, Rhory. Anyone. But not Calix. Not any of the Grey's."

"Let go of me, Mother," I demanded, refusing to fight her off. It was not only this moment I longed release from her. I wanted her to let me go entirely. I wished nothing more than her to allow me to walk out this house without a fight. But if it was a fight she desired, I would do it. "If you love me, you will step aside and allow me to finally claim my life. My way."

She recoiled, my words striking true. Through the material of my shirt, I felt her nails scratch lightly over skin before she did the unthinkable. She withdrew her hands and returned them to her side.

"Is this truly what you want?" Sadness crept across her face, ageing her before my eyes.

"Yes," I said. It was the easiest word I could muster. "*Calix* is who I want."

Mother paused, taking my words in. My heart broke seeing her so sad. So defeated. I knew, deep down, she cared for my best interests. But she would learn that I was in safe hands. We would prove it to her.

"Okay," she said finally. "If this is what you want from me."

Mother looked to Eamon and nodded, dismissing him with the faint flick of her head.

"Thank you," I said, gripping the pack of clothes again as tears pricked in my eyes.

We stared at one another, mother and son. I felt guilty for leaving her to care for Father alone, but I knew he would want this for me. Before his mind was claimed by his sickness, Father had always encouraged me to follow my heart, and now I was finally able to heed his desire for me. I would make him proud.

"Rhory, before you go," she said, eyes brimming with tears. "At least permit me to hold my son for one last time?"

I nodded, selfishly allowing myself to fall into her

open arms. She pulled me to her, grasping the back of my head with her hands and keeping me to her. We were of equal height, but there was something about being in her arms that made me feel small again.

I pinched my eyes closed and held her close.

"I love you, Rhory," she whispered into my ear. "Which is why I am not sorry."

A talon of panic sliced down my spine. I tried to withdraw, but Mother dug her nails into my hair and held on tight. I couldn't begin to fight, not as Eamon's hands were suddenly on me. Both of them applied pressure to keep me locked in place.

"You are hurting me," I gasped out, feeling the skin of my scalp sting from the scrape of her nails. My power reared its head, but even it refused me in the presence of Mother.

"I promise it will not last. I must do what is necessary," Mother said. "I vowed to keep you safe, but you continue to defy me."

"Get off of me," I pleaded, unsure if I spoke to Mother or Eamon, for both of them treated me with equally unkind hands. "Fucking let me go!"

"Quiet now," Mother sang. Somewhere in our struggle, she had passed me into Eamon's arms. He held me strong, with my arms bent behind my back and his body forced up against mine. I felt his mouth near my ear, but I didn't dare move for fear of getting closer to him. His proximity made me sick.

All I could do was look at my mother as cold light brewed from the tips of her fingers and covered her hands in the flame of her power. Our magic was forbidden to be used, especially in front of someone. Eamon didn't flinch as Mother revealed her magic, nor did she care. Her gaze was entirely focused on me.

My own magic awoke in response, but the way Eamon held me prevented me from touching his skin. Which could only mean he had been warned. In that moment, I knew one thing for certain. *This had been planned.*

Mother stepped towards me, her sharp face cast in the light from beneath her. It elongated her features, making her frown look more like a menacing smile. Seeing her open display of magic stifled me. In all my years, I had never seen her use her power. She had kept it hidden from me, never daring to speak about it.

As she brought her glowing hands towards me, I longed to call out for Calix. His name filled my mouth, but I couldn't muster the breath to speak it.

"If it is freedom you search for," Mother said, eyes glowing unnaturally with the reflection of her power, her determination, "Then I, as your mother, will be the one to give it to you."

I turned my face as much as Eamon allowed. Mother continued raising the glow of her hands towards me until I felt the frozen bite of her magic grace the skin of my cheeks.

"It is time I rid your mind of the poison that is Calix Grey."

"You can't," I breathed, stilling completely in their grasp.

"Yes," Ana said, tracing her nails up the sides of my face until the tips rested over my temples. She laid pressure on them and pierced her nails into the soft skin. "Yes, I can. Do not worry, my darling boy. This will only hurt a little, and then you will be free…"

"No!" I squirmed.

"Eamon, hold him," Ana snapped.

"Mother, please don't!"

"You left me no choice, Rhory. You forced my hand. You made me do this. But I promise, when it is over, you will be happy. I know what is best for you. Mothers know best. And I refuse to let you squander your life away with a monster when there are others who would better suit you. Others who would do as I please to keep you safe."

"Calix!" I screamed his name with every fibre of strength in my being. "Calix *is* what is best for me!"

"Shh," Eamon murmured into my ear, lips caressing the skin as he tightened his hold. "I've got you now."

There wasn't a moment to fathom Eamon's words as Mother pressed her hands to my skull and pierced it with her power.

I gasped out, a single tear tracking a cool river down my cheek as her cold fingers of magic rooted through my mind. Then, the room fell away from me. The world faded from view. There, in the darkness of my mind, stood Calix. Waiting, just as he promised. He was before me, smile illuminated by the light of Mother's power as it raced towards him in a tidal wave. I cried out for him as the power swept over the vision of Calix and engulfed him entirely.

I blinked, and he was gone. Swallowed whole by her magic. Then, when the light finally settled, there was no one left standing before me. In fact, I didn't know who it was. Who did I see only moments before? I focused on the shadows, willing them to reveal themselves, to calm the confusion and panic that gripped me from feeling so lost and out of sorts.

Out of the darkness, the figure stepped forward.

Eamon materialised, smiling and corporeal. My deep inhale lifted the weight of panic from me. *He had come back.* No darkness could ever hide him from me. No light could wash him away from my mind.

He was there.

My love.

*My Eamon.*

## ❊ 47 ❊

I knew, without a doubt, where to find Calix—now more so than ever before. Because it was one of the first memories that had come back to me. Perhaps it was because I was searching for it, but I knew with complete certainty Calix would be waiting, just as he had promised all those years ago.

The red cloak of the Crimson Guard whipped behind me as I ran from Castle Dread, my feet pounding against the pavement with the same fury as my heart in my chest. Marius and Jak had gifted the cloak to me, Jak even going so far as to tie it around my neck.

Darkmourn passed in a blur, as did the forest that separated Darkmourn from Tithe. My journey didn't matter, it was the destination I was focused on.

Jak's gift to me felt like reading a book backwards. The flooding of memories as they returned was strange. One after the other, I was in the eye of a storm as the winds of the past battered into me. I could have let them knock me down, but I didn't. I held firm and drank them all in.

I remembered the *before*. It was both painful and beautiful, like breathing in fresh air after being stuck in a room infested of smoke.

Auriol's cottage revealed itself before me. I had reached it without truly thinking. I slowed, panting viciously. But at no point did I stop. If I was not running with purpose, I was walking with desperation to reach him. To reach Calix.

The cottage was as I remembered it. Crumbling white-weathered walls, and vines that left scars across its surface. There was the flickering of orange light from the window at the side of the house. He was here, just as Calix promised before my mother had altered my mind to suit her own purpose.

W armth crashed into me as I pushed open the front door. It squealed on its hinges, signalling my arrival. Maybe I should have called out that it was me. But I knew Calix was here, and he knew who entered his grandmother's home. I couldn't explain it, but we knew. We always would.

It was only when I walked up the hallway and turned into the room awash in candlelight did I truly feel like I exhaled for the first time.

Calix was lying across Auriol's bed. His long body stretched out, with a pillow propping up his head. His lips parted as he regarded me, blinking a few times as though the vision of me would quickly fade.

"Rhory?" My name was a question, encompassing every thought that passed behind his bright, gleaming eyes. He shuffled up, regarding me with suspicion.

I inhaled deeply through my nose. There so much I longed to say to him. So many words and promises which I felt as though I could drown willingly in. Instead, I picked three words which held the most power.

"I remember you," I murmured.

Calix sat up, powerful arms straining as he righted himself. "Tell me, Rhory. Tell me it all."

I blinked and the tears I fought hard to hold back spilled without restraint. They ran down my face, leaking between my upturned lips until all I could taste was salt.

"You," I whispered.

Questions passed across Calix's golden stare. He pressed his hand across his chest, long fingers splaying directly over his heart. "Please, don't play tricks with me."

I stepped to the end of the bed. "You... you asked me to run away with you. The last time I saw you, you asked me to meet you here and we would run from it all." I kicked off my shoes and climbed onto the bed between his legs. "I was coming to see you when Mother stopped me. That is when... when she stole you from my mind. But I was coming to you, Calix. I was."

Calix broke. He reached over for me, taking my face

in his hands and kissing me with years of passion he was forced to keep to himself. I melted into him, letting his strength pull me further onto the bed and into his lap.

"Shh," he hushed, lips pressed to mine. "It doesn't matter anymore. You are here. You came back for me, just as you promised you would."

My greedy hands touched him with years of my buried passion for him. I traced them across his torso and chest, his shoulders and upper arms. I longed to feel him, just as I remembered from before. This differed from sleeping with him in Jak's house, or on the grounds of the forest. This was familiar. Because now, I knew him. Truly knew him, and I couldn't imagine a curse powerful enough to ever remove him from my mind again.

"I waited for you," Calix said, pressing his forehead to mine. He brushed red curls from my forehead, ensuring not a single strand fell over my eyes. Calix wanted me to see him just as he saw me. Entirely.

"That night, I waited for you. Every noise I heard outside, I thought it was you finally coming. But you never did. Then, when I came to find you that following day, it was to see you in the arms of Eamon. It…" Calix took a shuddering breath in. For such a large, powerful man, he wore his emotions across him with pride. It was one of the many most wonderous things about him. "It destroyed me, but I loved you enough to give you what I thought you wanted. And, Rhory, I would do it again and again. Over and over, no matter the agony. If it meant you lived the life you choose."

"But I never chose that life," I said, grasping his face and holding it so he could look only in my eyes. "The one I wanted was with you. I would have escaped that night and found you. We would have been leagues away now, years deep into the life we wanted. That was what I desired. I choose you, always."

Calix smiled through his sorrow. He brushed a tear from my cheek with the pad of his thumb. The feeling was so gentle; I leaned into it and closed my eyes.

"There is so much time we must make up for missing," I murmured, "Starting now."

"Tell me, Little Red. Where do you wish to start?" Calix asked, his voice a soft purr.

I took Calix's hands and pried them from my face. Gently, I placed them down on his lap. Then I moved myself down to the end of the bed where I stood freely.

"Such large eyes you have." I lifted my fingers to the clasp of my cloak and untied it. It fell to the ground, like a puddle of blood beneath my feet.

Calix inhaled deeply through his nose. His eyes widened at my words, words only he would know. "You *do* remember."

"Answer me," I demanded, my stomach jolting with excitement.

Calix raised a single brow. "All the better for seeing you with, every inch and all."

Slowly, I unbuttoned my shirt, stopping only when I felt Calix would look away. He knew, as before, that I deserved his entire focus. And he gave it to me, licking his lips and rubbing his hands up and down his thighs with unspent excitement.

"Such big hands you have," I sang out, mouth watering as Calix moved his hands from his thigh onto the growing mound protruding between his thighs.

"All the better to touch you with," he replied, gaze narrowing with desire and hunger.

I wiggled free of my trousers, undershorts and all the remaining clothes until I was completely naked.

Calix trailed his eyes up and down my entire body three times. By the fourth, he lifted his finger and curled it inward. "Come to me."

The bed creaked as I climbed back on it. I crawled over to him on all fours, watching him as he drank me in. His mouth parted, pink tongue spreading out over his lower lip.

"Such a big tongue you have," I said, forcing Calix to flatten beneath me. I stopped only when my face was above his. A shiver passed over my skin as he lifted a hand to my thigh and slowly crawled his fingers up towards my ass.

"All the better to taste you with," he replied. "Now, are you going to let me do that?"

"All in due course," I replied.

"Do you remember how much you loved when I would fuck you with my tongue?"

Calix stuck it out. I brought my lips around it. He groaned into my mouth as I sucked his tongue up and down. When I pulled away, he grinned like a cat who found the cream.

"I want those lips around my cock," Calix said.

"Why wait?" I asked, tilting my head and raising my brows. "Tell me if I remembered this wrong, but I recall a time when we pleasured one another at the same time."

"You do?"

"Hmm, maybe I am wrong," I said with a sly grin, knowing I was, in fact, not wrong at all.

Calix brought both hands to my hips and brought me down hard on his cock. With his guidance, I rocked across the lump of muscle, enjoying the press of it against my ass.

"Now you mention it," Calix said, lifting his hips beneath me so every single inch of his cock had the pleasure of rubbing against me. "I think you are right."

"Oh, I am. Aren't I?"

"Turn around," Calix commanded.

I did as he asked. Calix released me enough to shift my position on him. I stopped when I faced his cock, and my bare ass was pressed directly before his mouth. We laughed as his long limbs knocked into me awkwardly while he frantically took off his clothes. When his teeth nipped at my skin, followed by the wet lap of his tongue, excitement rushed him, throwing every item of clothing into a forgotten pile on the floor beside his grandmother's bed.

I gripped the base of Calix's cock. My fingers couldn't touch around its width. I opened my mouth to make a comment but failed spectacularly as Calix brought his tongue to my ass and drew it upwards, slowly and tenderly. All I could do was release a long, breathy moan.

It would have been easier to give into the pleasure and forget the world. But I wanted Calix to experience it alongside me. So, I brought him into my mouth and wrapped my lips around the curved tip of his cock. My cheeks were entirely soaked with spit, making it easier to take him in, deeper and deeper. My jaw ached slightly, but that only encouraged me more.

Calix had each of my ass cheeks in his hands, separating them so he could bury himself deeper into me. He fucked me with his tongue. It slipped in, spreading warmth across my lower half. If he didn't hold me up in place, I would have fallen on top of him.

Calix made my knees weak with his devouring.

We competed with one another. I longed to make him groan as I moved up and down his length, sucking the tip and caressing as many of his inches as I could with my tongue. He breathed into my ass, exhaling his pleasure, which also spilled from the tip of his cock and sweetened the insides of my cheeks.

I loved how his taste filled me. And I wondered what I tasted like to him. Whatever it was, he must have craved it, because he was prepared to devour me all the way to my core. Whatever it was, he must have craved it because he ate, nipped and devoured me without breath.

"Careful," Calix said suddenly, shifting his hips and pulling his cock away from my mouth. "If you carry on like that, I will have another unfortunate accident."

"Unfortunate?" I asked, breathless.

Calix released my ass and allowed me to crawl into a different position. This time I turned to face him, sitting upon his hips and rocking across his hard cock with my spit-glistened ass.

"For whom?" I murmured. "I want to taste your cum. I want it all."

"And I *want* many things," Calix replied, his face pinched in a thrilling scowl.

"Like?" I teased.

"Like burying my cock in that tight hole. Your little mouth can't take all of me, but your ass can. And I want to submerge myself in you."

"*I want. I want,*" I repeated, mockingly. "That is all I hear from you."

"Oh, don't play coy. You will beg for it the second you feel the head of my cock so much as flirt with your hole."

"Is that so?" I countered.

"Care to test my theory?"

Calix reached beside him and produced a vial of lubrication from the beside dresser.

"Tell me that is not Auriol's own stash?"

A deep laugh rumbled out of Calix. "This is mine. Call it a precaution for if Jak unlocked your memories and you came back to me. Which he did, and one cannot be caught unprepared."

I smiled, licking my lips as they turned up. "Care to do the honours?"

Calix quickly uncorked the vial with his teeth, spat it

out and emptied the contents until his hand, crotch and cock glistened with lube.

I reached beneath me, taking his length in my hand and positioned it before my entrance. Calix was right, of course. The second I felt the curved tip of his cock brush against the heart of me, I felt myself open and the muscles relax.

I lowered myself upon Calix, welcoming every inch of him as I did so. The further I sat on him, consciously tightening the muscles around my hole to provide him as much enjoyment as possible, Calix's eyes glazed over. His mouth parted, tongue swelling as he exhaled a groan of pure pleasure.

At some point, he pressed both hands on either side of my ass, spread my cheeks with his grip and slammed the final inch inside of me. The force of it took my breath away.

"Rock for me, Little Red." Calix urged me to do as he asked, moving my hips as I familiarised myself with the swell of him inside of me. "Ease into it. I don't want to hurt you."

I leaned down over him, pressing my forehead to his. Breathless, I replied softly under my breath, "Fuck me."

"What was that you said?" Calix asked; I could hear the grin buried in his tone.

Our faces were so close that my eyes crossed when I looked into his pits of gold. "Fuck me, I said fuck me."

A growl rumbled out of Calix's throat, conjuring a new wave of shivers to race across my skin. He released his hands from my ass and raised them behind his head.

When he replied, it was with all the cocky arrogance I had first fallen in love with all those years ago. "From my vantage point, you are the one sitting on me. Ride it, if you want it. Fuck me yourself."

And I did just that.

Lifting myself up on my knees, I moved carefully to ensure his hard cock couldn't retreat from me. I contorted myself into a squatting positioning. For leverage, I grasped onto my thighs, which already burned from the position. It was a pleasant feeling, one that sang in harmony with the pleasure of his length inside me.

"Try not to finish too quickly," I warned, winking as I pinched my nails into the skin of my thigh.

"That," Calix said, narrowing his gaze at me, which mirrored the smirk plastered on his handsome face, "Was a onetime thing. And believe me, if I cum inside of you, that will not stop me from continuing. We have years of catching up to do."

"Thank my lucky stars," I breathed.

There was no more talking as I bounced myself upon Calix's length. He threw his head back, thumping into the pillow as I moved myself up and down. Soon enough, the discomfort in my thighs vanished as the swell of indulgence enraptured me. Deep inside, I felt the tip of his cock play with the soft spot of my centre. Each time they joined as one, it sent a jolt across every bone, muscle and vein, threatening to undo me.

Sweat spread across my forehead, running down the sides of my face and dampening my hairline. At some point, I fell backwards onto the bed. I was afforded only a moment's break from his cock until Calix took over. With my legs still bent between us and my arms holding up the rest of my weight, Calix thrust skyward. The faint muscles across my stomach rippled as I lost myself to my heavy breathing.

Somewhere in the back of my mind, I was thankful that we hid in the belly of a forest with no one around. Because I screamed and Calix howled. The symphony of our pleasure would have frightened birds from nests and sent burrowing creatures back into the holes in the ground they called home.

A rush of blood flooded my head as Calix shot forward and spun me around. It happened so quickly, I almost didn't hear the sloppy pop sound his cock made as it fell out of me.

"Rhory…" Calix whispered. "Look in my eyes."

I hadn't even realised I had closed my eyes. My mind was far too lost to the euphoria that the world seemed somewhat detached. Only when I opened my eyes and saw him did it all rush back into focus.

Calix had laid me on my back. My knees were brought up to my stomach and held in place by his hand. He had not yet entered me again. Instead, he watched me from his perch above as he leaned over. His hair fell over each side of his face, shadowing his expression but never dimming the glow of gold that was in his eyes.

"Are you okay?" I asked.

"I have never been better."

I craned my neck upwards and looked down the length of our bodies. In the shadows he created his muscles looked huge across his torso and stomach. His cock hung between his legs, only an inch from brushing the sticky sheets of the bed.

"Then why have we stopped?" I asked him, unable to hide the disappointment in my voice.

Calix shifted his entire body weight onto one hand and balanced on it whilst he took the other and brushed the side of my face. He was warm and slick with sweat. I didn't care. I wanted it all.

"I want to see you," he said. My heart stung at the sadness in his voice. "And I want to look into your eyes and see you seeing me. It's all I have wanted for years. Not your body, not your sex. You."

I leaned up as much as his body's imprisonment allowed. My hands were free, so I spread them across his head, digging my fingers into his scalp. I used his hair as leverage, making sure he couldn't look away from me even if he desired to.

Which, we both knew, he didn't.

"I am here," I replied finally, feeling my chest swell with his shared sorrow. "And I see you."

"Rhory," Calix breathed my name out as though it were the heaviest of burdens.

"Calix," I replied.

"From now, until you decide you no longer desire it… I wish to give you my love."

"How can you give me your love?" I asked, pulling his face down towards mine. Warm light spilled from my hands and cast the surrounding room in a halo of my power. Calix's eyes widened as I opened him up to my emotions. I took nothing from him this time. Instead, I showed him just how I felt through our connection, so he not only heard everything I had to say but believed it, with no room for disbelief.

"I stole it for myself years ago. I love you, Calix. I love what you are, who you are and everything in-between. I have loved you when my mind belonged to you, and loved you even when it was taken and given to someone else. There is no curse in the world strong enough to ever make me forget that."

Calix crashed his mouth into mine. The kiss was powerful with passion, but soft in equal measure. It was all lips and tongue, and the silence allowed me to read his response through my touch as he drove his emotions into me.

*Love. Warmth. Happiness. Joy.*

There was not enough time in the world for me to name everything I felt coming from him.

"You love me?" he asked once he pulled away. I smiled at the bruising of his mouth and the swelling of my own. "Even though I am the big bad wolf of Darkmourn?"

"I love you," I replied, aware that Calix took his cock in his hand and brought it back to my ass. "Big bad and all."

"Say it again," Calix groaned, slowly easing his cock back inside my hole. "I want to hear you scream it."

"I love you," I moaned as I felt every inch of him sheath within me.

"Then I'm the luckiest man in Darkmourn and beyond." Calix lowered himself atop me, pressing his chest to my chest and his lips to my lips. His pace was softer. He moved his hips in circles, the motion like the shore of a lake during the calmest of winds. He didn't fuck me now. He made love to me and I lost myself to it entirely.

'Then say it, tell me you love me.'

"I *do* love you, Rhory Coleman," Calix whispered. "Completely, entirely and with every fibre of my being. I love you."

As he spoke those final words, I truly understood their meaning. They no longer hurt. Those words were once my undoing, but now made me whole again.

ALSO BY BEN ALDERSON

**Indie Published Books**

**The *Dragori* Trilogy**

*Cloaked in Shadow*

*Found in Night*

*Poisoned in Light*

**Darkmourn Universe**

*Lord of Eternal Night*

*King of Immortal Tithe*

*Alpha of Mortal Flesh*

**A Realm of Fey Series**

*A Betrayal of Storms*

*A Kingdom of Lies*

*A Deception of Courts*

*A War of Monsters - Out Soon*

**Traditionally Published Books**

*Heir to Thorn and Flame*